The
Angel's
Mark

The Angel's Mark

S. W. PERRY

CORVUS

Published in hardback in Great Britain in 2018 by Corvus,
an imprint of Atlantic Books Ltd.

10 9 8 7 6 5 4 3 2 1

A CIP catalogue record for this book is available
from the British Library.

Paperback ISBN: 978 1 78649 494 8
E-book ISBN: 978 1 78649 493 1

Printed and bound by CPI Group (UK) Ltd, Croydon, CR0 4YY

Corvus
An imprint of Atlantic Books Ltd
Ormond House
26–27 Boswell Street
London
WC1N 3JZ

www.corvus-books.co.uk

For Jane

Medicine is the most noble of the Arts,
but through the ignorance of those who practise it...
it is at present far behind all the others.

HIPPOCRATES

... lay that damned book aside,
and gaze not on it, lest it tempt thy soul.

CHRISTOPHER MARLOWE,
The Tragicall History of Dr Faustus

1

London, August 1590

He lies on a single sheet of fine white Flanders linen. Eyelids closed, plump arms folded across his swollen infant belly, he could be a sleeping cherub painted upon the ceiling of a Romish chapel – all he lacks is a harp and a pastel cloud to float upon. The sisters at St Bartholomew's have prepared him as best they can. They've washed away the river mud, plucked the nesting elvers from his mouth, scrubbed him cleaner than he ever was in life. Now he stinks no worse than anything else the watermen might haul out of the Thames on a hot Lammas Day such as this.

Male child, malformed in the lower limbs, some four years of age. Taken up drowned at the Wildgoose stairs on Bankside. Name unknown, save unto God. So says the brief report from the office of the Queen's Coroner, into whose busy orbit – twelve miles around the royal presence – this child has so impertinently strayed.

The chamber is dark, unbearably stuffy. A miasma of horse-dung, salted fish and human filth spills through the closed shutters from the street outside. Somewhere beyond Finsbury Fields a summer thunderstorm is boiling up noisily. Plague weather, says present opinion. If we escape it this year, we'll be luckier than we deserve.

The chamber door opens with a soft moan of its ancient hinges. A cheery-looking little fellow in a leather apron enters, his bald head gleaming with sweat. He carries a canvas satchel trapped defensively against his body by his right arm, as though it were stuffed full of contraband. Approaching the child on the table, he begins to whistle a jaunty song, popular in the taverns this season: 'On high the merry pipit trills'. Then, with the exaggerated care of a servant preparing his master's table for a feast, he places the satchel beside the corpse, throws open the flap and proceeds to lay out his collection of saws, cleavers, dilators, tongs and scalpels. As he does so, he polishes each one on a corner of the linen, peering into the metal as though searching for hidden flaws. He is a precise man. Everything must be just so. He has standards to maintain. After all, he's a member of the Worshipful Company of Barber-Surgeons, and while he's here in the Guildhall of the College of Physicians – a surprisingly modest timber-framed building wedged between the fishmongers' stalls and bakers' shops to the south of St Paul's churchyard – he's on enemy ground. This rivalry between the meat-cutters and the balm-dispensers has existed, or so they say, since the great Hippocrates began tending patients on his dusty Aegean island.

After two verses, the man stops whistling and engages the child in a pleasant, one-way conversation. He talks about the weather; about what's playing at the Rose; whether the Spanish will try their hand against England again this summer. It's a ritual of his. Like a compassionate executioner, he likes to imagine he's strengthening his subject's resolve for what lies ahead. When he's done, he leans over the child as though to bestow a parting kiss. He places his left cheek close to the tiny nostrils. It's the final part of his ritual: making sure his subject is really dead. After all, it won't reflect well if he wakes up at the first slice of the scalpel.

✠

'Who are you planning to cut up for public sport today, Nick?' shouts Eleanor Shelby to the lathe-and-plaster wall that separates her from her husband. 'Some poor starving fellow hanged for stealing a mackerel, I shouldn't wonder.'

For several days now Eleanor and Nicholas have communicated only through this wall, or via scribbled note passed secretively by their maid Harriet. Whenever Nicholas approaches the door of the lying-in chamber, Eleanor's mother Ann – who's come down from Suffolk to oversee the birth and ensure the midwife doesn't steal the pewter – snarls him away. She's convinced that if he gets so much as a glimpse of his wife he'll let in the foulness of the London streets, not to mention extreme bad luck. Besides, she tells him crossly whenever she gets the chance, who's ever heard of a husband setting eyes on his wife during her confinement? Imagine the scandal!

To add to Nicholas's present misery, every church bell from St Bride's to St Botolph's begins to chime the noonday hour, the latecomers making up by effort what they've lost in time-keeping. Now he must shout even louder if his wife is to hear him.

'It's *learning*, Sweet. Cutting up is what East Cheap butchers do in their shambles. This is a lecture, for the advancement of science.'

'Where any passing rogue may peer in over the casement for free. It's worse than a Southwark bear-baiting.'

'At least our subjects are dead already, not like those poor tormented creatures. Anyway, it's a private dissertation. No public allowed.'

'Insides are insides, Nick. And, in my opinion, that's where they should stay.'

Nicholas slips his stockinged feet into his new leather boots, tugs out the creases in his Venetian hose and wonders how to say farewell before the bells make conversation through the wall impossible. Normally there'd be the usual passionate endearments, followed by a lot of letting go and grabbing back, kisses interrupted and then jealously resumed, breathless promises to hurry home, a final reluctant parting. After all, they've been married scarcely two years. But not today. Today there is the wall.

'I can't tarry, Love. You know what Sir Fulke Vaesy thinks of tardiness. There's bound to be a line somewhere in the Bible about punctuality.'

'Don't let him bully you, Nick. I know his sort,' comes Eleanor's voice, as if from a great distance.

'What sort is that?'

'When you're the queen's physician, he'll grovel to you like a lapdog.'

'I'll be seventy by then! Vaesy will be a hundred. What kind of physician makes a centenarian grovel?'

'The kind whose patients don't pay their bills!'

Smiling at the muffled peal of Eleanor's laughter, Nicholas shouts a final farewell. Nevertheless, his leave-taking feels hurried and incomplete, practically ill-starred.

At first sight, you would not take the young fellow stepping out of his lodgings at the sign of the Stag and into the dusty heat for a man of physic. Beneath a plain white canvas doublet, whose points today are left unlaced for ventilation, his body is that of a hardy young countryman. A coil of black hair spills ungovernably beneath the broad rim of his leather hat. And even if this were midwinter and not blazing August, his doctoral gown – won after a lengthy struggle against a whole battery of disapproving Cambridge eyebrows – would still be tucked away, as it is now, in the leather bag slung over one shoulder.

Why this unusual modesty, given that in London a man's status is known by what he wears? He would probably tell you it's to protect the expensive gown from the ravages of the street. A truer answer would be that even after two years of practising medicine in the city, Nicholas Shelby can't quite help thinking that a

Suffolk yeoman's son has no right to wear such exotic apparel.

Keeping up a sweaty trot in the heat, Nicholas passes the Grass church herb-market and heads down Fish Street Hill, towards the College Guildhall. He squirms with embarrassment when the clerks there bow extravagantly. He's still finds such deference uncomfortable. In a side-chamber he takes the gown from his bag and, like a guilty secret, wraps it around his body. He enters the dissection room by one door, just as Sir Fulke Vaesy comes in by the other.

He's made it, with barely moments to spare.

Edging in beside his friend Simon Cowper, Nicholas expects to find the subject of today's lecture is one of the four adult felons fresh from the gallows that the College is licensed to dissect each year, just as Eleanor had indicated. Only now does he see the tiny figure lying on the linen sheet, surrounded by the barber-surgeon's instruments.

And Simon Cowper, knowing that Nicholas is an expectant father, cannot bring himself to look his friend in the eye.

Sir Fulke reminds Nicholas of a Roman proconsul preparing to inspect hostages from a conquered tribe. Resplendent in his fellow's gown with its fur trim, a pearl-encrusted silk cap upon his head, he's a large man with a fabled appetite for sack, goose and venison. He rises from his official chair and towers over the tiny white figure on the table. But Vaesy has no intention of getting his hands bloody today. It is not for the holder of the Lumleian chair of anatomy to behave like a common butcher jointing a carcass in the parish shambles. The actual cutting of flesh will be done by Master Dunnich, the cheery little bald fellow from the Worshipful Company of Barber-Surgeons.

'A healthy womb is like the fertile soil in Eden's blessed garden,'

Vaesy begins, to the biblical accompaniment of summer thunder, much closer now. 'It is the wholesome furrow in which the seed of Adam may take root—'

Is he delivering a lecture or a sermon? Sometimes Nicholas finds it hard to tell the difference. Through the now un-shuttered windows comes the smell of the street: fish stalls and fresh horse-dung. On each sill rest the chins of passers-by, craning their necks to peer in and gawp. The heat has made this lecture less private than Nicholas imagined.

'However, this infant, found by the watermen in mid-river just yesterday, is the inevitable issue of disease, physical and spiritual. The child has clearly been born' – the great anatomist pauses for effect – 'monstrous!'

The beams of the Guildhall roof seem almost to flinch. Nicholas has a sudden protective urge to wrap the naked child in the linen sheet and tell Vaesy to stop frightening him.

By 'monstrous', Vaesy means crippled. The description seems overly brutal to Nicholas, who tries hard to study the child dispassionately. He notes how the withered legs arch inwards below the knees. How the yellowing toes entwine like stunted vines. Clearly he could not have walked into the river by himself. Did he crawl in whilst playing on the bank? Perhaps he fell off one of the wherries or tilt-boats that ply their trade on the water. Or maybe he was thrown in, like an unwanted sickly dog. Whatever the truth, something about the little body strikes Nicholas as odd. Most corpses fished from the river, he knows, are found floating face-down, weighted by the mass of the head. The blood should pool in the cheeks and the forehead. But this boy's face is waxy white. Maybe it's because he hasn't been in the water long, he thinks, noting the absence of bite-marks from pike or water rat.

Is that a small tear on one side of the throat? And there's a second, deeper wound – low down on the calf of the right leg, like a cross cut into old cheese. A dreadful image enters Nicholas's mind: the infant being hauled out of the water on the end of a boathook.

'The causes of deformity such as we see here, gentlemen, are familiar enough to us, are they not?' says Vaesy, breaking into his thoughts. 'Perhaps one of you would be so good as to list them? You, sirrah—'

Instantly the eyes of every physician in the room drop to the laces of their boots, to the condition of their hose, in Nicholas's case to the scars of boyhood harvesting etched into his fingers, to anything but Vaesy's awful stare. They know the great anatomist will expect at least ten minutes' dissertation on the subject, all in faultless Latin.

'Mr Cowper, is it not?'

Of all the victims Vaesy could have chosen, poor Simon Cowper is the easiest: forever muddling his Galen with his Vesalius; ineptly transposing his astrological houses when drawing up a prognosis; when letting blood, more likely to cut himself than the patient. He stands now in the full glare of Vacsy's attention like a man condemned. Nicholas's heart weeps for him.

'The *first*, according to the Frenchman, Paré,' Cowper begins nervously, wisely choosing a standard text for safety, 'is too great a quantity of seed in the father—'

A snigger from amongst the young physicians. Vaesy kills it with a look of thunder. But it's too late for Simon Cowper; his delicate fingers begin to drum nervously against his thighs. 'S-s-s-secondly: the mother having sat too long upon a stool... with her legs crossed... or... having her belly bound too tight... or by the narrowness of the womb.'

For what seems like an age, Vaesy torments the poor man by doing nothing but arching one bushy eyebrow. When Cowper exhausts his slim fund of knowledge, the great anatomist calls him a fuddle-cap and reminds him of his own favourite medical catch-all. 'The wrath of God, man! The wrath of God!' To Vaesy, sickness is mostly explained by divine displeasure.

Cowper sits down. He looks ready to weep. Nicholas wonders how wrathful God has to be to allow a crippled child to end up on Vaesy's dissection table.

Two attendants step forward. One removes the starched Flanders linen, the other the corpse. Now Nicholas can see that the table it covered is little more than a butcher's block with a drain drilled through it, a wooden bucket set beneath the hole. In place of the linen is set a sheet of waxed sailcloth, a vent stitched into the centre. From the stains visible on it, it's been employed in this role before. The dead child is set down again, like an offering upon an altar.

'The first incision into the thorax, Master Dunnich, if you'd be so kind,' orders Vaesy to the little bald-headed barber-surgeon.

Immediately the stench of putrefaction fills the air like an old familiar sin. Nicholas knows it well. Even now, it never fails to turn his stomach. At once he's back in the Low Countries, his first post after leaving Cambridge.

'Isn't there enough sickness for you here in Suffolk?' Eleanor had asked him when he'd told her he was off to Holland to enlist as a physician in the army of the Prince of Orange, thus postponing their marriage.

'The Spanish are butchering faithful Protestants in their own homes.'

'Yes, in Holland. Besides, you're not a soldier, you're a physician.'

'I can do some good. It's why I trained. I fought hard for my doctorate. I won't waste it prescribing cures for indigestion.'

'But, Nicholas, it's dangerous. The crossing alone—'

'No more dangerous than Ipswich on market day. I'll be back in six months.'

She had pummelled his arm in frustration, and the knowledge that she was refusing to weep until he'd gone only compounded his guilt.

In the course of that summer campaign Nicholas had witnessed things no man with a soul should ever have to see. Things he will never tell Eleanor about. Sometimes he still dreams of the babe he'd found on a dung heap, tossed there on the tines of a pitchfork for sport by the men of Spain's Popish army; and the starved corpses of children after the lifting of a siege. When the smell of roasting meat reaches him, he remembers the remains of women and greybeards herded into Protestant chapels and burned alive.

Not that the Dutch troops and their mercenaries had all been saints, not by any means. But he'd learned a lot that summer: how to tell a man his wound is nothing, that he'll soon be up and supping ale in Antwerp, and sound convincing, when in fact you know he's dying; how to drink with German mercenaries and still keep a steady hold on a scalpel; how never, *ever* to gamble with the Swiss... No one had cared then whether he belonged to the appropriate guild. There was no distinction made between physicians who diagnose and surgeons who get their hands bloody. No time to study the astrological implications when a man is bleeding to death before your eyes.

'Now, gentlemen,' Vaesy's voice pulls Nicholas back to the present, 'if you have studied your Vesalius diligently, you will note the following—'

With the help of his ivory wand and numerous quotations from the Old Testament, the great anatomist takes his audience on a journey around the infant's organs, muscles and sinews. By the time he finishes, the dead child is little more than a filleted carcass. Dunnich, the barber-surgeon, has opened him up like a spatchcock.

To his own surprise, Nicholas is in a state bordering on numb terror. He thinks, God protect the child Eleanor is carrying from such a fate as this.

But there's more. There's the bucket beneath the dissecting table. It's almost empty. There's scarcely a pint of blood in it. And then there's that second wound, the one on the child's lower right leg, which Vaesy has apparently missed altogether, for the great anatomist has failed to utter a single word about it in all the time he's been standing over the corpse. Nicholas describes it now in his mind, as if he were giving evidence before the coroner: one very deep laceration, Your Honour, made deliberately with a sharp blade. And a second made transversely across the first – towards its lower point.

An inverted cross.

The mark of necromancy. The Devil's signature.

✝

The Tollworth brook, Surrey, the same afternoon

The hind turns her head as she sups from the ford, ears pricked for danger. Her arched neck gives a sudden tremble, the way Elise's own neck used to tremble when little Ralph clung too tight and she could feel his warm breath upon her skin.

She knows I'm close, thinks Elise. And yet she does not fear me. We are the same, this fallow deer and I. We are fellow creatures of the forest, driven by thirst to forget there may be hunters watching us from the trees.

Dragonflies dart amongst the columns of sunlight that pierce the canopy of branches. She can hear the thrumming of their iridescent wings even above the noise the stream makes as it courses over the mossy stones, even above the rumble of distant summer thunder. She sinks to her knees, puts her lips gingerly to the water. It burbles over her tongue, over her skin, flows into her. Cold and sharp. Bliss made liquid.

Elise recalls it was by a stream like this, on another hot summer's day not long past, that she first succumbed to the delirium that only this cool water can keep at bay. Exhausted, starving, she had imagined the weight she was bearing upon her young back was not her crippled infant brother but the holy cross, and that she was dragging her sacred burden through the dust towards Golgotha...

By a stream like this... on a day like this...

The figure had appeared from nowhere, a silhouette as black as that sudden flash of oblivion you get when, by mistake, you glance into the sun. An angel come down from heaven to save them.

'Help us,' Elise had pleaded, peeling poor little Ralph's withered legs from her back as the desperation overwhelmed her. 'He cannot walk, and I cannot carry him another step. In the name of mercy, take him—'

Forcing the memory from her mind, Elise slakes her thirst in the ford like the wild animal she has become. And as she drinks, she cannot forget that it was her own desperate wail of need that had alerted the angel to their presence. If she had not cried out, perhaps the angel would not have seen them. Perhaps all that followed would have stayed firmly in the realm of bad dreams.

If she were able, Elise would shout a warning to the hind: 'Drink swiftly, little one – the hunters may be nearer than you think!'

But Elise cannot cry out. Elise must remain silent; if needs be, for ever. A single careless word, and the angel might hear her and return – for her.

2

Vaesy's desk is strewn with sheets of parchment covered with symbols and figures. At one end stands a collection of glass vessels. Some, notes Nicholas, contain the desiccated remains of animals, others coloured oils and strange liquids. At the other end is an astrologer's astrolabe and a beaker of what looks suspiciously like urine – the astrolabe to measure the position of the heavenly bodies when the owner of the bladder relieved himself, the urine to reveal by its colour whether his bodily humours are in balance. Nicholas can make out, seen through the beaker's glass, the skeletal hand of a monkey held together with wire, distorted by the yellow liquid into a demon's claw. He has entered a place where medicine and alchemy mix – a perfectly unremarkable physician's study.

'You asked to see me, Dr Shelby,' the great anatomist says pleasantly. Out of the dissection room, he seems almost amiable. 'How may I be of service?'

Nicholas comes straight to the point. 'I believe the subject of your lecture today was murdered, Sir Fulke.'

'Mercy, sirrah! That's a brave charge,' Vaesy says, easing himself out of his gown and setting down his pearl-trimmed cap.

'The child was thrown into the river to hide the crime.'

'I think you'd best explain yourself, Dr Shelby.'

'I can't imagine how the coroner failed to notice the wound, sir,' Nicholas says. He can, of course – laziness.

'Wound? What wound?'

'On the right calf, sir. Small, but very deep. I suspect it might have severed the posterior tibial canal. If not staunched quickly, it would eventually have proved fatal.'

'Oh, *that* wound,' says Vaesy breezily. 'A hungry pike, most likely. Or a boathook. Immaterial.'

'Immaterial?'

'The Queen's Coroner did not make the child available for dissection so that you, sirrah, could study wounds. The wound was immaterial to the substance of my lecture.'

'But there was almost no blood left in the body, sir,' Nicholas points out, as diplomatically as he can. 'The child must have bled out while alive. Blood does not flow *post mortem*.'

'I'm perfectly well aware of that, thank you, Dr Shelby,' says Vaesy, his easy manner beginning to harden.

'I do not believe the wound was made by any fish, sir. There were no other bite marks on the body.'

'So you've decided the alternative is murder, have you? Are all your diagnoses made so swiftly?'

'Well, he didn't drown. That's obvious. There was very little water in the lungs.'

'Are you suggesting the Queen's Coroner does not know his job?' asks Vaesy icily.

'Of course not,' says Nicholas. 'But how are we to explain—'

Vaesy raises a hand to stop him. 'The note from Coroner Danby's clerk was clear: the child was drowned. How he came to such an end is no concern of ours.'

'But if he was bled before death, then he was murdered.'

'And what if he was? The infant was an unclaimed vagrant. He was of no consequence.'

If Vaesy is so familiar with the good book, thinks Nicholas, how is it that mercy and compassion are apparently such alien concepts to him?

'Shouldn't we at least try to identify him – find out if he had a name?'

'I know exactly what his name is, young man.'

'You do?' says Nicholas, caught off-balance.

'Why, yes. His name is Disorder. His name is Lawlessness. He was the offspring of the itinerant poor, Dr Shelby. What does it matter to us if he drowned or was struck down by a thunderbolt? Had he lived, he would surely have hanged before he was twenty. At least now he has made a contribution to the advancement of physic!'

Nicholas tries to curb his growing anger. 'He was once flesh and blood, Sir Fulke. He was an innocent child!'

'Never fear, there'll be plenty more where he came from. They breed like flies on a midden, Dr Shelby.'

'He was someone's son, Sir Fulke. And I believe he was murdered. You have influence – delay the interment of the remains. Ask the coroner to convene a proper jury.'

'It's far too late for that, sirrah. The child is already delivered to St Bride's.' Vaesy's veined cheeks swell as he gives Nicholas a patronizing smile. 'He should thank us, Dr Shelby. He's better off in consecrated ground than as carrion cast up on the riverbank.' He takes Nicholas by the elbow. For a moment the young physician thinks he's found some previously unsuspected empathy in the great anatomist. He's wrong, of course. 'Your wife, Dr Shelby – I hear she is expecting a child.'

'Our first, Sir Fulke.'

'Well, sirrah, there you have it: the wholly natural sensitivities of the expectant father.'

'Sensitivities?'

'Come now, Shelby, you're not the first man to get in a lather at a time like this. I once knew a fellow who became convinced his wife would miscarry if he ate sturgeon on a Wednesday.'

'You think this is all in my imagination?'

Vaesy puts a hand on Nicholas's shoulder. The sleeve of his gown smells of aqua vitae. 'Dr Shelby,' he says unctuously, 'I hope one day to see you as a senior fellow of this College. I trust by then you will have learned to lay aside all unprofitable concern for those whom we physicians are in no position to help – else we would weep tears for all the world, would we not?'

✠

The wholly natural sensitivities of the expectant father.

'The arrogant, over-stuffed tyrant!' mutters Nicholas as he runs towards Trinity church, the brim of his leather hat pulled tight over his brow. It's raining hard now, one of those intense summer squalls that mist the narrow lanes and send the coney-catchers and the purse-divers heading for the nearest tavern to pursue their thievery in the dry. A crack of thunder rolls like a cannonade down Thames Street. 'He thinks I'm overwrought. He thinks I'm no tougher than one of those novice sisters at St Bartholomew's.'

But there's a fragment of truth in what Vaesy has said. In his heart Nicholas knows it. The memory of that pitchforked child; his witnessing of the dissection; the Grass Street wall he cannot breach – all these have done nothing to ease his fears for Eleanor and the child she carries.

✠

After one of Vaesy's lectures it is the habit of the young physicians to celebrate their survival by getting fabulously drunk. Their favoured tavern is to be found at the sign of the White Swan, close by Trinity churchyard. The knock-down has been flowing a while when Nicholas arrives, eliciting angry mutterings from the other customers about young medical men being more ungovernable than apprentice boys on a feast day. Nicholas throws his dripping hat onto the table as he sits down, noting morosely the once-jaunty feather drooping like the banner of a defeated army. 'Am I the only one?' he asks as he signs to a passing tap-boy. 'Did anyone else see those wounds?'

'Wounds?' echoes Michael Gardener, a Kentish fellow who's already looking like a well-fed country doctor at the age of twenty-four. 'What wounds?'

'Two deep incisions on the poor little tot's leg. The right leg. Vaesy missed them completely.'

'Master Dunnich probably made them by accident; you know how careless barber-surgeons are,' says Gardener, running his fingers through his luxuriant beard. 'That's why I never let them near this.'

'Did you see them, Simon?'

'Not I,' says Cowper, his face shiny from the ale. 'I was too busy trying not to catch Vaesy's eye again.'

Gardener raises his jug to Nicholas and, with a hideously lewd grin on his face, calls out, 'Enough of physic! A toast to our fine bully-boy! Not long now and he'll be back in the saddle.'

'He's a physician,' someone in the group laughs. 'It'll be the jumping-shops of Bankside for our Nick!'

Simon Cowper, now quite in his cups, affects an effeminate simper. 'Oh, sweet Nicholas, why must you pass the hours in such low company, while I must content myself with sewing and the psalter?'

Nicholas is about to tell Simon just how wrong he is to caricature Eleanor in such a manner, but the words dissolve on his tongue. Why spur his friends to further teasing? He sighs, gives a good-natured smile and empties his tankard.

And, just for a while, the dead child on Vaesy's dissection table fades from his thoughts.

✙

Dusk, and Grass Street little more than a dark slash of overhanging timber-framed houses cutting through the city towards the river near Fish Hill.

Nicholas lies alone on his bed, his head resting on the bolster, his eyes towards the wall. He pictures Eleanor lying snugly on the other side, barely inches from him but so inaccessible that she might as well be in far-off Muscovy. She's asleep now, a welcome respite from the heaviness that keeps stirring within her.

Eleanor is the thread in the weave of his soul. She is the sunlight on the water, the sigh in the warm wind. The lines are not his. He's borrowed them from the overly poetic Cowper, his own sonnets being distinctly wooden. Eleanor is the perfect bride that his elder brother Jack used to describe in their moments of hot youthful fancy: impossibly beautiful, wholly devoid of any amorous restraint, in need of urgent rescue and usually with a name from mythology.

For Jack, the myth turned out to be a yeoman's daughter named Faith: extremities like the boughs of a sturdy oak, popping out acorns regularly every other year. But Nicholas, to his immense and perpetual astonishment, has found the real thing; though if there was any rescuing needed, it was Eleanor who performed it. He can't quite believe his luck.

Often, in his mind, he relives the moment they first danced a *pavane* together. It was at the Barnthorpe May Fair. Thirteen years of age, within a week of each other. He the prickly second son of a Suffolk yeoman, she the lithe-limbed, freckled meadow sprite, as hard to hold in one place as gossamer caught on a summer breeze. They'd known each other since infancy. Nicholas calls it his first lesson in medicine: sometimes the remedy for a malady can be staring you in the face, but you're just too stupid to see it.

For the past two hours now Harriet, their servant, has played a secret game of go-between. Whenever Ann and the midwife insist that Nicholas and Eleanor stop talking, Harriet finds a reason to visit the two chambers: a little warm broth for Eleanor... some mutton and bread for Nicholas... floor rushes that need changing before morning... piss-pots to be emptied... She uses these excuses to carry whispered messages, taking to these tasks with all the furtive skill of a government intelligencer carrying encrypted dispatches.

'How is young Jack, my sweet?' Nicholas had asked in the last spoken exchange between husband and wife, sensing the growing drowsiness in Eleanor's voice even through the wall.

'Grace is fine, Husband – thank you.'

Jack, if it's a boy – named for Nicholas's elder brother; Grace, if it's a girl, in memory of Eleanor's grandmother.

When he'd spoken again he'd received no reply, only a muttered, 'For mercy's sake, hush!' from his mother-in-law.

At the end of the working day Nicholas Shelby has never hesitated to discuss a difficult diagnosis with his wife, or to make her laugh loudly by mimicking some particularly pompous or difficult patient. But tonight, with Eleanor so close to her time, how can he even mention what he's seen at the Guildhall? He must endure it alone, with only the sound of his own breathing for company.

He touches the plaster, letting his fingertips rest there a while. Though the wall is barely thicker than the span of his hand, it feels as cold and as impenetrable as a castle's.

Suddenly, he fears the night to come. He fears he will have bad dreams. Dreams of dead infants hoisted on Spanish pitchforks. Dreams of a child bled dry and floating on the tide. Whole columns of grey, empty-eyed, lifeless children marching across a barren landscape that is half muddy Thames riverbank, half flat Dutch polder. And every one of them his and Eleanor's. More than anything, he fears his own imagination.

In fact, he sleeps surprisingly soundly. He stirs only when the lodging's prize cockerel beats – by a good half-hour – the bell at Trinity church.

✠

Unable to see Eleanor, and with no patients to visit the next morning, Nicholas seeks out the clerk to William Danby, the Queen's Coroner. While it might not matter to Fulke Vaesy that a nameless little boy could end his short life in such a manner, in the present circumstances it matters greatly to Nicholas Shelby.

The wholly natural sensitivities of the expectant father.

Damn me for it, if you dare, he tells an imaginary Sir Fulke as he heads for Whitehall. Some of us still remember why we chose healing for a profession.

The clerk to the Queen's Coroner is a precise, bespectacled man in a gown of legal black. Nicholas finds him in a room more like a cell than an office, filling out the weekly city mortuary roll. He writes with a slow, methodical hand on a thin ribbon of parchment, carefully transferring the names of the dead from the individual parish reports.

What must it be like, Nicholas wonders as he waits for the man to acknowledge him, to spend your day tallying up the deceased? What happens if you misspell a name? If a Tyler in life becomes a Tailor in death, simply through inattention, are they still the same person to posterity that a wife or a brother remembers? Such mistakes can easily happen, especially in times of plague, when the clerks can't write fast enough to keep accurate records.

Names... Jack for a boy. Grace for a girl. Names unknown, save unto God...

'The boy they found at the Wildgoose stairs—' he begins, when at last the clerk looks up.

The man lays down his nib. He places it well to one side of the parchment roll to prevent an inky splatter obliterating some-one's existence. He ponders a moment, trying to place one child amongst so many. Then, as though he's recalling some unwanted piece of furniture, 'Ah yes, the one we allowed to the College of Physicians—'

'I wondered if he had a name yet.'

'If he had, I can assure you we would not have agreed to the request for dissection.'

'Someone must know who he was, surely.'

The clerk shrugs. 'We asked the watermen who found him. And the tenants in the nearby houses. None admitted to knowing the boy. Perhaps he was a vagrant's brat. Or a mariner's child, fallen off one of the barques moored in the Pool. Sadly, there are many such taken from the Thames at this time of year: fishing for eels, grubbing for meat scraps at the shambles. They wander into the water and the next thing they know—' He makes a little explosive puff through his lips to signify the sudden watery end to someone's life.

Nicholas waits a moment before he says, 'I believe he was murdered.'

A defensive flicker of the clerk's eyes. 'Murdered? On what evidence do you make such a claim?'

'I can't prove it, but I'm almost certain he was dead before he went into the water. If nothing else, justice demands an investigation.'

'Too late for justice to worry herself much now,' the clerk says with a shrug. 'I assume the College has already had the remains shriven and buried at St Bride's.'

'So I am told.'

'Then what do you expect me to do – beg the Bishop of London for a shovel, so we can dig him out from Abraham's bosom?'

The pain on Nicholas's face is clear, even in the gloom of the little chamber. 'He was somebody's son,' he says falteringly. 'He had a father, and a mother. A family. He should at least have a proper headstone.'

The clerk is not an uncaring man. The names he writes on the mortuary rolls are more to him than just a meaningless assembly of letters. His voice softens. 'Have you passed by the Aldgate or Bishopsgate recently, Dr Shelby? There are more beggars and vagrants coming into the city from the country parishes than ever before. Some bring disease with them. Many will die, especially their infants. That is a sad fact indeed. But it is God's will.'

'I know that,' says Nicholas.

'Then there's the tavern brawls, the street-fights after the curfew bell rings, children and women falling under waggon wheels, wherry passengers slipping on the river stairs...'

'I appreciate Coroner Danby is a busy man—'

The clerk picks up his pen. 'And thank Jesu the pestilence has spared us so far this summer. No, sir, I fear there will be no time to spare for investigating the death of a nameless vagrant child. There are barely enough hours in the day to arrange inquests for those who *do* have a name.'

✠

Nicholas has often treated patients whose grasp on reality is failing. He's prescribed easements for those who hear voices, or see great cities in the sky where the rest of us see only clouds. He's treated over-pious virgins who say they converse nightly with an archangel, and stolid haberdashers who tell him a succubus visits them in bed after sermon every Sunday to relieve them of their seed. He doesn't believe in possession. He believes in it about as much as he believes it necessary for a physician to cast an astrological table before making a diagnosis, something most doctors he knows seem to consider indispensable. Yet, as he leaves Whitehall, it has not occurred to him that his natural concern for Eleanor's safety is a tiny breach in the wall of his own sanity. Or that the soul of a dead infant boy might have discovered the crack.

Their father has taught the Shelby boys never to leave a task unfinished. Sown fields do not reap themselves. Nicholas visits the sisters at St Bartholomew's hospital who prepared the infant for Vaesy's examination. Their recollection is hazy. They welcomed three dead infants to the mortuary crypt on the day before the lecture, none of them memorable.

He speaks to the watermen down by the Wildgoose stairs on Bankside, where the child was pulled from the river.

'Why, sir, we know the very fellows who found the body,' one of the watermen tells him. Then, with heartfelt regret, 'But working on the water don't pay for itself, Master—'

It costs Nicholas twice the price of a wherry fare to get the names. And when he locates them, the men turn out to have been somewhere else on the day.

I thought I'd been in London long enough not to get gulled so easily, he thinks as he walks back across the bridge. He feels dispirited. Oddly ill-at-ease. He longs to share his fears with the one person he knows would listen sympathetically. But that's impossible. How can he dare even whisper of child-murder when Eleanor is so close to her time?

✠

Three days after his visit to Coroner Danby's clerk at Whitehall, Nicholas attends a formal lunch at the College of Physicians. Harriet has strict instructions not to linger if the baby comes – she is to hurry by the fastest route to the Guildhall, and no stopping to gossip on the way.

Today's guest of honour is John Lumley, Baron Lumley of the county of Durham and of various estates in Sussex and Surrey. It is Lord Lumley who, by the queen's gracious licence, had endowed the College of Physicians with an annuity of forty pounds a year – from his own purse, of course, not hers. It pays for a reader in anatomy. Sir Fulke Vaesy is the present incumbent.

The agenda is wearyingly familiar to Nicholas: first the prayers, then the food – roasted pigeon, salmon and plum porridge. Then an address by the College's distinguished president, William Baronsdale. The heat of the day and the heaviness of his formal gown lead Nicholas to wonder if he can fall asleep without anyone noticing.

Baronsdale rises with ponderous solemnity, his ruff starched to the unyielding hardness of ivory. He's barely able to move his head. He looks to Nicholas like a ferret stuck, up to the chin, in a drainpipe.

'My noble lord, sirs, gentlemen,' he begins sonorously, 'it is my duty to acquaint you with the gravest threat to face this College in all its long and august history.'

His drowsiness instantly banished, Nicholas wonders what impending calamity Baronsdale means. Has there been an outbreak of pestilence he hasn't heard about? Has Spain sent another Armada? Surely Baronsdale isn't going to mention the chaos everyone fears will come with the queen's death, given that she cannot now be expected to provide the realm with an heir. Discussion of the subject is forbidden by law. Not even old Dr Lopez, Elizabeth's physician, who at this very moment is wiping his plate with his bread, dares mention it.

This lunch might yet prove more entertaining than I'd expected, thinks Nicholas.

In fact, it transpires that Baronsdale is warning them of a far greater hazard than any of those Nicholas has contemplated. It is this: how to stop the barber-surgeons passing themselves off as professional practitioners, thus impertinently considering themselves the equal of learned physicians.

An hour later, with Nicholas's eyelids again feeling like lead, the great men of medicine agree on their defence. The nub of it, according to Baronsdale, is that the barber-surgeon uses tools in the practice of his work. He must therefore be a tradesman. In other words, little better than a blacksmith. 'Why, if everyone who wields a sharp point in their daily toil considers themselves a professional,' proclaims Baronsdale, 'there'd be a guildhall, a chapel and a chain of office for the seamstresses!'

Nicholas has an urgent need to talk to the wall at Grass Street again. But there's no escape for him. Not yet. Baronsdale hasn't finished. It appears the barber-surgeons are not the only threat facing the College.

'On Candlewick Street, a fishmonger named Crepin is alleged to be selling unauthorized cures for lameness, at two pennies a pot,' he whines. 'On Pentecost Lane, one Elvery – whose trade is that of nail-maker – is said to be concocting a syrup to cure the flux. He prescribes it without charge. Doesn't expect so much as a farthing.'

Mutters of disapproval from around the table.

'There is even a *woman*—'

More than a few gasps of horror.

'Yes, a common Bankside tavern-mistress. Goes by the name of Merton. They say she concocts diverse unlicensed remedies, without any learning whatsoever!' Baronsdale wags a finger to signify the Christian world is teetering of the edge of the pit of hell. His neck twists rigidly in his ruff as though he's trying to unscrew his head. 'We must put an end to these charlatans,' he says gravely, 'lest the learning of fifteen centuries be hawked outside St Paul's Cross for a loaf of bread or a pot of ale!'

The applause is warm and appreciative. But Nicholas notices the guest of honour, John Lumley, seems unperturbed by these dire warnings of impending catastrophe. In fact, is that a yawn the rather sorrowful-looking patron of the chair of anatomy is trying to stifle?

Though Nicholas has only observed John Lumley from his own lowly orbit, Lumley's reputation is well known to him. He is the queen's friend, though he's served time in the Tower for once desiring a Catholic monarchy. He's a man of the old faith, yet in possession of a mind always on the search for new knowledge. His great library at Nonsuch Palace is said to be the match for any university library in Europe. And though he funds the chair of anatomy from his own purse, he's not a physician. Which, thinks Nicholas, might just make him the perfect man to turn to.

But how, exactly, does a junior member of the College raise the subject of infanticide with one of its most senior – especially after his betters have gorged themselves on roasted pigeon and salmon, fine Rhenish wine and flagons of self-congratulation?

With confidence. That's the answer, Nicholas decides as he waits in the Guildhall yard while around him the servants of the more successful physicians prepare for their masters to depart. Get to the point right away. Don't hang back. Tell him what you saw.

He spots Lord Lumley's secretary, Gabriel Quigley, standing aloof to one side. Quigley is a bookish fellow in his mid-thirties. The severe folds of his gown serve only to accentuate his angular frame. His thinning hair falls loosely over a brow marked by traces of the small-pox. He looks more like a fallen priest than a lord's secretary.

'Would you do me a service, Master Quigley?' Nicholas asks. 'I'd be grateful for a brief audience with Lord Lumley.'

Quigley's reply tells Nicholas in no uncertain terms that a

lord's secretary is considerably nearer to God than a mere phy-sician, any day of the week. 'His lordship is a busy man. What would be the subject of this audience, were he to grant it?'

'A matter of great interest to an eminent man of physic,' says Nicholas, biting his tongue. It's better than 'The violent over-throw of this place and all who dwell in it', which is what he's been considering since before the plum porridge was served.

'My lord, I wondered if I might speak to you about Sir Fulke Vaesy's recent lecture,' Nicholas begins, with a respectful bend of the knee, when Quigley brokers the meeting.

'The drowned boy-child?' Lumley recalls. 'Coroner Danby took not a little convincing over him.'

'A most unusual subject, my lord.'

'Indeed, Dr Shelby. One likes to feel that when Sir Fulke dissects a hanged criminal, the fellow is making some sort of reparation for his offences by adding to our understanding of nature. But a poor drowned child is quite another matter. Still, I always say we men of learning should not let our natural sensitivities get in the way of discovery.'

Natural sensitivities. Nicholas prays Lumley isn't going to turn out to be as lacking in them as his protégé. 'My lord, on the subject of the infant – I couldn't help but notice—'

At that very moment, to his horror, Sir Fulke Vaesy himself emerges from the College hall. Striding over, he bows as gra-ciously as his girth will allow and booms, 'A grand lunch, my lord! And all the better for the dessert: barber-surgeons cooked in a pie!' He glances at Nicholas. 'How now, Shelby? Wife foaled yet?'

'Any day, Sir Fulke,' Nicholas says lamely. He can hear the sound of doors slamming. Doors to his career. And it will be Vaesy who'll be doing the slamming, if Nicholas says in the great anatomist's hearing what's been on his mind these past few days.

'Dr Shelby was about to mention your lecture, Fulke.'

'Was he now?'

Nicholas bites his tongue. 'I was going to say how instructive I found it, Sir Fulke.'

Vaesy beams, thinking good reviews can only make Lumley's forty pounds a year that bit more secure.

Lumley pulls on the hem of his gloves in preparation for departure. 'Was there anything else, sirrah? Master Quigley suggested you wished to speak to me on an important matter.'

Nicholas clutches at the only straw left to him: delay. 'Perhaps I might be allowed to correspond with you, my lord – to seek your views on matters of new physic. I'd value them greatly.'

To his relief, Lumley seems flattered. 'By all means, Dr Shelby. I shall look forward to it. I always like to hear from the younger men in the profession – minds less set. Don't you, Fulke?'

Vaesy doesn't seem to understand the question.

As Nicholas walks away he can almost hear the drowned boy whispering his approval: *You are my only voice. Don't let them silence me. Don't give up.*

✠

On his way home Nicholas stops by the East Cheap cistern to wash the dust from his face. It's hot, he's eaten too much, listened to enough worthy back-slapping to last him a decade. Close to the fountain stands a religious firebrand reciting the gospels, punctuating his readings with dire warnings of man's imminent destruction, to anyone who will listen. Few bother. A lad in a leather apron leads a fractious ram by a chain in the direction of Old Exchange Lane. A rook alights on the branches of a nearby tree and begins to caw loudly.

These are the minor details that will stay seared into Nicholas's mind for ever. They have no particular importance. They are mere dressing for the centrepiece of the masque: Harriet.

She's hurrying towards him, not even bothering to lift the hem of her dress from the filth of the street. He opens his mouth to call out.

Boy or girl? Jack or Grace?

He doesn't care which. A boy will be the greatest physician in Europe, a girl the mirror of her mother. But the words cannot fly his mouth. They are glued there by the awful expression on Harriet's flushed face.

✝

Silence.

Elise has sworn never to allow a single word to pass her lips, no matter how long she lives or how desperate she becomes. A single careless word might bring the angel back.

Silence is a hard restraint. It is by no means her natural state. Her mother used to tell her that God Himself would soon go deaf from her constant chattering. But that was before Mary Cullen had descended into her own mute world of drunken insensibility, informing her on the way that God had crippled her little brother Ralph as a punishment for Elise's ungovernable tongue. Now silence is Elise's only protector.

She would beg for food, but she knows what will happen if she does: people will spit at her, throw stones that buzz like bees past her head or strike her painfully in the back. They will call for a man with a whip to chase her away, or threaten her with a branding, even having an ear sliced from her head to mark her for the vagrant they say she is.

So Elise does not beg. Instead, she lives off scraps of food thieved from window ledges and unattended tables, sleeps on the hard earth beneath the briars. She is utterly alone, without even little Ralph for company now. The only human voice she hears and does not flee from is her mother's, whispering to her the old story: that there is somewhere better than here, my darling, and if you go down to the Tabard and beg a cup of arak on credit, I will tell you how to get there.

3

What follows Nicholas Shelby's return to Grass Street is as predictable as the unravelling of a scarf when an errant thread is tugged, and just as unstoppable.

Ann cannot meet his wildly searching gaze. She turns from her son-in-law as though he's a ranting madman. But this time neither she nor the midwife bars his entrance to the lying-in chamber.

Eleanor's skin is feverish to the touch. His fingers come away chilled by her sweat. The flesh around her belly is as hard as iron. It does not yield to the pressure of his palm. Her eyes are closed, her breathing little more than the panting after a lost fight. She seems already to have put a great distance between them.

'There is no sign of imminent birth,' the midwife tells him. 'Barely a single drop of blood discharged from the privy region – just some small quantity of her water.' She makes it sound as though things are only a little awry, not quite as expected, no real need to worry. Do I sound like that, he wonders, when I'm delivering grim news?

It's the first time he's entered this chamber since it was closed off for the birthing. It feels like a foreign land to him. He glances to a collection of dark-red pebbles at the foot of the bed. 'What are those supposed to do?'

'They are holy stones, stained by the blood of St Margaret,' the midwife replies, not a little frightened by the intensity in his stare.

'She needs medicine, woman, not superstition,' he shouts, sweeping them away with an angry wave of his hand. They rattle on the uneven floorboards like noisy accusations. 'Harriet!' he calls. The girl appears at his side. She seems to have caught some of Eleanor's deathly pallor. 'Run to the apothecary by All Hallows for a balm of lady mantle and wort. Hurry!'

'No balm can alter God's will, Nicholas,' says Ann, laying a hand on his shoulder. 'It is not good to fight what is ordained.'

Ann is not a thoughtless woman; she's already lost two children of her own, a boy in childbirth, another daughter who lived less than a month. Trials, she believes, are sent by God to test our mettle. Her words are intended to bring strength to her son-in-law. Instead, they only make him angrier.

'It might help induce the birth,' he shouts. 'It has to be better than prayer and holy stones!'

Eleanor is fading away before his eyes. But it takes almost two full days. And not once during that time does Nicholas get so much as the paltry comfort of knowing she's aware he's beside her – not a squeeze of his hand, not even a slack smile of recognition. Nothing.

When he's not sitting on a stool by the bed, moistening her lips with a wet cloth, he's to be found leafing frantically through his books: Galen's Art of Physic, Vesalius's Fabrica, half a dozen more. He's searching for some scrap of redeeming knowledge that he thinks he might have forgotten. But he's forgotten nothing. Eleanor is going to die not because of what Nicholas has forgotten, but what he never knew.

On the second day, around eight in the evening, in his desperation he even considers a caesarean delivery. He's heard about such a procedure, though he's never actually seen one performed. And he knows that even if the child is saved, the mother will die. To his knowledge, there has only ever been one instance of both surviving, and that was in Switzerland. How can he possibly plunge a knife into the belly of his beloved Eleanor in order to save their child? But if he doesn't...

Her breathing is getting slower and deeper. Now and again comes a sound like the one his winter boots make when he steps by mistake into the mud of the Finsbury fields. He grips Eleanor's cold hand and screws his eyes as though peering into the sun.

Why did they wait so long to call me?

Why did I go to that wretched feast?

Why do the swiftly passing minutes of her final struggle mock me so cruelly? What good is my knowledge now?

Why can't I *do* anything?

Why?... why?... why?

✠

The day after the funeral service for mother and child, held at Trinity church, Nicholas stands in the lying-in chamber at Grass Street. Now it's just another empty room – a sloping floor that creaks when you walk on it, irregular pillars of oak holding up a low sagging ceiling, a small leaded window giving onto the lane, the shutters open for the first time in weeks.

Just another room.

He puts out one hand to touch the uneven plaster. He thinks of the recent nights he's spent on the other side of this wall, straining his senses to catch Eleanor's soft, feminine murmurs, longing to be with her. He stares at his splayed fingers pressed against the surface, barely recognizing them as his own. The room is silent now, empty. He could call to the wall for eternity and never receive a reply. Weak with grief, he lets go of the wall and sinks to his knees.

Just another room.

Someone else's hand.

Someone else's tragedy.

His gaze comes to rest on a patch of plaster beside the door frame, where he and Eleanor had planned to make a mark each birthday to record their child's growth. They'd agreed to stop at thirteen. If it's a boy, they'd decided, he'll grow too fast. If it's a girl, at thirteen she'll think such fancies childish. Now the wall will stay unmarked for ever.

Time has become something ugly and distorted for him now. Minutes have become confused with years. Crouching by the door, he remembers the incredibly slow pace of their betrothal. Their parents had given them a year's indulgence, to see if their attachment was anything but a foolish passing fever. When it had become clear it was not, the serious business had begun: acreages measured for the dowry, searches conducted to ensure there were no undeclared mortgages hanging over houses or holdings, no errant uncles with papist tendencies, no undisclosed cattle thieves amongst recent ancestors. Day passing slowly into day, with always another day to wait. It all seems so long ago now, yet at the same time it's unfolding in his mind as though for the first time. Years, days, hours – how it is that time tricks you so?

The next day a letter arrives at Grass Street. He has Harriet read it to him because his eyes don't seem able to focus the way they used to:

> ... the harvest is well in hand... your brother Jack is a tower
> of strength, as usual... your mother is well... she's received
> the fine psalter you sent her and reads a psalm from it
> each night before we sleep. It looks expensive. You must be
> doing well. Eleanor's father asks you to kiss his daughter
> for him. And the best of news: your sister-in-law has been
> safely delivered of another sturdy acorn.

4

Across the gentle slopes of the North Downs three men ride out to fly their hawks and bring home coney and pigeon for the pot. It's early September, feels more like autumn. The air is still, the sky shroud-white. When the birds fly from the glove they instantly become mere darting shadows, almost lost against the trees. The world's span has shrunk to the next hedgerow.

Down sunken lanes and across meadows strung with bejewelled spider-silk, past manor house and parish church, through fords that Caesar's legions once muddied with their boots, the hunters follow a long, lazy circuit from Ewell through Epsom and back across Cheam Common. The fruit-pickers in the orchards appear from the mist like ghosts, hoping for a glimpse of them.

For these riders are no ordinary men. Servants hurry after them across the fields, bearing hampers of mutton and cheese, skins of the best Rhenish wine. This is not hunting as any humble man might imagine it.

'Tis beyond doubt, Master Robert, you have a fine bird there,' says John Lumley to his nearest companion, as a sudden flurry of bloody feathers drifts on the slack air. 'Your Juno is putting my Paris to shame.'

Lumley is the host of today's agreeable expedition. His long, mournful Northumbrian face seems made for the weather, his deep shovel-cut beard glistens with dew. In addition to being patron of the College of Physicians' chair of anatomy, Lumley is also the over-mortgaged owner of Nonsuch, the magnificent hunting lodge built in the rolling Surrey countryside by Elizabeth's father, King Henry. Nonsuch. So beautiful there is *none such* place to match it. *Nonpareil*, as the Frenchies would have it. Prettier by far than Greenwich, more striking even than Cardinal Wolsey's vast temple to vanity at Hampton Court. And what its owner really means, when he compliments young Robert Cecil on the quality of his falcon, is: I wonder if you're training her to pluck out my heart, so you can steal Nonsuch from me and hand it to the queen as a gift? You think it would raise your stock in her estimation.

Just because you hunt with a fellow, it doesn't mean you trust him. Not in these uncertain times.

Juno settles on her master's outstretched glove with a blurred thrashing of her wings and a tinny peal of the little bells tied to her leather jesses.

'Did you see how artfully she took her prey?' Robert Cecil asks boastfully, reaching into his saddlebag and rewarding the bird with a morsel of raw rabbit flesh, while a servant runs across the muddy field to recover the corpse. 'I'll warrant my Juno can open up a body a deal more swiftly than even your friend Fulke Vaesy. And she doesn't cost me forty pounds per annum, either.'

Lumley thinks, I wonder if you've also taught her to spy on me, count the size of the debts I owe the Crown. Save yourself the trouble – just ask your father.

In his seventy-first year, and by no means in the best of health after long and arduous service to his monarch, Robert's father William Cecil sits upon his horse so comfortably that you'd think they'd been joined since birth, which in private moments the horse probably laments they have been. When lesser men wish to compliment William Cecil on how audaciously his falcon has plucked a pigeon out of the sky, or sent a coney tumbling stone-dead through the grass, they do not cry, 'Well done, William!' Most call him 'Your Grace' or 'my noble Lord Burghley', the pre-eminent of his numerous titles. At Whitehall they call him 'my Lord Treasurer', which is his office of state. There's only one person in all England who calls him whatever she pleases, and that is the queen. Mostly she calls him 'Spirit'. Nicknames are a favourite game of hers. At court a nickname means you've arrived. At twenty-seven, Robert Cecil is still waiting for his. He considers it long overdue – along with his knighthood.

'Is it true what I hear, Lord Lumley – that Sir Fulke is the greatest anatomist in all England?' Robert asks casually.

'I believe so, Master Robert.'

'It must be most instructive – observing at such close quarters God's miraculous handiwork. I should like to attend one of his lectures, if court duties afford me the leisure.'

'The College would be honoured, I'm sure.'

Old Burghley chuckles. 'Slicing a man to pieces on the dissection table... court business – much the same basket of apples, if you ask me! What say you, Lumley?'

Lumley, who has spent a lifetime at court bending to the wind of the queen's changeable temper, merely smiles.

'And who was the subject of Vaesy's recent lecture, my lord?' Robert Cecil asks. 'Some hanged felon? It's right, don't you think, that those who refuse to be governed should give something back at the end? Lord knows, they thieve enough from us while they're alive.'

'A young boy – about four or five.'

'Are we hanging children now?' asks Burghley with a scowl.

'A drowned vagrant, Your Grace, taken from the river. Of no name or consequence, as far as we could determine.'

'Where's the benefit in cutting up a child?' asks Robert Cecil.

'Is there not more to be learned from the body of a grown man? Are the organs not closer to perfection?'

'Sir Fulke recently travelled to Padua, where he was able to observe the professors there dissect a crippled child,' Lumley explains. 'The infant taken from the water was similarly afflicted. Sir Fulke is trying to discover if deformed limbs are God's intention or merely a result of our own human imperfection.'

John Lumley's words fall heavily, like a whole flock of downed pigeons. Lumley might be a seasoned courtier, but he's just proved he's not above stepping in dog-shit when he's not looking where he's going. For Robert Cecil's body is not streamlined like Juno's, or as effortlessly agile. He's crook-backed. His splayed legs do not rest comfortably on the flanks of his horse. He's not made as elegantly as a courtier should be made. As a consequence, he feeds hungrily on insults. Even unintended ones.

'So Vaesy's been to papist Padua, has he?' he asks icily. 'On *your* commission?'

Lumley wonders why his mouth has suddenly dried up. He appeals to Burghley to get him off the hook. 'He went there purely for matters of academic discovery – to the university. I can assure Your Grace, Sir Fulke is unswervingly true to the queen's faith.'

Robert Cecil smiles wanly. But there is steel in the smile, nonetheless. 'All I know, my lord, is that when Juno opens up a carcass with her talons, she does it not for the discovery, but for the thrill of it.'

✠

The dream comes to him every night without fail.

When it wakes him, always at the same point, Nicholas knows there will be no more sleep to be had. He will toss and turn until dawn. So, in an effort to stop the dream plaguing him, he demands that Harriet bring him a jug of arak from the pantry. He keeps it by his bed, refusing to let her remove the bottle except to replenish it – which she now does every morning.

The dream is not a dream of loss. It's a call to follow. And it's always the same: Eleanor walking along the riverbank, stepping carefully across the pebbles, her bare feet splashing through the pools and rivulets. She is accompanied by a child who clings to her hand – the little boy from Fulke Vaesy's dissection table. He's been stuck back together as if he were made from clay. Always they are too far ahead of him to reach.

And what wakes him is the sound of the tide rushing in between.

✠

For some time now, Nicholas Shelby has absented himself from sermon. It has been noted.

'We feel most sorely for our brother in Christ,' says the priest at Trinity church to Nicholas's mother-in-law, Ann. 'But is it not unduly wilful for a man to deny himself God's healing balm when he hath most need of it?'

'He is beyond all reason, Father,' Ann replies sadly.

She is not an uncaring woman, but she knows she can do no more for her son-in-law. She decides to return to Barnthorpe. She tells herself it's because the roads will soon become impassable. But in truth, winter is still a good while away.

When Nicholas is again absent for Sunday sermon, the church authorities decide – regrettably – that grief is an insufficient excuse for wilful non-attendance. They write to him at Grass Street.

'What does it say?' Nicholas asks, ordering Harriet to open the letter.

He has moved his bed into the room they'd used for the lying-in chamber. He's refused to let Harriet remove the thick woollen drapes from the little window, parting them enough to let in only a single shaft of dusty light. Harriet is too afraid to clean the room now, and Nicholas hasn't appeared to notice. It's mid-morning. He's still abed. The jug is empty. She speaks to him from the doorway because he stinks of sweat and arak. And he hasn't been near the Grass Street barber in a fortnight.

'They're fining you a shilling, Master, for recusancy. They say they're being compassionate – they could have fined you twelve.'

'Tear it up,' Nicholas tells her brusquely. He's decided he has no wish to worship a God as uncaring as theirs. They belong to a world that is already alien to him. He pulls the bed sheet over his head, desperately seeking a few more moments' anguished sleep.

Receiving no response, the churchwardens send another letter. It is rather less compassionate than the first. In it they warn Nicholas that if they find any hint of a refusal to accept the queen's religion, they have it in their power to fine him more than he earns in a whole year. This threat moves him no more than the first.

On Holy Cross Day, in the middle of September, Simon Cowper spots him coming out of the Star on Fish Street Hill. The bell at St Margaret's has just tolled five in the afternoon. His friend's white canvas doublet looks as though its owner has been rolling about in the street. He's obviously drunk.

'I thought you favoured the White Swan,' Simon says amiably.

'Full of sour-faced Puritans averse to dice, loud debate and dancing. No fun at all,' Nicholas growls, by which he means he's been thrown out on his ear.

'People have been asking after you; Michael Gardener and the others...'

'Why?' It's a challenge rather than a question. Nicholas doesn't care about the answer; his present concern is making it across

Fish Street Hill to the sign of the Troubadour. Simon has to pull him out of the way of an oncoming waggon.

'We understand the sore hurt you endure, Nick. Really we do,' Simon tells him, holding on to his friend's arm to stop him falling where he stands.

'Do you now? Is that a fact?'

His eyes are raw, Simon Cowper notes, as though he hasn't slept for days. 'Nicholas, I know this is a grievous trial for you—'

Nicholas's interruption is harsh and contemptuous. 'Tell me, Simon, what precisely *do* you think you know?'

'I don't understand—'

'What does any doctor know? What does Fulke Vaesy know? God's blood! The man can't tell a stab wound from a hernia.' He stares at Simon like a madman, spitting out the words. 'And what about me? What sort of physician am I? What do I know?'

'Nick, perhaps if you went to sermon again—'

But Nicholas isn't listening. 'I'll tell you what Dr Nicholas Shelby knows,' he says, pulling his arm away from Simon's grasp and holding up the thumb and forefinger of his right hand to make a crooked zero, 'he knows about this much of nothing.'

The last Simon Cowper sees of his friend is Nicholas's back as he staggers off in the direction of the Troubadour – save for the moment when he turns and shouts back at him cruelly, 'If you know so much, Simon, you'll know to leave me be... and stick to writing shitty poems to your mistress!'

✠

If you look beyond the grief, you'll find it's not self-pity that is destroying Nicholas Shelby. He is not the self-pitying kind. Rather, it is rage. Rage pure and simple. Rage against an uncaring God. Rage against his discovery that everything he's learned – from the teachings of Aristotle, Hippocrates and Galen, to the practical physic he picked up in Holland – is worth nothing at all. When he'd chided the midwife for placing holy medals on Eleanor's birthing bed, for putting sprigs of betony and vervain on the sills of the little shuttered window, for any number of her frivolous superstitions, he could just as well have kept silent. His own vaunted knowledge has proved to be no better than any of it.

And he's developing a dangerous confusion as he drinks and rages, losing the patience of one landlord after another. The dead infant on Fulke Vaesy's dissecting table has somehow widened the breach in his sanity. It has wormed its way deep inside his head. Now he's beginning to believe that the child was his and Eleanor's.

His wild demeanour begins to alarm even Harriet. Tearfully, she finds employment with a draper's family on Distaff Lane. Nicholas barely notices. Nor does it seem to trouble him when, with increasing rapidity, his clients start to seek the safer counsel of other doctors.

✠

The leaves are turning. It's autumn. The curfew bells ring out at nine prompt. Then the taverns empty, the city gates slam shut, and men and women of modesty and goodly keeping bolt their doors. They read from their psalters, talk over the day's business, tuck themselves up in their beds like hens in the coop. To keep the foxes at bay they have the bellmen, stout fellows who roam the empty streets bearing horn lanterns and accompanied by dogs the size of three-headed Cerberus. In the lanes of Grass Street ward, these watchmen save Nicholas from a kicking or a purse-cutting on more than one occasion. They are gentle with him. They know him. After all, didn't he cure Ned Tate's wife of the quatrain fever last Candlemas? When Davy Trow got that dose of French gout from a bawdy-house in Southwark, didn't Nicholas prescribe mercury at half the usual price? With increasing concern for his safety they pick him up, brush him down and send him home.

His clients, however, are all gone now. They'd rather trust their symptoms to the fall of a dice than to a wild-eyed madman, a Tom-o-Bedlam, a fellow with the suffering of Christ in his eyes. Who'd want to be bled by a physician who can barely stand up, let alone hold a blade still?

'I swear Lucifer has him by the throat,' says the last one to go, a haberdasher named Hawes, whose child Nicholas cured last Easter of painfully inflamed gums. 'Does he think he'll not marry again? She was only a wife, for Jesu's sake. A fine and comely one, I'll grant you, but the way he's carrying on, you'd think he'd lost the blessed Virgin herself.'

London is a dangerous place in which to lose your mind. Almost every second man carries a blade of some sort. Thus far, Nicholas has escaped with little worse than bruises as he gets expelled from almost every tavern between the Fleet ditch and Fish Street Hill. He picks quarrels for no apparent reason. He gives no thought as to how long his luck might hold.

At the sign of the Green Falcon he gets thrown into the gutter when he discovers – after more jugs of stitch-back than he can accurately count – that an expert cut-purse has neatly filleted away his coin, leaving no evidence of the attack other than a neat tear in his cloak. Given the number of people Nicholas had barged into on the way there, it could have happened at any point over a distance of quarter of a mile, say between the Old Jewry and the top of St Clements Lane.

His closest brush with a prison cell comes on a windy Friday afternoon in early October. On a drunken whim he returns to the office of Coroner William Danby at Whitehall. He's become convinced that the child on Vaesy's dissection table was Eleanor's child – *their* child – delivered before her death. He also imagines, for no reason a sane man might entertain, that Coroner Danby gave the boy to Fulke Vaesy to cut up so that Nicholas would never learn the name of his only son. Wild-eyed amongst the sober lawyers and functionaries of Whitehall, he somehow gets as far as the office of the coroner's clerk.

'I want a headstone, at St Bride's churchyard, where he's buried,' he cries, remembering that Vaesy had told him that's where the remains had been taken. 'But I need a name to put on it! Why won't you tell me his name? Why is Coroner Danby hiding it? Why did Fulke Vaesy bleed him empty before I got to the Guildhall?'

Why?... why?... why?

The clerk is so terrified he drops his pen and his mortuary rolls and flees.

Madmen are not generally welcome at Whitehall. Nicholas escapes being thrown into the dungeons only because he's put on his doctoral gown in an effort to give himself more dignity. As it is, the halberdiers who throw him out ensure he crawls away like a whipped dog.

He returns to the riverbank. He stands in the shallows as though he's waiting for converts to baptize. He's indifferent to the ice-cold water and the bruises the Whitehall halberdiers have inflicted. The arak is coursing through him like fire.

He's contrived to convince himself this is the spot where the child was pulled from the river – the Wildgoose stairs on Bankside. It's not. He's on the northern shore, a little east of the Queenhithe moorings, at the foot of Garlic Hill. But in his present state he could be standing on the banks of the Rhine and still believe he was in Southwark.

Only now he's in possession of a name.

'Were you there when they pulled my Jack from the river?' he shouts alarmingly to a stout woman grubbing for shellfish on the shingle.

Jack, if it's a boy... Grace, if it's a girl...

To the inhabitants of the tenements along the riverbank, raving drunks and madmen are as common as the tide. The woman lays down her basket of whelks and oysters, straightens up and massages her aching back with her muddy hands.

Nicholas wades out of the water like a survivor from a shipwreck. 'A boy of about four or five,' he says, slapping his thighs with hands turned rosy by the cold. 'Crippled in the legs—'

To his amazement, she answers, 'Oh, aye. I remember such a fellow.'

The heat of the arak in his veins turns into a warm flood of hope and yearning. 'You *do*?'

'In the summer – around last St Swithun's Day, if I recall.'

'Did he tell you his name?'

'I thought you said his name was Jack,' the woman says, frowning.

'Did you speak to him?'

The woman gives him a sly squint. 'D'you think these here cockles jump into this basket by themselves?'

Nicholas fumbles in his purse for a penny. The woman turns the coin over in her hand to see if it's been clipped. Apparently satisfied, she nods across the broad expanse of grey-brown water to where the low roofs of Bankside stand like a palisade before the Rose theatre and the bear-pit.

'It wasn't on this shore,' she explains. 'I'd gone across the bridge to fish the other bank. That's when I set eyes on them.'

Something akin to joy surges in Nicholas's deluded breast. '*Them*? You saw Eleanor, too?'

'Was that her name – Eleanor?'

'She was my wife.'

The woman gives him a suspicious stare. 'Your wife? Mercy, she can't have been more than thirteen. I thought at the time, how can a maid of such tender years bear the weight of a crippled young boy on her back without complaint?'

Even in his present delirium Nicholas is still able to distinguish the difference between Eleanor and a thirteen-year-old maid. His heart sinks. 'I want to know about the child,' he demands, reaching out to clutch the woman's arm.

'What is there to tell?' she asks nervously, avoiding his outstretched hand and causing him to lose his balance on the shingle. She's decided she doesn't like the look of him after all. Too much of a zealot by half, she thinks. She shrugs. 'He had the marks of Christ's crucifixion on his limbs, and a lamb with a halo trotting at his side, for all I know. What's it got to do with me?'

Now believing that she's been trying to gull him all along, Nicholas tries to snatch back his coin. The woman evades his grasp. She throws down the penny as if it's burning her palm and puts as much distance between herself and the madman as she can, leaving her basket where it lies – and Nicholas with no notion of how close he's come to the truth.

The descent is not yet complete, there is still a little way to fall.

A chill autumn night, a little after one. The drizzle turns the stones of Greyfriars a slick, dark silver. The watch hears muffled curses from the adjacent cemetery. They arrive just in time to prevent Nicholas Shelby being beaten to a pulp and what's left of him being thrown into the river. His assailants disappear into the lanes.

Every watchman's dog knows Nicholas as an old friend now. When they encounter him, they wag rather than snarl. He wakes painfully to the slippery kiss of snuffling jowls. He groans, curses and rolls over on his face, like a man trying to find a more comfortable position in which to sleep. One arm stretches out to grub at the soaking earth, as if he's trying to pull a sheet over him.

If it was somewhere other than Greyfriars churchyard, the watch might let it pass. But Nicholas has been brawling on holy ground. The local justice of the peace is a very godly man and a great champion of the Vagrancy Act. So the watchmen haul Nicholas off to the Wood Street counter, where he spends the night on hard boards amongst a score of other prisoners, insensible to the stench and the squalor. He lies on his back, snoring like a parson. The watch leaves tuppence with the gaoler, so at least he'll have some breakfast when he sobers up.

At Barnthorpe, the family has been troubled by the absence of letters. With the harvest safely gathered in, brother Jack borrows his father's horse and rides down to London to investigate. Ann has told him what to expect, though she hasn't revealed the worrying details to his parents. Jack visits the lodgings on Grass Street. Someone else is living there now.

He doesn't give up easily. He finds his way to the Swan. There he talks to a brace of young physicians. We rather hoped you might tell us where he is, they say. If you see him, tell him Simon Cowper bears him no grudge.

Where else to look? There must be upwards of two hundred thousand souls in London. How do you find just one amongst such a multitude? Especially if – as it seems – he doesn't want to be found.

For Nicholas Shelby, lapsed member of the College of Physicians, seems to have disappeared from the face of the earth as though he'd never existed.

5

Cold Oak manor lies in a meadow bordering the Thames at Vauxhall, west of Lambeth Palace. Like many of the nearby houses and white-painted weatherboard cottages, it serves as a bolthole from the noise and stench of the city, and as a place of comparative safety should pestilence come. It is a fine house with mullioned windows, a tiled roof and a long meadow sloping gently down towards the river. Cold Oak belongs to Sir Fulke Vaesy, though he is seldom here. It is where he has all but incarcerated his wife, Lady Katherine – a nunnery no longer being available, since the late King Henry threw down the religious houses. For Kat's part, the arrangement suits her just fine. She has her own household; she is well regarded by the neighbouring families. It is a pleasant enough life, except when *he* comes to visit.

Vaesy is here now. He's been ambushed into it by the President of the College of Physicians, William Baronsdale, who expects his senior fellows to have tidy domestic lives.

'Your place at Vauxhall would be ideal,' Baronsdale had told Vaesy, when the question had been raised of how the College should celebrate the forthcoming Accession Day in a style fitting to Her Majesty. 'We'll all meet at Cold Oak to make our plans. What say you, Sir Fulke?'

What *could* he say? 'To the Devil with that, I can't bear to be in the same room as that witch of a wife'?

So here he stands, playing the part of the eminent man of physic, while the servants unwrap the newly arrived visitors like gift parcels on New Year's Day. Looking on, while they bear away cloaks and hats for safe-keeping. Tutting when they leave little puddles of rainwater on the floor.

'Come, Wife, and greet our guests,' he calls to Kat, as though he and Lady Katherine are paragons of domestic harmony. In his heart he wonders what size of brick Kat will drop into the mill-pond this time, just to humiliate him. He already suspects the fellows of the College snigger behind his back: *Have you heard? Fulke Vaesy can't keep his wife in her proper place. And a man who can't control his wife has only himself to blame if his servants thumb their noses at him and call him 'sirrah'.*

Kat has dressed in a simple gown of blue taffeta, the collar drawn back to show the lace sitting modestly around her neck. Her once-golden hair is bound severely beneath an embroidered French hood. She knows, from observing herself in the mirror glass in her chamber, and by the dove-like cooing of her maid, that enough of her once considerable beauty is on show today to turn the heads of her husband's guests. If any of them shows so much as a gelding's interest in her, she will flirt. Just to infuriate him.

At the foot of the stairs she pauses briefly to give John Lumley a dutiful curtsey. She's known Lord Lumley for more than twenty years. She was a bridesmaid at his wedding to the late Jane FitzAlan, his first wife. Jane was Kat's dearest friend, and she still misses her wise counsel. So John Lumley she will not flirt with. They are too close.

'Welcome, gentlemen all,' she says, addressing the assembled men of medicine. 'It is a great sadness to feel so well in the presence of so many eminent physicians. Think of the wisdom I am denied!' Her smile broadens with the appreciative murmur of laughter. 'There are meats and pies in the parlour, and malmsey for those not too Puritan to drink at noontime. My husband will show the way.'

The guest parlour is a spacious wood-panelled room with a view over the orchard. On the table the servants have set plates of brawn, pastry chewets stuffed with minced lamb and dishes of spiced comfits. A maid is on hand to pour malmsey and small-beer from pewter jugs. Some of the physicians wish to smoke, so a dish of embers is sent for, as they take out their clay pipes and stuff the bowls with nicotiana.

'Lady Katherine is clearly a woman of rare facility, Sir Fulke,' says Baronsdale as he indicates the laden table, without looking at her.

'Proverbs tells us that a good wife is like a merchant's argosy, bringing bread from distant places,' Vaesy says with a wan smile.

Katherine replies with her eyes: in that case, Husband, may you founder on the sharpest reef and drown in the deepest of depths, where the worms that slither in the mud can feast on your bones. What she actually says is only a little less inflammatory.

'Then how long must we wait, Mr Baronsdale, until a woman's "rare facility" allows her to practise medicine?'

Baronsdale's face is a picture of bewilderment. She might as well have asked him when the College could expect to license a monkey, or one of those strange beasts they keep in the menagerie at the Tower. Her husband seems equally nonplussed. The anger flares in his eyes.

'I do not quite understand, Lady Katherine,' says Samuel Beston, who once treated her father for pebbles in the bladder. 'A *woman*, you say—'

'Wife, be attentive to the serving, if you please,' Vaesy warns with a smile as empty as her own.

Out of the corner of her eye, Kat notices John Lumley's usually dour face crease with a barely constrained smile. He is the one person in this room she has no need to convince.

'Come, Mr Beston,' she says, revelling in her husband's

discomfort, 'have I suggested we turn the world on its head?'

'But, madam, there is an order in all things that must be observed,' says Baronsdale. 'And that is God's order. Besides, a woman would not have the learning—'

'But she could acquire the learning, couldn't she?'

'How so, Lady Vaesy?' asks old Lopez, the Portuguese Jew, one of the queen's doctors.

'Lady Vaesy is not suggesting the impossible,' says Lumley. He seems to be enjoying this. 'Abbess Hildegard was practising medicine in the Palatine five hundred years ago. Before the Moors were ejected from Spain, they could count any number of female physicians. Yet all we have in England are a few practitioners of folk law.'

'Whom we shall shut down, just as soon as the Lord Mayor and the Bishop of London allow us,' says Beston, who's utterly misunderstood John Lumley's meaning.

'It is not right to challenge the order God has imposed upon us,' says Baronsdale firmly. 'On the way here, I saw a band of itinerants grubbing for food in the ditches. Would you have them raised to the state of princes?'

'I would have them fed,' says Kat.

Beston pulls a face, suggesting Kat's got it all wrong. 'And they are fed, madam.'

'Have you asked them, sir?'

'There is no need. For those who have fallen upon calamity through no fault of their own, the state and the Church provide alms and charity. The ones Master Baronsdale was referring to were of another sort entirely.'

'Ah, yes,' says Kat. 'The undeserving poor. I wondered when we'd get around to them.'

'Exactly, madam – tinkers, feckless vagabonds and the like. For them, there is the law: the scourge and the whip.'

'God's order?'

'Incontrovertibly,' says Baronsdale.

The physicians leave. John Lumley is almost the last to go. He kisses Kat's hand and gives her a conspiratorial smile. 'Thank you, Kat. Deliciously *piquant*, as usual – the food, I mean.'

'Commend my affections to Lizzy, my lord,' she replies. She likes John's new wife almost as much as she liked Jane.

'I shall, madam, gladly.'

As Lumley turns away, Fulke Vaesy favours his wife with no leave-taking other a hard stare of reproach. He calls angrily for a servant to saddle his horse.

Once more mistress of Cold Oak manor, Kat walks in the orchard to rid herself of the cloying remembrance of her husband and his companions. She pauses before the row of beehives standing like white headstones amongst the trees. She thinks back to when she was fifteen, the year she married Fulke. He'd been thirty-five then, the very age she is now, and physician to John Lumley. She can still picture her father's letter. He'd not even had the courage to tell her to her face:

> Daughter, be dutiful unto me and agree to my will, which is that you make a marriage...

Kat cannot make that young girl fit the person she is now. That person – that child – had harboured fanciful dreams of a life rich with bliss, a handsome gallant of a husband by her side, a house full of children, a life married to the man she already adored – a man most certainly *not* Fulke Vaesy.

And then, with that letter, her father had slammed the door on every one of them.

She wonders idly if Fulke still wants her, the way he did when she was fifteen. She hopes so. Twenty years of hunger would be small enough penance for what he did to her.

6

A little before noon on a dreary Wednesday in mid-October, a young man in a dirty canvas doublet, his beard and coarse black hair matted and wild, fights his way through the crowds on London Bridge. A band of apprentice boys going south for some sport amongst the stews and taverns on Bankside call him a vagabond and kick out at his shins as he passes, but most people make way for him. He looks like a fellow you'd not care to tussle with.

Several times already he's been stopped by the city's law officers, who touch their cudgels discreetly, to let him know they will take no nonsense from a vagrant. With these men he becomes deferential, somehow smaller, fills less space. He means them no trouble. He's not a peddler or a purse-diver, he assures them – just an honest man who's fallen on difficult times. They let him pass.

He carries no visible possessions other than the clothes he wears and a leather bag slung over his left shoulder. It used to hide his physician's gown, when he was drinking in the White Swan and didn't want every man and his dog stopping by to discuss their maladies. But he threw away the gown a few paces back, not even bothering to watch as it sailed out on the wind through a narrow gap between the timber-framed houses that cling precariously to the side of the bridge. It's probably wrapped now around the mast of some salt-bleached Baltic trader moored in the Pool. All that remains in the bag is a parcel wrapped in cloth. He'd throw that after the gown, too, but the houses here are too close-packed to get a decent shot.

He emerges into Southwark beneath the great stone gatehouse that guards the southern end of the bridge. Ringed about its top, like the points of a crown, is a grinning crop of traitors' heads, all the colours of an artist's palette, from bleached white to the purple-black of rotting plums. Used to people staring at him now, he senses the eyeless sockets peering down at him as he passes below. Pop up here with us, Nicholas Shelby, they seem to be saying to him. You're dead anyway, so what does it matter? The view's grand and there's all the maggots you can eat.

Southwark is its usual venal self today: the mud and shingle rising towards the houses along the bank, the occasional grand building poking above the hovels like a pearl sitting in horse-shit. The drabs, the cats and the flesh-brokers have braved the cold to ply for business. The more successful of them wear winter cloaks neatly trimmed with rabbit fur; the rest look as grey as the sky and close to starvation. They don't trouble him; they know wild men are dangerous. And though he longs for the warmth of female arms around him, they could only ever be Eleanor's, so that comfort has gone for ever. Besides, he has no money left to pay for a whore. He doesn't even have enough for a jug of knock-down. For the first time in weeks he's sober.

With the wind at his back, he heads deeper into Bankside, skirting St Mary's church, making for the bear-garden and the open fields beyond. The flags flying skittishly above the Rose theatre signal there's a play on: The Lord Admiral's Men are per-forming Marlowe's *Tamburlaine*. If he had just a penny left, he'd pay to stand in the pit with the groundlings, hoping the warmth of their bodies might comfort him.

The cold drizzle washes the colour out of Bankside. It beads the painted signs above the shop fronts and lodging houses with strings of watery pearls. The air smells of fresh horse-dung and the marrow scent of butchered bones emanating from the Mutton Lane shambles.

He pauses beneath the sign of a winged god holding a quill – Hermes, the guardian deity of writers and poets. He knows that most of the city's booksellers lie behind St Paul's, north of the river, where the Stationers' Company can keep an eye open for proscribed writings or anything that might offend the Puritan Bishop of London. So perhaps this one has something to hide: Romish tracts or Italian erotica.

Inside, the shop is dingy. It smells of rag pulp and ink. Nicholas pulls the cloth-bound parcel out of his bag and opens it for the shop owner's inspection.

'How much will you give me for these?' he asks, looking down at his once-treasured collection of medical books.

✠

A narrow lane ghostly with river mist. The upper storeys of the timbered buildings loom over him like the interwoven boughs of some dense, dark arbour. Raindrops cling to the jutting beams, unsure whether to freeze or fall. *Jesu*, the night is wicked cold.

Nicholas blows on his numb fingertips. He's tired of pacing the lanes, tired of killing time. Time means memories. And the only way to kill the memories is more *mad-dog*.

The gaming house is called the Blackjack. Firelight beckons to him through the leaded windows. Inside, a young fellow with a fiddle is sawing out a jig. The tapster eyes Nicholas suspiciously, but wild men are not uncommon on Bankside, and this one at least has a little money to spend. It's not a tapster's job to ask how he came by it. 'You're not from the lane, are you?' he asks casually.

'I've come across the bridge.'

'Searching for something? Work? A woman?'

'The Wildgoose stairs. It's hard to find them in the dark. I got lost,' says Nicholas, realizing this exchange and his brief conversation with the bookseller earlier in the day are the nearest he's come to normal human contact in weeks.

'Follow the riverbank,' the tapster says, signalling the direction with one thumb. 'It's that way.'

The lanes are tomb-dark when Nicholas leaves the Blackjack, with only the occasional candle burning in a window to steer by.

He's following the course the tapster gave him. At one point he wonders if he should head inland for the Pike Garden. But he can imagine what discomfort awaits him there, vainly seeking sleep beneath a hedge. He's bound to wake every half-hour or so with biting cramp brought on by the hard earth and the cold. He can't remember when he last had the luxury of undisturbed sleep on a comfortable bed. Sometime in late July, he imagines.

The river mist is thickening. The inhabited world has somehow faded away while he was looking elsewhere. The vapour writhes around his legs like steam bubbling on the surface of a boiling cauldron. It plays tricks with him, making him hesitate, slowing him down. In the stillness he begins to hear voices in his head. At first the words are indistinct, ghost-like, then clearer:

Go away, Master Nicholas! It's unseemly for you to see her.

It's the Grass Street midwife he can hear. Then Eleanor's mother Ann:

You'll let the miasma in! You'll bring misfortune! Away with you!

Suddenly, out of the mist, comes the rattle of the midwife's holy stones as he casts them onto the floor of the lying-in chamber. He hears Fulke Vaesy's voice like the tolling of doom's own bell: *A healthy womb is the fertile soil... the wholesome furrow in which the seed of Adam may take root.*

The seed of Adam. Or the seed of a sinful father?

Nicholas finds himself at the bottom of an alleyway. He has no precise memory of how he got here. Ahead of him a wooden jetty thrusts out into the mist, weed-encrusted mooring poles set on either side at intervals of perhaps ten feet. Empty wherries bob on the tide, straining at their mooring ropes. Beyond them: blackness, and deep water. He realizes, with an odd sense of homecoming, that he's reached the Wildgoose stairs.

You killed them, Nicholas, says his own voice in his head. You know you did. You put Eleanor's child – your child – on the dissecting table for Fulke Vaesy to butcher. Accept it. Take the punishment.

Without hesitating, Nicholas Shelby steps onto the jetty and begins to walk out into the darkness.

✝

The hedgerows are a different world in autumn. Her coat is too large. It lets in the wind and rain. Old when she stole it, it's now in tatters. Elise longs for the days when the sunlight dazzled her as she kept watch over little Ralph, warmed her limbs, eased the muscles of her legs from the weariness of the road. She longs to go back to the time before the angel came.

She dreams of an early summer two years ago: she is lying on a truckle, the pull-out platform at the foot of a bed where a servant sleeps. But Elise is not a servant, though she suspects she'd be better off if she were. It has taken her all of a minute to realize that the Cardinal's Hat is not the mystical place of imagined safety her mother is always telling her about. It is, in fact, a bawdy-house. The family have decamped here from their Bankside tenement, due to her mother's inability to stay sober long enough to pay the rent.

They have come here with nothing. Her mother, Mary, does not even own the bed – though she is apparently trying to buy it. Elise knows this because several times a day her mother takes total strangers into it for money. This laborious purchase requires a religious devotion that even the Bishop of London would admire, with a great deal of devout groaning and grunting, and cries of Jesu! Jesu! Jesu!

With little Ralph left to crawl around the floor like a crippled crab, Elise has assumed all responsibility for him. She begs scraps from the Cardinal's whores to feed him when Mary is too drunk or too busy to remember. She bathes him with water from the stone jug in the corner when Mary would happily let him stink. She even

*pours her mother's arak out of the window when Mary is keeping
the Cardinal's Hat afloat all by herself.*

*When one of Mary's customers knocks a tallow candle onto the
truckle bed where Elise is sleeping, setting fire to the straw mattress and giving her a livid burn down one side of her young cheek,
her mother seems indifferent. Elise, in extreme pain, has to go to
St Thomas's hospital by herself to beg for treatment. On the way, she
decides things have to change.*

*Even then she waits. She is unwilling to abandon her mother
entirely. She waits another eighteen months. By then Mary is clearly
afflicted with a terrible malady that Elise can do nothing about.
There is no money for physic.*

A bright Bankside morning in June. Mary is snoring like a saint.

*'Remember that story Mam was always telling us, about there
being somewhere better than this, somewhere where we'll sleep on a
goose-down bed and eat mutton every day?' Elise asks as she hoists
Ralph onto her shoulders, kissing his uncomprehending face on the
way. 'Well, I've remembered where it is. So it's just you and me now,
Ralphie. Don't look back. We're off to Cuddington!'*

7

Until the moment he decided to go into that pitch-black river, Nicholas Shelby had believed in the Church's teaching: that cutting off one's own life before the allotted time is a great sin. And sin is easy enough to fall into, isn't it? That's why we need priests. So why has the sin of suicide proven so difficult to commit?

There was no fear that he can recall, just the darkness and the rank water pouring into his mouth. He remembers choking. He remembers praying that the end would come quickly, the sooner to be with Eleanor. But then, to his surprise, his body had begun to wrestle control away from his will. The ancient, instinctive fight to live had begun. He remembers his arms and legs thrashing and flailing, as though his body would have none of his mind's wickedness. He remembers being carried on a strong current, the water roaring in his ears like the tormented howls of a bear in the baiting pit.

And the image of Eleanor drifting not nearer, but ever further away.

It's been close. The disgusting sludge he's ingested while he's been in the water almost does the job for him. But even in his delirium, he understands what's happened: the river has vomited him out as though it can't stand the taste of him.

For long, tortuous days he struggles against the fever, too weak to do much except lie in a bed he doesn't recognize, sweating and puking like a child with the flux. He has no idea where he is.

Indistinct figures administer to him. Through eyes inflamed by the river's filth he can see them only vaguely. Sometimes Eleanor is amongst them. She tells him this spineless capitulation is not what she expects from a husband. Slowly, he begins to fight back.

✠

At Nonsuch, John Lumley says to his wife Elizabeth, 'He won't have forgotten the slight, Mouse. It'll fester in that scheming head of his like a pustule. I could kick myself for it.'

He calls her Mouse out of deep affection. A less mouse-like woman would be hard to imagine. Lizzy is twenty-five years his junior and as skilled as the chatelaine of a grand household should be. She wears her fair hair seemingly, beneath a white-linen coif, but her grey eyes glint with good humour and generosity. She buys trinkets for the chamber-maids when she goes to London. She treats the grooms, the kitchen scullions and the gardeners like friends. Lizzy Lumley is the perfect remedy for her husband's northern chill – literally so, for she's always chiding him about his reluctance to have the many Nonsuch hearths lit.

They are together in his reading chamber, a cosy room set off the great library. John is attending to his correspondence. Lizzy is at her needlework, a small white spaniel snoring contentedly on her lap. From the window the Lumleys can look down into the inner court, where a marble fountain in the form of a rearing horse flows with clear spring-water. The fountain is not just for show, the water being piped into the house so that the Lumleys may wash their hands under a spigot when they prepare for bed. No need for a servant to bring them bowls when they wake. When King Henry built Nonsuch, he built it for luxury.

'What slight is that, Husband?' asks Lizzy, looking up from her sewing. 'And who won't forget it?'

'Do you remember in the summer I spoke of the little boy they took from the river – the drowned vagrant child?'

'How could I forget, John?'

Indeed, how could she forget? The subject of children is one of the few thorns marring the otherwise-perfect bloom of their marriage. The other being her husband's colossal debts to the Crown. When he'd told her of the drowned infant destined for Fulke Vaesy's dissection table, she'd almost wept. Such talk of a young life cruelly ended brought back the ghostly presence at Nonsuch of the three infants borne by John's late wife Jane, all dead in infancy, and the very real absence of any from her own womb to replace them.

'When the Cecils last came hawking,' John continues, 'I somewhat carelessly mentioned that Sir Fulke's lecture was about deformity in the limbs of crippled infants.'

'Ah,' sighs Lizzy, imagining the crook-backed Robert Cecil she knows: full of thin-skinned Protestant zeal for sniffing out insults to himself and the realm – especially to himself. 'But that was ages ago. I'm sure by now he'll have forgotten all about it,' she says bravely. 'Besides, you meant him no slight – did you?'

'Intention is not the point, Mouse. You know what he's like: for a Christian man, Robert Cecil has a strange understanding of mercy and forgiveness.'

'Well, if anyone's deserving of God's mercy, it's the poor little mite Sir Fulke cut up into pottage-meat.'

'You're right, of course, Mouse.'

'Anyway, why do you bring it up now?'

'His father's written to me again,' he says, lifting the letter as if it's a particularly soiled rag, 'regarding the Henrician loan. It set me thinking.'

'Oh, that,' says Lizzy despondently. 'I thought the queen had agreed to another easement of terms.'

'She has, but that won't stop Robert Cecil trying to steal Nonsuch from me and making her a present of it.'

John Lumley's fears are warranted. He's inherited Nonsuch from his late father-in-law, Henry FitzAlan, Earl of Arundel. One of old Arundel's parting gifts was to embroil him in a plan to buy up on the open market an ancient loan the late King Henry had made to a cartel of Florentine bankers. 'We'll cream a percentage off the interest by taking on the paper risk,' Arundel had told him. 'After all, who can you trust in this world if not a Florentine banker?'

But the Florentines had paid just one instalment, and that was thirty years ago. They haven't answered Lumley's letters since. With Arundel now in the grave, John Lumley is the sole debtor. It's only his friendship with the queen that forces Burghley to sign these waivers on the interest.

'All I know is that John Lumley is more than a match for little crook-backed Robert Cecil,' says Lizzy to the snoring spaniel. 'Isn't that so, Nug?'

'You're a wondrous boon to me, Mouse. I'd go down without you – you know that?'

'The queen is steadfast in her friendships, John,' Lizzy assures him with a smile. 'She'll not abandon you, whatever the Cecils tell her.'

Through the window John Lumley watches the wind snatching at the water in the courtyard fountain. The spray makes the marble horse look as though it's in full gallop, barely a stride away from dashing itself into oblivion against the white ashlar walls of Nonsuch. He can almost feel the fatal impact of sinew and bone against stone. 'Aye, Mouse,' he says. 'But these days there are so many plots against her. I fear she cannot risk being as steadfast as once she was.'

Lizzy fixes him with a concerned eye. 'There's nothing else, is there, John – other than the money? You'd tell me if there was?'

Lumley doesn't answer at first, though by the tone of Lizzy's voice, he ought to. He just stares at the fountain. Then he says, almost to himself, 'No, Mouse. Nothing. But that won't deter Robert Cecil.'

Elise dreams of the angel again.

First comes the blinding sunlight, then the silhouette of a woman stepping out of the trees on that country lane. Next, the blessed relief as the angel lifts Ralph from her shoulders and hugs him to her breast, soothing his fractious mewling. 'Rest awhile, child,' the angel says. 'What are you doing out here alone with such a burden?'

'I am running away from my mother, who is a bawd and often in drink,' Elise replies in her dream. 'It is not safe to live with her any more.'

'But where are you running to, child?'

'Ever since I was a little girl, my mother has told me stories of a grand house and a rich relative, in a place called Cuddington,' Elise says, reciting the tale Mary had told her so often, before her descent into arak-induced silence. 'That is where we're going. But God has crippled my little brother Ralph because I talk too much, so as a penance I'm taking him there on my shoulders. We shall sleep on a goose-down mattress and not have to eat scraps that make my insides hurt.'

'But I know an even better place,' the angel tells her.

Waking from the dream, Elise remembers wanting so much to believe the angel that she'd never thought twice about following her.

In the angel's house she'd been baptized in a tub of warm soapy water. Elise had never had a bath before. At first she refused to climb in, terrified it had no bottom and that she would sink without trace into the depths. With almost unbearable gentleness, the angel had calmed her, bathing the right side of Elise's face where the skin was gnarled like tree bark from the time that customer of her mother's had set fire to the truckle bed.

When the angel had come to her again a few days later with the news it was time to move elsewhere, Elise had offered not the slightest objection.

Why should she? Who on earth would not trust an angel to lead you to heaven?

8

The second day of November, All Souls' Day. The day to remember the deceased. The perfect day on which to return from the dead.

He is lying on a straw mattress, half-wrapped in a crumpled sweat-stained sheet, wearing someone else's patched nightshirt. A splash of grey light slants across his chest. When he searches for its source, he sees a small leaded window set into the wall. And he sees it clearly.

Pressing his face to the glass, Nicholas imagines he's weeping. Then he realizes he's staring at raindrops pattering on the outside.

The window opens easily. He breathes in the chill air. Raindrops strike his face, run down his cheek. He is too exhausted to know whether to give thanks for his salvation or let the torment return. So he remains in a state of undecided numbness.

He's looking out over the low rooftops towards the Thames. For an age he stares at the great grey watery beast that stalks across his field of vision, the tide tugging at the anchor chains of the little ships moored upriver of the bridge, the Long Ferry heading east towards Gravesend, carrying outbound passengers to the traders moored in the Hope Reach.

He can hear the bellowing of cattle. He looks to his left and down. Is that the entrance to Mutton Lane? If it is, then the sound must be coming from the slaughtermen at work in the Mutton Lane shambles. Close by, a church bell rings eight. If he's right about the shambles, then it's the bell at St Mary Overie. He can't be more than a few hundred yards from where he went into the river.

But when *was* that? How much time has passed since then? He has no idea.

And then the door opens.

For a while he just stares at the young woman standing in the frame, not knowing what to say. He wants so desperately for her to be Eleanor.

But, of course, she isn't.

She is, though, a comely young woman, Nicholas notes in a detached way, as if he were registering the beauty of a flower or a sunset. How else is he to regard feminine attractions now, after Eleanor?

She's not conventionally beautiful in the English style perhaps. You couldn't lose her amongst a throng of rosy cheeks, flaxen curls and freckles. Rather, her skin has the smooth olive sheen of a Spaniard or an Italian. She has a strong, gamine face that narrows to a defiant chin. It could be stern, if it wasn't for the generous mouth and the astonishingly brilliant amber eyes. Her hair is a rich ebony, burnished by a foreign sun. It flows back in unruly waves from a high forehead. And though his interest may be merely academic, his senses cannot be completely indifferent to the way the green brocade kirtle she wears flatters those straight shoulders and that slender waist. He notes, too, the narrow wrists and slender fingers – not at all like the village girls from Barnthorpe. The word that springs into his mind is 'exotic'. An exotic flower, blooming in the wasteland that is his recent memory.

'You're awake,' she observes dispassionately in a faint accent he can't quite place. 'I image you must be hungry. Can you manage a little breakfast? There's larded pullet. We have some baked sprats left over, too. I'll have my maid Rose lay out a trencher downstairs.'

'How long have I been' – he looks down, casting an uncomprehending eye over the unfamiliar nightshirt – 'like this?'

'Two weeks. At first we really thought we'd lost you. I'm glad we didn't.'

When he doesn't answer, she turns to leave.

'Forgive me, I don't even know who you are,' he calls after her, feeling suddenly very foolish and only too conscious of the unkempt state he's in.

She looks back and bestows a bright smile on him. 'I'm Mistress Merton. Seeing as how I've been nursing you like a sickly babe, you may as well call me Bianca.'

✠

He chooses the baked sprats. Then the larded pullet. Then some manchet bread, hot from the oven. His long fight against the river has left him ravenous.

He's sitting in the taproom of the Jackdaw tavern. He knows it's the Jackdaw because through the rain-streaked window he can see the painted sign hanging over the lane. A tail of water cascades from one corner, splashing onto the churned-up mud and horse-dung below. He observes his distorted reflection in the little lozenges of glass. It is not a good sight. He looks like a man who's survived the pestilence – just.

A tankard of small-beer sits before him on the table, set down a moment ago with a smile by Rose, a full-bodied lass with a head of unruly curls. Not so long ago he would have emptied it in a moment, cursed the world, its maker and everyone in it and angrily demanded another. Now he just turns the tankard slowly, inspecting it. On his face flickers a sad half-smile that hints at remorse, or perhaps self-loathing.

He remembers something that happened to him when he was a boy. He'd been walking down a Suffolk lane, leading his grandfather's old gelding punch, Hotspur. The horse was the largest and strongest on the farm, but as passive and biddable as a blind old hearth-dog. Nicholas had been leading him by the halter when, foolishly, he'd managed to put his right foot directly under one of Hotspur's descending hooves. The pain had been beyond anything he'd known. 'Hotspur, *whoa!* Whoa!' he'd yelled. True to his nature, the horse had obeyed. Stationary, Hotspur's entire weight began to bear down on Nicholas's pinned boot. 'Whoa!' he'd yelled again, the tears springing into his eyes. *'Whoa!'*

And just when he'd thought every bone in his foot was about to be ground into dust, his grandfather had said softly, 'When you've 'ad enough, my lad, just you tell old 'Spur to *giddy-up.'*

Sometimes, he thinks, we can be the agent of our own pain.

He pushes the tankard away.

At Nonsuch, Kat Vaesy has come to celebrate All Souls' with John and Lizzy. She's come alone, save for a single groom, contemptuous of the cut-purses who sometimes prey upon travellers on the London road. When she arrived yesterday afternoon, her cheeks flushed from the ride from Vauxhall, John and Lizzy had met her at the outer gatehouse. Taking John's hand, she'd dismounted and greeted him with a respectful 'my lord'. Protocol satisfied, she'd hugged him, kissed his cheek and cried, 'Oh, John, it does my heart good to see you again! And *you,* Lizzy! And little Nug!'

The spaniel had raced around the courtyard, yelping ecstatically, until Gabriel Quigley, John's secretary, had been forced to scoop it up and return it to Lizzy's waiting arms.

This morning the two women stand together in the empty royal apartments and peer through the windows at the Italian gardens, waiting for the rain to lift so they can walk up to the pretty grove of Diana the huntress and let Nug chase pheasants.

They are much alike, Kat Vaesy and Lizzy Lumley: of a similar age, married to men a good deal older, both unable to bear children... and yet so utterly different.

Lizzy had once considered Kat a rival. When she'd wed John Lumley, the friendship between her new husband and the anatomist's banished wife had been so close she'd felt shut out. She'd even wondered if Kat wasn't John's mistress. It had taken some time for him to convince her that the unbreakable bond they shared was one of grief. For Kat Vaesy and John's first wife – Jane FitzAlan – had been the closest of friends, sisters almost. Even so, the knowledge hadn't done much to blunt the other thorn on the bloom: the knowledge that Jane FitzAlan's ghost would always be a constant reminder to Lizzy of her own limitations.

Raised by her father, the Earl of Arundel, on the extraordinary premise that a woman's intellect is in every respect the equal of a man's, Jane FitzAlan had won renown as a scholar in her own right. She'd even translated books by Euripides into English. No wonder John had loved her so, thinks Lizzy. She often imagines Jane standing by the Nonsuch library shelves, understanding effortlessly the contents of whatever volume she plucks from the shelves. Jane would never have had to ask Gabriel Quigley what they mean – as Lizzy sometimes does. Jane would never have feared appearing foolish in John's eyes. Late wives, she thinks, can cast such dreadfully long shadows.

'You have no notion of how good it is to be here again,' Kat says, lifting a finger to trace the rain running down the leaded windowpane. 'Sometimes I miss Nonsuch dreadfully.'

'You should stay – join the household. It would make John happy.' Lizzy laughs. 'It would make me even happier.'

'I can't, Lizzy.'

'Why not? Cold Oak is a pleasant enough house, but I know how much it pains you when Fulke comes.'

'That's where the problem lies, Lizzy. Fulke would never allow it. And I have no means of my own.'

'You wouldn't need *means*.'

'Oh, Lizzy, we both know John wouldn't be content unless he was maintaining me in the manner of a grand lady – and he's already got one of those!'

'But you'd be so welcome.'

'I'd be a burden on his purse, that's what I'd be. Besides, Fulke would accuse me of trying to turn John against him.' Kat takes her fingertip from the glass and studies it, as if she expects her skin to have absorbed the rain outside. 'Thank you, but no. Cold Oak suits me fine.'

'John told me Fulke was vile to you, as usual, when Baronsdale and the others came down to plan the Accession Day banquet,' Lizzy says, petting Nug as he begins to whine.

Kat grins. 'You know me, Lizzy: I gave as good as I took. You should have seen Baronsdale's face, when I asked him how long it would be before the College would allow a woman to practise physic. You'd have thought I'd suggested he make Lucifer a senior fellow.'

'I envy you, Kat, I really do – having the courage to make those boring old men squirm in their ruffs,' says Lizzy, the spectre of Jane FitzAlan tapping her on the shoulder once again. 'I'd give anything to have the knowledge that John has, to be able to discuss physic with him on equal terms. But it's just not the way God has made things, is it? At least, it's not the way He made *me*.'

'Look, the rain's easing,' says Kat. 'And Nug's weary of listening to women's chatter.'

✠

The bell at St Mary Overie has just rung nine. The Jackdaw is almost empty, save for a pair of strong-armed wherrymen taking a late breakfast, and a fellow with a bald pate and a rash on his thin neck, who sits on his own, staring mournfully into his small-beer. Nicholas reckons he's a chapter-clerk from the Bishop of Winchester's palace across the way. He's probably wondering how he'll explain to his dean the painful irritation that heralds a dose of the French gout. Not for nothing does Southwark call its whores 'Winchester geese'. *Mercury – administered by catheter, or burned over a flame and inhaled.* The remedy pops into Nicholas's head unbidden. But what use is such knowledge to him now? What does Nicholas Shelby know about anything, other than how not to drown?

'How did you find me?' he asks Bianca Merton a while later.

'It was Timothy, our tap-boy. He went down to the river one morning with the slops and found you lying on the shore. He said you looked like a drowned bear, like one of those poor creatures they bait in the bear-garden.'

He assumes she wants an explanation. He can't give one – not yet. 'I'm sorry, but I can't pay you,' he says, knowing few along the river will save you out of pure compassion. 'I have nothing.'

She shrugs. 'Then that's exactly what you owe me. You've taken barely a bowl of broth every other day – and you purged most of that.'

'There's not much I can remember—'

'I don't doubt it. There's not many who go into the river around here and come out alive. You were racked with the ague, even yesterday morning. I thought a syrup of lobelia might help. It did – a little. Not enough, though. So I gave you theriac. A few drops, and a day later... well, here we are.'

She smiles warmly. It's a broad, open smile – not the eyes-lowered, modest twitch of the mouth that a tavern-mistress would usually give a physician. Then he remembers that a physician is probably the last person on earth he resembles. 'Theriac? Are you an apothecary, then?'

Those intense amber eyes hold his for a moment, challenging him. If circumstances were different, he thinks, they're the sort of eyes that might entice a man into any number of betrayals.

'Does that tell you I'm an apothecary?' she asks wryly, glancing towards the window and the wooden sign hanging beyond. It still shows a painted jackdaw. There's not a unicorn's horn – the apothecary's traditional sign – anywhere in sight. 'How could I be such a thing, when the Grocers' Guild refuses to admit a woman to the trade? No, Mr Shelby, I am a tavern-mistress, plain and simple.'

He's more aware now of the slight accent in her voice, though her English is faultless, gentle even. At rest, her upper lip is downturned slightly at the corners, which gives her mouth an impatient set. Her jaw is given to sudden tensions that come without warning when she speaks. What causes these sudden hardenings of the expression? he wonders. What do they hide?

He can think of a score of questions he should ask her. Simple ones like: why did you choose to administer mercy to a total stranger? Or, why did you not call a constable and have this half-drowned vagabond taken to the Bridewell prison? But what he really wants to ask Bianca Merton, the owner of the Jackdaw tavern who says she's no apothecary – and is clearly neither plain nor simple – is how she got her hands on theriac?

To make it properly, it is said you need ingredients bordering on the magical. It's also the most expensive physic money can buy.

In an empty byre that still stinks of its former occupants, Elise shelters from the rain and tries not to remember. But now that Ralph is no longer with her, memory is her only companion. And memory can cling tighter than Ralph's little fingers ever did.

In her mind, it is once again early summer. They have spent five days in the angel's house. Elise thinks it is as close to heaven as you can get without actually being dead.

Out of the blue, the angel comes to her with news that she and Ralph are to leave. 'Please, not to Bankside,' Elise begs, while Ralph sinks his fingers into her like the monkey she'd seen clinging to its trainer at the Bermondsey fair. 'If we can't stay here, we wish only to go to Cuddington – to the great house my mother was always telling me about, the one with the goose-down bed and mutton to eat every day. Otherwise, we would rather die.'

If Cuddington is where you'll be happy, then that is where we're going, the angel replies kindly.

Why did I not take up Ralphie and flee again before it was too late? Elise asks herself, as the guilty tears stream down her cheek and the wind whines through the gaps in the wall of the byre. She knows the answer now: the angel was working her magic upon her, making her compliant, bending Elise to her will. And that night she must have used a particularly potent magic, because after supper Elise found herself so confused that if the angel had told her she was going to Greenwich, where the queen had personally asked to see her, she would have believed it and gone like a lamb.

This new place had turned out to be as dark and noisome as the stew she'd run away from. But somehow by then she had lost all ability to think and act for herself. She had strange, vivid dreams, even in the daylight. Often, she could not tell when she was dreaming and when she was awake. Again, now, she knows that was the angel's magic at work.

But there had been one sliver of hope before the descent into terror: Elise had discovered that she and Ralph were not alone. There were others here in this new place, others the angel had rescued.

Other victims trapped in the angel's cage.

9

S tay for a while,' Bianca suggests. 'I could use the help.'
Finding a man who can haul casks and labour in the brew-
house – which Nicholas finds ever easier as his strength
recovers – and can also read and write is a tall order south of the
river. She's glad when he accepts.

She already suspects that the man she and Timothy fished
from the river is no run-of-the-mill vagrant. He's educated. She
knows this because, in his delirium, she'd heard him curse God –
in Latin.

She thinks perhaps he's a fallen priest, though as he fills out
again, he looks more like a sturdy yeoman's son than a man of
God. But then how many farmers' boys have a churchman's Latin?
Still, she does not pry. In the two years she's lived on Bankside,
she's learned that many who come here do not wish to be the
people they once were. Besides, his presence helps keep Rose's
eyes off the better-looking customers.

As for Nicholas, where else does he have to go?

Not back to his old life. That's gone for ever. To Suffolk, then?
Back to his family, back to brother Jack and his sister-in-law
Faith, adoring parents to a hearty new acorn? No, he couldn't
stand the pity. Or the constant reminder of what he's lost.

He thinks perhaps when the spring comes he'll head for
the Low Countries again, re-enlist in the army of the Prince of
Orange, go back to patching up wounds and strapping shattered
bones. You don't even need to be a physician for that. They're

desperate enough in their fight against the Spanish to take a monkey, if it could learn the right tricks.

So, while he waits for the season, Nicholas retains his place in the attic. The little window becomes his spyhole to the past. He closes it when the sounds of the slaughtering in the Mutton Lane shambles become too intrusive. But when it's open, and the air is clear enough, he can just make out the spire of Trinity church across the river. He imagines Eleanor sitting there alone, waiting for him to join her on his way home from administering to some jumped-up alderman's self-induced dyspepsia. But when he slides onto the pew beside her, he discovers she is someone else entirely.

✠

On most days the Jackdaw heaves with dice-players, coney-catchers, purse-cleavers and every other sort of hard-drinking, loud-throated sharp-trick you can put a name to. They sup raucously from leather bottle and tankard until their cheeks bloom. They play *primero* and *hazard*, the cards and the dice going down between the laden trenchers while young Timothy, the tap-boy, strums his cittern and sings sorrowful songs in a high voice about slain lovers and broken hearts. Sometimes Nicholas wants to tear the instrument from his fingers and throw it into the fire.

He dines in a corner of the taproom on pottage and maslin bread. Bianca joins him when she can. They develop an easy friendship, though he senses in her, too, an unspoken wariness that prevents anything deeper. Some pains are too expensively purchased to be traded carelessly, he thinks.

Bianca Merton.

Why does the name seem oddly familiar to him? For several days now he's racked his memory. But it's too brim-full of pain to see to the bottom clearly. It takes a while for the tiny nugget of recollection to float clear. Even then, it seems to have come from someone else's memory, for it is surely a different Nicholas Shelby struggling to stay awake after the feast at the Guildhall on Knightrider Street, while he listens to President Baronsdale fulminating against the tricksters and fraudsters who practise illegal physic: *Imagine it: a woman! A common Bankside tavern-mistress by the name of Merton. They say she concocts diverse unlicensed remedies, without any learning whatsoever!*

A broad smile creases his face as he imagines Baronsdale learning the truth. And smiling seems just as much of a new experience as all the others he's encountered recently.

Yet still Bianca does not volunteer where she got the theriac from.

*

He likes the simple tasks she sets him. They require no thought. Thought leads him inevitably to the darker places.

He realizes life cannot be easy for an unmarried maid trying her best to carve out a place for herself on Bankside. He's noticed how her temper flares when she thinks some would-be gallant is paying her attention solely because he finds appealing the idea of a wife who could bring a profitable tavern to a marriage. But how to learn a little more about Bianca Merton, without it sounding like an interrogation?

She solves the dilemma for him. Over a late bowl of pottage one evening she lets slip that she's been in England barely two years. 'From Padua,' she tells him when he gently probes further. She places her hands either side of her face, sets the thumbs at her jaw, then pushes the fingers back along the crown, running them through her hair as if she's clearing the deck for action. 'My father was an English merchant there,' she tells him.

'That explains the accent I can hear in your voice. It was puzzling me.'

'My mother was Italian, but my father made me speak English always. He wanted me to assist him in his business with the Englishmen who came to Italy to trade,' she explains. 'And what of you?'

'Me? I was born in Suffolk.'

'Is that in England?'

'Almost.'

'And does *everyone* speak Latin there?'

He looks at her blankly. 'Latin?'

'You rambled in it – when I bathed your fever. You cursed too profanely to be a priest, and you're not rich enough to be a lawyer. So I wondered if all Suffolk folk have it.'

This startles him. Until now he had not imagined the intimacy of her bathing his sweat-drenched body. He doesn't know whether to be embarrassed or grateful. So he blusters.

'Oh, every man who has ambitions for his son has him learn Latin,' he tells her breezily, looking at his fingertips. 'We start at petty school. We're reading Ovid by ten. If you can recite a few verses of the Bible in Latin, the magistrates will let you off your first capital crime with no more than a branding. Not that I've actually committed a capital crime – nothing above the occasional misdemeanour, really.'

'So definitely not a bishop then?'

He shares her laughter. 'And your father and mother – are they still in Padua?'

'They're both dead: my mother of the sweating sickness, these eight years past. My father died on the voyage to England. He was old, and it was a hard sea.'

'Why did you leave?'

'The authorities in Padua may claim it's an open city, but

underneath they mistrust anyone from outside the Veneto, especially an Englishman. They thought him a threat. It was only a matter of time.'

'It's the same here. If the apprentice boys can't push a foreigner off London Bridge when they parade, they count it a very poor year.'

She says, 'I'll make a note not to cross on feast days.'

✠

First light on a raw November morning. Nicholas dreams that Eleanor lies beside him. She whispers softly that if he should ever sup in the Jackdaw's taproom with Bianca Merton again, she will marry the wool merchant from Woodbridge with the comely calves who tried to court her while he was away in Holland. Nicholas is midway through his promise never to do so again when some sound, some groan or creak the Jackdaw makes as it emerges from its nightly torpor, wakes him. As he opens his eyes, the absence of Eleanor tugs at him like a retreating wave.

The attic is bathed in a watery grey light that spills grudgingly through the leaded window. He throws the latch to let in the cold morning air. Looking down, he sees the alley is empty, the houses opposite emerging only slowly from the shadows.

Then, below him, he hears the door of the Jackdaw open.

Even wrapped in a thick cloak and hood, he knows it's Bianca. She looks up and down the lane, as though checking to see if she's alone. Then, apparently satisfied, she sets off in the direction of the Mutton Lane shambles.

Where is she going at this early hour? he wonders idly. If it's an errand, she'd send Timothy, or Rose. And why has she lowered the latch so carefully as she steps out into the new morning, as though she wants to avoid making the slightest noise? Is it because she fears someone will, by pure chance, look out of a window and see her?

It happens again – three times over the following week. Three times he watches her slip furtively away from the Jackdaw in the early hours. On each occasion he's woken by the soft creak of her feet on the stairs. The latest was this morning, just as dawn was breaking. His last glimpse of her – before cursing himself for a suspicious busybody and carefully closing the window, lest she hear him – was as a fleeting shadow, barely visible beneath the sign of the basket-maker on the corner of Black Bull Alley.

Why do I do it? he asks himself. Why do I ease open the window with a guilty heart, just so I can peer out into the lane to observe her? The old Nicholas wasn't a snoop. Why does the new one want to spy on his benefactor? Perhaps it's for the same reason I want to know where she got the theriac from, he tells himself. Or perhaps it's because simple trust is no longer enough.

✠

Later, when the Jackdaw is fully awake, he finds Bianca in the kitchen. She's making entries in her tally book in a small, confident hand. She looks up, framing her brow with slender fingers and running them back through her hair. It's a habit, he's noticed.

'Ah, Nicholas. I'm glad to see you up and about. Will you do me a small service?'

'Of course. Name it.'

'Go down to the Mutton Lane stairs. Meet a wherry for me. About eleven, depending on the tide.'

'Visitors?'

'A merchant coming across from the Vintry. He's got a shipment of imported malmsey. My present supplier's decided he wants an additional sixpence a cask just for the risk of doing business in Southwark. I don't want this one falling prey to the dabs and purse-divers before I get the chance to wring a good price out of him.'

He asks, as casually as he knows how, 'Sleep well, last night?'

The answer is a pretty smile and a flash of those brilliant amber eyes.

'Like the infant Jesus in the arms of Mary. And you?'

✠

When Nicholas steps out of the Jackdaw he finds Bankside teeming with people. What's brought them onto the street? he wonders. A new play on at the Rose? A bear-baiting in the Paris Garden? Then he remembers the date. It's the seventeenth day of November: Accession Day. We're celebrating the anointing of our sovereign lady, England's *Gloriana*, our most noble, high and puissant Elizabeth.

For warmth he's borrowed a buffin-lined coat, a forfeit for an unpaid tab at the Jackdaw. The frost snaps noisily beneath his boots. Outside St Mary Overie the urchins are begging alms from passers-by, their young faces as hard and grey as the winter sky. In the doorways of the stews the doxies huddle together and hope for trade, if only for a few brief moments of promised heat. A flat smoke-haze hangs above the chimneys. The Tabard is doing a brisk trade in steaming sack-posset; but Nicholas knows he'll have to hurry if he's to make the Mutton Lane stairs on time.

In the pale mid-morning light, the houses hugging the far bank of the Thames look no more solid than their watery reflections. They're the frontier of a foreign land he can't remember visiting.

On the way to the Mutton Lane stairs he passes the old Lazar House. Once home to Southwark's lepers, it stands now like an empty prison amongst the close-packed tenements of uneven timber beams and sagging brickwork. It's lain empty and abandoned since before Elizabeth's reign even began. Yet its grim, forbidding air remains. Not even vagrants seek shelter here, as Nicholas himself can attest. He's not superstitious, but he can't help muttering as he hurries by, '*Requiem aeternam dona eis, Domine*' – grant them eternal rest, O Lord.

His use of the Latin makes him realize how free he is, here in Southwark. If anyone across the river heard him muttering prayers in Latin, they'd probably denounce him for a papist.

At the Mutton Lane shambles they're preparing the last of the winter pigs driven in from the Kentish fields. The steam from their slaughtered carcasses billows into the still air. The lane reeks of blood, offal and damp hog-skin. There's a small knot of people on the jetty, waiting to catch a boat across or, like Nicholas, for a passenger to arrive.

No one pays him much attention. And why should they? He looks a deal better today than the last time he came this way. Beneath the buffin-lined coat he's still wearing his white canvas doublet, but Rose has managed to get most of the stains out of it, pounding away with the black-soap as though she was trying to exorcise his demons for him. She's darned his hose. Timothy has brushed his boots. His hair is still unkempt and there's a lingering look in his eyes that warns you to step aside, but his beard is trimmed tight against his jaw and neat enough. These days the watchmen hardly recognize him. And he doesn't stink of knock-down any more.

As he approaches the end of the jetty he hears a shout, swiftly followed by another. He looks out over the ranks of spiteful little wave-crests. A wherry is holding off just beyond the shore.

And between the boat and the stairs, arms outstretched as though exhausted after swimming a vast distance, a body falls and rises on the tide.

✝

Elise squats by an empty crossroad, watchful like the hind in the forest. She is watching for the Devil.

The Devil has many disguises. If he can assume the form of a woman, an angel even, then how easy will it be for him to take the form of the waggoner who passed by a few moments ago, or whoever next comes down the road?

There are only a few people Elise can be certain are definitely not the Devil. The widow Alice Welford is one of them.

In the days before Mary took them off to the Cardinal's Hat, Alice Welford would look after her and Ralph when Mary either couldn't or wouldn't. No, Alice would have been a disguise even the Devil could not have contrived.

Then there were those whom Elise had met in the Devil's cage. She acquits them now in her memory: first, the two women who sat from dawn to dusk just hugging each other. One had empty sockets in her face where her eyes should have been. She wore a little bell on a cord around her neck, which tinkled softy as she rocked back and forth smiling sightlessly at nothing. Then the young fellow, spindly and warped, who endlessly brushed the palm of one hand across his cheek. And she can acquit, too, the old man with the wispy beard and just one hand, who'd asked her name four times before she realized he forgot the instant she told him.

And, lastly, the one person who – to her surprise and delight – she knew: Jacob Monkton, the moon-faced poulterer's lad from Scrope Alley.

'Did the angel save you too, Jacob?' she'd asked innocently. But he'd merely greeted her with sharp little noises, as though angry sprites were pinching his flesh. That was Jacob's way. Most people in Southwark called him an addle-pate, though Elise knew he wouldn't hurt a fly.

No, none of these could have been the Devil, thinks Elise, as she scurries over the crossroads and into the bushes beyond.

But that hadn't meant the Devil wasn't on his way.

10

D o you think we can trust him?' askes Bianca as Rose laces her into her best carnelian bodice. They're in Bianca's chamber above the taproom of the Jackdaw. Rose is preparing her mistress for the meeting with the vintner from across the river. For the occasion Bianca has donned her blouse of Haarlem linen – no one can get linen as white and as fine as the Dutch – a kirtle of green brocade and her favourite bodice. The blouse will show off what remains of her Italian colour, and the green and the carnelian will flatter her amber eyes. If the finished article can't get her a penny off a cask of imported malmsey, she thinks, she might as well pack up and go back to Padua.

'If he's even half a man, he'll forsake the Vintry and take up residence here on Bankside at the first sight of you,' giggles Rose as she moves in to tie off the last of Bianca's points. 'He won't give a whirligig for the price of malmsey!'

'I was speaking of our Master Nicholas, actually. We still know so very little about him. What say you?'

'Master Nicholas? I think he's a young gentleman dispossessed of his inheritance and unrequited in love,' says Rose, a perpetually cheery young woman with a mass of brown curls that she's forever brushing from her eyes.

'Don't be foolish, girl.' Bianca lifts one arm so that Rose can tug the folds of the blouse straight.

'Then he's a lonely troubadour, searching for a mysterious

damsel who comes to him in his dreams,' suggests Rose, who in her spare time likes nothing better than to have Bianca recite romantic penny-ballads to her.

'I can't imagine they have troubadours in Suffolk, Rose. There's little there but swamp and sheep. I know; I asked him.'

'Then perhaps he's sold his soul to save the woman he loves; condemned to wander eternity alone,' says Rose, with more perspicacity than she knows.

'At least we know now he wasn't sent by the Grocers' Guild to shut me down,' says Bianca. 'And not even the Bishop of London would go to the trouble of having his spy throw himself into the river, just to convince.'

'I say a pox on the pizzles of the Bishop of London *and* the Grocers' Guild,' declares Rose.

'He has physic, that much I'm sure of.'

'How do you know, Mistress?'

'You should have seen the look in his eye when I said I'd treated him with theriac.'

'You said you were down to the last vial your father left you, Mistress.'

Bianca spreads her arms and turns a circle for Rose to check that all is correctly laced and in good order. 'But we couldn't let him die, could we? He'll be our talisman. I know he will. And under that rough exterior he's quite the gallant, don't you think?'

'Marry, Mistress!' says Rose, feigning innocence through her curls. 'And there was I, thinking it was the vintner you wanted to distract.'

✠

On the Mutton Lane stairs no one seems to know what to do. They stare at the pale spreadeagled thing in the water and cover their mouths in shock. Someone mutters a prayer. Eventually a wherryman manages to snag the corpse with his boathook. He shouts for assistance, but no one – save Nicholas – wants to help fish a half-frozen corpse out of the river.

Alerted by the commotion, two slaughtermen in blood-stained leather aprons arrive from the shambles. They have the body out of the water in no time, laying it on the planks like a grotesque and sodden mannequin. It's then that the waiting wherry passengers find an urgent need to choose another landing place. In a moment, the only living people left on the Mutton stairs are the two slaughtermen and Nicholas Shelby.

Nicholas is looking into the pale, bloated face of a young lad of maybe fifteen years. It has a bovine simplicity about it, a gentle moon of a face. The gulls have had the eyes. There are gnaw-marks where perhaps a pike has had a nibble. But decay has not yet fully set in.

He must have been in deep water for a day or two before rising to the surface, Nicholas thinks. The veins show darkly below the mottled skin, as though he's already begun his journey of trans-formation into a creature of the river.

But the most striking thing of all is the torso. It's been opened up, the chest and upper abdomen little more than a gaping cavern the colour of rotten salt-meat. Inside, through the snapped-off ends of the ribs, the spine is clearly visible, tied in with cords of yellow fat. There is no heart, no entrails, nothing but a few gobbets of dark flesh where the knife has passed them by. The lad has been eviscerated.

'You could 'ang that up in East Cheap market. I'd ask five shillings for it,' one of the slaughtermen says.

'He's a bit ripe,' says the other, laughing cruelly. 'Call it game, an' charge six.'

Nicholas Shelby doesn't hear them. He's too busy staring at the corpse. On the side of the left calf – deep enough to show a glint of white bone – the knife that did the filleting has also carved an inverted cross, deep into the alabaster flesh.

11

The parish constable arrives without anyone having appeared to summons him, as though he has a nose for the anonymous dead the river throws up almost daily. He's a savage-looking fellow with a permanently suspicious frown and an unkempt beard. He carries a wooden cudgel, his unofficial mace of office. He's accompanied by one of the parish watchmen: on Bankside, the law officers go around in pairs even in daylight. Nicholas doesn't recognize them. They're not the friendly fellows who took pity on him during his fall.

'Anyone know who he was?' the constable asks in a disinterested voice, glancing at the corpse leaking river water and live elvers that squirm on the jetty.

'Looks a bit like young Jacob Monkton,' says one of the bystanders who's found the courage to return for a closer look at what the tide has cast up, 'the poulterer's son from Scrope Alley. The lad with the addled wits.'

'Aye, it's him aright,' says another. 'Someone should run and tell his brother, Ned. He's been looking for Jacob a goodly while. Best cover him up before he gets here, though. If Ned sees him like this, he'll start knocking holes in the brickwork. You know what he's like.'

'Whoever he is, he's a treasonous young fellow, by the state of him,' laughs one of the slaughtermen. 'Looks like he got restless after they hanged and drawed him – decided to hop it before they got round to the quartering.' He roars with laughter at his own great humour.

'The internal organs have been excised,' Nicholas Shelby tells the constable quietly.

'Knowledgeable, are you?' asks the constable.

'No, not really.'

'He must have fell off the bridge, got caught up in one of *them*—' the constable says, pointing downriver to where the waterwheels are turning in the arches of London Bridge. Even at this distance, the noise they make as they spin in the current is clearly audible, an ominous whump... whump...

'Probably,' is all Nicholas says, keeping his own counsel. He knows the lad didn't die from crush injuries sustained by falling into a waterwheel. But he can also guess why the constable has already made up his mind that he did. The alderman will want a report; the justice of the Queen's Peace will want a report; the coroner will want a report. Everyone will want a report – hours of work, and all for less than a shilling, to a man barely able to write his own name. Add to that the fact that the lad was of humble background and is known to have suffered from a malady of the wits, and an accident is by far the best verdict.

Besides, now is probably not the time to start shouting about murder. It's not uncommon for a witness to end up in the Counter while the judiciary takes its time deciding if they know more than they're saying. Some can languish there for months before a magistrate decides they're innocent. And despite the best efforts of Bianca and Rose, Nicholas still doesn't look entirely reputable.

Nevertheless, he offers to accompany the body to the mortuary at St Thomas's, speak to the coroner to confirm the constable's conclusion, if needs be. At least that will buy him time. The constable looks him up and down, declines his offer and tells him to be on his way.

Nicholas has seen enough anyway. Enough to tell him the wound on the lad's leg is just like the one on the dead infant at Vaesy's lecture, only larger. As for the evisceration, it looks as though someone has torn away the poor soul's innards in a hurried search for swallowed treasure.

He's also noted – with a professional interest he can't shake off – the raw wheals on wrist and ankle. The killer must have strapped the poor lad down before he went to work. A dark image enters his mind unbidden: a struggling, arching young body writhing in terror as the knife begins to cut – slowly, deliberately, as carefully as an obvious lack of skill allows.

Nicholas turns and walks back up Mutton Lane. There's almost a spring in his step – the joy that comes from knowing at last that while the rest of the world thought you a raving madman, you were in fact right.

He can hear Fulke Vaesy's very words in his head – only now there's a sweetness to them that brings a grim smile to his lips:

So you've decided the alternative is murder, have you? Are all your diagnoses made so swiftly?

And now he has a name to work with: Jacob Monkton, the poulterer's son from Scrope Alley.

A boy with addled wits.

An infant with withered legs.

And a killer with a hungry knife.

12

A stiff wind tears at the crests of the jagged little waves, sending icy spume into the faces of the oarsmen. As the barge approaches the Whitehall stairs, Sir Fulke Vaesy readies himself for the jump onto the jetty. He is a large man, not given to agility. When he hesitates, alarmed by the pitching deck beneath his feet, someone gives him an insulting shove in the rear and he almost tumbles onto the slippery timbers.

Vaesy has no idea why he'd been summoned to Cecil House. The barge-master – who wears Lord Burghley's ermine lion-emblem on his jerkin – has spoken not a word to him throughout the journey. He has a nagging fear that Lady Katherine has found some way to cause trouble for him; she's loosely connected to the Cecils on her mother's side and he wouldn't put it past either of them.

Burghley's London home is a showy offshoot of Whitehall Palace, set between the Strand and Covent Garden. The weak sunlight gleams in the high windows of the great hall, the yard busy with hurrying secretaries and clerks. This is as much a place of government as a family residence.

'How gracious of you to come, Sir Fulke,' the crook-backed young Robert says as Vaesy is ushered into his audience chamber. 'And on such an inclement tide.'

For a moment Vaesy finds the protocol confusing. Robert Cecil – who has yet to wear the ermine – should by rights make courtesy to a knight. But he merely observes Sir Fulke from behind his desk; doesn't even attempt to stand. And he is the Lord Treasurer's son. So Vaesy make the smallest bend of the knee that he can stomach and hopes it will do. It seems to suffice.

Cecil motions the great anatomist to a fine, high-backed oak chair. The arras cushions bear the Cecil crest picked out in golden thread.

Silence – ominous and lingering.

Vaesy wonders if he is expected to say something: engage in some ritual none of the liveried servants have thought to mention to him. He consoles himself with the knowledge that if Katherine had wanted to cause him real trouble, he'd be facing Burghley himself and not the son. When the question comes, it's as unexpected as a pistol shot.

'You were physician to John Lumley once, were you not?'

It takes Vaesy a moment to compose his answer.

'Indeed I was, Master Robert – fresh from Oxford. Eager as a lamb in springtime.'

'You were lucky. With his entrée at court, Lumley could have had his pick of medical men.'

'Lord Lumley is ever generous,' says Vaesy, stung by the thinly veiled insult.

'And you have remained close ever since?'

'I count myself fortunate in holding Lord Lumley's trust, yes.'

'You were his physician when his children died – is that not so?'

'I was.'

'All three of them?'

Vaesy tries hard not to bristle at the charge implicit in Robert Cecil's words. 'The daughters were lost to the sweating sickness, the boy to the small-pox,' he says. 'We men of medicine treat the symptoms of a malady as diligently as we can. It is up to God to determine whether the body recovers or fails. I did my utmost.'

'I don't doubt it, Sir Fulke. Not for a moment.' Robert Cecil turns his attention back to the parchment in front of him. He dips the nib of his pen into a fine horn inkwell and puts his signature to the document. He adds, softly, 'Speaking for myself, had I been your client, I should have hoped for better odds.'

Vaesy swallows the insult. He can do little else.

After what seems like an age, Robert Cecil says casually, 'Forty pounds – a useful sum for a physician, I expect.'

'Sir—?'

'Lord Lumley's endowment to the College of Physicians – forty pounds per annum for a reader in anatomy.'

'Ah, yes, of course. Very useful, Master Robert.'

'For which he sometimes requires you to travel across the Narrow Sea, I understand – into Europe.'

'There is much new work being undertaken there. England should not fall behind. I'm sure Lord Burghley would agree.'

Robert Cecil gives Vaesy a cold smile. 'I rather think my father considers physicians in much the same way he considers cutpurses: he thinks both should hang. The last such visit was to Italy, was it not?'

'Yes, to Padua, Master Robert,' replies Vaesy, determined not to let Robert Cecil stick yet another pin in him. 'To the university there.'

'And for what purpose?'

'To learn of the latest advances made by the Italian masters of physic in the subject of human defor—' Vaesy break off as Robert Cecil looks up from his desk, hunching his crooked shoulders as though challenging the anatomist to continue. But what he actually says takes Vaesy by surprise.

'Surely, Sir Fulke, as a physician you comprehend the danger of contagion?'

'Contagion? There was no plague in Padua, Master Robert. I should not have gone otherwise.'

'I refer to contagion of the soul, Sir Fulke.'

'The soul?'

'I assume the Pope's writ still runs in Padua, does it not?'

So that's why I've been summonsed, thinks the great anatomist. This isn't a casual chat about anatomy, this is an interrogation. A cold stone of fear suddenly hardens in his stomach. He can name men who have come to Cecil House and left their liberty at the door. There are cells – probably directly below where he's sitting now – for those Lord Burghley considers enemies of the realm. The power of the Cecils is almost unlimited. And Robert Cecil thinks he's a traitor because he's been to Padua.

'Master Robert,' he says, suddenly full of humility, 'I can assure you that physic was my only motive for going.'

'And did you carry any letters between the noble lord and Padua, Sir Fulke? Any *sealed* letters?'

'Only an introduction to the university chancellor. It was quite innocent, I promise you. I showed it to our president, William Baronsdale. He said it was the very model of such intercourse.'

'Did it not occur to you it might have been encrypted?'

'Encrypted? Why?'

'To serve as secret communication between heretics!'

'No!'

Vaesy feels the floor beneath his feet begin to crumble. He thinks he's about to plummet conveniently into one of Burghley's cells, where the manacles will be awaiting him. 'Lord Lumley's loyalty to the Crown is unimpeachable,' he insists, somewhat croakily. 'As is mine, Master Robert. Ask anyone!'

Burghley's son draws himself up as though about to present a prosecution – a capital prosecution.

'Your friend John Lumley has flown far too close to the wrong sun for his own good,' he says. 'By rights, he should have met a traitor's end years ago!'

'If Lord Lumley has ever been in error, Master Robert—'

Robert raises a hand to stop him. 'John Lumley's error – no, let us call it what it truly was: his *treason* – was to plot with his father-in-law, the Earl of Arundel, to marry the Scots whore, Mary Stuart, to the Duke of Norfolk. How easily some people forget. But not me, Sir Fulke. Not me.'

Vaesy fidgets uncomfortably. All this was years ago; Robert Cecil would have been barely out of his cot. But guilt by association, he knows, has been the undoing of many an innocent man. 'That was all in the past, Master Robert,' he says. 'Norfolk paid with his life. Lord Lumley with his liberty. At the time I was merely Lord Lumley's doctor.'

'Even so, that marriage, Sir Fulke, would have established a Catholic claim to the throne. One lucky shot – one assassin's ball fired though Elizabeth's heart – and the Pope would have had England presented to him like a New Year's Day present.'

'I was never part of the faction, I swear it. I only ever saw the duke from a distance. We never exchanged but a word. And I would point out the queen was pleased to forgive Lord Lumley his... his... error.'

Robert Cecil laughs, though to Fulke Vaesy it sounds more like a bark.

'My father's hair is white and his constitution much troubled by Her Grace's habit of forgiveness!' He tests the tip of his quill. A small blob of ink blooms on his fingertip. It suggests to Vaesy the prick of a poisoned thorn. 'You are oftentimes in Lord Lumley's presence, in his house at Tower Hill, and at Nonsuch Palace. Is that not so?'

'I am, Master Robert. But I would desist if you thought it best—'

'He is open in your company?'

'As any man is to his doctor.'

'Exactly.'

So that's it, thinks Vaesy. That's why Robert Cecil has summoned me. He wants me to be his informer. He wants to make me his paid snoop, like the rogues he and his father employ to hang around in taverns listening out for careless drunken sedition. I'm to *spy* on John Lumley.

And if I refuse?

But Vaesy already knows the answer to that question: he will have made certain enemies of the two most powerful men in England.

✳

Halfway up Black Bull Alley, Nicholas hears someone call his name.

'Master Shelby!'

He stops, turns around.

'It *is* Nicholas Shelby, the physician? I fancied I might bump into you soon enough!'

It takes a while for Nicholas to place the barrel chest, the ginger beard streaked with white, the wide forehead beneath the woollen cap. Faces seen during his fall have an uncertain claim on his memory. This one is no different.

'It's Isaac Bredwell, sir – the bookseller. Surely you must remember—'

And then Nicholas has him fixed: Isaac Bredwell is the man with the sign of Hermes hanging above his shop. He's the bookseller who bought Nicholas's collection of medical volumes, the man who has the last tangible pieces of the old Dr Shelby.

'How do you know my name, Master Bookseller?' he asks.

'It was written in your volumes, sir. And fine volumes they were, too. Forgive me for saying so, but I did wonder later if they'd been stolen. You didn't look much like a doctor when you entered my humble shop.'

Nicholas has only hazy memories of that day, but Isaac Bredwell's strange little shop stands out more clearly than the rest.

He'd been surprised to find the bookshop there at all, wondering how the owner could possibly make a living in a place where barely one man or woman in five had the skill to read. The tiny place had smelled of linen pulp and of ink. Next to the piles of penny-ballads Nicholas had noticed a heavy wooden cudgel. Bredwell had told him it was to ward off the Puritan evangelicals, but Nicholas had reckoned he needed the weapon because either he was selling imported Italian erotica or papist tracts and he wanted a chance to fight his way clear of the government searchers, if they came calling.

'If you're in need of physic, Master Bredwell, I'm sorry, but I no longer practise,' Nicholas says, as pleasantly as he can. 'And if you want me to buy those books back, I fear I haven't the coin.'

'Not at all, sir,' says the bookseller with a merchant's smile as he falls in beside Nicholas. 'I sold them on for a goodly profit, thank you all the same.'

'Then I fail to see how I can be of service to you.'

'It's more a question of how I can be of service to you, sir,' Bredwell says, apparently steeling himself to broach a difficult subject. 'I hear you're now in the service of Mistress Merton, at the sign of the Jackdaw.'

'What of it?'

'It occurred to me, sir, when you came into my shop, that you were a man in what I shall call *extremis*—'

'It was raining. I was cold.'

'Of course, sir. But let me put it this way: you won't be the first man to enter Bankside as one fellow and leave as another.'

'I fear you have me at a loss, Master Bredwell. Can you please speak plainly; I have business—'

'Sir, if any man wants to practise the art of reinvention – which by the look of you now, I assume you do – there's nowhere better in all London than here. We get all types, Master Shelby: purveyors of smuggled papist tracts, felons on the run from justice, foreign intelligencers off the barques moored in the river. And because of them, we get the Bishop of London's men. Privy Council spies, too – all searching for the seditious and the heretical. It's a simple case of filth attracting rats.'

'Is that so? Thank you for the warning.'

'Sometimes the innocent find themselves taken up in error, if you follow my meaning.'

'I'll bear that in mind,' says Nicholas. 'But what does any of this have to do with Mistress Merton?'

Bredwell's next questions stops Nicholas in his tracks.

'How much do you really know about her?'

'Bianca?'

'Ah, so now it's *Bianca*—'

'If you have something to tell me, Master Bredwell, I charge you: be open or take your leave.'

Bredwell looks around theatrically. 'They say she has the healing touch of St Brigid. She can make a talisman to ward off almost every known medical trial, short of rigor mortis. It's even rumoured she took baptism as a cloak, and in secret venerates the old gods, practises magical cures learned in ancient times.'

'Is that so?' asks Nicholas, who happens to know the going rate for denouncing your neighbour as a secret Catholic or a witch. As a physician, he'd received more than one letter that began 'In the discharge of my Duty to our Sovereign Majesty, I must draw your attention to Diverse Faults in the conduct of the said mistress...' Usually they were from spurned suitors or jealous neighbours.

'Someone at the Tabard told me he'd seen her – with his own eyes, mind – in the dead of night, sailing in the sky in the shape of a bat with a woman's face!'

Nicholas tries not to laugh, but fails. 'I'm sorry, Master Bredwell, I don't wish to offend, but I suggest you ask the quarter sessions to investigate what the Tabard is putting in its ale.'

'You may mock me, Mister Shelby,' Bredwell says in a hurt voice, 'but no heretic can escape the bonfire for long, nor any witch for that matter. Just remember this: they burned a woman in the Spital fields last Pentecost, for casting a charm that poisoned her master's Rhenish wine.'

'Blame bad wine on the vintner, Master Bredwell; not on some poor woman who can scarcely afford small-beer,' says Nicholas, trying to keep the anger from his voice and not entirely succeeding.

But Bredwell isn't to be deflected. He leans a little too close for Nicholas's comfort and warns, 'Take my advice, Physician: when that bonfire is lit, make sure you're not standing too close to the flames.'

✳

When the vintner from across the river walks into the Jackdaw – alone – Bianca confines her anger to a secret jab with her heel against the foot of the bench. Her sideways glance at Rose says, 'We should have expected as much – Nicholas has run off with my penny!'

She knows her temper is somewhat volatile. In Padua, her mother used to call her *Signora Zanzara*, after the biting insects that plagued their summers. Trying to be rational, she asks herself if Nicholas would really make a run for it with just one penny of her hard-earned coin in his pocket. *Frettoloso* – hasty. Something else her mother used to say of her.

As the vintner extols the quality of his malmsey, Bianca finds herself blushing. She fans her face with one hand; resolves to have Timothy damp down the fire. But underneath she's cursing.

It's dawned on her that she hasn't put on her white Haarlem blouse and the cornelian bodice for the vintner's benefit at all. Rose was right, damn her to perdition. I must be going soft in the head, she tells herself.

In Padua there had been any number of fellows seeking her father's permission to pay suit to her. But God had given her eyes, hadn't He? She'd seen how Italian men were, once all the over-elaborate *corteggiamento* was done with – interested in nothing but their guilds, their societies and their reputations.

When she'd left Italy, she'd been interested to see the mettle of her father's own race. The only ones she'd had any contact with before that were the merchants who passed through her father's house, bringing their spices, plants and curiosities from foreign lands. They were all serious-minded men of business, full of charters, bonds, conditions and parcels vendible. Dull, dull, dull, dull, dull.

On the voyage she'd been astonished by the English sailors: strange, weather-beaten little men who could climb rigging like monkeys, who carried charms of aquamarine to calm the waves and the storms, but whose speech she couldn't understand – apart from the profanities and blasphemies that seemed to make up most of their vocabulary.

They can't all be like this, she'd told herself. And indeed, when they docked at Tilbury, she'd discovered they weren't. But they weren't much better.

She had rapidly come to the conclusion that there appeared to be only two types of native male: silk-gloved gallants who thought God had made woman solely to provide a subject for their sonnets or to breed their sons; and the rest – pasty, ill-mannered rogues with a fondness for bear-baiting, cock-fighting, thieving and falling over drunk. And to think she'd begun to hope that Nicholas Shelby might be different—

The vintner is looking at her with a satisfied gleam in his eyes. God's wounds! She's just agreed a price a full ha'penny a barrel above what she'd intended. She curses Nicholas and all his works.

'I wonder if the Mutton Lane stairs are open again,' the vintner says as he gets up to leave. 'We had to land by the Falcon tavern. There was a body in the water – off Mutton Lane.'

Bianca starts as if she's just been slapped: hard.

'A body? What sort of body?' she asks, a cold stone of dread forming in her stomach.

'I don't know. I was too far off to see.'

She keeps her composure barely long enough for the vintner to reach the door. As he disappears down the lane, Rose has to steady her. It's a while before she can persuade her mistress to take her hand from in front of her mouth.

'Jesu, Rose,' Bianca whispers, 'you don't think he's gone and—'

'Don't be foolish, Mistress,' Rose says, giving her a gentle shake that at any other time would be unforgivably familiar. 'He'll be back, by and by.' She pours her mistress a shot of the malmsey sample the vintner has left behind.

And then, as if on cue, Nicholas walks in.

Bianca's expression travels from relief to rage and back to somewhere in between. He's too far away to hear her muttered welcome: *stupido farabutto!*

'They shut the Mutton Lane stairs,' he says apologetically. 'Somebody drowned.'

He says no more than that, knowing the details will be common knowledge by sunset. He's not yet ready to trust her with his conviction there's a killer on the loose on Bankside. He thinks to himself, there's too much I don't know about you, not least where you go when you slip away so furtively from the Jackdaw when you think no one is looking.

✠

When he wakes the next morning the attic is flooded with a bright winter light. Opening the little window, he breathes the crisp, cold air surging in like a wave foaming into a rock-pool. Across the river the church spires stand out sharply against the early sunshine. From somewhere close by comes the sound of Bianca singing as she and Rose air the lodging-room sheets. She has a fine voice, he notices. The faint accent of the Veneto gives it a richness he hasn't heard before.

At breakfast she tells him she has no urgent tasks; the morning is his own. He thinks he will visit the parish authorities, tell them what he knows: that the little lad taken from the Wildgoose stairs and Jacob Monkton were killed by the same person. Perhaps they might listen to him now. But then Bianca suggests a walk to the Paris Garden.

The notion appeals. The fresh air might help him think. He can't remember the last occasion he made time for simple pleasures. Surely a few idle hours passed in pleasant company can't hurt.

As they walk their breath hangs in the air like ghostly smoke. If you didn't know better, you might take them for a couple at the tentative beginnings of a courtship. They have an easy way about them: he in the buffin coat, walking with a slow swing of his Suffolk yeoman son's shoulders; she in the green brocade kirtle, occasionally dipping her head as she laughs at something he's said. But that is where it ends. Each of them has secrecy in their blood. Perhaps today is the day to wash a little of it out.

And indeed – to his surprise and joy – Nicholas finds himself beginning to smile at little things again; like the drayman they pass at the riverbank who's trying to force an unwilling mare to drink, or the creaking of the sails of a windmill that sounds to Bianca like a parrot calling *ee-nough... ee-nough...*, which is what

Timothy shouts at closing time. If it wasn't for the ever-present dark current drifting sluggishly in the well of his soul, Nicholas might even feel carefree.

'Will you stay long?' Bianca asks as they follow the riverbank towards the Paris Garden. 'You seem much recovered.'

'I don't know,' he replies. 'I had thought of perhaps going into Holland in the spring.'

'For trade?'

He laughs. 'No, I have no head for business.'

'Then to fight – against the Spanish?'

This amuses him even more. 'I'm not a soldier. I *was* a physician.'

'Ah,' she says, looking down at the hem of her gown. She has kept a list of possible occupations in her head. She's been crossing them off as she's grown to know him better. 'I knew it would be something learned.'

'I wasn't much good at it. There was someone I couldn't cure – someone very dear to me.'

She nods wisely. 'Is that why you went into the river?'

A bold question. To his surprise, he finds it comforting, rather than intrusive. It's the comfort of invited confession.

'Yes. I think I wanted to pay God back, by committing the worst of sins – the self-destruction of His own creation. They say He loves us all. Well, I suppose I wanted to remind Him what it's like to lose someone you love deeply.'

'If a man should esteem me that much, I should think myself blessed.'

'But I couldn't even do that properly. The river spat me out.'

She looks at him in silence for a moment.

'Good,' she says, in a matter-of-fact voice. 'Good.'

✖

In the Paris Garden they eat coney roasted on a brazier. After-wards they watch a bear dance to a jig his master plays on a hurdy-gurdy. The beast has a sorrowful look in his yellow eyes, as though he's dreaming of distant forests. He seems quite tame. Bianca gives him an apple, which he chews with stumpy teeth.

As they walk back along the river, Nicholas picks his moment.

'There's something I've been meaning to ask you.'

'Then ask it. Like that poor bear, I do not bite. At least, not too sharply.'

'When I recovered from my fever, you told me you'd treated me with theriac.'

'It worked, didn't it? It appears not to have poisoned you.'

'Theriac is a medicine of the ancients. The great Galen him-self distilled it in the time of the Caesars. Its substance is known only to a few. I don't know of more than a couple of physicians in London who have it.'

'Is that so?' she says, with a nonchalant smile playing on her mouth.

'So how does a tavern-mistress come by it?'

'Come with me,' she says.

✠

The journey does not take long. She says nothing as they walk. Her movements are swift but still graceful. English women, he thinks, don't move like this. He has to hurry to keep up with her.

In the grim shadow of the Lazar House, just to the west of the Mutton Lane shambles, Bianca stops. Nicholas can smell the river, a pungent mix of mud and putrefaction just out of sight.

Perhaps it had been a house once, or a shop. All that remains of it now is a jumble of blackened bricks and charred timbers, left by the fire that destroyed it. Dead weeds and scraps of plaster lie around the rubble like grey silt. Rangy cats stalk rats amongst the wreckage. Bianca hoists up the hem of her gown. Nicholas follows her across the wasteland.

At the back of the plot is a wall of sagging brickwork and crooked timber, about ten feet high. He guesses it might have been the back wall of a courtyard once. It is pierced by a stone arch with an ancient door. Looming beyond the wall is the roof of the Lazar House itself.

Seen up close, the door looks as though it's not been opened since Henry was on the throne. Yet to his surprise, when Bianca takes a key from the sleeve of her gown, it swings easily on new hinges.

'Timothy's father is a locksmith,' she explains, seeing the look on his face. She beckons him through.

Immediately he is almost overwhelmed by the rich scents that even the November air cannot diminish: winter cherry, mugwort, asarabacca... He is standing in a small space between the adjacent buildings, open to the sky, perhaps thirty feet wide by twenty deep, bordered on the far side by the wall of the Lazar House garden.

'It's the poorest physic garden you ever will see,' she says proudly, spreading her arms to tell him that, however humble, it's still hers. 'I have agrimony, toadflax, goatsbeard and comfrey. I can make an infusion of cudweed for aching bones, or a paste of juniper for the dropsy. I've pennyroyal for cleansing water, and borage to banish melancholy. In summer I sometimes come here just for the smell.'

He's seen them before, of course, on his travels. He knows of a barber-surgeon named Gerard who has a garden in Holborn, mostly given over to medicinal herbs. He'd owned a copy of Turner's *Great Herbal* and an edition of Bankes's *Treatise* – until he sold them to Isaac Bredwell for sixpence each. But he's not visited the gardens of either man, and as far as he knows, there's not another private physic garden planted anywhere in England, and certainly not in a patch of waste ground beside the Thames. Now he understands where Bianca Merton goes when she slips away from the Jackdaw.

'You told me you weren't an apothecary,' he says, trying to suppress a grin as he rubs leaves of winter cherry in his palm, smelling the deep scents on his fingertips.

'I told you no such thing. I told you—'

'I know what you told me – that day at the Jackdaw, you told me to look out of the window at the tavern sign. You asked me if it was the sign of an apothecary.'

'And was it?'

'You know full well it wasn't.'

'So there was no lie, was there?'

'Bianca Merton, you dissemble worse than a fellow of the College of Physicians.'

She smiles sweetly.

'So why are you the mistress of a tavern on Bankside and not a licensed apothecary with a shop on Cheapside?'

'Because the Lord Mayor and the Bishop of London do not *approve* of women apothecaries,' she says hotly. 'Nor do the Grocers' Guild and the College of Physicians. They think women should have no place in physic, that we should confine ourselves to mixing paste to sooth the feet of sick cattle.' She brushes away a lock of hair that has fallen across her brow. Her fingers leave a small streak of dirt and crushed thyme leaf on her skin. 'And they have set those fine men of the Grocers' Guild to search out anyone who so much as dries a bunch of herbs in the fireplace.'

'The Grocers' Guild has been given its authority to license apothecaries by the queen, to stamp out—' He stops, realizing he's about to hurl a boulder into a millpond.

'Go on, say it,' she snaps. '*Charlatans*. That's the word you were thinking of, isn't it? If I were a charlatan, Nicholas Shelby, you'd be cold in your grave, not standing here defending those bores in the Grocers' Guild.'

'I'm not defending them,' he insists, holding up the palms of his hands as a gesture of peace. He can't help smiling at her vehemence.

'Perhaps if I were to wear a horse-hair beard and dress like a man,' she says, turning with her arms outstretched, so that he might imagine the unlikely spectacle, 'would that make me more acceptable to the Grocers' Guild?'

'Not really. But it might confuse a few at the Tabard.'

She stops turning and gives him a hard stare. 'The Tabard?'

'One Isaac Bredwell, bookseller, in particular. He's convinced you're a wise-woman, or worse. One of his drunken friends says he saw you flying down Black Bull Alley in the shape of a bat.'

Bianca peals with delight, her anger instantly forgotten. 'Oh, God's blood that I was able! I would sink my fangs into Master Bredwell and then refuse to make him a balm to relieve the sting.'

'You know him?'

'He paid court to me when I arrived on Bankside. He seemed to think I would beg him to make me respectable. He's sixty, if he's a day. And he smells of ink. If he touches anything, he leaves a smudge.'

'What happened?'

'What do you think happened? I spurned him.'

'Kindly?'

'Not really.'

'That explains a lot.'

'Why must people like him always think that a maid who seeks her own path must have a familiar and... and... fly across the face of the moon at midnight?'

'You own a tavern, you tell me. Perhaps you should water your ale a little.'

She gives him a friendly push. It's the first time a woman has touched him since Eleanor. Then he thinks of the hours she must have spent mopping the sweat from his body and feeding him her healing potions. A warm wave of gratitude flows over him.

'You still haven't told me how you make the theriac,' he says. 'There's more to it than just herbs. Galen put snake-flesh into his. Don't tell me you have your own pit of serpents – I think I'd believe you, if you did.'

'I brought some vials with me from Italy. They were my father's.'

'So you come from a line of apothecaries—'

'A proud line.'

'You told me your father was a merchant.'

'Well, in a manner of speaking, he was. We lived in rooms above his warehouse full of dried plants, spices, alligator skins, horns of the narwhal – you name it, Father probably had a sack of it somewhere. You could call him a merchant of cures.'

✖

As the light begins to fade, Bianca suggests they return to the Jackdaw. By the time they reach Black Bull Alley, Nicholas has rehearsed the words sufficiently to tell her about the child on Vaesy's dissection table and the real nature of Jacob Monkton's death. Just telling someone will be a huge relief. But he knows that once those rehearsed words are out of his mouth, the bond he has begun to forge with Bianca will change for ever. It will not be a gift he is giving her, it will be a terrible burden. He's about to speak – reluctantly – when a voice suddenly breaks into his thoughts.

'Mercy, what have we here?'

'Well, talk of the Devil,' whispers Bianca.

At the end of the lane stands the bookseller, Isaac Bredwell. Beside him is a huge fellow of about twenty with fiery auburn hair, his face red-veined and sweaty with drink. Around his great stomach is tied a grubby leather apron. He wears a cloth cap on his head and his great fists rest on his hips, elbows thrust aggressively wide.

'Ned Monkton,' Bianca whispers in Nicholas's ear, 'the brother of the boy they found at the Mutton Lane stairs yesterday. He looks drunk.' She gives the two men a direct and confident smile. 'Go back to your father, Ned,' she says calmly. 'He needs you. There's no profit for you here, troubling innocent folk out for a walk.'

Nicholas can't help staring at Ned Monkton. He looks the sort of fellow to steer clear of, especially when he's in his cups. Has he been on the ale because of Jacob? he wonders. He must know about his brother's death by now. Even if the constable didn't send him word personally, news travels fast on Bankside. He can hear the voice of the bystander on the jetty: *If Ned sees him like this, he'll start knocking holes in the brickwork. You know what he's like...*

Ned Monkton bares his teeth in a grin that's halfway towards a snarl. He swaggers closer, leering at Bianca, seemingly oblivious to Nicholas's presence. The ale has made him bold.

'If the witch here don't want you, Isaac,' he says, 'maybe she's ripe for a younger buck. What say you – *witch*?'

It has not escaped Nicholas's notice that, apart from the four of them, the lane is empty. Nor does he need to study Ned Monkton's flushed face or his belligerent posture to know he is not a man likely to be agreeable to reason. 'Be peaceable, friend,' he says softly. 'We mean you no ill. Let us pass.'

'Away, *friend*,' spits Ned Monkton, pushing Nicholas aside without even glancing at him.

'Ned, your father wouldn't like to see you like this,' Bianca says, standing her ground. 'Hasn't he suffered enough?'

But Ned isn't listening to her. 'Witch-whore,' he growls viciously. 'Papist witch-whore!'

Whatever sympathy Nicholas might have felt for this man vanishes instantly. It's been a while since he was in a proper fight. He'd been too drunk to remember much of the scrap that left him bloodied in the Greyfriars cemetery, and throwing the occasional rowdy out of the Jackdaw doesn't really count as serious face-to-face bloodletting. But he knows, from treating knife and sword wounds, that London street brawls can quickly turn fatal, and if he's learned anything in medicine it's that a speedy cure is usually the best cure. So without warning, he hits Ned Monkton just below the corner of the left eye with all the force he can throw into his fist.

It's a lucky shot. Monkton's legs give way like a poleaxed heifer. He sags in an untidy heap in the mud. Nick is about to give him a kick in the groin to make sure he's not going to get up in a hurry, when Isaac Bredwell strikes him on the back of his head with something very solid.

As Nicholas goes down, he's taunted by a fleeting image: a wooden cudgel lying against a volume of Italian poetry. He hears Bredwell's voice toll like a deep bell. 'You should have listened to me when you had the chance, Shelby. I tried to be charitable.'

Nicholas sprawls in the dirt, the stench of horse-dung rank in his nostrils. The back of his skull seems to be ablaze. Clusters of fireflies swarm across his vision. The whole lane seems to have filled with a red fog. Ned Monkton is back on his feet, bending over him. And that indistinct gleam where Monkton's hand should be must be the blade of a knife. He can almost feel the razor edge of it tearing through his stomach.

And then he hears Bianca's voice.

She is speaking in a strange, low monotone that chills his blood even more than the expectation of the knife. It's so far from the warm lilt of her singing that it seems to be coming from another woman entirely.

'I curse thee, Ned Monkton,' she is intoning, 'I curse thee so thy limbs shall become serpents and their venom turn thy blood to fire... I curse thee that thou shall crawl upon thy belly in blindness through the slime... I curse thee to be the Devil's sport and burn in brimstone for eternity... I curse thee, Ned Monkton, that thine eyes and thy privy member be made the feast of worms and all loathsome things that slither in the pit of hell...'

Now it is winter. Her bones are rods of ice that seem to chill her from within. The old burn on the right side of her face feels as though icy fingers are pinching and twisting the skin there. Sometimes the chattering of her teeth and the shivering of her body make Elise believe there is some frenzied creature trapped inside her, fighting to escape. When it rains, she cannot sleep for the rattling of the branches; when it's dry, the ground is too hard to give her comfort.

The cold has sapped her caution. She knows she is becoming careless, but she must eat soon. She longs for rest, but how can she rest when those dreams she'd kept leashed in the far corner of her mind have found a way to break loose?

Sometimes she's convinced that Ralph and the others from the Devil's house have escaped and are with her. She speaks to them: to Ralph, to the woman with no eyes and the little bell around her neck, to the old man with the stump for a hand, and always to dear Jacob Monkton, his innocent moon-face brimming with trust.

There are entire days when she believes she suckled the body she saw crucified upside-down in the Devil's house, suckled it until the life that had drained out of it returned.

And when these hunger-driven visions fade for a moment, Elise sometimes finds herself howling silently, head back, the raindrops streaming down her face, scratching an inverted crucifix with her fingertips in the wet earth.

13

'I never took you for a superstitious man, Nicholas Shelby. Now keep your head still or I shall summon up a goblin to bite you!' instructs Bianca, her eyes gleaming with concerned amusement.

It is a little after five in the evening. Timothy has set a good fire burning in the hearth. The air is sharp with the tang of wood-smoke. At the table in the private parlour at the Jackdaw, Bianca's slender fingers are rubbing a paste of crushed comfrey root and valerian mixed with a little water into back of Nicholas's skull. The wound is superficial, but the headache is not. He finds the pressure of her fingertips soothing. He can feel the warmth of her breath, gentle and feminine, on the back of his neck. The intimate contact dulls one ache, but reminds him of another. As she moves round in front of him to check her handiwork, he thinks, with a guilty start, how comely she looks. Her green brocade kirtle now appears wine-dark against her skin, her hair is loose and unruly. He thrusts this image of her from his mind. It is impossible. He even feels a short-lived anger – anger at her ability to excite senses he had only for Eleanor.

'I'm not at all superstitious,' he protests. 'And I don't believe you can conjure up goblins. But if Isaac Bredwell and Ned Monkton weren't convinced you were a witch a couple of hours ago, they certainly are now. Have you any idea how dangerous that might be?'

'It worked, didn't it?' she argues. 'If Isaac had been sober and surer on his feet, he might have done some real damage here.'

'Yes. I'll admit it. It worked. You put the holy terror into them.'

'They deserved it.'

'You even had me convinced for a while.' Nicholas laughs at the thought of two well-made men fleeing from this slight, almost boyish young woman. But his laughter is tinged with concern. 'You do realize that if they report you to the local justice of the peace, you could find yourself spending a day in the stocks, at the very least.'

'Those two rogues? Putting themselves within a hundred yards of a law officer? That will be the day, Nicholas.'

He finds her disdain in the face of danger admirable, but troubling. He wonders if she understands the risks of what she's done. 'You could even find yourself dragged before the Bishop of London. It might be commonplace in Padua, but here cursing a man in the street is tantamount to witchcraft.'

She laughs softly. 'We women from the Veneto are renowned for our cursing; the Holy Office of the Faith didn't even bother to place an edict against it on the church door. I'll tell the Bishop of London it's just my strange foreign ways.'

Inside, Bianca is less sure of herself than she sounds. From the moment of her arrival in England she'd been forced to ask herself: whose side are you on? Which nation has your heart?

In Padua, with its famous university drawing scholars from all over Europe – Catholic *and* Protestant – the thought had seldom occurred to her. She had an English surname, an Italian given name, spoke English almost all the time, except when conversing with her mother or her Italian friends. True, they'd owed their allegiance to the Doge in Venice, but in her own mind her father's house felt wholly English, even if she'd never actually travelled to the country and had to have England pointed out to her on a map.

But in London she hadn't felt English at all; at least not at first. Everything was so strange, so *foreign*. And, *Jesu*, how they mistrusted foreigners, even though the city itself – just like Padua – teemed with them. Within hours of her moving into lodgings in a merchant's house in Petty Wales by the Tower, two men had arrived demanding to know if any foreigners were staying there. They claimed to be servants of a man called Burghley. Bianca had escaped their interest because of her English surname, though the landlord had immediately doubled her rent. 'You have no man with you,' he'd said. 'I don't need the Bishop of London accusing me of running a bawdy-house.'

Then there was the time she'd witnessed a group of apprentice boys, woollen caps pulled down over their brows, chasing a poor fellow down the street. When she'd asked someone if he was a cut-purse, they had said no, he was a Dutchman. This had confused her mightily, as she'd thought the Dutch were allies of the English. Apparently that was only the Protestant ones.

Even here in Southwark she'd found suspicion rife. She'd soon learned that the queen's ministers and advisors sent informers into the taverns to listen for foreign sedition and religious dissent. She'd found it easy to spot them – there being few things more obvious than a man trying hard to pretend he's not eavesdropping.

She wasn't overly troubled by such snoopers. The spies of the Holy Office of the Faith in Italy were a hundred times more dangerous. Besides, if she'd sent them packing, the Privy Council would simply have sent new ones. A few weeks later they left of their own accord, apparently satisfied she was running an orderly house. When she'd asked Timothy why foreigners were distrusted so, he'd laughed at her ignorance and said, 'That's easy to answer, Mistress. The Pope in Rome says our Elizabeth is a heretic. It's every foreigner's wish to send her to hell.'

While Bianca rubs the balm into his skull, her reflective silence makes Nicholas think he might have offended her.

'I just think you should take care,' he says kindly, interrupting her thoughts.

She snaps her long fingers contemptuously, then follows with that habit he's noticed: running her hands from the sides of her brow and back through her hair – part self-consciousness, part belligerence.

'What care I for Ned Monkton and Isaac Bredwell?' she says bravely. 'Or the Bishop of London, for that matter? If Englishmen are so afeared of a woman's voice when it's raised against them, the queen must have a pretty easy time of it. I'm surprised she needs a Privy Council at all.'

'I'm just advising caution,' says Nicholas, raising his palms in conciliation and trying not to grin. 'But however badly Ned Monkton is grieving for his brother, he had no cause to speak to you so... so... discourteously.'

'Oh, Nicholas, really! I've been called a witch oftentimes before now and lived. Worse, too. Try *whore*... a vain sister of Satan... the mare that Lucifer rides by night... I've even been called a papist trull, because I look a little less than English-born. Mostly it's by men who covet me above their wives, or who don't want to pay their ale account. Is it any surprise that curses come fluently to me?'

Is that hurt he can detect behind the defiance in her voice? Is Bianca Merton not quite as redoubtable as she likes to think? An image pops into his head: Ned Monkton trampling her herbs under his great heavy boots. He thinks, perhaps I will not go to Holland in the spring after all. I might be of use here.

'Anyway,' Bianca says, dabbing off the excess comfrey and valerian paste and wiping her fingers on a linen rag, 'it was just a little spat. They were drunk. I don't think Ned Monkton intended to use that blade. He's not a killer. He's grieving. That was his little brother they fished out of the river at the Mutton Lane stairs on Accession Day, after all.'

Her words remind Nicholas of what he'd been about to tell her on Black Bull Alley. 'I know – I heard someone on the jetty say so.'

'Poor little sprat. The way he was found – isn't that's enough to drive any brother to madness?'

'The constable decided he fell into one of the waterwheels beneath the bridge. That's what the coroner's verdict will say. That's the version that will go down in the parish mortuary roll.'

Nicholas hears her place the balm pot on the table a little more forcefully than perhaps she'd intended. 'What do you mean by "version", Nicholas? Do you imply that's not how he died?'

'Jacob's death had nothing to do with any waterwheel.'

'How do you know?'

'I was a physician, once. I know what I saw.'

'You are a physician still, Nicholas Shelby. You do not un-become something simply by crossing a river – or casting yourself into one, for that matter. You cannot unstitch yourself like an old shirt in order to make a new one. Now, tell me what you mean by "version".'

'You clearly know the Monktons,' he says, the ache in his skull slowly fading. 'If you tell me everything you know about young Jacob, then I'll tell you how he really died. Do we have a compact?'

It appears they do. True to her word, Bianca tells him how Jacob was the darling of his older brother's eye, how Ned protected and cared for him because Jacob's brains didn't work the way other people's brains work – protected him with his considerable fists, if anyone so much as looked at Jacob the wrong way. Little Jacob, who gazed in wonderment at each new day as though nothing in it was even remotely familiar to him. Jacob, whom the unkind said should have a cell of his own in Bedlam. Jacob, who went missing from the hovel on Scrope Alley that the Monktons call home a whole month before his eviscerated body washed up at the Mutton Lane stairs.

When she has no more to tell him, Bianca puts away the balm and throws the linen rag into a basket for Rose to clean. There is a look of sadness on her face as she gazes out through the parlour window to the dark yard beyond. No matter what she thinks of Ned, she admires the loyalty in him, feels deep sadness for young Jacob. Sometimes, she thinks, you have to forgive a hurt if the one who causes it is suffering too.

'Now it's your turn,' she says. 'Tell me how young Jacob Monkton really died.'

✝

Joshua Pinchbeak has had an encounter with God. He can prove it. He bears the physical scars of it and he bears them proudly. He will tell anyone who'll listen how God spoke to him out of a whirlwind of fire and light. A physician once told him he was only suffering from a stroke of the palsy, but Joshua Pinchbeak knows better.

The encounter had blazed with such excoriating intensity that it was a whole day and a night before his senses returned. An entire month passed before his limbs regained some of their former strength. The ordeal has left him with one arm that does not work, and a tongue that can barely speak the warning God wants him to shout to all who will listen. His left leg drags as he walks and one side of his face has slipped, like a bank of earth after a heavy rain. But he has survived the whirlwind, and he understands why. Joshua, a simple weaver's son, has been chosen to bring God's warning to every man, woman and child he can reach. A terrible warning: the end of days is coming soon. Prepare!

Joshua has read the scriptures. He's devoured every word. He knows that God makes His chosen face a trial of faith. After all, didn't He make Job crawl on his belly like a worm, took every possession, every joy, every last hope away from him? But Job was up to the trial. Not once did Job deny his Lord, and in the end Job was rewarded. Every age must have its Job, and Joshua Pinchbeak, itinerant preacher and messenger of the end of days, believes he is this one's.

In market squares and on cathedral steps from York to Exeter, in sunlight that burned him and rain and wind that scoured him, he has tried to make them listen, to fear what is coming. His earthly reward has been nothing but more pain.

Because he is not ordained, because he doesn't have a doctorate of theology from Oxford or Cambridge, from Basle or Strasbourg, from Padua or Heidelberg, the clergy chase him from the church door. They have brought him before the assizes. They have tried to make him confess that he is a papist, a Presbyterian, an Anabaptist, a Lollard, that he's possessed by Devils, that he's a blasphemer, that he's just making it all up. He has languished in the filth of a dozen prison cells. But he will not stop shouting his warning. Prepare!

He has taken a great risk in coming to London to preach. If he is challenged, St Paul's Cross will be far harder to escape from than a country churchyard, or the crossroads at Kingston where he preached yesterday. He is exhausted from the long journey south. He is thirsty and half-starved. To sleep in the open tonight will be a great ordeal. But if just one man or woman heeds his warning, he will bear these trials willingly. He will not complain. What possible pain can Joshua Pinchbeak suffer that he has not already endured?

14

This evening at the Jackdaw the more observant customers notice an unusual quiet in Bianca Merton. This evening she does not go amiably from table to table exchanging pleasantries, delighting the crowd with her stinging put-downs when some fellow who's had a little too much cheer suggests she might like to accompany him to one of the Jackdaw's lodging rooms. Even Rose and Timothy find themselves spared the usual chivvying.

'You've asked her to be your mistress once too often,' says a wherryman named Slater to his companion, Walter Pemmel. 'Now you've ruined it for all of us.'

'Never!' protests Walter, who's old enough to remember the reign of Bloody Mary. 'It's 'cause I told her I was already wed. She's a-pining for what she can't 'ave.'

The truth, of course, is that this evening Bianca Merton is troubled as she's seldom been troubled before. She's finding the story Nicholas has told her almost impossible to bear. And tonight, like him, she will find sleep elusive; and, when it comes, disturbed by dark dreams.

✠

Lizzy Lumley has come down to Cold Oak manor. She does so every November, as close to Katherine Vaesy's name-day as her duties at Nonsuch or the Lumley town house on Tower Hill will allow. Her husband has insisted she bring Gabriel Quigley and

Francis Deniker, his clerk, with her. 'Bad roads and bad men, Lizzy,' he'd protested. 'There are more cut-purses between here and Vauxhall than there are trees.'

Tomorrow morning the two women will ride east to Long Southwark, dispensing alms from the Lumley rents to the destitute sick. It's what aristocratic women do, when sewing or reading their psalters fails to satisfy. Indeed, Lizzy's charitable nature is famed throughout Surrey. At every Sunday sermon the Reverend Watson assures Lord Lumley it will earn her a special place in heaven. Mindful of the new faith, he stops short of praying for her beatification.

'Remember, Lizzy, "He that hath mercy on a poor man lendeth to the Lord",' quotes Kat Vaesy at supper, deepening her voice to mimic her estranged husband's sonorous tone. They laugh. Both know that Fulke Vaesy is probably the least generous man in Christendom.

'And speaking of having mercy on a poor man,' Lizzy whispers, glancing to where the pox-faced Quigley is sitting with Deniker and the senior members of Kat's household at the servants' table, 'have you not noticed how Gabriel's eye has been wandering your way all evening?'

'Fie! You're imagining it,' Kat protests.

'You could do worse, if you look past his poor face. A perfect countenance isn't everything. John sometimes looks the saddest man in all England. But underneath—'

'Nonsense, Lizzy. He's John's secretary. I've known him for years. He's a dear man, but too stern for my tastes. I'm surprised you could drag him away from the Nonsuch library to accompany you.'

'It was John's idea. He insisted.'

'And he was right to worry – have you noticed how many more tinkers and vagabonds there are on the roads these days?'

'Then he made Francis join us, just to be sure.'

'I can imagine Gabriel putting up a defence of sorts. He has an iron streak beneath that monkish exterior of his,' says Kat. 'But *Francis*? Dear Francis, who recites parables of Our Lord's love for the poor whenever he gets the chance – and means it, unlike some I could name? What use would he be in a quarrel?'

'His heart is bold, bless him,' says Lizzy. 'He has more courage than you'd give him credit for. I know that for a fact.'

'You arrived safely, that's all that matters.'

'The only excitement we encountered was when we rested the horses at Kingston.'

'Oh, Lizzy, tell me, *please*. Excitement here at Cold Oak is when the bees refuse to swarm.'

'A religious firebrand. He was ranting at travellers passing by the crossroads. You should have heard him! We'll have to work fast tomorrow – apparently the world is about to end.'

'That's the problem with being so close to London. We get a lot of Puritans and Anabaptists on the road. Most are harmless enough.'

'Not this one, Kat. He seemed quite out of his wits,' Lizzy says. 'Kept shouting about how Armageddon was at hand. He looked more like a vagrant than a man of God, mind. I think he was half-starved, poor loon.'

'I'll make sure I avoid Kingston in future,' says Kat with a shudder.

'He said he was heading for the Cheapside Cross, to warn people of what was in store for the ungodly. His name was Joshua. Joshua Pinchbeak.'

'You *spoke* to him?' says Kat, her eyes widening in horror.

'Why not?'

'John would have the night-terrors if he knew.'

'He said his name was Joshua, and that if I didn't listen to him, the walls of Jericho would come tumbling down upon my head.'

Kat lays a hand on her friend's wrist. 'Then thanks be to God that John made you see sense. Imagine if you'd been alone—'

'What if this Joshua was right?'

'Lizzy!'

'What if the end of days really is near? The times are full of strife and bloodshed. The pestilence may come again. Who knows what God is planning for us?'

'Let's pray your friend Joshua was wrong, and Armageddon is still a way off,' says Kat in the tone of an elder sister. 'Besides, I've work to do; I'm planning more beehives in the orchard this spring.'

Lizzy says, 'Well, if he's right, I for one intend to go to my maker in the hope that my sins will be forgiven. And I shall be comforted, I like to believe, by the love of my husband.' An awful silence while she reflects on what she's just said. She colours. 'Oh, Kat, I'm so sorry. How thoughtless I can be sometimes! I really didn't mean—'

Kat smiles. 'Don't reproach yourself, Lizzy. The great anatomist is quite out of my thoughts. Has been for years. When he comes to Cold Oak, I pretend he's the fellow who takes away the night-soil from the chamber pots.'

It's a lie, of course. Fulke Vaesy slops around her mind like foul water at the bottom of a drain. Lady Katherine Vaesy is in a quandary. She cannot divorce her husband; the Church will not allow it. And, without money of her own, she cannot leave him. Her father made the contract and she must bear its unyielding terms year after year. Her husband cannot prove the marriage null, and so he too must suffer it – year after year. Thus husband and wife are bound inescapably to each other, bound not by love but by chains of ice. But she does not tell Lizzy Lumley this. She puts on a brave face.

'And I'm glad for you, Lizzy,' she says. 'I truly am. Glad for John, too. You've made him happy again.'

Lizzy looks down at her trencher, her meal half-eaten. 'But I'm not Jane FitzAlan, am I? I'm not the golden first wife. And I haven't given him children to replace the three darlings he lost.'

Kat shakes her by the arm, gently, so that Gabriel and Francis do not notice. In her mind is the thought that she, too, was once just like this, fearful of inadequacy in the face of almost unbearable infatuation.

'You must not speak like that, Lizzy. Jane is dead. John loves *you* – I know it.'

'Sometimes I wander in the library, when he's not there. He has so many books on physic that I hope I might find something amongst the pages, some secret knowledge that would give me the gift to read his innermost thoughts, to see deep inside him, to learn if he is happier with me than he was with Jane.'

By the light from the hearth and the candle flame on the table, Kat can see a silver trace of tears against the amber gleam of her friend's cheek.

'You have no need to do such a thing, Lizzy,' she says urgently. 'You must remember: I saw him married to Jane, and I've seen him married to you. Doubting him is a disservice John Lumley does not deserve.'

'But sometimes I fancy I might learn the answer to why I cannot give him children. There must be a reason, Kat, other than some sin I have committed in the eyes of God.'

'You're the most sinless woman I know, Lizzy. Besides, it's not too late. You're not an old maid, for mercy's sake. There's still time.'

Lizzy wipes away the tears on the sleeve of her kirtle. She smiles bravely. 'And nor are you, Kat. It would be such a wonderful thing to see you happy again. Dispensing charity to the needy might make you pleasing to God's sight, but it can't warm your body on a cold night the way a loving husband can.'

'That cannot be, Lizzy,' says Kat.

'What do you mean?'

'You must promise me one thing. Promise it as though tomorrow might *really* be the end of days. Promise me on your immortal soul.'

'Of course, Kat. I'll promise you anything,' Lizzy says, suddenly a little scared by her friend's intensity.

'If you ever do find yourself carrying John's child, do not let Fulke near the lying-in chamber. Even if he tells John it is good physic for him to be there, trust yourself *only* to the midwife. If you have to crawl out of bed and slam the door in his face yourself – keep him away!'

✠

When Nicholas enters the Jackdaw's parlour the following morning he finds Bianca balancing a large clay ewer precariously on one shoulder. She's trying to aim the neck at a wooden washing tub set on the table.

'I must get this linen clean or it won't be ready for tonight,' she says in a practical manner, as if their last conversation had involved not the slightest mention of violent death and mutilation.

'Here, let me take it,' he offers, lifting the jug from her. He waits while she crushes soapwort leaves in her palms and then, at her command, begins to pour the hot water into the tub. Then, as she starts to knead the steaming linen, he says in a resigned voice, 'You're going to tell me it's all in my imagination – what I said last night about Jacob Monkton and the little boy Sir Fulke Vaesy dissected. You're going to tell me I was seeing things – just like Vaesy himself told me.'

'Of course I'm not,' she says, drawing a soapy finger from the tub to brush a loose curl of hair from her face. 'Just as you cannot un-make a physician of yourself, you cannot un-see what you saw. I believe everything you told me. It's just rather hard to comprehend, that's all.'

'Sir Fulke Vaesy is a very eminent man of medicine,' Nicholas says, wondering why he's bothering to defend his former profession. What does he care for Vaesy now? Or the College of Physicians, for that matter? They are part of someone else's life. 'But what kind of anatomist can oversee a dissection and not even notice that someone's been there before him?'

'Perhaps he's just not as clever as he thinks he is. But I cannot say I'm surprised. All that learning, and still the barber-surgeons have to do the cutting for you. Years of study, yet you call upon apothecaries to mix your medicines. I sometimes wonder what you physicians actually *do* to earn those fancy gowns you wear.'

'I threw mine away. And you're not the only one to wonder.'

Bianca's soapy finger has left some suds clinging to her temple. She brushes them aside with the back of her wrist. 'Well, Master Lapsed-physician-without-a-gown, tell me again – just so I can take it all in.'

'This is what I know for sure: the infant on Vaesy's dissection table had been bled dry. Jacob Monkton had been eviscerated. Both had an inverted cross cut deep into their flesh, close to the extremities, severing a major blood vessel. I believe they were drained of blood via those wounds. Before they died.'

'How do you know the cross was inverted? Wouldn't that simply depend on which way were you looking at it?'

'The transverse cut was at the end nearest the ankle,' he tells her. 'It would be more natural to make it at the upper end or in the middle.'

'Unless the bodies were upside-down, suspended by their feet. Then the crosses would be the right way up, wouldn't they? There'd be nothing satanic about them at all.'

'Apart from the fact that they were made to drain out the victim's life-blood,' Nicholas murmurs to himself. He'd tell Bianca about the marks on Jacob Monkton's limbs; it adds weight to her suggestion that the bodies were suspended. But he doesn't want to risk distressing her further.

'And that's what killed them – the blood?' she asks.

'There was virtually none left in the infant, and Jacob's evisceration came after death – I'm pretty sure of that.'

'So why would the constable say Jacob fell into a waterwheel?'

'An easy life, most likely. I didn't recognize the man. He's probably newly appointed. He can probably barely write his name, so a report to the coroner would be a labour he'd most likely rather do without. Then there's the fact that there was no obvious culprit to hand, no witnesses to a killing. Much easier to tell the coroner it was an accident. Especially if you're right about Jacob's malady of the mind.'

'And you think the killer disposed of their bodies in the river, in the expectation they'd either sink or wash out into the Narrow Sea?'

He nodded. 'And if they didn't – well, who'd be interested in the remains of a crippled child and a boy with addled wits? In my practice at Grass Street we used to get two or three such unfortunates washed up in the Fleet ditch every month. The question you're going to ask me, I suppose, is why? Why kill them in such a manner?'

'Actually, I was going to ask if this child and Jacob Monkton are the only ones.'

He's been trying not to consider that possibility. 'You think there could be more? God grant that there are not.'

Bianca looks up from the tub. 'The child was crippled, Jacob addled in the wits. Perhaps the killer thinks the world would be better off without the weak. I've met more than a few in this parish who think like that.'

'He'll have his work cut out then,' says Nicholas. 'Think of all the men crippled by the wars in Ireland and the Low Countries, women ruined by disease and hunger, children blinded and maimed in accidents... He's got a fine choice in this city, if that's what he's killing for.'

'But bleeding one victim and gutting the other? Aren't there easier ways to dispose of a burden, if that's what the killer thought they were?'

'Of course there are. And they don't require a measure of medical knowledge.'

'You think he has a skill in surgery?'

'A very small skill,' Nicholas agrees. 'Either that or he's a supremely incompetent physician. The way Jacob Monkton's body was eviscerated would shame even a half-trained barber-surgeon.'

'Perhaps he was in a hurry, frightened of discovery—'

'In which case, exsanguination is a strange way to kill. Even a small child will take time to bleed out.' Again Nicholas sees the wheals on Jacob Monkton's limbs. 'No, he was in no hurry. In my judgement, he was taking his time. He had a purpose in mind. I just can't imagine what it was.'

'If those wounds really were made in the form of a satanic cross, Nicholas, the likes of Bredwell and Ned Monkton would say they're a sign of devilry. And they wouldn't be the only ones around here to think it.'

'Then they're superstitious fools,' Nicholas replies, remembering the apocalyptic sermons the vicar of Barnthorpe used to preach to his congregation each Sunday, warning that the Devil lurks behind every tree, waits on each dark country lane for the unwary and those who let their faith slip even for a moment. He'd been astonished by the congregation's open-mouthed acceptance, their readiness to blame the lameness of a cow or the confusion of a sick and bewildered old woman on some satanic agency.

Bianca confirms what he's thinking. 'That may be so, Nicholas, but I can tell you, if two women walk out together on a sunny afternoon on Bankside and it suddenly starts to rain, there's more than a few in this city will instantly call them a coven!'

'So going to the parish with this may not be the best of ideas,' he muses.

'Two corpses with the mark of Satan carved into them? There'll be a full-blown witch-hunt by sunset. They'll find some poor innocent, force a confession out of him and then we can all have a good hanging.' She adds harshly, 'That's always good for business, if nothing else.'

'We can't just do nothing, Bianca. We can't simply wait for the next poor soul to wash up on the tide. If there *have* been others, we need to find out.'

'And just how will you do that?' she asks.

'They took Jacob Monkton's body to the mortuary at St Tom's – I heard the constable say so. The mortuary porter there will have made a note of injuries and marks for the coroner and for the parish mortuary roll. If there have been others, perhaps they'll be on his records, too.'

Bianca drops the linen onto a nearby bench, where it lands with a heavy sodden thud – a little too much, for Nick's taste, like the sound Jacob Monkton's gutted corpse made on the Mutton Lane stairs.

'The mortuary porter?' she asks.

'Yes.'

'At St Tom's?'

'He should be able to tell me, if anyone can.'

Bianca raises her eyes to the ceiling. 'He might,' she says, 'if you hadn't punched him in the face, and I hadn't cursed him to the Devil. The mortuary porter at St Tom's is your old sparring partner, Ned Monkton.'

15

I need a peace envoy, thinks Nicholas. I'll send him with a letter. He enlists Timothy, the Jackdaw's taproom lad. But what exactly do you write to someone who called your friend a witch-whore and drew a knife on you – even if it *was* after you'd punched them in the eye.

By the sixth draft, he thinks he's got it. As a fall-back, he instructs Timothy that if Ned can't read, then he's to speak Nicholas's words as diplomatically as he can. 'Whatever you do, sound humble,' he tells the boy. 'Don't make it sound like a legal arraignment. And if he looks like replying with his fists – run!'

✠

The next day Nicholas sets off on the fifteen-minute walk from the Jackdaw to St Thomas's hospital. Passing beneath the rotting traitors' heads set on spikes around the roof of the grim stone gatehouse at the foot of London Bridge, he makes his way east along Bankside towards Thieves' Lane. Beneath his feet the winter mud oozes through the city's ulcerated skin like an incurable malady.

From a distance, St Tom's looks exactly like the monastery it once was. It sits on open ground amid a ragged collection of skeletal trees, as if the bones of those it has failed to save have been pressed into service as vegetation. But it is no mean establishment. In addition to its care of the general sick, it boasts a foul ward for those who fall prey to the French pox – as common in

Southwark as catching a cold – and a night-layers ward for the homeless. It is also the receiving point for the parish's vagrant dead.

The gatekeeper studies Nicholas warily. 'Show me your neck,' he orders.

Nicholas pulls back the collar of his linen shirt.

'Insane?' The question is delivered in a flat monotone.

'Medically speaking, no,' says Nicholas, raising an eyebrow. 'For coming here, very probably.'

The quip has no effect on the gatekeeper. He cares only that the visitor standing before him is not a lunatic, and that he's not showing signs of pestilence – sufferers of either being forbidden from entering. Apparently satisfied on both counts, he allows Nicholas through.

The mortuary crypt lies beneath the old monastery chapel, down a stairwell that looks more appropriate to a dungeon than a hospital. It reminds Nicholas of the hole that a wasp might bore into a rotten fruit: black and with something very likely unpleasant at the bottom of it. As he descends, the ripe scent of death and quicklime rises to greet him.

At the bottom of the shaft a lantern draws grudging detail from the darkness. Nicholas sees a row of long bundles, each wrapped in a dirty winding cloth. He counts six of them. And at the end of the row lies a single plain wooden coffin. He knows the score: the same casket used for every burial – roll the corpse into the grave, carry the box back for the next customer. If this is where Ned Monkton works, he thinks, no wonder he drinks too much and sees bats with women's faces.

A large figure looms out of the darkness. For a moment Nicholas almost expects it to be carrying a scythe. 'Ned – is that you?' he croaks, across a tongue that's almost too dry to let the words escape. 'It's me, Nicholas Shelby. I sent you a letter—'

Ned Monkton is as big as Nicholas remembers him, ruddy-faced and wearing a dirty full-length leather apron over his tunic and hose. He steps a little too close to Nicholas for comfort.

'You've got the fuckin' nerve of Old Nick, coming here,' he says, touching the livid bruise under one eye. Then, to Nicholas's astonishment, he smiles. 'But there's not many on Bankside as would chance a swing at Ned Monkton. You're a saucy fellow, ain't you?'

Nicholas is about to tell him it's a small enough payment for calling Bianca a witch-whore, but decides not to push his luck.

'What do you want with me, Shelby? Your letter said it was to do with my Jacob?'

'It is, Ned. I want to help.'

This takes Monkton aback. 'Help? How the fuck can you help Jacob now? Don't you know how he was found?'

'Of course I know. I helped pull him out of the river. I'm so sorry, Ned, about what happened to him. I hear he was a goodly lad; despite the trials he bore in life.'

This seems to change Monkton's mood. 'Aye, there's martyrs as don't bear their suffering as bravely.'

'I have some information, Ned. I also want some information. Call it a trade.'

'Are you after selling me some quackery to bring him back to life, Shelby? 'Cause if you is, there's a spare box right there what'd fit you just right,' Monkton says, glancing at the coffin.

'Why would I do that?'

Monkton studies him, an alarming squint of menace on his face. 'You're a physician, ain't you? I don't like physicians.'

'That's understandable. I'm not overly partial to them myself.'

'We got stung by a physician at St Saviour's market – my father and me,' Monkton explains. 'Standing on a box, he was, shouting as how he had all these secret mixtures what could cure all known ills.'

Nicholas winces. 'It's an easy gull, Ned, especially if some-one's desperate. You're not the first. You're not even in the first thousand.'

The news seems to satisfy Ned Monkton. He shrugs, as though he's remembering nothing weightier than being tricked at cards. 'Told us he'd study the alignment of the heavens to work out the best remedy.'

'How much did that cost?'

'With the mixtures he made? A week's income – every last farthing.'

'I'm guessing it didn't work.'

'Just left Jacob shitting like a goose for a week.'

'I'm sorry, Ned; there's a lot of charlatans about.'

'Not so many as was.'

'Please tell me you didn't—'

'No, nothing like that. Realigned his fucking heavens for him, though.'

Nicholas allows himself a brief, sympathetic laugh. 'I've wanted to do that myself, once or twice.'

'After I got out of the stocks, I went to see your Mistress Bianca. She'd just taken on the Jackdaw. People was saying as how she had the knowledge of apothecary. I begged her to make a potion for Jacob.'

'What did she say?'

'Oh, she had no time for the likes of me. Wouldn't even take my coin.'

'Did she tell you why?'

'She said nothing she could mix would help. I reckoned she thought a poulterer's son beneath her.'

To his surprise, Nicholas feels for this rough young fellow – so devoted to his brother, using his fists to protect him from the scorn and the cruel taunts of the uncaring. And what must it have cost him, he wonders, to see Jacob's butchered body carried into this very crypt, laid beside the corpses huddled together in their shrouds and waiting their turn in the single battered coffin?

'She gave you the soundest medical advice anyone in London has had for a while, Ned,' he says, as gently as he knows how. 'She was being honest with you. She was telling you the truth.'

When Ned Monkton nods thoughtfully, Nicholas knows he's made a breakthrough. 'And you know in your heart she's not a witch, don't you?' he adds. 'She can no more fly than we can.'

Ned Monkton's face reddens with shame. 'I knows it's a grievous fault, Master Shelby,' he admits, 'but I gets a bit mixed up when I'm in drink. It makes me think on Jacob so, and then I gets monstrously quarrelsome.'

'I don't blame you, Ned. If it was my brother, I'd probably be the same. Tell the truth, I *have* been the same.' He holds Ned's gaze a moment, before asking an uncomfortable question. 'Would you have used that knife on me, Ned?'

Ned's jaw works slowly as he considers his reply. 'Maybe... probably not.'

'I'm glad you didn't. Ugly things, knife-wounds. Even the smallest can prove fatal.' Nicholas nods towards the line of wrapped bodies. 'You think it's nothing worse than a small puncture, the next thing you know you're lying there with your lungs full of blood, dead. Besides, if you'd killed me, how would I find the man who murdered your Jacob?'

Ned Monkton stares at him. 'Murdered?'

The single word sounds, in this grim place, like the dead groaning in their winding sheets.

'Yes, Ned. Your Jacob didn't fall into a waterwheel, like the constable claimed. He was murdered. There's a killer loose on Bankside, Ned. And I need to stop him, before he kills again.'

✠

Out on the river a dung-boat makes its way on the tide, bearing the city's waste to the fields and gardens beyond the Fleet ditch. The oarsmen wear cloths across their faces to keep out the smell. On the south bank the sails of the grain mills turn in the wind like the hands of the fashionable new clocks that men like Robert Cecil and John Lumley keep in their studies to impress their friends. Nicholas Shelby, lapsed physician, hurries along Bankside towards the Jackdaw, carrying with him a dark and troubling burden.

Counting young Jacob and the infant from Vaesy's demonstration, there have been four corpses marked with an inverted cross taken from the river since August. There could be more, though Ned Monkton's partiality to ale makes accurate recollection troublesome.

'I know as well as any Christian man, that wound is the mark of Satan,' Ned had told him.

'Did anyone else notice them?'

'Perhaps some of the sisters might have, but they're mostly ex-patients, poor women with not the brains they was born with. One or two of them make my Jacob look like a scholar.'

'Did you tell anyone?'

'Aye, when Jacob came in and I saw he was marked in the same way, I told the hospital warden and the matron.'

'What was their reply?'

'They said I was imagining it. And if I wasn't, I should hold my peace anyway.'

Nicholas is not surprised. The hospital survives on charity and the goodwill of the aldermen and its benefactors. The very last thing it wants is to have the Bishop of London's men turn up in search of devilry. Besides, what does the city care for the dead poor who float up from the river's depths? Better to let them sink back down, undisturbed.

Two insubstantial visions jostle for attention in Nicholas Shelby's mind as he reaches the Jackdaw. They are Ned's description of the two other corpses. One is of a heavyset woman of around thirty. She has an eyeless, bovine face and a little bell on a cord tied around her neck.

'Are you telling me the killer put out her eyes?' Nicholas had asked.

'No,' Ned had replied, 'it must have happened long before – the sockets was healed over.'

The other vision is of an old, emaciated man with a wispy beard. 'Maybe an old cut-purse,' Ned had offered, describing in some detail the stump of ill-tailored flesh where one of the hands should have been.

Nicholas can imagine them laid out in the mortuary crypt – just as the little boy and Jacob Monkton were laid out. He can see the sisters washing the naked bodies, preparing the winding sheets, chattering inconsequentially to keep up their spirits as they lather over those deep, obscene lacerations. One vertical wound, the other slashed across it. The inverted cross. All that's godly, decent and good turned on its head.

✠

'At least now you can report what you've discovered to the parish aldermen,' Bianca tells him later that night when the Jackdaw has closed. Timothy and Rose are busy cleaning the pottage bowls and the wooden trenchers in the parlour. The embers are glowing like a hoard of golden treasure in the hearth. Outside in the lane the tavern's painted sign swings gently in a cold wind blowing off the river.

'Judging by Ned Monkton's efforts to get someone to listen, it's not going to be easy,' Nicholas replies. 'Think on it, Bianca: tavern brawls, duels between gallants, robberies, accidents, drunken husbands who beat their wives, souse-heads who fall under waggons or into the river, wildfowlers on Lambeth marshes who point their firing-pieces a little too carelessly... There aren't enough coroners in all England to deal with so much unexpected death. Who's going to have the time to care about a few vagrants?'

'But Jacob wasn't a vagrant,' Bianca says. 'The family is poor, but they're not vagabonds. Ned's father is a poulterer. Even Ned has a job, though only God knows how he's managed to hang on to it.'

'Probably because there's few else who'd do it,' says Nicholas with a shudder. 'By the way, I don't think you need to fear Ned any more. He's an honest enough sort of fellow in his own way. Grief and drink, that's all – enough to change any man for the worse.' He realizes he could be describing himself. He hopes that in the firelight Bianca hasn't noticed the colour flooding into his cheeks.

'And his little brother was a God-fearing subject of your sovereign majesty – our sovereign majesty – Elizabeth,' she says heatedly. 'Not the most gifted of them, I'll grant you, but whoever killed Jacob – and the others – and threw their bodies into that filthy river will have to answer for it. Isn't that what your vaunted English law says?'

'Yes, but it's the same law that will brand a poor man with a white-hot iron for straying from one parish into another without permission or gainful employment,' says Nicholas. 'It's the same law that excuses a rich one the scaffold for manslaughter, if he can recite from the Bible in Latin. I don't think the law is going to be much use when it comes to justice for Jacob Monkton.'

✠

His eyrie in the attic is warm and there is a smoky tang in the air from the smouldering fire downstairs. Rose has set a tallow candle by the mattress, a bowl of water and fresh linen in the corner. As Nicholas bathes his body he smells the bitter, aromatic scent of the wormwood and alum she has mixed with the water, on Bianca's instruction. He longs for sleep, but there is too much on his mind. Beyond the little window the lane is lost in darkness.

He remembers how he sat here no more than a few weeks ago – though it feels more like an age – staring out over the river and imagining Eleanor sitting alone in Trinity church, waiting for him to come to her. He accepts now that the distance between them is unbridgeable. It is wider than the greatest river any man could possibly imagine. His image of her has become tantalizingly indistinct. It trickles through his fingers like Rose's wormwood water. It flows down into the alley where it mixes with the rain. It streams towards the river where it mingles with the tide, and so to the Narrow Sea and the great ocean beyond. And as it flows, Nicholas realizes at last that she is becoming lost to him for ever.

In Holland, he recalls, he'd met a man named Jannsen, a maker of spectacles. This Jannsen had told him how his young son had been playing with some lenses in his workshop, when by chance he'd moved one lens in front of another. The boy had yelped in terror. Because seen through the two lenses, a tiny spider on the bench below had suddenly appeared the size of a rat. Jannsen believed it might be possible to make a device that would bring things too small to see with the naked eye into plain sight. What if that were really possible? Nicholas wonders. Perhaps then he could see across the vast gulf that separates him from Eleanor.

It is only a fancy; he knows that. And because it is only an impossible fancy, it fills him with an unbearable sense of loss.

✠

Bianca Merton pauses at the top of the narrow stairs. The door to the attic chamber is ajar, a gentle light from the tallow candle seeping past the frame. Treading softly, she moves closer. Through the narrow space she can just make out Nicholas Shelby's back as he sits on the mattress by the window. By the slow rise and fall of his shoulders she knows he is weeping.

Slipping silently away, she goes to her own chamber on the floor below. Rose is already asleep on the pull-out truckle bed, snoring softly. Careful not to wake her, Bianca crosses to the far side of her own bed, takes a key from the collection on the cord around her waist and kneels before a small iron-hooped chest by the wall. Slipping the key into the lock, she turns it cautiously to make no sound and lifts the lid.

On a nearby window ledge, just within reach, is the candle Rose has set as a night-light. Bianca reaches out and draws the sconce to her, setting it down on the floor by her left knee. The meagre light of the flame makes no impact on the dark depths of the chest. Familiarity alone makes Bianca's fingers explore the inside with accuracy. She inhales the scent of lavender, put there to keep the moths away.

Her fingers come to rest on a package wrapped in cloth. Using both hands – it is heavy, though barely the size of a small cushion – she lifts it out and places it on the floor. Her breathing matches the rhythm of Rose's gentle burbling. Untying the thick ribbon, she unfolds the cloth. The intricate wheels and pointers of her father's astrolabe catch the flickering candlelight.

Bianca smiles in reminiscence: she is eleven again, sitting on her father's knee in the sunny courtyard of their house in Padua. He is teaching her how to use the device to fix the position of the constellations, how to cast a horoscope.

Yet for all his skills at divination, he'd failed to predict that his life would end in a cold, dank cell. When the Holy Office of the

Faith had come hammering on his door, accusing him of heresy and sorcery, he'd been the only one taken by surprise.

She puts the astrolabe aside and pulls out a thick, leather-bound book. It is written in Latin – a language she cannot read. But she knows the title well enough: 'A miraculous insight into diverse and wondrous systems of physic'.

Next out of the parcel come three vials of liquid. Each is stopped and sealed with wax, an alchemical symbol painted on the glass. One contains *argento vivo*; the second *lignum sanctum*; the third, *theriac*. She stands them beside her father's book, three sentinels to protect his secrets.

A merchant of cures. That's how she'd described him to Nicholas. But to Bianca his merchandise had been dreams. Dreams of distant lands and wondrous sights. Dreams of unimaginable knowledge.

The last item she takes from the parcel feels heavy in her hand, though it is barely six inches long. It gleams as she lifts it to her mouth and kisses its cold silver majesty. She holds it to her heart.

It is her father's inverted crucifix.

✝

Joshua Pinchbeak sets down his pack by the Cross on Cheapside. He quenches his thirst from the fountain. He has never seen such a monument as the Cross before. It makes a considerable impression on him: three tiers rising almost thirty feet above the street, pillars on the corners framing shrines of the saints. He almost weeps to see how the reformers have smashed the statue of the Virgin and Child, hammering at the stone until the figures look as though they're made of cold grey gingerbread. Does the new religion really think it can save itself by vandalism? he wonders.

Around him, women queue to fill their pots from the fountain. They look at him askance, alarmed by his wild appearance and the fervour in his eyes. He shouts at them: You must prepare for the end! It is coming soon. You must prepare! The words struggle to leave his slack mouth, the cold water streams over his chin. The women move hurriedly away.

And then a shadow falls across the water in the fountain.

Instinctively Joshua flinches from the expected violence of a constable's hand laid heavily on his shoulder, or a watchman's staff jabbed painfully into his back. But the pain does not come. He looks up.

What he sees makes every trial he has suffered since God spoke to him out of the whirlwind worthwhile. His reward is at hand. His suffering has moved God to pity. The Holy Virgin has come down out of her shrine to tell him his ordeal is over!

Joshua Pinchbeak knows it's the Virgin, because she is hooded, and her head tilts slightly to one side, just like all the images he has ever

146

seen of her, before the heretics whitewashed them over or smashed the glass they were painted on. Her smile is the smile that only the saints possess. Her voice is the song of heaven. The touch of her hand on his arm is just as he imagined an angel's touch would be.

'Come,' she says softly, enticingly. 'Come with me. And I will give you rest.'

16

Nicholas does a lot of walking in the days following his visit to Ned Monkton.

It is the start of Advent. A weak winter sun silvers the river. The frost sparkles as it cracks underfoot. Bianca has given him the buffin-lined leather coat to keep; the original owner now troubles the Turk's Head for credit instead.

Rose has trimmed his beard tight against the cheek, and with some careful application of a wax that Bianca makes by boiling certain berries she picks near the river, even the hair on his head has been brought under a measure of control. He still doesn't look like any physician William Baronsdale and his friends at the College would recognize. But at least he no longer looks like an out-and-out Tom o' Bedlam.

In this new persona, Nicholas Shelby presents himself to the authorities. Perhaps now they'll listen to him, now that he can prove one man is responsible for at least four murders.

'It's not my master you need to talk to, sir,' says the clerk to the Southwark alderman, when Nicholas tracks him to his lair in Bridge House on the road to Bermondsey. 'You need the coroner. He'll have to inspect the bodies, sir, to determine if a crime has taken place.'

Nicholas explains calmly that the bodies have long since been given a Christian burial. 'But they'll have been entered in the parish mortuary rolls,' he assures the clerk. 'Jacob Monkton's name will certainly be there. And the infant is already listed in the records of the Queen's Coroner, William Danby.'

'You know that to be a fact, do you?'

'I was there when the child was cut up!'

Startled, the clerk seems to shrink into his chair. 'You were *party* to this murder?' he asks timorously.

'I was there at the anatomy lecture,' Nicholas explains, his tone slow and deliberate, 'when the boy was dissected.' He adds, for good measure so there can be no misunderstanding, 'At the College of Physicians.'

'I *see*,' says the clerk, breathing a sigh of evident relief that he's not in the presence of a self-confessed killer. 'And what exactly is it you want Alderman Hawse to do?'

'We want him to organize a search of empty buildings along Bankside. We think the murderer may be holding his victims somewhere for a time before he kills them.'

'We? Who is *we*, if may I enquire?'

'Myself and Mistress Merton.'

'Merton?' The clerk frowns as he ponders the name. 'Isn't she the mistress of the Jackdaw? The woman the Grocers' Guild were trying to arraign a couple of months back for making unlicensed physic?'

'She doesn't need a licence,' Nicholas says, a little more sharply than he intends. 'This is the liberty of Southwark. The city corporation's writ doesn't run here. You know that as well as I. Now, if we can return to the matter of the killings—'

A look of official regret comes over the clerk's face. 'I really would like to assist, Master Shelby. But if Alderman Hawse is to raise a muster of men to seek out a felon, he will need more than the suspicions of a potion-maker and someone who attends public dissections for pleasure. Might I suggest you try the warder at the Marshalsea. After all, if it's a felony...'

But Nicholas is already halfway to the exit.

✠

It is late afternoon when he reaches the open fields of St George's parish. Rooks call to him from the bare branches, the ground is hard underfoot. His feet are cold and they ache. He's walked almost from one end of Southwark to the other.

Ahead of him are the White Lyon, the Marshalsea and the Queen's Bench gaols. From a distance, they look like a row of ordinary houses, though not remotely welcoming. This is where Southwark keeps its debtors, its miscreants, its heretics and its traitors.

The Marshalsea has a grim lassitude about it. For the luckier inmates, a fine will secure their freedom. Others will languish here until age or sickness releases them to their maker. Some await the next assizes, to hear if they are to be burned with a brand about the face, or lose an ear, an eye or a hand, in payment for some misdemeanour. For a few – the heretics and the traitors, the Jesuit priests denounced or caught up in the random sweeps – incarceration is only a pause on the road. Their final destination will be Tyburn, where they will hang until half-strangled, then watch while their entrails are cut out and burned before their fading sight. Their eviscerated bodies will then be quartered, the pieces nailed up where they can best serve to remind the citizenry of the benefits of remaining obedient to Elizabeth's law. There is a melancholy lying on the land here, a melancholy that will long outlast the winter.

'Listen to me, friend,' says the warder, his voice not remotely amiable, 'I've got five warrants outstanding for suspected papist agents. I've another three for unlicensed preachers. On top of all that, I've a villainous Jesuit in the condemned cell, who keeps me awake all night chanting his vile Masses. And you want me to launch a hue and cry for the killer of four vagabonds? If you ask me, the fellow's doing us a public service. What's his name? He should get a pension.'

Nicholas braces himself for the long walk back to the Jackdaw. There's a biting wind blowing up. It carries the hard scent of dashed hopes.

✠

On the other side of the river – beneath the same cold December sky – the Bishop of London, John Aylmer, has brought his open-air sermon at St Paul's Cross to a thunderous close. Resplendent in his cope and mitre, he has preached from the enclosed wooden pulpit between the north transept and the churchyard for over an hour and a half, fulminating against papist infiltrators, witches, equivocators, heretical philosophies, licentious behaviour, playhouses and general unspecified sin. His audience has loved every word, even the ones that put the fear of damnation into them.

On Paternoster Row, having made his courtesies to the bishop, Robert Cecil sits alone in his expensive imported Italian carriage. He's waiting for Sir Fulke Vaesy to be brought to him.

Burghley's son doesn't care for physicians any more than does Ned Monkton. Nothing any of them have ever suggested has worked on his crooked back. Not their potions, not the wooden poles they'd strapped to his back to straighten it, not a single moment of the pain they'd inflicted on him. But Robert Cecil is not a man to let self-pity stand in his way. He does not see his crookedness as a weakness; rather as scar-tissue, hard and protective, like armour. That's what you need for this job, he thinks: scar-tissue, outside and in.

'Master Robert, I give you good day,' says Vaesy with an elaborate bow, appearing at the carriage door.

Robert beckons him inside. 'A goodly sermon, I thought, Sir Fulke,' he says, his voice deadened by the plush velvet and the curtains. 'Was that Lady Lumley I saw you with?'

'Indeed it was. She's in London for a few days.'

'But the noble lord himself was absent, I noticed.'

'Still at Nonsuch, Master Robert,' Vaesy says. 'He told me that if the queen sends word she intends to Christmas there this year, he wants as much warning as he may contrive. He'll need to talk to his bankers.'

'He can rest easy. She intends to Christmas at Greenwich,' says Robert Cecil with a sardonic laugh. The Cecils know full well the cost of playing host to Elizabeth and the court. It can run into thousands. 'And was that Secretary Quigley I saw with you?'

'Yes, he's accompanying Lady Lumley.'

'I didn't recognize the other fellow. His name?'

The question could be mistaken for polite small-talk, but Vaesy knows that when Robert Cecil asks for a man's name there is usually an ulterior motive. For the Lord Treasurer's son, names are currency: some worth little, some worth a lot, but always worth storing away in case they might be found to have a greater value at some later date. 'Francis Deniker – Lord Lumley's clerk at Durham,' Vaesy tells him, with the uncomfortable feeling that he's committing a minor act of betrayal. 'He's been called down to make an inventory.'

'An inventory? Of what?'

'The contents of Nonsuch, Master Robert.'

'Ah yes, all those books. All those fine hangings, all those paintings, all that silverware. A man could buy a lot of friends with what he could sell those for. Foreign friends, for instance. Romish friends.'

'I think it's just an inventory, Master Robert.'

'I'm sure you're right,' says Robert Cecil, taking up a document from beside him on the seat. It is a digest that his intelligencers have prepared for him. 'You have been with Lord Lumley several times since we last spoke, Sir Fulke. Yet this is all you have for me: "sermon at Cheam church with the Reverend Watson" ... "visit to a bookseller at St Paul's" ... "Lady Elizabeth to Southwark, to distribute alms to the needy" ... Not exactly earth-shaking, is it?'

Fulke Vaesy looks around the plush interior of the coach – anywhere other than at Robert Cecil. *What does he want me to say? Am I to invent an accusation? Am I supposed to denounce my patron, my friend, without the slightest evidence? Is that what it's going to take to win favour from the Cecils?*

'You tell me this man Deniker is only making lists; you tell me you have seen nothing out of the ordinary,' Robert Cecil continues, 'but you should know that adherents to the old faith are practised in their cunning, Sir Fulke. *Very* practised. They are adept at maintaining a façade of compliance with the proper religion, whilst in secret they go about their disgusting superstitious rituals.'

'I really haven't seen anything like that.'

'Innocent-looking inventories can hide papist Masses between the pages, Sir Fulke. We've even unearthed their filthy pamphlets from the bottom of barrels full of Dutch herring!'

'Master Robert, I can assure you, I have seen no—'

Robert Cecil raises a hand to silence him. Vaesy stares at the hand and thinks, *I could live for years off the gemstones on those gloves.*

'The papists do not make loud with their heretical Masses, Sir Fulke, they *hide* them. They have been known to contrive miniature altar stones and other tokens, which they carry disguised as trinkets beneath the clothes in travelling chests. Their priests scuttle through this land in the guise of ordinary men, unseen. You may have witnessed no *obvious* signs of heresy, Sir Fulke, but that does not mean John Lumley has given up his old ways. Look yonder' – he points at the ancient Caen stones of the minster on the other side of the street – 'they say that in the reign of the second Edward, the monks dug up a whole cemetery of animal bones from beneath the Lady Chapel: skulls, jaws, ribs, scores of wormy bones.'

'Is that so?' says Vaesy, wondering why Burghley's son is telling him the sort of trivia the vergers usually reserve for tourists.

'It is believed St Paul's is built upon a pagan temple, Sir Fulke – a place where sacrifices were performed. And shall I tell you what happens on the saint's day, even now, in our modern times?'

Vaesy knows Robert Cecil is going to, whether or not he's interested.

'The head of a buck – antlers and all – is paraded at the front of the procession! Paraded like some heathen trophy! Do you see *now*, Sir Fulke, how long it takes to eradicate heretical belief?' Robert Cecil's stare is so fanatical that Vaesy wonders if he's in the grip of some spiritual paroxysm. 'The roots we must tear out – if our new religion is to survive – they go deep indeed. *Very* deep. So, Sir Fulke, if you wish to be numbered amongst those who kept our queen's faith alive, against all the legions the Antichrist in Rome could send against her, I suggest you redouble your efforts.'

✠

If an alderman's clerk and the warder of the Queen's Bench won't listen, perhaps a church officer might. The following day Nicholas seeks the help of the vestrymen at St Saviour's, the Bankside parish church. It's their responsibility to administer to the poor and vagrant of Southwark. Perhaps they will take an interest in what he has to say.

But instead of a spirit of selfless Christian charity, what he actually finds is a clique of comfortable burghers whose idea of looking after the destitute is to ensure that as few of them as possible settle in the ward and become a drain on its coffers. This, they tell him vehemently, is best achieved by a whipping and scourging of biblical proportions, a task for which they are only too ready. Twice on Sundays, if necessary.

'But young Jacob Monkton was no vagrant,' Nicholas protests. 'His father's a poulterer on Scrope Alley. His brother is the mortuary porter at St Thomas's. He deserved the protection of the law as much as you or I.'

One of the vestrymen is a prosperous little pug of a man named Cheyney. Nicholas has seen him frequenting the Turk's Head, the tavern across the lane from the Jackdaw. Cheyney, he knows, is a haberdasher, a man of some considerable standing in his guild. He considers himself the arbiter of parish morals, and he has a deep and very partisan understanding of the Poor Laws. Cheyney tells him bluntly, 'The Monkton lad went missing for over a month. Is that not so, Master Shelby?'

'So I am told.'

'Then he was out of the parish without licence. *Ergo*, the boy is a vagrant, as defined under the Vagrancy Act, passed by our sovereign lady's Privy Council in Parliament.' His beady eyes gleam in bureaucratic triumph. 'And just between you and me, Master Shelby, you really ought to consider whether it's in your long-term interests to cleave quite so closely to an employer like Mistress Merton.'

✠

Under a pale sky streaked with white mare's tails of cloud, Lizzy Lumley returns to Nonsuch accompanied by Francis Deniker and a groom from the Lumley town house behind Tower Hill. Gabriel Quigley has remained in London on his master's business. Lord Lumley assembles the household in the inner court to welcome her, the grooms and servants along one wall, the maids and scullions along the other. It's what he always does when his wife comes home: makes an occasion of it.

'An uneventful journey, I trust, Mouse?' he enquires of his wife as the stable lads lead away the mud-splattered horses.

'We crossed the river at Richmond, on the ferry, Husband,' says Lizzy, accepting her husband's kiss on the back of her hand with a gentle smile. 'It was an unusually smooth passage for the season.'

'Lizzy, you know how much it troubles me when you cross by ferry,' John says, a concerned frown on his face. 'The river is very strong at this time of year. What if the ferry had been carried away?'

'Husband, the ferry is perfectly safe. Had I crossed by the London Bridge, you'd be waiting here in the cold till nightfall. And the Portsmouth road is a veritable swamp the other side of Morden.'

'I would have sent a coach.'

'You don't *have* a coach, Husband.'

'Then I shall get one, Mouse. One like Robert Cecil's – from Italy, full of plump cushions.'

I wonder if you would have thought to send a coach for Jane? she asks him in her private thoughts. Probably not. Jane FitzAlan could have walked from Nonsuch to Constantinople and back without the need of a coach. *And* she'd have presented you with another child on her return. She lifts a gloved hand to his cheek and says, 'I'm just happy to be home.'

✠

With Lizzy Lumley returned to Nonsuch, Kat Vaesy has time on her hands. Time to do what she so often does when she's alone at Cold Oak with none but her maid and cooks for company: dwell amongst her memories.

She sits by the window of her privy chamber, looking out at the beehives in the orchard. It's been months now since the last insect dawdled sleepily along the window ledge. When they come again, it will be spring.

She's been rummaging through her small collection of books: psalters, uplifting tracts on the duties of women, pamphlets on modesty, all the tedious constraints her father had sought to impose upon her so she would make Fulke Vaesy the sort of wife he expected.

One book had stood out amongst the others, like a signal from a time before her misery had begun. It lies open on her lap now: Pliny's *Naturalis Historia*.

Twenty long years ago Jane FitzAlan, John Lumley's first wife and – at that time – Kat's closest friend, had plucked this very book from a shelf at Nonsuch and thrust it into her hands. Every time she goes there, or Lizzy comes to visit, Kat always intends to return it. Yet somehow she's never quite got round to it.

As Kat stares at the tight line of print, she is transported back to that hot summer's day: she and Jane in the library, John away in London, the gleaming white walls of Nonsuch sending blazing light through the high windows.

'You have to give me something – a book I'll understand enough to sound clever,' she is saying to Jane, her voice tinged with desperation.

'Don't be so foolish, Kat,' Jane says, sounding as though she wants to shake the young Katherine by the collar of her stammel shift. 'You *are* clever. That's one of the reasons he loves you.'

'Jane, I mean it. Please. Look – that one there, with the red leather binding.'

'You're wasting your time,' Jane says as she picks the closest book she can reach. 'I've never seen a man so reduced by passion. You've won him, Kat, and quite without recourse to' – she glances down at the cover – 'Master Pliny.'

Reluctantly, Kat Vaesy puts away the memories and slowly

closes the book. She rises from her chair and takes up an ornate wooden Bible-box that she keeps by her bed. It has an intricate pattern of entwined leaves carved into the side. Jane – dead for over a decade now – gave it to her for a wedding present. Fulke has always believed she keeps her psalter in it. She takes a key from the bundle she carries on her belt and opens the box. Reaching in by instinct, just as Bianca Merton had done with her own box of mysteries, Kat touches her treasures with trembling fingertips. She feels the tightly wound swaddling sheet; the coral-handled bell whose gentle trilling would have lulled her daughter to sleep; the length of hollowed-out horn through which she would have blown soap bubbles, to delight... What would it really matter if her husband knew of this sad cache of lost hopes? He'd call it the over-sentimentality of women. He'd say she's kept them because she's too bitter to forget.

But how *can* she forget? The day he came to her as she lay in her birthing bed and committed butchery upon her and her child – butchery he passed off as merely unsuccessful physic – will stay with her until her last living moment, probably beyond.

One day, she thinks. One day I shall show him the contents of this Bible-box. And when he laughs and calls me a fool for not letting go of the past, I shall tell him the truth: that these treasures were meant for a child I planned – no, *longed* – to have.

By another man. By Mathew.

✠

A *primero* game at a nearby table is progressing noisily towards its climax, the music of Timothy's lute almost drowned out by the shouts of the players as they throw down their cards. Every part of Nicholas's body yearns for the soothing oblivion of a couple of quarts of knock-down. He can feel it calling to him in the tingling in his fingers, making them curl as though they were already clasping the jug. He feels as though he's walked a pilgrim trail and back again. And it's not just the din of the tavern and the throbbing of his feet he wants to drown out, it's also the questions in his head.

'If the parish authorities won't take action, then *we* have to,' Bianca says blithely, doing what she always does when she's trying to solve a tricky problem: running those long fingers through her unruly hair as though preparing herself for whatever battle – large or small – lies ahead. The bloom of the taproom fire on her skin, the brilliant white of her Haarlem-linen collar against the carnelian of her bodice, the green brocade of her kirtle that looks as deep as an ocean in the semi-darkness, all these would make her unbearably desirable, thinks Nicholas, were it not for one inescapable fact—

He pushes the thought from his mind. 'And what exactly are you proposing?'

'Let's face it, no one is going to listen to a taverner with a hint of Romish in her voice, and her labourer. One of us is going to have to raise their station a little.'

'And who did you have in mind?' he asks.

With a challenging tilt of the head she looks him straight in the eye and says, 'Well, you're the one with the Latin.'

17

The first light snowfall of winter turns into a slippery grey gruel underfoot. On Bankside the lanes are busy as Christmas approaches. Despite the chill, most of the Jackdaw's customers are outside, watching a man in bright-yellow Venetians and a gaudy coat festooned with ribbons. He's attempting to walk along a rope strung between two carts, while breathing fire like a dragon.

The street entertainer is almost at the end of the rope when he begins to teeter. The crowd responds with the usual cacophony of jeers and cat-calls that it saves for poor performances at the Rose playhouse. He falls, landing with a stomach-turning thud on the hard ground. The torch he employs to provide the dragon's fire sails through the air and lands spluttering in the snow.

By the time Nicholas gets to him, the man has been propped up against the wheel of the nearest cart. Squatting down beside him, Nicholas pulls back his coat and shirt to inspect the damage. One shoulder sags like a half-empty sack of flour. The neck muscles twitch alarmingly under the skin. His face is as pallid as the December clouds.

'You're lucky – nothing's broken,' Nicholas tells him. 'But you've dislocated that shoulder.'

'Are you a physician?' the man snarls, his face creasing in agony. 'A pox on you then. I don't have coin to waste on a quack.'

'Nor did my father when he sent me to Cambridge,' Nicholas retorts. 'Listen to me: I served in the Low Countries with the army of the Prince of Orange, treating the wounded. I can help you. It'll cost you nothing. Tricky way to earn a living – a one-armed rope-walker.'

The man leans back his head and laughs through the pain. 'The Low Countries – where?'

'Brabant… Delft… what does it matter? A dislocated shoulder is a dislocated shoulder in any state.'

'I was at the fall of Antwerp in eighty-five. In Sir William Parvis's company.'

'Ah, a most fine gentleman.'

'Yes, he was. You know he died?'

'Yes, he did. But I wasn't his surgeon.'

The rope-walker grits his teeth and gives Nicholas a maniacal grin. 'Then do what you must, Surgeon, and by the holy Virgin's tit, do it fast!'

Nicholas unlaces his left boot and sets it aside. The slush against his bare foot feels like a thousand icy pin-pricks. He swiftly removes the fellow's coat so that he can get a good purchase on the arm. He leaves the shirt alone, in the interests of speed. Making a quick check with his fingers, he determines which way the shoulder has dislocated. He's lost count of the reductions – the reseating of dislocated joints – he's performed in Holland: young recruits who'd not been trained to shoulder their firing-pieces correctly and got caught by the recoil; pike-blows taken against the steel pauldron-plate in the heat of battle; riders thrown from their horses. The trick lies in moving fast. He places a comforting hand on the man's sound shoulder. 'Ready?'

'Ready when you are,' his patient replies, closing his eyes.

Nicholas lifts the patient's arm. Another pitiful groan. The audience begins to cheer – on Bankside, pain and suffering are valuable public attractions; the bear-pit is only five minutes' walk away. At the Turk's Head there's cock-fighting in the yard every Thursday. If I really wanted to, thinks Nicholas, I could send Timothy around the crowd with a cap for tips. He puts his foot as deep into his patient's armpit as it will go. The man's mouth gapes like a fish's as he groans in agony. His chest heaves.

Nicholas hauls on the arm like a sailor hoisting a sail. A scream rips through the crisp air like a scalpel. More cheers. And then he feels resistance. The screaming stops. The limb has reseated itself. The rope-walker's face is that of a prisoner who'd just been told he's being spared the rack. Nicholas even gets a round of applause.

'Easy as falling off a rope,' he says to himself in a satisfied tone. 'And you don't need to read Galen for seven years to do that.'

Perhaps Bianca was speaking the truth, he thinks. Perhaps you can't just un-become a physician.

✳

The next day, Nicholas goes to St Thomas's and asks to see the warden.

He's kept waiting an hour. He passes the time in observation. When he enters one of the wards, where ten patients lie on mattresses covered with surprisingly clean linen, the sisters pay him no attention whatsoever. He gets the impression that the barber-surgeon on duty knows how to perform the simple stuff – the letting of blood to balance the body's humours, the treatment of fractures – but when he contrives to talk to the hospital's only resident physician, he discovers the man prefers the ease of the dice-houses and taverns on Thieves' Lane to labouring on the wards at St Tom's. He says he plans to set himself up in practice in Woolwich. It appears there's an opening.

The warden's office is a poky little cell in the oldest part of the hospital, occupying what was once a corner of the monks' beer cellar. Nicholas stands in the open doorway, filling it even though he is not overly tall, waiting for the warden to look up from his work. 'I hear you might have need of a new physician,' he says.

The warden looks as sickly and as impoverished as his patients. But he's canny enough to know the young fellow asking for a position could quite easily be a self-taught charlatan seeking an easy salary and a bed. He wouldn't be the first. 'Name for me the four dictums of surgery,' he says, his attention returning to his accounts.

'Firstly—'

'In the Latin – if you wouldn't mind.'

This man is no Fulke Vaesy. He looks more like a pensioned-off Bankside rat-catcher. But Nicholas does his best to oblige, though his grasp of the classical languages is somewhat rusty.

'Firstly, to unite the parts disjointed. Secondly, to sunder such parts joined unnaturally. Thirdly, to cut out those parts superfluous...' His Latin falters as he looks at the warden and sees that the man appears not to have heard a word. He's still scratching away with his nib on a parchment. But then he looks up, a faint trace of admiration on his face.

'And lastly?'

'Lastly, to supply those parts wanting.'

Nicholas thinks of adding, 'And fifthly, to charge an arm and a leg for the doing of it', but he suspects the warden's sense of humour is as susceptible to shock as his inmates.

Only when he has listed the symptoms of quinsy, swine-pox, tissick and dropsy, along with their cures, does the warden finally decide he's heard enough. He engages Nicholas for two days a week, salary one shilling and fourpence per session – minus the fourpence, when Nicholas politely turns down the offer of bed and board in one of St Tom's damp corners.

And so – in a manner somewhat less grand than before – Nicholas Shelby once again takes up the profession of physician. On Tuesdays and Thursdays he forsakes the Jackdaw and is to be found sitting in the cloisters at St Thomas's, warmed by a brazier, while a seemingly never-ending file of Southwark's shivering, sneezing, limping and spluttering pass before him. He treats tavern spit-turners for burns, weaver women for aching wrists, draymen for crushed fingers. For cases requiring minor surgery he uses the hospital's collection of ancient and battered saws, lancets, drills, sewing-quills and rasps. To the astonishment of the barber-surgeon, he cleans them with brandy appropriated from the warden's private store. It's a trick he'd picked up in the Low Countries. Not once does he cast a patient's horoscope before he makes a diagnosis, even if they ask him to.

He knows he's sailing close to the wind – practising surgery with his bare hands. Even to touch a patient's body is regarded by some of the older fellows of the College of Physicians as a breach of professional standards. But it seems the writ of neither the College nor the Worshipful Company of Barber-Surgeons runs in Southwark, as happens north of the river. Besides, the warden appears only too happy to have someone qualified – and more importantly sober – to carry out the work, and the barber-surgeon seems only too glad of the help.

So Nicholas keeps his head down. He minds his own business. He tends to his patients as diligently as if they were paying him. Those in need of an apothecary he directs to Bianca Merton, trusting neither the competency of the sisters at St Tom's nor the efficacy of their balms and potions.

And he chooses carefully the sister, the patient and, indeed, the moment to ask, 'Do you recall if there was ever a woman who brought a young boy here, four or five years of age – a little boy with deformed legs?'

✠

As Christmas approaches, Bianca musters her forces to ensure the Jackdaw outdoes its rivals in the lane, the Turk's Head and the Good Husband. The taproom is garlanded with mistletoe and holly, some of it bought from hawkers, the rest cut illicitly from the hedges and banks around the Pike Garden and the orchards by the Barge House stairs. Hot spiced wine is prepared. Using a recipe she brought with her from Padua, Bianca has Rose prepare dainties of pastry and marchpane, which fly off the tray. When the landlord of the Turk's Head suggests they're papist wafers and threatens to report her, she lets him try one. Then another. He forgets the Church and offers her a shilling for the secret.

Christmas in London, she thinks, is a world away from Padua. Here there are no tableaux of the nativity paraded through the streets and squares, no swelling voices spilling out of the churches as Mass is celebrated. Here, despite the strictures of the new religion, the festivities seem more steeped in a pagan past. It has a dangerous edge to it, as though it wouldn't take much to tear away the thin façade of propriety and expose a whole ensemble of fawns and sprites, antlers on their heads, cavorting in a woodland glade. No wonder the Pope thinks the English heretical.

✠

Nicholas is troubled.

This will be his first Christmas without Eleanor. The approaching festivities serve only to heighten the pain he feels at her absence. He tallies in his mind the passing of the milestones: her death in the first week of August... his attempt at self-destruction in mid-October... He realizes his sanctuary with Bianca has lasted barely ten weeks. He wonders if the fragile start to his recovery will hold. And he dreads the prospect of a message from Ned Monkton, telling him another victim has arrived in the mortuary crypt at St Thomas's. So he tries to keep his mind occupied. He willingly joins in the preparations. When he's not at St Tom's, he's to be found busying himself with all manner of tasks: cutting a Yule log from a felled tree in the fields beyond the Rose playhouse, doing deals with vintners and brewers on Bianca's behalf, visiting the markets and shops of Bankside for the ingredients with which Bianca will prepare leech and frumenty, brawn and souse for the Christmas table.

And the Jackdaw is gaining a reputation for something other than good fare and cheap ale. Often now, when a customer orders his stitch-back, he might ask Bianca if she will make a salve for his bunions, or seek advice from Nicholas on his wife's backache. Some of the better-off even pay.

Three days before Christmas, Timothy announces that he thinks government watchers have returned to the Jackdaw, just as they did when Bianca first bought the tavern. From the parlour door, he points out two rough-looking fellows drinking in the taproom.

'They say they're wherrymen, but I've asked around and no one who works on the river seems to know who they are.'

'Well, we've had a good run,' says Bianca. 'It's over a year since I threw the last lot out.'

'Aren't you worried?' Nicholas asks.

'Of course not,' she replies blithely. 'There's no sedition preached at the Jackdaw.'

If they are informers, who has sent them? Has the Grocers' Guild or the Barber-Surgeons' Company caught word that he and Bianca are practising without licences? Or are they Privy Council watchers, on the lookout for Romish intrigue and Jesuit priests in disguise?

'Do you want me to throw them out?' Nicholas asks.

Bianca just smiles nonchalantly. 'Why draw attention to ourselves?'

And to show how contemptuous she is of these supposed spies, she at once names them 'Leicester' and 'Walsingham', after the two towering pillars – both now dead – of the queen's secret state.

✣

On Christmas Eve a mummers' play comes to the lane. A crowd gathers to watch St George slay the dragon. St George is played by a handsome fellow with an earring, the dragon by a skinny boy with a paper hat in the shape of a serpent's head. He hisses menacingly, terrifying the women and children and drawing volleys of good-natured abuse from the men. His face is painted with burnt cork, as it is a well-known fact that dragons come from either Turkey or Ethiopia, and hence are customarily dark-skinned.

When darkness falls, candles are lit. More of them, swears Rose, than there are stars in the night sky. The Yule log blazes merrily in the taproom hearth. Measures are danced to the accompaniment of cittern and tambour, songs lustily sung, games of Hoodman Blind and Hot Cockles played.

For the holiday, a king of Bankside is required. It's traditional. So Timothy is duly enthroned. Anointed with a crown of laurel, he goes about the tavern like a tyrant, waving his sceptre – a pig's bladder on a stick – and sentencing even the wholly innocent to dreadful and bloodthirsty punishments, redeemable only on immediate payment of a rosewater and sugar-paste sweetmeat.

Nicholas joins in as best he can, though he feels as if he's watching a play being performed in a language he doesn't understand. When the Jackdaw has emptied and they've cleaned up, he offers to tamp the fire and set the locks. After all, Bianca and Rose are all but exhausted, and as Timothy is now king of Southwark, however temporary his reign, he is to be excused such menial tasks. They all wish him happy Christmas. Bianca gives him a chaste kiss on the cheek. The firelight turns her amber eyes to brilliant gold; but only Rose wonders if the way they gleam when Nicholas is around might be due to something more than just the season's cheer.

Later, alone, Nicholas sits by the fire, fighting the desperate desire to drink himself into stupefaction. He cannot face the climb up the stairs to the attic while sober, but fears what will happen if he weakens.

When he's sure everyone is asleep, he takes the key that Bianca has now entrusted to him and slips out into the lane, locking the door behind him. There's a crescent moon in the sky, glimpsed fleetingly beyond scudding clouds that threaten more snow. The wind off the river bites like a snapping terrier. From the lanes around the Jackdaw come the occasional muffled cries of revellers. The watch will have its work cut out tonight. Nicholas heads north towards the bridge, his stride purposeful, his heart resolved.

When the priest of Trinity church in Grass Street ward wakes with the dawn on Christmas Day, he sees through the window a figure huddled in the porch, still as a statue, staring out at the churchyard. In the dark, Nicholas has been unable to find the correct grave and, in keeping his uncertain vigil, he's damned near frozen to death.

'I went for an early walk,' he tells Bianca on his return.

'Of course you did,' she replies, as she helps him peel off the frost-hardened buffin coat. And she lets her hand linger on his arm to let him know she understands.

✠

One year slips into another. Epiphany approaches. On Twelfth Night the Jackdaw is witness to celebrations that outdo even Christmas. For Bankside, there is only one disappointment this year: the river has failed to freeze. The jugglers, fire-eaters, rope-walkers, acrobats and dancing bears must remain firmly on dry land.

There have been no more bodies washed up on Southwark's disreputable shore, save for a drowned cat and an ancient pike that the less scrupulous inhabitants of St Saviour's parish try to pass off as a sea monster. They charge a penny a peep through an aperture cut into a dark cloth. Inside, the head with its fearsome teeth has been set before an ale cask that some enterprising fellow has painted with scales to suggest the monster's body. They do quite well until the pike begins to rot.

Has the killer's appetite been satiated at last? Nicholas wonders. Where is he? What is he doing? Is he at home, watching his children play with their New Year's presents – just an ordinary man? Is he helping his wife to take down the garlands of holly and ivy, swearing on his soul that whatever he's done, he'll never again let Lucifer make him embrace such terrible evil again?

Or is he merely waiting for the weather to change?

＋

For Joshua Pinchbeak there has been no Christmas, no Twelfth Night, only periods of half-waking from the slumber of the ages. He has lost almost all coherent memory of his life before he came to the Cross on Cheapside. Even the time between then and now – is it days, or years? – is little more than a procession of vague fragments, dreams almost.

Is he dreaming now? He's not sure.

He is bound to a Cross, pinioned by leather straps around his wrists and ankles. What remains of his senses tells him he is upside-down, for his insignificant weight is being taken by the muscles in his calves and thighs. He can hear the soft, familiar cadences of prayer, a man's voice very close by. His mind tells him it will be an easy thing to untie the straps and rise to heaven. All he has to do is give himself up to the desire.

He turns his head, and the blur of his vision eases just enough for him to see a table with strange implements on it: spirals of iron, razor-sharp blades, an old hourglass with the lower bulb full of white sand...

Then a sudden icy fire floods through his body. He cannot move his head enough to see where the blade is piercing his flesh, but what little remains of his reason tells Joshua the pain is coming from some-where on his left leg. He tries to pull away, but he can't. The limb is held fast against the timber. He screams as the blade cuts deep down towards the bone.

Almost as quickly as it comes, the pain vanishes, replaced by a warmth that seems to cover his knee in a pulsing tide. He can hear a splashing sound, like the falling of raindrops.

Just before his eyes close for ever, Joshua Pinchbeak – itinerant preacher, carrier of God's warning that the end of days is coming – again turns his face to the table.

His gaze comes to rest on the hourglass.

The bulb has been turned. The grains of sand are flowing.

18

Epiphany, the formal end of Christmas. Nicholas is at his place in the cloisters of St Tom's, expecting to be kept busy with the aftermath of the Twelfth Night festivities. What he gets is the first chink in the curtain.

As the chapel bell strikes midday he's summoned to the foul ward. It is here that patients afflicted by the pox are cared for, a disease rife this side of the river. Bankside even has its own language for it: French gout... flap-dragon... The whores who suffer from it are fire-ships and blowers.

A woman has been brought in. Nicholas can only guess her age. Her ruined face is covered in ulcers; she's blind, delirious. A dreadful noise comes from the hole where her nostrils used to be before the disease ate away the cartilage. It's far too late to treat her. All he can do is try to ease her pain with a decoction of guaiac, and call a priest to comfort her when the end comes. What he is looking at is the human cost of what Southwark likes to call its 'liberty'.

A heavyset woman of about fifty sits on a stool beside the patient, watching her anxiously while singing a calming repetitive ditty. She wears a simple woollen kirtle, her grey hair spilling from beneath her coif. At first Nicholas assumes she's the bawd, and the poor creature on the mattress is one of her drabs. The anger rises in him like a fire. Why has she waited so long before bringing her to a physician? She can't possibly have been making any money out of this miserable wretch for a good year or more.

He's about to tell the bawd harshly that she's lost her invest-
ment and, if that's the only good thing to come out of the poor
woman's affliction, he's glad. But then he sees that the woman
on the stool is close to tears.

'Who is this?' he asks the foul-ward sister, indicating the patient.

'Mistress Mary Cullen, sir. Brought in from Pale Lane in
Bermondsey.'

He turns to the woman on the stool. 'And you are?'

'Widow Welford, Your Honour,' says the woman on the stool,
wiping her eyes on her sleeve. 'Alice Welford. A neighbour.'

'A neighbour – is that what you call yourself?' asks Nicholas,
wondering what kind of neighbour would wait until someone
was close to dying of syphilis before seeking help.

Alice Welford smiles nervously, softening her boxy features
and becoming almost motherly. 'I used to look after Mary here
when she was a squeaker, no higher than my knee. She used to
come round for her bowl of paplar, regular. She'd have starved
otherwise – her own mother was cup-shot by ten in the morning
most days.' She raises an imaginary glass to her mouth. 'Runs
in the Cullen family, I fear. I ended up doing the same for Mary,
looking after her daughter – before this happened.' She tilts her
head to study Mary's ravaged face. 'Poor little duck. Is there any
hope for her?'

Nicholas draws Alice aside. Mary Cullen may be blind and
delirious, but who's to say her hearing's not acute?

'I'm sorry, but there's really nothing to be done,' he says. 'It
was too late months ago. Why didn't you bring her here earlier?'

Alice Welford frowns. 'Mercy, sir, I would have done, I swear.
But I haven't seen Mary for a year at least. She turned up on my
step just over a week ago. Hardly recognized her, the state she
was in.'

'She came to you for help?'

'I tried – God's precious wounds, I did. I paid out of my own purse for a balm from some napper in St Saviour's market. Said he'd studied physic in Vienna. Didn't work, of course.'

'Well, you've done your best.'

'How long – can you tell?'

Nicholas gives a sad shrug. 'It's hard to say. No longer than a few days.'

'Only I can't really afford to pay for a bed here, you see.'

'I'll make sure it's put down to the parish.'

'I should have taken her in years ago,' the woman tells Nicholas vehemently, 'before that sharper Michael Riordan showed up.'

'Is that the husband?'

'Mercy, no! Even Mary wasn't that addle-brained. One of the canting crew, Michael was. A thief. Have your purse away faster than you could blink.'

'Don't tell me he put her on the street for money?'

'No, but he might as well have. Left her with two sprats and nothing else. Not even a pot to piss in – saving Your Honour's pardon.'

Nicholas smiles. 'I'm not an Honour, I'm just Nicholas.'

He's used to hearing the life stories of his patients. If this is the only epitaph Mary Cullen will ever get, well, what's a couple of minutes spent listening to it?

Alice Welford studies him with eyes made wise by endurance. 'Well, *Nicholas*,' she says, savouring the name as though it's something exotic – which to her it probably is, given that she's unlikely to be on first-name terms with any other physician in London, 'you can't blame Mary for turning to the jumping-house to earn a crust, seeing as how that bastard Riordan left her with an infant son what couldn't even stand on the two legs God gave him – can you?'

19

At Nonsuch, Fulke Vaesy has come for a morning's hawking. Lizzy Lumley sends word to the kitchens to prepare for a man so intimately acquainted with flesh. The anatomist's visits are seldom a comfortable experience for her; there will be endless talk of medicine, the College, the latest discoveries in science. She fears most of it will be beyond her comprehension. It will remind her she is not another Jane FitzAlan.

The Nonsuch cooks prepare a fine meal of pulled hare in blood-and-claret sauce, but to Lizzy's despair, even the food cannot escape being pressed into the service of scientific debate.

'Answer me this, Fulke,' says John, lifting the fine pewter sauce jug from the table and examining it, 'when the blood in this sauce was in the hare, it carried the animal's life-force, did it not?'

'Indeed it did,' answers Vaesy. But in his head he replies with a question of his own: *Have you laid aside your papist sympathies, John, or have you been consorting with England's enemies again in secret? It's important I know, lest Robert Cecil holds me guilty by association.*

'Yet once the blood is in the sauce,' Lumley continues blithely, 'it has no vitality whatsoever.'

'That also is true.'

'You and I could swallow a gallon of it, yet we wouldn't suddenly leap up and start trading blows like two hares in springtime.'

Vaesy gives his host an indulgent smile. He explains that, in his medical opinion, the life-force does *not* leave the body with the blood. It remains within the organs, an invisible residue from the God-given life-force that's carried on the air we breathe. But once again, like a spy's cipher, every word of this explanation has an alternative meaning: *You're not hiding fugitive Jesuit priests at Nonsuch, are you, John? Only if you are and I'm to have any hope of becoming a queen's physician one day, I'll have to tell Robert Cecil about it.*

'Must we talk of blood at the table, Husband?' asks Lizzy, eyelids tight shut.

'But this is scientific discourse, Sweet,' Lumley says, laying a fond hand on his wife's shoulder. 'You'll find it interesting.' Then, to Vaesy, 'Take the sickness described by Abulcasis of Cordoba, for example – are you familiar with him?'

'The Moor describes many maladies in his writings. Can you be more specific?'

'I'm talking of the bleeding sickness, Fulke. When those who suffer from it cut themselves, the flow is most profuse, almost unstoppable. It can only be quenched with difficulty. Sometimes the bleeding cannot be stopped at all, and the afflicted die.'

'That's quite enough blood for one supper!' cries Lizzy, rising from the table. 'I'm going to invigorate *my* life-force with a stroll in the privy garden.'

The two men barely notice her leave, or her parting sigh of exasperation. Lumley calls a servant to pour more Rhenish.

'Surely, Fulke, that must prove that the invigorating life-force is contained within the blood itself,' says Lumley ardently. 'After all, when the tyrant Nero sent word to the philosopher Seneca that he should open his veins and die, that's *exactly* what happened – he died! And the same would happen to you or I. So the secret must lie somewhere in the *blood*.'

Vaesy lifts his spoon and waggles it in front of his chest to indicate his lungs. 'But you discount something important, John: before the blood can become vitalized, first it must mix with what we physicians call in the Greek *pneuma* – the vital spirit with which God has filled the air around us.'

Lumley nods to show he's keeping up, crosses his arms over his stomach and leans back comfortably in his chair. He enjoys these exchanges. It's why he's a patron of the College.

'This *pneuma* is drawn in with every breath we take,' continues Vaesy. 'It is then boiled in the liver by the heat of the body, into what we term a *concoction*.' He lays the spoon face-down on the table. Little rivulets of blood-and-claret sauce trickle down its back. He points to them. 'Thus the enriched fluid flows in a tidal motion from the liver to the organs, as they may require it.'

'Is that so?'

'Very simple. Very elegant. One of Our Lord's cleverer creations.'

'And the medical authority for this comes from where?' asks Lumley as he gestures for a servant to remove his trencher.

The words slip out of Vaesy's mouth as though someone else has control of his tongue. 'Robert Cecil.'

Silence.

Lumley stares at his friend in bewilderment. 'I had no idea Robert Cecil was a man knowledgeable of physic,' he says. 'I thought the law was more his field.'

Almost gagging on a morsel of hare, Vaesy splutters, 'A s-s-slip of the tongue, John. The hawking must have tired me out. I meant to say *Galen*. It was most definitely Galen; he described the flow of the blood throughout the body! Twelve hundred years ago. It was indisputably Galen. I can't imagine what prompted me to say otherwise.' He takes a hurried sip from his glass. 'Must be this excellent Rhenish.'

Lumley scoops up a little of the sauce on his right index finger. 'Aye, I'm sure you're right,' he says, licking his fingertip. 'As you say, all very simple and elegant. The problem I have is this, Fulke: is it true?'

✠

Out in the cloisters, away from the grim oppression of the foul ward, Alice Welford seems altogether a lighter woman. She moves with a fluidity Nicholas hadn't noticed before. As they walk he listens intently to the story of Mary Cullen's short and troubled life.

'Mary was a good girl – better than you'd think, considering this great trial she's come to,' Alice says wistfully. 'That rogue Riordan came whistling through when she'd barely turned fifteen. Handsome bastard, he was – told everyone he'd fought almost to the death in the Irish wars. Truth was, he'd never been further west than Oxford.'

'How old would this boy of hers be now?' Nicholas tries hard to keep his voice slow and even.

'Little Ralph? He was born the summer the harvest failed—'

Ralph.

To Nicholas, the name arrives like the view seen from the top of a hard-climbed hill. *Ralph Cullen.* 'That would make him, what: four?' he says, remembering the year his father had struggled to pay for his tuition at Cambridge because the fields at Barnthorpe had yielded half what was expected of them.

Alice Welford nods.

'And Ralph was born with a malformation of the legs?'

'As if the good Lord hadn't given him enough to contend with, what with Michael Riordan for a sire and a souse-head for a dam.'

Nicholas allows himself a pause; he doesn't want to sound too eager for information. Although he trusts Alice Welford not to invent, this is still Bankside. 'You mentioned Mary had two children by this Michael Riordan. Who was the second?'

'Oh, that was Elise, God bless her soul.'

Another name. Another slight lifting of the curtain's edge.

'Only she wasn't the second,' says Alice, 'she was the first, if you follow me. By about eight or nine years.'

'Elise was Ralph Cullen's older sister?'

'That's right. Though whether Michael Riordan was the father is anyone's guess – what with him travelling the road or getting taken up in the Bridewell. His visits were more erratic than the plague. And about as welcome, as far as we were all concerned.'

'So that would make Elise about thirteen or so now?'

'Give or take.'

The answer to his next question, he knows, might pass a sentence of death on Elise, daughter of Mary Cullen. If it's 'yes', there might well be a fifth victim. 'Tell me, Alice, was Elise Cullen also born crippled?'

Alice Welford takes his arm, like an aunt reminiscing with a favourite nephew. 'Elise? Mercy, no! That child was born bonny. She has the constitution of a lion's cub, like them they keep in the menagerie at the Tower. Needed it, mind.'

'So she's alive?'

'No thanks to her mother. One of her customers at the Cardinal's Hat managed to set fire to the mattress Elise was sleeping on, burned her on the face. I think that was enough for the poor lass. One morning, while Mary was in her stupors, Elise took up little Ralphie and left.'

'Where is she now?' Nicholas asks, as calmly as his racing thoughts will allow. 'She ought to have the chance to make a settling with her mother, before she's taken up.'

'That I do not know, Master Nicholas. Honest, I don't.'

'Someone must know where's she gone,' Nicholas says, the tantalizing image of Elise Cullen already beginning to evade his grasp. 'She can't just have vanished.'

'All I could learn from Mary was that sometime around last Pentecost the two little conies just disappeared.'

'I have to find her,' Nicholas says, now beyond caring what Alice Welford might make of his sudden interest in a young girl he has apparently never heard of until this moment.

Alice shakes her head. 'I wish I could help you, truly I do. The thought of poor Elise carrying little Ralph on her young back down some dangerous road all by herself breaks my heart. I just hope she's found somewhere safe for them both. They was always inseparable. Yes, that's what she'd do – find a haven. And I'll tell you this, Elise wouldn't let nothing this side of Satan's front door stop her.'

✠

When Nicholas returns to the Jackdaw, Bianca says, 'They're back again.'

'Who's back?'

'Leicester and Walsingham. The two snoopers Timothy spotted before Christmas. They're sitting in the taproom as bold as two toads on a waterlily.' She's managed to make her face a mask of indifference, but she can't disguise the concern in her eyes, or the tightening of her jaw. She leads him to the door. And there they are, huddled together at a corner bench; dressed like watermen, yet ignored by the other wherry crews.

Bianca has seen men like this before; she knows the type well enough. They're tyranny's minor mercenaries; little men who grow large off the fear their masters instil in others. She'd seen their sort in Padua, when the Office of the Holy Faith had come to her father's house to accuse him of writing books contrary to God's teachings. Only then they'd worn the rough brown cloaks of the clergy, not the assumed garb of Thames wherrymen. But they had the same look in their eyes: *You might turn your noses up at us, but if you know what's good for you, fear us.*

'Perhaps they just like the ale here,' Nicholas says, trying to reassure her. 'What is there for them to find? The Jackdaw is the least seditious drinking house in Southwark. You said so yourself.'

'I just don't like them, Nicholas. They offend me.'

'Shall I throw them out?'

'No, I suppose we'll just have to suffer them. But I'm not having them run up credit. And tell Timothy to serve them last, from the old casks.' She gathers her kirtle around her and steps boldly into the taproom, but not before saying, 'You were looking a proper Jack-o'-dandy when you came in just now.'

'Was I?'

'Something's happened, Nicholas, hasn't it? Are you going to tell me? Or is everyone in this tavern hiding their hearts from me?'

✻

'Of course I can't be absolutely certain that Ralph Cullen was the crippled infant taken from the river,' Nicholas admits later, when he's recounted his conversation with Alice Welford, 'but I'd wager money on it.'

'The poor little lambs,' Bianca whispers, holding the tips of her fingers against her lips. 'How they must have suffered so.'

The Jackdaw is almost empty, Rose and Timothy are tidying away. And although they left a good hour ago, the presence of the two informers still lingers. They seem far more threatening in the absence, as though the walls, the floor and the ceiling beams have become their proxy eavesdroppers.

'Do you really think Elise Cullen is still alive?' Bianca asks.

'It's a possibility. She left the Cardinal's Hat with Ralph sometime around Pentecost. He was found at Wildgoose stairs some two months later. And we have to face the possibility that his sister is one of the victims Ned Monkton missed, or who hasn't yet washed up on the riverbank.'

'But she could have escaped?'

'Yes, she could. Elise Cullen may still be alive. But what she knows of the other deaths – who can say?'

Bianca leans across the table towards him, resting her chin in her hands, studying his face carefully. Her skin gleams with a sheen of perspiration from the heat of the taproom fire. An unruly twist of ebony-coloured hair has broken loose from beneath her simple linen coif. It hangs over her right temple, a brave standard waiting to be unfurled when battle is joined. Her eyes challenge him as she says, 'A diagnosis, please, Dr Shelby.'

He considers his answer for a moment in silence, then says, 'Ralph Cullen – if that's really the little boy on Vaesy's dissection table – was taken from the river at Wildgoose Lane. Jacob Monkton was taken out by the Mutton Lane stairs. Of the two other bodies Ned Monkton told me about, one washed up just this side of Winchester House, the other in front of St Mary's.'

'Is that significant?'

'I believe it is.' He looks around the taproom as though searching for someone. Then he rises to his feet, saying, 'Be patient. Wait here a moment. I'll find out if I'm right.'

Bianca's gaze follows him as he walks over to one of the few remaining drinkers, a wherryman named Slater whose daughter Nicholas has treated for an excess of phlegm. The two men exchange words, though she cannot hear what is said. When Nicholas returns, there's a grim smile of satisfaction on his face.

'Well, I've been *patient* – in my own tavern,' Bianca says, with a challenging frown on her face.

'Will Slater said that if you throw a barrel into the river any further upstream than Lambeth marshes, the current could take it to either bank before it reached the bridge. But if you throw it in closer, the chances are it'll come ashore on Bankside.'

'Fascinating, Nicholas. But what does it mean?'

'It means this: he's putting them into the water somewhere between here and Lambeth. If we went up to the attic now and looked out of the window, there's an outside chance he might actually be looking back at us.'

✳

On a blustery January morning Nicholas watches, head bowed, as Mary Cullen's body is carried from the mortuary crypt at St Tom's to the chapel graveyard. The hospital's assistant chaplain reads the lesson with almost indecent haste: *for-she-that-suffereth-in-the-flesh-shall-cease-from-sin*...

Nicholas doesn't hear the rest. The hurried words are carried away on the wind almost before they leave the chaplain's mouth. He wonders if such brevity is the lot of all who leave St Tom's this way.

The only other witnesses to Mary Cullen's speedy exit from this world – save for Nicholas, the assistant chaplain and the gravedigger – are Ned Monkton and Alice Welford. Ned has come because he's custodian of the single coffin and must return it to the mortuary crypt, once Mary has no further need of it. But he's also here because Nicholas has told him Mary Cullen's story, as recounted by Alice, and he wants to pay his respects to the mother of the child who may – perhaps – have shared Jacob's last days with him.

As Nicholas walks away to his next duty, Alice asks to speak to him.

'Call me an addle-pate if you will, Master Nicholas,' she says, pulling her patched gown tighter around her shoulders and sniffing through a nose made rosy by the chill, 'but it's only just come back to me. You know how it is when someone dies; suddenly you start remembering old exchanges, conversations—'

Of course I know, Nicholas wants to say, I've done little else since August. But the retort would be needlessly harsh, so he just nods.

'When we spoke last, you asked me where little Elise Cullen might have gone—'

For Nicholas, the blustery chill is instantly forgotten. 'You've remembered?'

'After a fashion.'

'Tell me,' he demands with almost indecent urgency.

'It was knowing poor Mary's gone to a better place that set me thinking. There was a tale she used to tell Elise and little Ralph, almost from before they was out of swaddling...'

A *tale*. Almost as soon as it's born, the hope begins to wither. On Bankside, tales and lies are coins of the same currency. Nicholas is about to tell Alice Welford he has a pressing appointment. But then something makes him hold back. It is an all-but-obliterated memory from his fall; the faint recollection of an encounter with a woman on the riverbank at the foot of Garlic Hill by Queenhithe, an encounter he'd dismissed either because he was too drunk or too angry to take it for what it might have been – genuine.

'If I recall aright, it was like this,' begins Alice. 'Mary's mother – old souse-head that she was – used to claim the Cullens had a cousin who farmed at Cuddington. Apparently he was a yeoman of some measure. Whenever times got really hard, Mary used to tell everyone that one day she'd take herself and the two sprats away to live with him. Now I recall it, it was definitely Cuddington.'

'Are you telling me that's where Elise might have been heading when she and Ralph left the Cardinal's Hat?'

Alice shrugs. 'Who can say? Maybe there really was a piece of proper meat in the pottage. Elise certainly thought so. I remember her jumping up and down and trilling like a pipit with excitement every time Mary spoke of how they'd all sleep on a big feather bed, eat roast meat every day of the week and travel to the Guildford fair in a grand carriage.'

'Do you know where this place Cuddington is, Alice?'

'Of course I do. Surrey, by Cheam Common. Everyone knows that.'

'I'm from Suffolk, Alice,' Nicholas says, gauging whether he can afford to hire a horse from one of the Bankside livery stables. 'I've never been any further into Surrey than Long Southwark.'

'Suffolk or not, you'd be wasting your time trying to,' Alice tells him. 'And so will Elise.'

A shadow of disappointment clouds Nicholas's voice as he asks why.

'Marry now, Master Nicholas, there can't be Cullens still farming at Cuddington, can there? It's not possible.'

'Why not?'

'Well, they tore down every stone, didn't they? Pulled up the very foundations.'

For a moment Nicholas thinks Alice Welford is talking about one of the plague villages, razed and ploughed over after the pestilence scoured it so unmercifully that the few survivors took themselves off to start their lives again from scratch somewhere new.

But then Alice says, 'It was old King Cod-piece what did it. The eighth Henry. Had Cuddington scrubbed out, every last piece of it. Put up that great palace of his in its place – the one they call Nonsuch.'

20

The funeral over, Nicholas receives a summons from the hospital warden.

'I have a task for you – it's civic,' he announces in a tone that suggests to Nicholas he can't find anyone less important to carry it out. He gives Nicholas an address barely ten minutes' walk from the Jackdaw. 'Be there by ten. You'll be met by one of the bishop's clerks from Winchester House. And remember, you're the hospital's emissary.' He looks Nicholas up and down and sighs with disappointment. 'Don't you at least have a gown?'

Nicholas reaches his assigned destination in good time. But he almost walks straight past the low, straggling line of ancient herringbone brickwork and half-rotted beams, so busy is his mind with what Alice Welford has told him. He has to stop, turn back and take a second look, just to convince himself this is the right place.

Raised in the reign of the second Edward, the old St Magdalene almshouse now resembles those it was built to shelter: decrepit, destined for inevitable disintegration and death, and a drain on parish resources.

How can this place possibly be the location of the strange little ceremony Nicholas has been sent here to perform, a ceremony that – the warden of St Tom's was careful to point out before he left – dates back several hundred years and is an honoured tradition? According to the warden, the Magdalene almshouse does not actually belong to the hospital, yet by some ancient concord, drawn up so long ago that the original document is in French, a physician must be delegated on one particular day each summer and winter to administer free medical care to the inhabitants. Apparently, says the warden, it's something to do with the bishopric of Winchester, which used to own the land the almshouse is built on. The hospital's reward is a basket of perch.

London is full of such odd little contracts, not all of them observed, especially when real coin is required as settlement. Today's duty has fallen to Nicholas, as St Tom's only physician. He wonders idly how he's meant to carry a basket full of fish all the way back to Thieves' Lane. It is only when he's joined by two men and a woman that he can be sure the warden hasn't played a practical joke on him.

One of the men is a dun-robed clerk from Winchester House, presumably here to ensure the ceremony is carried out according to custom. With him is a woman in a winter gown of russell worsted, worn over an unassuming farthingale. Nicholas has the impression he's seen her before, but he can't place where or when. But he certainly recognizes her companion. It's Gabriel Quigley, Lord Lumley's secretary. Nicholas hasn't seen him since the lunch at the Guildhall the previous summer.

Quigley is a stick of a man in a severe legal gown and ox-leather boots buttoned and pointed at the sides, his skin pitted by the small-pox – grey in body and mind, by the look of him. He stands beside the Winchester House clerk with a sour expression on his face, like a third-tier lawyer hired to fight a suit he doesn't believe in.

At first Quigley doesn't recognize Nicholas. And why should he? Nicholas has changed dramatically since they last met. Only when Nicholas gives his name and calls himself *doctor*, for the first time he can remember since his fall, does Quigley nod in vague and dismissive recollection. Nicholas knows what he's thinking: what transgression have you committed, what dreadful professional failure, to end up working at a place like St Thomas's on Bankside?

'And what brings *you* to the liberty of Southwark, Master Quigley?' Nicholas enquires pleasantly.

'I am here upon Lord Lumley's business,' Quigley says, implying that if he were not, he wouldn't come within a mile of the place. 'His Grace's late wife – the Lady Jane FitzAlan – made a charitable annuity to this place. Lord Lumley has seen fit to maintain it, in her memory – and as a favour to Lady Vaesy, who first brought the needs of these poor souls to Lady FitzAlan's attention. I am here to escort Lady Vaesy as his proxy.'

'And the bishop is most honoured by her presence,' says the clerk from Winchester House, whose own master is also far too busy to attend in person.

Now Nicholas realizes why the woman looks familiar to him. He makes an extravagant knee to her. He might be in Southwark, he might no longer be welcome at the grand ceremonies of the College of Physicians, but he hasn't forgotten his manners.

Katherine Vaesy nods in appreciation. She is a comely woman, he can't help but notice, though her features carry a brittle sharpness about them, like someone familiar with pain, a survivor perhaps of a cruel illness that has left its traces in her eyes and the lines around them.

'Gentles, please – time is pressing,' says the Winchester House clerk impatiently. 'May we begin?'

Nicholas does what he can for the inmates, their faces blank and uncomprehending as he treats rashes, scalds and lesions with some of Bianca's potions he's brought with him in his bag. Lady Vaesy and Gabriel Quigley hand out a single farthing to each one he treats.

'This is a strange place in which to find the man my husband once told me might make a fine physician,' Katherine says, as a patient offers Nicholas an elbow to inspect – a raw chafe that looks as though it's been allowed to fester for weeks.

'It suits me, madam – for the present. Besides, I'm sure Sir Fulke was being unnecessarily generous.'

'They say you came to Southwark out of grief, Dr Shelby. Is that so?'

Her directness causes him to press too hard on the limb he's inspecting. The patient yelps. Nicholas mutters an apology. 'Would you rather have had me come for the gaming and the bear-pit, madam?'

She shakes her head. 'Not if your grief is so shallow it can be eased by such distractions. There is nobility in suffering. There is God's grace in it. Don't you agree?'

'Not particularly, madam. Do these poor souls look noble to you? The rest of the world seems to have forgotten all about them.'

Katherine's brow lifts a little. 'To bear great tribulations with a martyr's grace, Dr Shelby? To be frank, I find that an inspiration.'

'And to be equally frank, as far as tribulations are concerned, I'd happily have done without mine, however noble they might make me.' Nicholas lets go of the elbow. Katherine rewards the woman with a farthing from her alms bag.

'I heard you'd given up physic altogether,' she says. 'Not that you can call this physic, of course.'

'Why not? It's doing more good than treating some comfortable fellow who's feeling a little down because his mistress won't reply to his letters. And *yes*, I have had patients like that.'

Katherine Vaesy's laughter sounds as out of place in the Magdalene as rough soldiers' song in a chapel. 'Forgive me, Dr Shelby,' she says, 'in the presence of physicians, I'm in the habit of speaking plainly. I've found it the only way of being listened to.'

'Cruel, madam – but probably justified.'

'You may not know it, Dr Shelby, but *you* were the topic of plain speaking amongst my husband's friends and their wives last summer – just for a day or two.'

'Really?'

'Oh yes. The men thought you dangerously over-sentimental. The women all wanted to cradle your head upon their bosoms.'

'It's nice to be appreciated.'

She smiles. 'I think we have something in common, Dr Shelby: you in your exile in Southwark, me in mine at Cold Oak manor. Perhaps we should get together and celebrate the benefits of solitude.'

Is the great anatomist's wife suggesting an *association*? Nicholas wonders. He remembers it was common knowledge amongst the young physicians that Vaesy and Lady Katherine were on barely better terms than Spain and England. He decides the best course of action is to pretend he hasn't heard her.

Once the physic is dispensed and the alms distributed, Nicholas assumes that the ritual is complete. He can't wait to escape. The dark interior of the Magdalene stinks, and the overseer seems more interested in the ale jug on his table than the inmates he's supposed to care for. Nicholas is also worried Katherine Vaesy might ask another of her uncomfortably direct questions. But there remains one final piece of the ritual that must be observed.

'It's time for the fish,' says the Winchester House clerk sonorously. 'And the signing.'

'I have to sign – for *fish*?'

'The representative of the benefactor – that is Lady Vaesy, acting for His Grace, Lord Lumley – together with the agent of St Thomas's – that is *you*, Doctor – must make their avowals in the covenant record,' says the clerk, as though it's a treaty between nations that Nicholas is required to sign, rather than some dusty ledger he's certain no bishop since the days of the second Edward has ever bothered to read. 'Then you may choose five fine carp from the Winchester House carp pond.'

Nicholas hopes there's a meal afterwards, but somehow he doubts it.

✠

Once back in daylight and almost in fresh air, Nicholas accompanies the little party at a brisk pace along Black Bull Alley in the direction of Winchester House. Almost immediately his sense of place and danger – he's been a Banksider long enough now to pick up these things – sends his brain a warning message: you're being followed.

The lad is barely out of childhood. He has a lean and hungry face washed clean of colour and hope. He's not even fast on his feet. He moves with a forward-and-aft lurch, like a sick pigeon. His head – crowned with a dirty woollen cap – bobs intently with each ungainly stride. He's just about keeping up with them, a little off to their side in the middle of the lane. It's partly his dodging of the carts and the pedestrians, the labourers with wicker panniers slung over their shoulders, the women carrying sacks of winter fruit, that's given him away to Nicholas in the first place. He's a cut-purse, and he's chosen Kat Vaesy as his target because she's carrying the alms bag on a cord over her shoulder. Nicholas is about to suggest that she hands the bag to Gabriel Quigley when the lad makes his move.

It should take a practised thief no more than a dozen heartbeats to complete the click, leaving the victim – the buzzard or the hick – to walk on unaware that anything is amiss until the time comes to reach for the purse. But this young lad is not practised. As he darts behind the clerk, his hand already reaching out towards Katherine Vaesy, Nicholas turns and, with a deftness that surprises even him, seizes the outstretched wrist with the hardest grip he can bring to bear.

It's like grasping the body of a small bird. The bones seem so delicate beneath his fingers that Nicholas instinctively eases his grip. The lad stares at him in astonishment, wild-eyed, terrified. A small knife lands almost silently in the mud.

For a moment no one knows quite what to do. The clerk, Quigley and Katherine Vaesy all stare at Nicholas and the lad, as if the pair are putting on some form of entertainment. Then Quigley shouts, 'Call for the bellmen! It's a branding for you, rogue, at the very least. You deserve the gallows!'

'Bring him to Westminster House,' says the clerk sternly. 'We'll hold him there for the constable.' He adds his weight to Quigley's threats. 'It's the Counter for you, my fine lad, and a hot iron on the cheek, so that godly folk might read such sinfulness plainly in your face!'

Nicholas and Katherine Vaesy say nothing. She's watching Nicholas intently. She seems to understand what he's thinking: this boy will be lucky if he escapes with the trimming of an ear, the judicial knife leaving him for ever marked as a felon. He looks half-starved, there are tears in his eyes. He probably wanted the purse so that he could buy food.

But what is really in Nicholas's thoughts is this: this pitiful member of what Quigley and the clerk would probably label 'the undeserving poor' might be the very next eviscerated corpse that washes up on the riverbank. When he lets go of the boy's wrist, it's not only with a sense of compassion, but also of fear. Released, the lad vanishes into the crowd like a fish thrown back into the stream.

'He twisted loose,' says Nicholas lamely.

Katherine Vaesy purses her lips in a wry smile of comprehension and approval. She knows exactly what he's done.

And then Nicholas senses a second disturbance close by. A rough male voice is calling out his name. Looking up, he sees Ned Monkton's impressive bulk breasting its way towards him through the crowd.

21

How long do we have, Ned?' Nicholas asks. The oily flame of a tallow lantern casts furtive pools of light over the uneven arch of the mortuary crypt ceiling at St Tom's. He thinks he and Ned must look like grave-robbers.

'Long enough,' Ned replies. 'The sisters will want to clean him up, so that the warden can write a report to the coroner, but I can hold them off for a time. I'll say you thought you'd seen marks of the contagion.'

'Where was he found?'

'The creek by the old Battle Abbey ruins. The watch brought him in about an hour ago – it took me a while to find out where you'd gone.'

'Battle Abbey? That's this side of the river—'

'Aye. He was found by a couple of lads from the stews out searching for trinkets on the shore.'

The body has a broken, purposeless frailty about it. It's slicked with mud and river-filth, a creature of the water dragged out of its element. Only the lower legs look made of flesh, where Ned has washed away the slime in search of the telltale incisions – and found them.

'Bring that lantern closer, Ned,' says Nicholas as he sees the raw edges of the wounds gaping like mouths stopped at the moment of blasphemy.

'Don't look much, does he? Thin as a sick greyhound.'

'Have you got whatever it was you used to clean the legs?'

Ned picks up one corner of the winding sheet that's been

folded, surprisingly carefully, at the feet of the corpse. 'It was all I could lay my hands on in a hurry.'

Knowing Ned's reputedly fearsome temper, Nicholas wonders how he's staying so unnervingly calm as he looks upon another victim of his brother's killer. With a good deal of scrubbing, they remove most of the watery grime from the body. Only then does Nicholas see the full picture.

His first cursory glance at the face has already shown him the telltale slippage of the flesh and muscle around the left side. For confirmation, he inspects the shoulders and the arms. 'Apoplexy,' he says, as much to himself as Ned.

'What's that?' asks Ned. 'Some sort of pox?'

'It's from the Greek – to strike suddenly. It's when the body is felled without any warning. Sometimes it's fatal, sometimes not. If you survive, you can be left without speech, or motion in the limbs.'

'My uncle Harry was taken like that,' Ned says, almost in awe of Nicholas's diagnosis. 'Lingered a couple of days afterwards, couldn't speak nor move. Aunt Hilda said it was God what struck him down for his blaspheming tongue.'

'And there's a deep laceration – just here – beside the windpipe.'

'Looks like someone started to cut his throat, then thought better of it.'

'It might have been done after the incisions on the leg, to finish the bleeding process.'

'There was the same wound on Jacob's neck.'

'And on the child at Vaesy's lecture – Ralph Cullen.' Nicholas purses his lips. 'Help me turn him over.'

The body makes a noise like a fish on a slab as they roll it. Nicholas sees at once the deep tear in the small of the back. It takes him no more than a few moments to establish that the liver has been removed, not at all precisely.

'Is that what killed him?' Ned asks.

'No. I suspect it was done *post mortem*, like the cut to the neck. Like what he did to Jacob.' Nicholas lifts up the cadaver's left leg. 'This is what killed him. A little bit closer with the lantern, please, Ned.'

For the first time since Fulke Vaesy's anatomy lecture, Nicholas can sense the killer's breath on his cheek.

There is nothing random about the two incisions. They were not made in anger, but deliberately, the tip of the blade cutting deeper into the flesh as the hand grew steadily more confident. Nicholas can see how the direction and depth change, how a slight twist or turn of the wrist has left a small promontory of flesh hanging here and there. He is so close that the smell of decay and river mud is overpowering, but he hardly notices it.

'He's searching for something, with the tip of his knife,' Nicholas says, to no one but himself. 'But he's holding too tight. He knows what he's looking for, but he has little skill.' He beckons to Ned to bring the lantern even closer. 'Ah! And then he finds it—'

'He does?' asks Ned at his shoulder, wondering how someone can read another man's thoughts in a tear in the flesh.

'Then the other cut – transversely, just to make sure.'

'To make sure of what?'

'That he's fully severed the tibial artery.'

'And what's that, to a simple man?'

'It's a vessel in the body that carries the blood. Like a pipe.'

'I just mind the bodies, I don't ask what's in them,' says Ned defensively.

'You remember the last time I came here, and I told you how lethal a simple knife-wound could be? Well, this is a perfect example. He's severed one of the major vessels that brings the blood down to the extremities. Cut through this, and eventually you'll lose enough blood to kill you.'

'But when I used to get a bit fractious and ended up with bloody knuckles – or when you got that lucky shot at me – my blood would dry up and stop the wound.'

'It does, Ned, but a tear in an artery or vein is too great a breach. And it could be that the killer is administering something to thin the blood, so it won't coagulate.'

'So what makes the blood flow out, then?'

'According to the ancients, there's a tidal flow between the liver and the organs. If you can get to the tear quick enough, you can hold it back.'

'How?'

'Most physicians will cauterize the vessel's severed ends with hot oil or tar to seal them. I prefer silk.'

'Silk?' echoes Ned, who can't even begin to imagine how an expensive fabric he's only ever seen adorning the gowns and doublets of the rich could possibly have a place in the treatment of a knife-wound.

'In Holland I used silk a lot: two ribbons, but they have to be really fine. Looped around the cut vessel, they'll tie off the ends nicely. Causes far less pain, too. But to be truthful, usually there's so much of an outflow of blood that it's impossible to find the tear in the artery before the patient bleeds to death. These incisions were made deliberately, to do just that. The wound on the neck was made to drain the body completely. But the man who did it would make a better slaughterman than a surgeon.'

'What kind of devil are we dealing with here?' Ned asks.

'Oh, I don't think he's a devil, Ned. He's just a man, fallible, like any other. He's already made one mistake: he thinks the tide is carrying the bodies downriver and out to sea. And he's arrogant enough to believe that if one should wash up on the riverbank, no one will care enough to take much notice.'

'But he leaves the Devil's mark behind him: the Cross, stood on its head.'

'That's what I thought – at first. But it's not a crucifix, Ned. At least, I don't think it is.'

'Then what is it?'

'It's just the way he uses the knife; a surgical technique. Like the way a man signs his name.'

'Funny kind of name-mark,' says Ned.

'But it's the same every time. This is a creature of habit, Ned – a very tidy man. But where did he get his knowledge from? Does he go to Tyburn and take note of the way the executioner cuts the body? Is he a barber-surgeon? Is he one of those people who attends the public demonstrations at the College of Physicians?'

At once Nicholas is back in Knightrider Street at the Guildhall, shoulder-to-shoulder with Simon Cowper, Ned Wooley and the rest, listening to Fulke Vaesy's biblical thundering.

'Or is he a *physician*?' he whispers as the dark, appalling notion strikes him. 'An incompetent physician – or one who's disguising his hand? Whoever he is, I have absolutely no idea how to stop him.'

When two nurses come down to prepare the body for the winding sheet, the corpse from Battle Abbey creek is given back his name. 'Mercy! It's that Pinchbeak fellow,' one says, recognizing the face. 'I heard him ranting like a zealot outside St Antholin's towards the end of Advent. Put the very dread of Judgement Day in me for a week or more. Spoilt my whole Christmas!'

22

Mercy, what's the matter with you?' asks Bianca, when Nicholas returns to the Jackdaw that evening.

'There's been another killing. Only this time I got a proper chance to inspect the body.'

Ashen-faced, she draws him to a quiet bench. She's been dreading this moment as much as he has.

Nicholas tells her about his visit to the Magdalene – how he'd seen Ned Monkton forcing his way through the crowd and had known that this time it was going to be different. This time he would be no helpless bystander.

'This one fits the pattern exactly,' he tells her. 'Always he chooses someone afflicted with a malady. Always someone weak, someone unable to protect themselves.'

'Look on the bright side,' she says.

'This has a bright side, does it?'

'At least now they'll have to listen to you,' she tells him, laying one hand on Nicholas's arm to tell him he's not fighting this battle alone.

✠

With a written testimony in which he describes the wounds made upon the preacher's body, Nicholas returns to the alderman's clerk at Bridge House. He stands over the man while he pens a report for the Surrey coroner, who – with surprising speed – sends a deputy the very next day to convene a jury.

Nicholas is even invited to sit upon it.

'He is not the first,' Nicholas assures the jury foreman, a stout baker named Royston with rosy-veined cheeks and a duck's tail of ginger hair at the nape of his neck. 'There have been others.'

'But if we know not from whence this fellow came,' says Royston, with the weary casualness of a man who is being kept too long from his proper calling, 'then he is of no concern of ours. He is a vagrant. What does it matter how he died?'

'An honest man can scarcely travel the queen's highway these days without encountering all manner of brigands and beggars!' complains another of the jurymen. 'Better they slay each other than honest folk.'

Nicholas fights, but he is outnumbered. The brief and inconclusive life of the jury barely spans the period between the bell at St Olave's tolling eight and then nine. Its verdict is brutally short: *Unknown man of some forty years, slain by knife-wound to the liver, probably in dispute with a fellow vagrant on the road.*

Nicholas can do nothing but place it beside those other forlorn conclusions stored away in his mind: *Male child... taken up drowned at the Wildgoose stairs on Bankside. Name unknown, save unto God... The wholly natural sensitivities of the expectant father...*

Having decided the killer must be keeping his victims somewhere secluded before he butchers them, Nicholas asks Royston to include in his report to the coroner a request that a search be made of all disused buildings along the south bank of the river between the bridge and the start of the Lambeth marshes.

'Perhaps you'd like me to ask the Privy Council to raise a muster while I'm about it, Dr Shelby,' is the dismissive reply. 'I'll ask them to call out the trained bands, shall I? – all for some unknown vagabond who's taken umbrage against another.'

'They'd do it to catch a Jesuit priest or a Spanish agent,' Nicholas tells him bitterly, wondering if the murderer is going to have to kill his next victim in public at St Paul's Cross during Sunday sermon before anyone shows a passing interest.

✼

Nicholas has one last hope. It springs from Gabriel Quigley's unexpected presence at the St Magdalene's almshouse, and something Katherine Vaesy had said to him.

'You've never struck me as someone who's on cordial terms with a lord,' Bianca says, when he tells her what he plans to do. They are sitting by the taproom fire. Timothy and Rose hurry past with jugs of ale and trenchers of food for the customers. 'Perhaps I should consider charging you rent, Master Shelby.'

'Lord Lumley might not even reply to the letter. I'd be surprised if he remembers who I am,' Nicholas replies with a forlorn laugh. 'We only spoke about a dozen words to each other, in the yard at the College of Physicians last August.'

'Then why do you think he will listen to you now?'

'It's just a feeling I have. He's not like Baronsdale and the others at the College. If he was of a mind to, he could just turn up for the feasts and admire his portrait hanging in the Guildhall. After all, he doesn't have a doctorate in medicine. But no, he sends Vaesy all the way to Padua, at his own expense, to learn about the latest advances from the experts. Isn't that the mark of a man with an open mind?'

'But what are you going to tell him?'

'That someone has been doing exactly what Sir Fulke does, only on living bodies rather than dead ones.'

'Is that really what you think?' Bianca asks with a shudder.

'Sometimes he removes just one organ, sometimes all of them. In Ralph Cullen's case he didn't take any, just the blood. But in every case I've seen so far he's severed the tibial artery – while his victims are still alive.'

'I'm an apothecary, Nicholas; I grow plants and mix balms and distillations. I haven't read your precious Galen. I don't know what a tibial artery is.'

'It's a blood vessel, in the leg. Close to the bone. And actually Realdo Colombo is the man to consult. In his *De Re Anatomica* he contradicts Galen on a number of points.'

'I'm sure that's very brave of him, Nicholas. Contradiction must be such a dreadful trial for a physician.'

'We bear it when we must,' he says, to let her know he can take a joke.

'These vessels – what is their purpose?'

'They carry the blood around the body,' he explains. 'The Greeks used to think they carried only air, but that's because they were studying cadavers. Now we know they carry the tide of the blood.'

'Our blood has a *tide*? I just assumed we were full of it, like a jug is full of ale.'

'Oh, quite the opposite. It's a river, inside us. That's what Galen says. He states that the blood is made in the liver, and our organs pull it towards themselves when they need nourishment, the way a lodestone attracts metal. That creates a tide. On the way, the blood passes through the heart—'

'And what does the heart do? Apart from being the seat of love and valour.'

'Think of it as being rather like an oven,' he says, trying not to sound as though he's giving her the blessing of a diagnosis. 'The heart heats the blood together with the divine spirit in the air we breathe: what we call *pneuma*. The mixture flows back from the heart to the liver. That's what causes the heart to vibrate – it's being moved by the tidal flow of the blood, a bit like an open door moving to the wind.'

'Rivers, ovens and doors? And wind?'

'Yes.'

She gives him a look of unimpeachable innocence. 'And that's what makes *your* heart flutter, is it?'

'According to the ancients.'

'I think I understand now why you don't write sonnets, Nicholas,' she says, raising one eyebrow in gentle mockery.

'Of course, Vesalius and Servetus disagree with Galen over the precise nature of how the blood flows across the heart,' he continues blithely. 'One of them thinks there are tiny holes which allow it to pass through, the other doesn't.'

Bianca throws back her head and stares at the sagging beams of the taproom ceiling. 'Rivers, ovens, doors and wind. And a disagreement between physicians over holes. Who could ever imagine such a thing?'

'You're laughing at me, aren't you?'

She looks straight at him, the core of each eye a droplet of molten amber in the light from the taproom fire. She reaches out and lays one hand against his cheek. 'Never think it, dear Nicholas. Never *ever* think it.'

✠

Later, Nicholas calls Timothy to bring him paper, nib and ink. By the light of the tallow candle Rose has placed in the attic, he begins his letter to John Lumley. He chooses his words carefully, knowing that each day Lord Lumley will receive any number of requests for favour and patronage:

> I humbly beseech my noble lord to recall with favour our short meeting at the College of Physicians this summer past, and I hope to find Your Grace still amenable to the offer of correspondence on matters of physic...

Then, expressing an academic interest in the workings of the human blood system as described and debated by Vesalius, Colombo and Servetus, he asks the patron of the Lumleian chair of anatomy if perhaps he might even be allowed to study at the Nonsuch library. In truth, he means to tell John Lumley his story face-to-face.

At no point in the letter does he refer, even obliquely, to the presence on Bankside of a murderer with an interest in draining his victims of their blood. Nor does he write of Elise Cullen, even though he knows Lumley will have people about him – his servants, his tenant farmers, the tradesmen and merchants who keep Nonsuch functioning – who would know if a girl of some thirteen years, alone and helpless, had recently been taken up by the authorities, or given alms and shelter by the local churches. Despite Alice Welford's belief that Elise might have tried to reach Cuddington, these lines of enquiry must wait until he's learned the measure of the man he hopes will be his salvation.

When he's finished, he folds the paper over on itself, seals it with wax from the candle and places it beside his mattress.

When the dawn begins to pluck the outline of the northern bank of the river from the darkness, Nicholas rises and goes downstairs. Bianca and Rose are already up, preparing the Jackdaw for the day. He asks if he can borrow Timothy, send him on an errand across the bridge to Lord Lumley's town house on Woodroffe Lane behind Tower Hill. He will not carry the letter himself. He no longer belongs to the city to the north.

23

I f Fulke Vaesy could have just one of the Cecils' fine possessions, it would not be Burghley House at Covent Garden, or
the vast estate at Theobalds; not even the Cecils' apparently
endless treasury. At this precise moment it would be Master
Robert's fine Italian carriage. For Vaesy is no born horseman.
And the road to Nonsuch has suffered much this winter.

He'd prefer by far to stay in London. But John Lumley is his
friend and – more important – his patron. If he hopes one day to
succeed the old Jew Lopez as the queen's physician, then he must
come when summoned, like a lapdog to its mistress.

Besides, he has work to do for Robert Cecil; an informer's work.
So he grits his teeth, swears at his horse and consoles himself
with the knowledge that at least Lady Katherine will not be there
today. He knows this because, before accepting any invitation
from John Lumley, he sends a servant to Cold Oak, to discover
from his wife's household if she's been invited, too. For not even
Nonsuch, with its multitude of chambers and corridors, is large
enough to rule out the possibility of an encounter. Cock-fights,
thinks Vaesy, are best kept where they belong – in the tavern yard.
He laughs brutally at the image of a feathered Katherine squawk-
ing viciously and lashing out with spurred talons. The noise is
loud enough for his servant, riding beside him, to look across
in alarm.

When he'd married the young Katherine Warren, twenty years
ago, Vaesy had savoured the difference in their ages. He had
looked forward to playing the master to the maid, forming his

young bride into the perfect, dutiful mistress of his household. A biddable wife. An example of dutiful, healthy Christian womanhood – just the type of bride a future President of the College of Physicians and a queen's doctor should possess.

On their wedding night he had told her what he tells his young men of physic today: that a healthy womb is like the fertile soil in Eden's garden, the wholesome furrow in which the seed of Adam might take root. *Jesu*, how wrong he'd been with Katherine. If only he'd known the corruption hiding inside her, he'd have left the marriage unconsummated. At least that way he'd have had an escape route – annulment. Not even Baronsdale, President of the College, the man who likes his fellows to have unimpeachable marriages, would hold him to the contract then.

Looking back, the signs had been there from the start: wilfulness, a lack of modesty, an unhealthy desire to enquire into things that a girl of fifteen had no business knowing. He'd blamed John Lumley's first wife for that. If Jane FitzAlan hadn't infected Katherine with those abominable ideas when they were together in the early days at Nonsuch, perhaps she would have remained the innocent he had once believed her to be.

He'd done his best to warn Katherine, God would be his judge on that. Finding her alone one afternoon in the Nonsuch library, he had told her angrily, 'It is not pleasing to Him for a woman to seek to know such things as are found here!'

She had merely glanced at him and carried on reading.

Had she not understood that she was being blasphemous as well as disobedient? Did she not comprehend that when God creates us, he places each of us to his appointed sphere? For a woman to inhabit the realm of learning and reason – a *man's* realm – is an abomination, one that sadly Jane FitzAlan had seemed all too willing to embrace.

In the years since then, he's often wondered if God hadn't

taken the three Lumley children from Jane as a warning. Perhaps that was why he'd been unable to save them, despite his command of physic. A punishment not just for Jane, but also for him – for failing to make her see the risks she was taking with her wilfulness. And knowing full well the extent of God's wrath when He'd been defied, Vaesy thinks now that the punishment continued with Katherine.

He feels the sweat break out on his forehead as he remembers that awful day when he'd discovered the true extent of his own wife's internal corruption. The sin of disobedience to God's ordained order had grown inside her until it had become a living entity.

Blasphemy and disobedience – that's what had swallowed the wholesomeness growing inside Katherine's body, swallowing it as surely as the serpent swallows a helpless chick fallen from the nest.

He recalls now with horror the wailing of the midwife as the monster sought to force its way out into the world like a slithering contagion, twisted and vile. His own son, made into a serpent by Katherine's rebellion against God's order!

He had thought that if he acted swiftly, if he excised this thing inside her, all might still be saved. Katherine would see how dangerous her wilfulness could be. She would repent. God would be merciful and allow her womb to heal. In time, if she prayed enough, she might still bear him healthy offspring.

He'd known immediately what he had to do.

It would be a fight between the light and the darkness. But he would not enter the battle unarmed.

The weapon was his secret; no other physician knew of it. He'd made sure of that. It had cost him a king's ransom to buy the silence of the exiled Huguenot physician who'd shown him the apparatus. His greatest fear had been that it might become public knowledge. If that were to happen, its use would quickly become commonplace – a blacksmith could fashion one in minutes. Before you knew it, farriers would be delivering babies. There'd be no profit for a physician at all.

Hurrying to his medical chest, Vaesy had retrieved the scissor-like device and, without taking it from its silk bag lest anyone see it, had carried it to his wife's birthing bed. There he'd shouted at the midwife to remove her miserable carcass at once. Then he'd set to work.

But the sin was embedded so deep in Katherine that it had proved unwilling to leave. The struggle had been like an exorcism. She had screamed in torment as he'd fought to grip that monstrously deformed head between the prongs of the device. He'd closed his eyes and called up a passage from the Book of Mark to strengthen his resolve: *blasphemies, pride, folly... all these evils come from within...*

Looking at his hands now, as they grip the reins of the horse so tightly that its head tosses against the pull of the bit, Fulke Vaesy recalls how they shook that day – until at last they'd felt the resistance end and the sin leave Katherine's body in a slithering, bloody tumble.

Wasn't that proof enough? Vaesy asks himself as his horse steps reluctantly over a little bridge across a racing stream. What other physician could have won such an infernal battle, save one favoured by God?

✠

The court has spent Christmas at Greenwich Palace. The Cecils, father and son, wait on the broad water-front terrace for the barge that will carry them upriver to their house at Covent Garden. The drizzle has turned the land, the sky and the river into a world of unpolished pewter.

'I'm not sorry to have seen the back of that year, Robert,' Burghley tells his son as he pulls his cloak closer to keep out the damp. His age and failing health have made dealing with Elizabeth's ever-growing cantankerousness a trial he can do without. 'I suppose we may thank our Saviour for keeping the Spanish too busy with their meddling in the Low Countries to send a fleet against us again. And Ireland is relatively quiet for once. I will pray long and hard for God's help to endure whatever this new year has planned for us.'

'My prayers are simple, Father, and brief,' says Robert. 'No plague. No plots.'

'Ah, the simplicity of youthful hopes,' Burghley says with a wry smile. 'Perhaps I should consider casting off some of the burden the queen expects me to carry. I might even seek her leave to retire to Theobalds – hand it all to those who still have the vigour.'

Vigour. Never is Robert Cecil more conscious of his crooked back and his twisted legs than when his father tries not to mention them. Through gritted teeth he says, 'You'd miss it, Father – the thrill of the battle. It's in your blood. And there's still work to be done.'

'There's always work in England for a queen's servant, Robert.'

'Do I not work, Father? She knows how hard, yet there is not even a knighthood in sight. I am Burghley's son, yet I am unrecognized.'

'It will come, Robert. Be patient. Perhaps this year.'

'Does she not understand the extent of the labour? How long does she think it will take us to smoke the last of the Bishop of Rome's vermin out of their priest-holes?'

Burghley favours his son with a wise but quizzical frown. 'Does any one of these vermin have a name, perchance?'

'Aye, John Lumley.' Robert chews the name like a sour fruit. 'Perhaps if I make a present of Nonsuch to the queen, she'll be a little more appreciative of my efforts on her behalf.'

'Well, we both know how much she likes presents. But remember, greed is a mortal sin,' warns old Burghley with just the hint of a chuckle. His own piety has not prevented him making a fortune out of serving Elizabeth.

'Her father built Nonsuch. It was her favourite house when she was a child. Imagine how grateful she'll be when a Cecil gives it back to her.'

'And you expect John Lumley simply to hand you the keys?'

'I live in the hope; but I also plan.'

'And what of Lumley himself? What do you intend for him?'

'Cast down for the papist traitor we both know him to be.'

The Burghley barge, a gilded Venetian wonder festooned with silk cushions and curtains, glides up to a flight of stone steps. The barge-master reaches out to help the Lord Treasurer aboard. Robert jumps onto the deck behind him, as agile as a monkey. He likes to show the liveried crew that a crook-back can be as nimble as any waterman.

As the two men settle onto the cushions, a liveried servant brings Robert Cecil a leather satchel. 'The latest news from our intelligencers, sir,' he says, handing over the report harvested from the Cecils' small army of watchers, searchers and informers. Robert Cecil scans the sheets of paper quickly.

'No plague, no papist plots?' askes Burghley, whose eyesight is not what it once was.

'Apparently not today, my lord father. Nothing of import anyway. A wool merchant from Holland has taken lodgings at the sign of the Fox by Aldgate. He may or may not have passed through the Romish seminary at Rouen on his way here. I'll make sure we keep an eye on him.'

'Is that all we have for our money?'

'A carpenter named Fladbury was heard by the West Cheap cross proclaiming he would give the queen a son – if they let him into her privy chamber and paid him five shillings. Drunk, apparently.' He shuffles the leaves of paper. The barge-master gives the order and six sets of oars break the surface of the river. 'Oh, and two of our watchers in Southwark have been informed there is a tavern-mistress there who was apparently born in Italy, or possibly Spain. She may be allowing seditious intercourse in her establishment. And the Grocers' Guild would like her arrested for unlicensed practice of apothecary. Not that that interests us, unless of course she's planning to poison the queen with an excess of aqua vitae, should Her Grace ever stop by for a jug or two of ale.' He stuffs the papers unceremoniously back into the satchel.

Old Burghley looks through the cabin window as the riverbank slides past. 'Judged against what we *have* faced, Robert, I think we may infer that for the moment the realm is enjoying a considerable measure of tranquillity.'

'We may,' agrees Robert through pursed lips. 'But sometimes the greatest plots hide behind the most ordinary of masks. I think we can safely ignore the drunk carpenter. But the merchant, and the tavern-keeper? Perhaps a stick thrust into the ants' nest might be in order – see what comes out. Just to err on the safe side.'

✳

Upriver from Greenwich the same damp grey mist wreathes Kat Vaesy's silent Vauxhall orchard. She walks alone, passing the beehives standing like old headstones in the grass. The orchard is where she comes when the thoughts in her head become so loud that she fears the servants will overhear them and tell her husband: *Even in her exile, you have not tamed her, Sir Fulke... she still desires the world to know what sort of man you are, and twenty years is not long enough to quench her thirst for revenge...* She has already dismissed one of her cooks because she believed the woman was in

Fulke's pay, though Lizzy Lumley told her she was imagining it.

What does Fulke want to know that he doesn't already know? Does he think she takes lovers to her bed here at Cold Oak manor? She imagines writing to Nicholas Shelby, inviting him here, even perhaps lying with him. He would understand the grief that's so thoroughly insinuated itself into every part of her, like holly strangles the bough over which it spreads. But Fulke Vaesy took even that possibility away from her, the day he destroyed their child – the day he almost destroyed her.

At first, when it became clear she was going to survive Fulke's brutal ineptitude, she'd tried to tell John Lumley how mistaken he was to put his trust in her new husband. But John had just counselled her gently not to let bitterness at losing the child colour her judgement. 'I'm sure Fulke did everything he could,' John had told her. She had realized then that if she even hinted that Fulke had been responsible for the deaths of the three Lumley infants – something she could not actually prove, even if her hatred of her new husband clamorously suggested it – she would lose John's sympathy, and very probably Jane's friendship with it. And that Kat would never have risked.

When her father had first sent her to Jane, she'd been little more than a child. She'd been expected to serve the baron's young wife as a lady-in-waiting, learn the arcane mysteries of running a great household. She'd learned fast, watching in awe as Jane deftly played the chatelaine. She'd joined Jane at grand occasions, danced the *pavane* and the *volta* in the great hall when John Lumley threw revels for his aristocratic friends. She'd even been in attendance when the queen and the court came to visit. Not for a moment had she been homesick. Who could think of a home such as hers – with a stern Puritan father and a mother so cowed that she barely said a word from dawn till dusk – when all around her was the unimaginable beauty of Nonsuch? Who would not want to live for ever within those gleaming white walls? Who would not be happy playing chase between the statues of gods and heroes, or strolling in the sunshine through the Italian gardens while the gently drifting mist from the fountains cooled your skin?

And to cap it all, as if being set down in the most fabulous place in all England was not enough, Jane had contrived to bring her together with the man she would later fall in love with. A man who was most definitely not Fulke Vaesy. In truth, Mathew was as unlike Fulke as it was possible to be. It was his stoic endurance of suffering that had so overwhelmed her. He was her very own Christ, she his Mary Magdalene bringing spices to anoint his poor body. The way he braved his malady was the most courageous thing she had ever witnessed. She and Jane Lumley had spent long hours in the Nonsuch library searching the volumes for an answer to the questions that tormented her: why had God punished such a good man? Was there anywhere in the world a secret knowledge that would save him? And could she find it?

Before she could get anywhere close to discovering the answers, her father – in an act of astounding indifference to his daughter's happiness – had ordered her to marry Fulke.

'Where is the wisdom in loving a man who could die tomorrow from a simple scratch?' he had asked her, as if Katherine were considering buying a sickly horse. 'You will marry Lord Lumley's physician. He will bring the family within the orbit of a man who has the ear of our sovereign lady, which may profit us greatly.' By *us* he had, of course, meant *me*.

Katherine Vaesy imagines herself a girl of fifteen again, standing not in her lonely Vauxhall orchard, but amongst the neat box hedges and Italian-style flowerbeds of the Nonsuch privy garden. She is embracing Jane, weeping uncontrollably like the sole survivor of a massacre. She is so inconsolable that even Jane is unable to comfort her.

'He's so much older than I am. And the size of him—'

She sobs into Jane's gown, her nose streaming with such a flood of misery that she's left a small section of her friend's bodice looking as though the jowls of an old and sickly lapdog have rested there.

'I've never seen Fulke Vaesy laugh, not once!' she sniffs. 'And he's so loud when he speaks, as though he's delivering a sermon!'

So loud in fact that she barely hears the shattering of the dreams inside her own head.

And then had come the wedding night. No one had warned her what to expect, not even her mother. 'You will do your duty to your husband, and to God,' was all her mother had told her, as though Kat were being sent on a difficult but necessary pilgrimage.

Of course she'd heard all sorts of fanciful stories, seen the animals in the fields in springtime, but nothing could have prepared her for Fulke's sweaty grappling, for the panting like a rutting hog, for the gasped obscenities while he tried to chew her ear off. Imagine – obscenities from a man who boasted of his piety!

And the pain! And the *weight* of him!

Perhaps Kat could have found the fortitude to suffer even that lewd indignity once every couple of years or so, if it had meant children to nurture and love. But he had taken even that from her, with his damnable physic.

She would weep now, but the tears stopped flowing long ago. That well is dry. There is only the silt of hatred in it now. How can it be, she wonders, that a poisoning that has continued for so long does not kill?

As if to escape to a better place, Kat's thoughts carry her to the time before the pain began. She is fifteen years old again. The season is summer, not winter. She is racing through the deer park on one of John Lumley's horses, Jane barely an arm's length away. Their galloping mounts are neck-and-neck, spume flying from the bridles. Grazing deer scatter wildly before them. As she rides, Kat is shouting out the name of the man she loves, shouting it against the roar of the wind as her horse flies across the park, yelling it like a hosanna, in the certainty that no one but Jane can hear it. Jane Lumley is laughing too, infected by her friend's joy.

Two young women delighting in a conspiracy of love.

For the moment, the name Kat shouts is a secret only they share. But in two days' time, when John Lumley returns from business in London, Lady Jane is going to reveal it to her husband on Katherine's behalf, in the sure and certain knowledge it will bring them all the greatest happiness.

Two days.

Such a small morsel of time. Not much of a prelude before the chill wind ushers in two long decades of darkness.

✠

On a chilly afternoon that same week, Nicholas and Bianca take a bracing stroll along the riverbank towards the Paris Garden. Bianca thinks a brisk walk in the cold might put at least a temporary stop to his infernal edginess.

He's been like this ever since he sent Timothy across the bridge with the letter. Out on the water the wherries and tilt-boats ply back and forth between the river stairs and the wharves. The passengers huddle in their cloaks.

'How can you be sure Lord Lumley will help? He may be just like all the others,' she asks.

'John Lumley is a man who likes uncovering mysteries,' Nicholas replies. 'That's why he built his library at Nonsuch. That's why he sent Fulke Vaesy to Italy to study anatomy. From what I know about him, he's not the sort of man to shut his mind to a proposition without first studying the facts.'

Bianca wonders what Nicholas will do if John Lumley turns him down. She knows his recovery is still incomplete. Whenever they walk along the river like this, she catches him sneaking the occasional melancholy glance across the water. Who is he searching for, when he steals these private glances into the distance? Now she thinks she knows.

There was someone I couldn't cure – someone very dear to me.

Just for a moment an unexpected jealousy comes over her.

Reaching the Falcon stairs, they see a young lad of about Jacob Monkton's age fishing from the end of the jetty. He wears a tattered wool jerkin. His hands and face are grubby. He's probably from one of the Bankside tenements. Nicholas watches him for a while. Then he turns and looks back along the river towards the bridge, scanning the buildings along the southern bank.

'When did Ned Monkton's brother go missing?' he asks suddenly, turning to her.

'Jacob? A good month before he was found,' she answers, brushing a curl of hair from over one eye.

'But I saw his body. He'd only been in the water a couple of days at the most. So where was he in the meantime?'

'You think Jacob was kept a prisoner somewhere?'

He nods. 'And perhaps the others, too.'

'But where?'

'Remember what Slater, the waterman, said about how the bodies might wash ashore?'

'So it must be somewhere between here and the Lambeth marshes.'

'Otherwise the killer would have to risk bringing an eviscerated body some distance to the river, wouldn't he? He wouldn't chance that, surely.'

Bianca puts a hand over her mouth, as if to stop her thoughts from escaping. 'What a horrible thought – poor Jacob in chains, confined like a condemned prisoner.'

'I didn't tell you this the day I found him, but Jacob certainly struggled at the end. I saw the wheals on his wrists and ankles. How do you keep a strong young lad like that compliant for a whole month? Or stop him from calling for help?'

'I could make a potion to take away the power of speech – easily,' Bianca tells him confidently, though inside her, the image of what Nicholas has just described starts a cold entanglement of terror in her stomach.

'But also make them compliant to your will – for that long?'

'It's simple, if you know the right plants. I'd probably use hemlock or wolfsbane, maybe a few others – keep the mix subtle, so that it didn't kill the subject outright. You'd have to keep administering it, of course.'

Nicholas looks towards the great bridge with its lofty parapet of timbered houses, the waterwheels turning in the current beneath the arches. Then he slowly lets his gaze return along the jumble of buildings clinging to the riverbank.

And stops.

As though he's caught a glimpse of something he had not expected to see.

He stands almost motionless, just a gentle nod indicating that he's not entered some form of trance. Bianca realizes he's looking in the general direction of the Jackdaw.

In fact his eyes have settled on a distant roof. He can just make it out above the surrounding tenements. It's the building he passed that Accession Day in November, when Jacob Monkton's eviscerated body came to him on the tide. The building adjacent to Bianca's physic garden. The deserted Lazar House.

'Jesu and all the angels,' he whispers, his voice almost drowned out by the shouts of the wherrymen on the river. 'How could we have been so blind? He's been doing it right under our noses!'

✝

The tattered remnants of the stolen coat, now padded out with discarded rags, flap around her in the wind as she scuttles, giving her body the appearance of a crippled rook struggling to take flight. She sleeps in cattle byres and under fardels of brushwood. She speaks without words to Ralph and Jacob, to the two women who sit and hug each other whenever she stops to rest, and to the old man with a stump for one hand who needs constant reminding of his surroundings.

They have been with her throughout her otherwise solitary passage through Christmas into Twelfth Night, Epiphany and beyond. They only disappear when a real human presence sends her scurrying deeper under cover.

From her hiding place, Elise observes these other creatures – the ones of her former kind – with the uncomprehending eyes of a wild animal. She has learned the temerity of the mouse, the ferocity of the fox. Like the wild dog, she has learned to scavenge. And despite the cold and the hunger she has survived.

And she has discovered, to her joy, that her mother has not lied to her. The great house Mary told her about really does exist. It is a palace so magnificent that Elise believes she has reached the very gates of heaven.

From the edge of a coppiced wood she can see minarets towering towards the winter sky, gleaming the way she imagines mountains made of snow must gleam – though she has never seen such a thing as a mountain or a minaret in her life.

And having come all this way, it breaks Elise's heart to think she dare not enter – because the Devil is so adept at disguise that he might even now be watching her from any one of the countless glittering windows.

24

In the lengthening shadows the greyhounds wait patiently, leashed in and lolling-tongued, tired and muddied after a long day hunting coney in the Surrey fields. On the lane, the liveried grooms calm the steaming horses. Everyone waiting. Guest, servant, horse or greyhound – each knows that before you can return to Nonsuch and rest, first you have to pause at the Lumley family chapel so that your master can pray before the mausoleum he's raised to Jane FitzAlan and their three dead children. God's blood, thinks Sir Fulke Vaesy, why can't some people leave their dead to sleep untroubled?

As the two men walk back through the little churchyard towards the waiting horses, John Lumley says, 'Tell me, Fulke, in the summer – if you recall – I asked you about a young physician I was of a mind to employ on a private venture.'

'Nicholas Shelby?'

'Yes.'

'And I told you he had fallen from his station, descended into vagrancy. I trust you found someone else to send.'

'The venture came to nothing. I was misinformed – the books were not for sale.'

'Well, he would have been no use to you anyway. Sad, but an excess of emotion can unman a fellow, if he lets it.'

'He appears to have resurfaced – on Bankside. He's practising at St Thomas's.'

Vaesy raises an eyebrow. 'Has he really? Well, I hope he's.

rediscovered sobriety in the meantime. I shouldn't care to trust my health to him otherwise.'

'In fact, he's written to me.'

'The impertinence—'

'And I've replied.'

'Whatever for?'

'In truth, Fulke, I did encourage him to correspond – at the College, last August. He asked me then if he might communicate with me on matters of physic.'

'Is there no limit to his presumption?'

'Come now, Fulke, I enjoy hearing the views of the younger fellows. The passing years are inclined to dull one's sense of inquisitiveness, unless you guard against it – don't you find?'

Vaesy looks at his friend as if he's speaking Polack. He snorts loudly. 'Shelby was a good physician, I suppose. But he seemed to think it was a doctor's place to get his hands bloody. I believe he got that extraordinary notion serving in Holland. That's what comes from listening to people who wear wooden shoes.'

'Don't you think you're being a little harsh?'

'If it's debate you're after, I'm sure I could find you someone more appropriate. Someone whose learning is built on more traditional foundations.'

'No new knowledge, eh? Just the rediscovered wisdom we lost after Adam's fall?' says Lumley with a smile. It is Vaesy's firm conviction that all knowledge was handed by God to Adam, then lost after the first sin. He thinks medical discoveries are merely God's way of letting us have a little of it back.

'That is the opinion favoured by the Church,' says Vaesy loftily.

'Did you not tell me Shelby's young wife had died, along with their child?'

'Yes, but what reason is that to come to vagrancy?' Vaesy asks. 'It happens all the time.'

'Perhaps it does, Fulke. But that doesn't stop us asking why is it that, for all its accomplishments, medicine cannot always save even the innocent.'

It's a question Vaesy has never once asked himself. It takes a moment for him to think of a suitable answer.

'It is not the role of a physician to *save* life, John,' he says with utter conviction. 'We simply apply our knowledge. The rest lies in God's hands alone.'

'Are you suggesting that, in physic, prayer is more efficacious than study?'

'For the answer to that question I fear you must ask a bishop,' says Vaesy, placing one hand on his breast, 'not a humble physician.'

Lumley allows a waiting groom to assist him into the saddle. Vaesy is hoisted unceremoniously into his. From this swaying, unreliable perch the great anatomist glances back at the little church from which they have so recently emerged. It looks exactly as it did all those years ago, when John Lumley buried Charles, Thomas and Mary here: insignificant. Just a simple English parish chapel.

Why does Vaesy feel the old stones are watching him, silent but accusing? He'd done all he could for the infants, hadn't he? He'd used the knowledge with which his studies had equipped him. It was true – the rest really *was* up to God, wasn't it?

The groom steps away from Vaesy's horse like a ship's master casting adrift a mutinous sailor. John Lumley raises a gloved hand and the party prepares to set off towards the glistening ashlar walls of Nonsuch. The greyhounds begin yelping ecstatically, in anticipation of dinner.

But before they've travelled further than the end of the church-yard, out of the corner of his eye John Lumley sees his apprentice falconer Thomas Parker running towards him down the lane.

The lad comes to a halt beside Lumley's mare, breathless, one arm outthrust in the general direction of the church.

'There, my lord! Look – *there!*'

And as John Lumley turns his head to follow the boy's outstretched hand, he sees two of the Nonsuch servants dragging something out of the hedge – something that at first glance bears more than a passing resemblance to a sack full of writhing serpents.

✠

It is dusk when Nicholas returns to the Jackdaw. When he does, Timothy tells him breathlessly about a rich man's servant who arrived on horseback barely an hour since.

'Grand he was, in a fine tunic with martlets woven on it! Dare say Southwark will have *that* off his back, if he's not across the bridge by nightfall,' the lad says gleefully. Reluctantly he hands Nicholas the letter, as if he fears that by relinquishing the precious thing with its fine wax seal he'll give up some of the magic that has mysteriously entered him from the touching of it.

Nicholas takes the letter to an empty bench and opens it. Before he's read even a word, he prepares himself for polite rejection, or Secretary Quigley's terse apology that his master is far too busy to correspond with a mere dispenser of potions to the poor. His eyes skim the letter quickly. Get it over with:

> ... and I commend such goodly endeavours to increase scientific discourse amongst men of learning... you are most heartily welcome at Nonsuch to avail yourself of the wisdom to be found in my humble library there...

He almost laughs out loud. *Humble.* The library at Nonsuch is rumoured to contain more knowledge than those of Oxford and Cambridge combined.

'It's from John Lumley!' he announces to Bianca with a broad grin. 'We're in.'

'And your other bright notion, Master Physician?' she asks with an inner shudder.

'Tomorrow. When we have the light to see what we're doing.'

As if that will make it more appealing, she thinks – as she considers his invitation to just about the last place on Bankside that anyone in their right mind would wish to visit.

In the months Elise has spent in hiding she's grown used to her own stink, the stink of the fugitive.

But now her captors have bathed her – just as the angel had bathed her. They have given her fresh clothes to wear: a linen undershirt and a simple woollen kirtle, both made for a considerably larger girl. The garments smell of soapwort. This new, overwhelmingly clean scent offends her. It frightens her, too. She wonders if perhaps she's been washed for the slaughter.

Now they have confined her in some sort of cellar, a place full of barrels and baskets, sacks of flour and carcasses hanging from the ceiling. After what she'd seen in the Devil's house, the carcasses sent her wild again – until she saw, by the light of the single candle they had allowed her, that they were only the salted joints of winter pork.

They have given her a proper mattress to sleep on – though naturally she has not slept at all. They have even given her food, laughing in wonderment as she stuffed it into her mouth with her hands.

But when they left, she noticed, they took care to lock the door.

25

T hey must have been truly great sinners to have been locked away in such a prison,' Bianca says in awe. She is standing in the physic garden, cloaked against the cold. The only colour in the whole of London appears to be the bright amber of her eyes. Beyond the old brick wall the snowflakes are starting to swirl about the grey, impassive face of the Lazar House like spray against a cliff.

'It wasn't a prison, it was a hospital,' Nicholas tells her. 'And leprosy is a sickness, not a sin. The Moor physician Avicenna wrote a treatise on the disease over five hundred years ago.'

'Have the English always been so enlightened?' she asks, her face pinched by the cold. 'In the Veneto we confined them on an island in the lagoon. People said they were cursed by God.'

'I'm just surprised they haven't pulled the place down yet, or turned it into tenements. Winchester House would make a tidy sum from the rents.'

'That's if they could persuade anyone to live in such a place,' Bianca says, keeping her hands firmly tucked inside her cloak, lest they feel the ghostly touch of leprous fingers. 'So where did they all go?'

'When the queen's father reformed the religious houses, the friars who looked after them left. The few patients who remained were sent to the confinement house at St Bartholomew's. As far as I know, there's not been a case of the disease reported in London since before I was born. The question is: how am I going to get in?'

He has already discounted the main entrance, an ancient stone archway facing south towards Winchester House, long ago bricked up to prevent cut-purses and vagabonds using the Lazar House as a refuge.

Bianca gives him a sharp look. 'You're not going inside?'

'Why else are we here?'

'Nicholas, don't be so foolish. He might still be in there.'

'If he is, he'd have lit a fire by now, just to keep warm. There'd be smoke coming from the chimneys.'

'But you can't be sure—'

'If I need help, I'll call to you.'

'And what am I supposed to do then?' she asks with an angry twist of her mouth. 'Prove Isaac Bredwell right – turn myself into a bat and fly to your aid? I'm coming with you.'

'No, you are not!'

'Why?'

'Because it might be dangerous.'

'You said there was no one inside.'

'It's derelict. Unsafe.'

She places her palms firmly on her waist. 'Am I now the hired man, and you the taverner?' she enquires ferociously.

'Look, if I'm not back before the bell at St Mary's chimes ten, go back to the Jackdaw and bring a couple of the handiest customers you can find. Failing that, send Timothy to St Tom's and fetch Ned Monkton. He'd be worth a couple of watchmen on his own.'

'And quite how do you propose to get inside?' she asks, nodding towards the physic garden wall, which must be at least ten feet high.

'If I can find a foothold—'

'Listen to me, Nicholas,' she says impatiently, 'if you're right and this is where he confined those poor creatures, then he has to bring them in from the river – unless he's found a way of passing through brickwork or hauling the weight of a human being over this wall. Wouldn't it be more sensible if we went down to the shore to see if there's an entrance between here and the Mutton Lane stairs?'

✴

Further east, towards the bridge, the riverbank is planked and piled. But at the end of Black Bull Alley it spills out onto gently shelving ground. The Thames hurries by, muddy brown and utterly indifferent, fragments of foliage torn from the bank upriver by the Lambeth marsh bobbing gently on the current. Further out, the wherries and tilt-boats ply their trade. On the watery horizon Nicholas and Bianca can make out the masts of Queenhithe and the roofs of the buildings around the Vintry. Turning right, they begin to follow the boundary of the Lazar House grounds, a wall as old and sturdy as the one in the physic garden. It looks as though it's been here since Brutus was king of Albion, seems to have grown out of the river silt like the black stumps of ancient trees that appear when the tide is unusually low. The brickwork is a dense, dark green with a thick coating of damp moss, the top capped with a deep greyish-white patina of filth from the gulls that perch there. Nicholas walks barely fifteen paces before he sees a gully running from the wall to the water, long ribbons of gulls' mess pointing downwards like arrows indicating the way on a map. He stops.

'Hurry up, I'm freezing,' calls Bianca against the shrieking of the gulls.

Moving closer, Nicholas notices a stout lintel set into the brickwork. Below it is a black break in the wall – the entrance to a culvert.

The lintel is just about head-height, and when he peers in,

Nicholas sees walls some six feet high, made of the same slippery, moss-covered stone as the riverside boundary itself. The floor is littered with pebbles that pierce the puddles of watery slime like tiny islands.

At the far end of the culvert a flight of stone steps leads upwards to ground level. And at its foot, lying like a bier in some ancient sepulchre, is a small wooden skiff, tethered by a loose rope to a ring set into the brickwork. Inside are two oars. There's an iron socket set in the prow, presumably to carry a lantern.

With the tide out, the stink of river mud is overpowering. Is this how Ralph Cullen, Jacob Monkton and the others were consigned to the water? Nicholas wonders. He imagines the river at night, a single lonely light burning out on the current, the soft splash of a gutted body rolled into the dark water.

'Perhaps it belongs to a fisherman,' suggests Bianca at his shoulder.

'I thought you said people avoid this place?'

'Perhaps your monks forgot it when they left.'

'In which case it would have rotted almost away by now,' says Nicholas, edging past the little boat towards the steps.

'Do we have to go in there *now*?' asks Bianca, wrinkling her nose at the pungent stink of river ooze.

'I thought you were intent on coming with me. Losing your nerve, Mistress Merton?'

She mutters something in Italian – an insult, by the way it's delivered. He hears it even above the noise of the gulls. But he's already climbing the steps.

✠

Nicholas is standing on a trodden path amid a wilderness of dead and dying vegetation. Some thirty paces off to his right is the wall that adjoins Bianca's physic garden. To his left – about the same distance away – he can make out the sagging roof of the Magdalene almshouse above the opposite wall. And ahead of him, rising like a grim stone bastion into the winter sky, is the river-facing side of the Lazar House itself. Only now can he truly appreciate the size of the place. The towering grey rag-stone is as solidly buttressed as a cathedral. A row of tiny windows pierces the wall high up below the eaves. Most are either empty or boarded up. What glass remains is grey and opaque, like the eyes of an old blind dog. In places the roof has fallen in, leaving gaping black wounds that let in the rain and the snow.

Steadying his nerves, he glances back to see that Bianca is close behind him, her face twisted in displeasure. As he begins to wade through the rotting ferns and stems of dogwood he imagines melancholy eyes watching him from the windows. He thinks he can hear the murmuring of long-dead monks praying for the desperate souls in their care, but it is only the sighing of the wind through the bare branches of an old hornbeam tree.

Reaching the louring face of the old hospital, he sees an ancient door, the timber faded to the colour of dust. One hand placed against the timbers tells him that although it may be ancient, it's as stout as the day it was hung. But when he inspects the lock, he discovers it's almost new. There's just a thin colouring of rust on the iron. And, judging by the bright edge to the barrel, it's been used recently.

And your diagnosis, Mr Shelby? says a voice in his head, sounding uncomfortably like Sir Fulke Vaesy's.

This is the door the killer uses. He's waiting behind it now. And though I told Bianca leprosy is a sickness, not a sin, now I'm not so sure. His skin is black like a toad's, his eyes ablaze with hatred for everything that is clean. And when I step across the threshold, he will cut out my organs and toss my carcass into the Thames.

'Nicholas, I'm really cold now,' says Bianca in his right ear.

'Have you seen enough? The door's locked. Can we leave?'

'We could get an iron crow from the Jackdaw: prise it open.'

Bianca's olive skin has taken on the same wintery grey as the sky. 'I suppose we might,' she says, drawing her cloak closer around her shoulders. 'But then we'll announce to everyone that we've been here – including, if you're right, the killer.'

'Does that matter?'

'He's not likely to drop by the Jackdaw and ask you to repair the door frame, is he? If he knows he's discovered, he'll put as much distance between himself and this place as he can. And, on that particular count, I wouldn't blame him.'

'I suppose you're right,' says Nicholas despondently. Looking around for another way in, all he can see is the great hornbeam tree rising to the Lazar House roof. He's never had a head for heights. He's not even sure the higher branches would bear his weight. Reluctantly, he steps back from the door.

A wooden skiff and a new lock. It's not a winning hand, and Nicholas knows it. Who's to say how long the skiff has been lying in the culvert? It could be a year or more. And the lock could have been put there by the parish, or by a vagabond to safeguard the profit of his felonies. The Lazar House might be hiding nothing more life-threatening than a house-diver's haul of stolen pewter.

But something tells him he's wrong to dismiss it so quickly. Perhaps it's just his sensitivity to its ancient, tortured atmosphere, but he can easily imagine the killer's next victim lying chained in the darkness somewhere beyond this locked door. He tries to put himself inside the killer's mind; asks himself what kind of place *he* would choose for a secret prison. Instantly, the Lazar House slips into place within the puzzle.

'There's no point in freezing to death out here in front of a locked door, Nicholas,' Bianca says, interrupting his thoughts. She claps herself vigorously for warmth. 'We need to think this through – form a plan.' Nodding in the direction of the river, she adds, 'And we need to go before the tide turns and traps us on the wrong side of that wall.'

He knows she's right. The answer to his questions will have to wait awhile. Reluctantly, he turns and follows Bianca back towards the culvert.

✝

The door opens so quickly that Elise barely has time to rise from the mattress before two men – she recognizes them as the Devil's minions she'd fought so tenaciously yesterday – tower over her.

She has spent the long hours since waking wondering when they might return, when they will show their true nature. But to her surprise, they appear to be bearing nothing more satanic than a trencher of bread and cheese. Behind them comes the tall, mournful-looking man with the spade-cut beard who, by his demeanour and the way the men defer to him, is clearly their master. He seems to Elise an unlikely disciple of Lucifer.

'God give you a good day, Mistress No-name,' he says with a surprisingly warm smile for one whose face looks so full of sorrow. 'Yesterday we feared we'd cornered a tigress. I trust we find you in a better humour this morning. Is it safe to lay this trencher down beside you? I'd prefer to keep my eyes in their sockets, if it's all the same to you.'

Elise recalls the battle proudly, as though she'd been the victor and not the vanquished. She had clawed and flailed and bitten. She had kicked out like a terrified foal until her legs felt as heavy as lead. Struck home, too – more than once – if the resulting cries and curses had been anything to go by. But the months of living like a feral creature had sapped her strength, robbed her of the capacity to resist for long. And as she had felt her strength fading, she had decided her only hope was to surrender herself so that these minions of the Devil might not think to search the hedge from which they had dragged *her, and where – in her fevered mind – little Ralph and moon-faced Jacob and the others are sheltering still, wondering where she's gone.*

'Come now, child,' says the mournful man with the beard, 'what shall we call you, if you won't tell us your name?'

But Elise knows how easy it is for the Devil to disguise himself. So she answers the question with the only weapon left to her: silence.

26

John Lumley does not know what to make of the bedraggled, half-starved young maid his servants have dragged from the hedge at Cheam church. His compassion, however, will not allow him to throw her back into whatever mire of misfortune he's plucked her from.

But what to do with her?

Clearly the girl is one of the vagrant poor. Should he hand her over to the parish authorities? He knows what they will do with her.

But a maid is not to be kept like a lost dog you might throw in with your hounds and forget about. If she won't say a single word about who she is, or where she's come from, what is a man to do?

Fulke Vaesy, on the other hand, has no doubts whatsoever about the maid's continuing silence.

'Devilry! That is the sole reason for her silence. The Devil is hanging on tight to her tongue. You should turn her over to the Church at the first opportunity. If you need a second opinion, ask your secretary, Master Quigley. He'll agree with me, mark my words.'

'Gabriel is in London on business of mine. But I think you'd find him as interested in the mute as I am,' says Lumley as the wind buffets the windows of the privy chamber, swirling the snowflakes around the statue of the leaping horse in the inner courtyard. The servants have set a fire in the hearth, a talisman to ward off the worsening weather. 'What do you make of her, Francis?' Lumley ask of his clerk, Francis Deniker.

'Sir Fulke may be right, my lord. A young maid of her age is highly susceptible to demonic possession,' says Deniker uncomfortably. 'I confess that in such cases I would have expected bodily spasms and utterings of the wildest sort, rather than silence. But if demons have stolen her powers of speech, then an exorcism may be in order.'

'Exorcism is mere papist trickery,' says Vaesy indignantly. 'A good Protestant scourging will suffice to free the child.' He studies his fingernails for a moment. 'Of course there may be a simpler reason a cat has got her tongue.'

'Which is?' Lumley asks his friend.

'Guilt – plain and simple. The child is a vagrant. I'd warrant she was skulking around the church to see what she could steal.'

'Fulke, she's a half-starved child!'

'The canting sort teach their brats to steal almost before they're out of swaddling wraps!' Vaesy says in a tone that suggests he's a man of the world and understands such things. 'The parents feed them on scraps to keep them lean. The smaller they are, the easier they slip through your window.'

Lizzy Lumley, who has been sitting quietly by the fire with needle and silk, looks up from her work. 'Come now, Sir Fulke, if those of us who are blessed with God's good fortune turn our backs on those who have nothing, His love will not abide long in our hearts. Is that not what the Bible says?'

Lumley's eyebrows narrow in triumph. 'Lizzy is right. Where is your sense of charity, Fulke?'

'Locked up safe, where brats like that can't steal it from me.'

'"He that hath mercy on a poor man honours his Maker" – Proverbs fourteen,' quotes Deniker.

But Vaesy can match anyone in a biblical tennis match. '"And if thy right hand offends, cut it away. It serves thee better that one of thy limbs perish than all thy body go into hell" – Mathew, chapter

five.' He favours Lumley with a self-satisfied smile. 'Give her to
the parish, my lord. They'll know what to do with a vagabond.'

'Oh, they will, Fulke. They'll flog her, perhaps even brand her
on the hand or face. Then they'll throw her back into the wilderness,' says Lumley. 'She'll starve before spring.'

'It looks as though someone has already branded her about the
face,' says Lizzy sadly. 'Poor child.'

'There we are, then,' says Vaesy. 'Surely you don't intend to
keep her?'

'Master Sprint can always use another pair of hands in the
kitchens,' says John Lumley.

'There will be thievery in her blood, mark my words,' Vaesy
warns.

'Mercy now, Sir Fulke,' says Lizzy, laying down her needlework, 'surely you don't begrudge the poor child a little shelter, at
least until the weather improves. Have we forgotten the message
of Christmas so quickly?'

Vaesy sighs and raises his hands in defeat. 'I concede the field.
Don't say I didn't attempt to warn you.'

John Lumley pours his friend a peace offering and hands him
the glass. 'There is nothing to warn us against, Fulke. The child
has been sent to me by God, as a test.'

'A test?' says Vaesy doubtfully as he sips the Rhenish. 'What
kind of test?'

'To discover whether a little of His love still abides in my heart.
I said so last night, at prayers. Didn't I, Lizzy?'

'You did, Husband,' says Lizzy, though neither man can tell by
her voice what she thinks of her husband's revelation.

'Yesterday was the nineteenth day of January – St Wulfstan's
Day. The child came to us at Cheam church, of all places. A most
providential conjunction, wouldn't you say?'

Only the mention of Cheam church saves Fulke Vaesy from the

unforgivable blunder of enquiring what St Wulfstan's Day has to do with anything. 'Ah, of course!' he says expansively, 'the anniversary of little Mary's death. My mind was quite elsewhere. I'm sorry—'

'So you will understand why I cannot possibly abandon a lost soul who came to me on that very day, and at the very place where her mortal remains now repose in God's blessed rest.'

Vaesy tilts his great head slightly and savours the wine as it flows into the back of this throat. He swallows noisily and says with a breathtaking lack of tact, 'Well, I only hope Master Deniker here is up-to-date with his inventory. You may need to consult it soon – to see what's missing.'

As Nicholas and Bianca approach the Jackdaw on their return from the Lazar House they see a small crowd has gathered outside. Profitable trade, Bianca thinks, happily noticing no similar gathering outside the Turk's Head. A few more shillings she can put aside for the day the pestilence returns and the Privy Council shuts the taverns and the playhouses.

And then she notices the two watchmen holding back their hounds on chain leashes. Nicholas casts her an uneasy glance.

The tavern door gapes open, almost off its hinges. And blocking the entrance – or perhaps to prevent escape – stand two men in crested militia helmets and steel breastplates, swords at their belts. Inside, another six are turning over the tavern from attic to cellar. One even carries a wheel-lock musket, as if the Jackdaw and its customers were a greater threat to England's safety than King Philip and all his Spaniards. They have descended upon the tavern with the brutal surprise they always employ when flushing Jesuit priests out of hiding, or traitors plotting in cellars. Inside, Rose is wailing like Mary at the foot of the Cross.

The man who appears to be conducting this unholy assault emerges, wearing a face like an unwritten page. Bianca knows the type at once: an official nobody prepared to do harm because someone much higher up has given him a commission; a man wielding someone else's power and consequently over-generous with it. Behind him comes a man-at-arms bearing Bianca's travelling chest like a trophy won in battle. Nicholas senses Bianca stiffen as she watches the officer hold aloft a warrant from which hangs a heavy wax seal. He addresses the crowd in a voice laden with arrogance.

'The herein named Mistress Merton is taken up by order of our sovereign majesty's Privy Council, for diverse infringements and omissions. She is arraigned for the crimes of heresy and witchcraft. Also sought is her accomplice, one Nicholas Shelby of the county of Suffolk, a former physician, currently present in this parish. God save the Queen!'

Someone cries out, 'Shame! Let the Privy Council find their own apothecary!' But even as the assenting murmurs swell, another voice calls out: 'There! There they are! There's the witch. And there's the one who calls himself a physician.'

For Bianca, a terrible recollection of Padua and the Holy Office of the Faith arriving to arrest her father; for Nicholas, a blinding flash of comprehension. He looks around for a glimpse of the watchers – the two men Bianca laughingly styled Leicester and Walsingham – but their work is done and they are nowhere to be seen. Instead Nicholas's searching eyes fall upon a florid, vengeful face laughing triumphantly in the crowd. The face of the man who has just denounced them. The face of the spurned bookseller Isaac Bredwell.

27

T he cold air makes pale phantoms of their breath as John Lumley and Fulke Vaesy cross the courtyard towards the Nonsuch kitchens. Above them an owl hunts, gliding silently over the roof-tiles.

'I thought the kitchens were the best place to put her,' Lumley explains. 'You can't keep up the pretence of silence for long in a kitchen – if, indeed, that is what it is.'

'Pretence, I assure you, John. And I shall delight in proving it,' counters Vaesy.

As they reach the open door a scullion darts out. She's carrying a haunch of meat over one shoulder, yet still contrives a passable curtsey. At Nonsuch the servants are adept. When the queen and her court are here and two hundred mouths need feeding, they display the fleetness of swifts on the wing at sunset. 'Have you come to see Betony, sir?' the girl asks.

'Betony?' echoes John Lumley, raising a quizzical brow.

'Seeing as how she won't tell us her name, sir, we've decided to call her Betony.'

It takes Lumley a moment to catch on. 'Betony – Lizzy planted it in the kitchen yard one spring,' he explains to Vaesy. 'It's run rampant ever since.'

He leads Vaesy into a plaster-walled cavern the size of a stable-block, lit by the glow from one of four huge fireplaces and a score of tallow candles set in heavy iron sconces. Before each hearth is a spit-iron for turning whole beasts. There are broad benches for preparing food, towering shelves laden with china, pewter and stoneware, smaller ovens set into one wall for baking bread. At the far end a door gives onto the pastry room and boiling house. Vaesy thinks to himself: I could fit my town house on Thames Street into this space and still have room for the garden.

Sprint, the head cook, is waiting for them, alerted by a servant sent in advance. He is a ruddy-faced fellow with a barrel chest and a good belly, as sound a testimonial to what flows from the Nonsuch kitchens as you could wish for. Unusually for one of England's great houses, he's not French.

'Has she spoken yet, Master Sprint?' asks Lumley.

'Not a word, my lord. At first it was like having a trapped starling in the place – flapping her arms like a proper Tom-o'-Bedlam. She's calmed now. I don't think she fears us any longer. But I keep young Will busy by the door, just in case she tries to flee.' He nods towards a tousle-haired lad in a woollen jerkin, who sits by the door salting stockfish.

'Does she respond to instruction, Master Sprint?'

'Most diligently, my lord.'

'Have you looked to see if she has a tongue?' Vaesy asks. 'Sometimes a deformity can occur—'

Sprint laughs. 'It appears she has a fine, strong tongue, sir. She's all but emptied the scullions' pottage bowl.'

'If she does indeed have a tongue, I could lay some irritant upon it – sting the organ back into function,' Vaesy suggests. 'I don't suppose there are nettles in your privy garden at this time of the year, my lord.'

'We'll have no need of nettles, thank you, Fulke,' says Lumley, appalled. 'We shall examine her with all gentleness. I suspect the child has known great suffering in her life. Let us not add to it.'

A breathless Francis Deniker arrives, a cloak thrown over his nightshirt. 'I understand you wish me to make a record, my lord,' he says, half-disbelieving the reason for the summons. 'It seems an odd time to study the child, if I may say so. Could it not wait until morning?'

'Sir Fulke and I have had a goodly supper. Fine food and Rhenish tend to put men of physic in an inquisitive frame of mind. Now is as good a time as any.'

'Yes, my lord,' the clerk replies, wishing that Gabriel Quigley was here to do the job instead.

'Well, Master Sprint,' says Lumley cheerfully, 'lead us to her.'

✠

Washed in a tub of water scented with camomile and marjoram, dressed in a clean linen kirtle, the girl who scrubs the bread-ovens looks an altogether different creature from the wildcat they dragged out of a hedge only yesterday. Her skin still carries the marks made by thorn and bramble, red wheals against skin that still bears the tan of a summer spent on the road. Her hair is not yet fit to be seen outside the Nonsuch kitchen yard, but the terror in her eyes has subsided to a tired wariness, like that of an exhausted bird caught in a net. She scrubs with a distant look on her face, pausing every now and then to look around her, as though she can't quite believe where she is.

'I've set Joanna to keep charge of her, my lord,' says Sprint, glancing at the plump woman in a freeze-smock who guides Betony at her labour. 'Shall I have her brought to you?'

'This gentleman is one of the finest physicians in all England,' Lumley says when the girl stands in front of him. 'I have asked him to examine you, so that together we might better understand the nature of your silence. Do you consent?'

The girl they have named Betony neither consents nor refuses. Instead she looks at Lumley the way a dog may look at a master it has not yet learned to trust.

'You're quite safe, lass,' says Sprint gently. 'This gentleman is the lord of Nonsuch Palace, which, as I've already told you, is where you find yourself. It is a goodly palace, and we in it are goodly people – at least we like to think so. Is that not so, my lord?'

'Indeed it is, Master Sprint,' says Lumley in what he hopes is his most reassuring tone.

'And just as our master, Lord Lumley, is obedient to God, so must *we* be obedient to him,' says Sprint. This causes John Lumley to smile. Sprint and his assistant, Joanna, are the least biddable servants in Nonsuch.

'Two stools, placed by the fire, please – just there,' orders Vaesy, indicating the great hearth with its spit-iron and the logs burning merrily behind. 'One for me, one for the child.'

It is uncomfortably hot in front of the fire. No sooner has Vaesy taken his place than he begins to sweat. He unlaces the topmost points of his shirt. He leans across the space between the stools and takes the girl by the arm, catching her off-guard. He does his best to make his face gentle, but he is a big man and his beard is impressive.

'Now then, my daughter, you have nothing whatsoever to fear from me,' he says with a forced smile, wiping his brow with the back of his free hand.

For a moment the anatomist and the vagrant girl simply stare at each other. Then, as Vaesy tells Betony that nothing she might say will get her into harm, he gently slides his hand down to her wrist, forcing her hand against the stool and effectively pinning her there.

'Tell us, child, what is your real name?'

Betony does not answer.

This surprises no one except Sir Fulke Vaesy, who is accustomed to being answered promptly and with reverence. He raises his voice. 'Child – your name?'

Silence.

Francis Deniker makes his first entry on the paper he has brought with him.

'Come now, Mistress Betony, did you not hear Master Sprint say we must all be obedient to those set over us?' Vaesy asks. 'We know you are not deaf. I am told you have taken instructions from that good lady yonder,' he says, glancing in the direction of Joanna. 'So I know you understand me when I say "obedient". Are you obedient, Betony – obedient to God and His ordained natural order?'

The girl nods. But she says nothing.

Sweating profusely now, Vaesy blusters on. He asks her where she came from, how she got to Cheam church. He tells her that she should feel honoured to be here. The queen comes to Nonsuch often, he explains. The queen eats food prepared in these very kitchens. Does Betony know the name of our sovereign majesty, the queen?

If Betony does, she's not of a mind to share the fact. The only sounds in the kitchen are Vaesy's increasingly frustrated voice, Francis Deniker's scribbling and the crackling of the fire.

'I think we should call a halt to this experiment,' says Lumley. 'We're getting nowhere.' He raises his left palm to indicate that Deniker may stop wasting paper.

Thus he fails to notice Vaesy's free hand seize the girl's other wrist, trapping it so firmly that it becomes a mere extension of his intent.

For a moment, only Vaesy and the girl share the bond of understanding. Her body locks into a spasm of fear as he draws her hand towards the smoking spit-iron. She twists away from the fire, away from the man whose grip she cannot escape. Her feet flail against his shins. He seems not to notice.

'Fulke, in the name of God's blood – no!' shouts Lumley.

Vaesy shoots him a silencing glance, as though Lumley were one of his junior physicians.

Sprint thinks: I know how to stop him. I'll hit him with the nearest heavy kitchen implement I can reach. But for all his independence, Sprint has never before considered assaulting a knight of the realm. So he, in company with Lumley and Deniker, remains frozen to the spot.

As if the will to resist has suddenly drained out of her body, Betony crumples. She looks into Vaesy's stern face, the tears streaming down her scrubbed cheeks. Her hand is so close to the burning spit-iron that were she to unclench her fist now, her fingertips would touch it. She bows her head, accepting the inevitable torment like a martyr going willingly to the flames. She closes her eyes.

But she does not speak.

The heat against her flesh is the warm sunlight spilling through the summer leaves. The stream burbles over the rocks. The air thrums with the beating of dragonfly wings.

Elise watches the hind supping from the water of the ford, its dappled skin the colour of pearls drenched in honey. *Drink swiftly, little one! The hunter is always nearer than you think.*

28

The kitchens are silent now, just the occasional *crack* from the logs glowing in the hearth and the soft snoring of the male scullions asleep on their mattresses.

Betony is with the female servants in their quarters in the outer court. John Lumley is confident she will be secure there. Even if she manages to slip away, the outer gatehouse is shut after dark. Unless she can fly over two storeys of brick and ashlar, she is effectively imprisoned.

Given the ordeal she'd been through, thinks Sprint as he makes his nightly rounds of the kitchens, she appeared oddly calm afterwards. Her mind seemed to have taken her to some distant place where none of them could follow.

Sprint's father had told him once about a burning he'd attended, back in the time before Elizabeth, when the realm was temporarily Catholic again and her half-sister Bloody Mary had sent three hundred Protestant martyrs to the flames. *It's like they welcomed it, eyes lifted to heaven, hymns on their lips right up till the moment they folded up and collapsed, like all the bones had suddenly been plucked out of their bodies.* Sprint has often wondered how anyone could face such a fearful death with equanimity. Now he thinks he knows.

He had enjoyed seeing Vaesy bested. When the physician had let go of the girl's wrist at the very last moment, his face had been crimson with humiliation. It had been a joy to watch the conflict in him. Inside two minutes he'd come up with more diagnoses than an ordinary man could have afforded in a lifetime: *The child is too dull-witted to speak... the child has never been taught the words... the child must be foreign and doesn't understand the simplest of questions...* The one diagnosis he'd refused to consider was that the girl was made of stronger stuff than he. By the look Sprint had seen on Lord Lumley's face, he suspects Nonsuch won't be seeing quite so much of the great anatomist for a while.

On the wooden counter over the bread-ovens stands a jug of small-beer. Sprint unties his apron like a crusader laying down his shield after a hard day's battling against the heathen, pours himself a larger measure than he intended. And as he drinks, the logs in the hearth behind him give out a last dying blaze of light, bringing the front of the bread-ovens into sharp relief.

At first he thinks one of the younger scullions has scratched his mark there, or scrawled some lewd doggerel into the sooty plaster. Lowering himself into a squat – not an easy thing for such a big man – he inspects the marks, the faces of the likely suspects already forming up in his mind, in order of culpability.

He's looking at a row of three inverted crosses, clawed into the soot in the very place where Joanna sct Betony to work, before Fulke Vaesy turned up and threw everything into riot. Betony must have made them when Joanna was at some other task, he thinks.

And below the third crucifix, a teardrop of spilt blood-sauce. Or perhaps just blood. From a fingernail – as it tore into the plaster.

Perhaps Sir Fulke Vaesy was right after all, Sprint thinks, as he wonders just what sort of creature John Lumley has let into Nonsuch.

✠

He looks so familiar to her – the man in the plain woollen tunic who sits behind the table. Familiar in the same way that

Leicester and Walsingham, the two watchers who'd come to the Jackdaw, were somehow already known to her. Even though Bianca has not set eyes on him before, he is already known to her in all his tedious detail. He is yet another of those minor men of government – the ones who toil to keep their masters' hands clean by taking to themselves the decision that a harsher degree of questioning might be in order. The ones who smile so regretfully while they show you the implements of torture you will *force* them to employ, because of your wholly unreasonable refusal to tell them what they want to hear. The gowned lawyers' clerks who draft the confession you never made. The men who say they're doing holy work, yet have something of the slaughterman in their eyes. The men who set their consciences subordinate to their service to the realm. As Bianca stands manacled before this very ordinary fellow – who will not tell her his name, but says only that he has come directly from the queen's Privy Council to examine her – she realizes that no matter which religion they think they're protecting from heresy, they are in essence the same.

She'd met her first one in Padua, when the Holy Office of the Faith had arrested her father. *Tell me, child – have you ever witnessed him laying out a circle with his staff, and there within making incantations to summon up Lucifer?* She had answered that her father was a good man and only interested in advancing physic. *Is your father in frequent correspondence with agents of the heretic Queen of England?* At that moment she'd understood how they worked: if they couldn't burn you for witchcraft, they would burn you for being a spy. It didn't matter to them which, only that you should burn.

'Mistress Merton, please tell me: where were you born?' says the man behind the table.

'Italy – in Padua.'

'So you are Italian?'

'I am both English *and* Italian.'

'Why did you come into England?'

'My father was murdered by the Holy Office of the Faith.'

'The Romish Inquisition?'

'Yes. He died of despair in his cell.'

'Then you are a true Protestant?'

Why should she tell this man what is in her heart?

'I was informed the queen has no desire to see into her subjects' souls.'

He writes down her answer carefully, mouthing it as he does so. Then he looks up at her, his face expressionless. 'So then you are a papist?'

'I am also informed that in England the old religion is tolerated, as long as it is practised privily.'

'Tell me, Mistress Merton, are you a witch?'

'No, I am not a witch.'

'Then are you a liar?'

Always the same even tone to the questions. Always the same slow, laborious writing of her answers. And when the session is over, they take her back to the cell she shares with a woman who is alleged to have consorted with demons in the Paris Garden by night, and with a mad girl who tells her conspiratorially that she is really the Christian martyr St Perpetua and expects the Romans to come for her at any moment.

And in this manner the days pass; six of them – until the night the cell door opens, and a short while later Bianca finds herself not in the little chamber facing the man in the woollen tunic, but standing on a jetty in the rain and the cold, Nicholas Shelby beside her – equally nonplussed – while out of the darkness the Thames roars at her like a proper interrogator should.

✠

They are rowing against the tide, heading upriver – though how the helmsman can steer a course in such relentless darkness, and with the barge pitching so violently, is anyone's guess. In the prow crouches a man-at-arms, holding a lantern. Its light turns the spray into a myriad tiny golden sparks that flare for an instant and are then swept away on the wind. Only the occasional beacon passing by to their right gives the slightest hint of where the bank is. To the left is nothing but darkness. Nicholas judges they must have reached the Lambeth marshes.

He sits uncomfortably on a wet wooden seat, trying to master the heaving of his stomach. The cold snatches the breath from his lungs. He's chilled to the bone. Bianca sits beside him. Her face is a mask he cannot read.

The oarsmen and the prisoners' escort – six men-at-arms – have shown no interest in either of them. It seems that conveying the doomed to unknown fates is apparently meat and drink to them.

There has been only one small moment of hope in their journey so far. It had come almost as soon as they slipped away from the bank. The helmsman had turned the barge west, upriver. At least their destination is not the Tower.

The noise of the wind and the waves makes conversation all but impossible. Bianca hasn't said a word since they were reunited, other than to ask if they'd harmed him. Nicholas replied that no, they had not – though he'd spent the days since their arrest in an uncomfortable cell in the Marshalsea. Then the sergeant of the men-at-arms had told them to mind their pox-blistered, profaning heretic tongues.

So now he holds his peace, and wonders why a tavern owner and a fallen physician are being taken for a ride on the river in the dead of night. And whether it is really intended that they should arrive anywhere.

✠

Without warning the barge lurches and swings across the current, rolling sickeningly. Out of the night drifts a substantial jetty, a glorious, gilded pleasure-barge moored on the far side. The starboard rowers raise their oars like well-drilled pike-men. With the merest of caresses, they are alongside the water-stairs. Nicholas closes his eyes and allows a little of the tension to drain out of his body. Whatever their destination, apparently it is intended they should reach it alive.

'Where are we?' whispers Bianca, risking the sergeant's wrath.

'Somewhere between Whitehall and St Martin's. It's hard to tell.'

Suddenly the lantern in the prow appears to leap into the night sky like a demented firefly, as the man holding it clambers onto the jetty. Nicholas and Bianca are invited to follow, by a barrage of oaths and vicious blows to the back.

Once on dry land, they follow the lantern as it dances through the darkness, hemmed in by their escort, encouraged to maintain a fast pace by the occasional savage kick to the heels. Nicholas judges they are heading away from the river. It's difficult to be certain. The buildings they pass are merely denser patches of night, pierced only by the occasional lighted window. From somewhere nearby a dog cries, a long, drawn-out sorrowful wail of loneliness.

And then out of the darkness looms a high brick wall. It stretches away into nothingness on either hand. They hear the thump of a gloved fist against timber. The low call of a challenge. The confident reply, 'Robert Cecil's men!' A pale wash of light spills out of the wall and a moment later they are inside Cecil House.

29

They are standing in a corridor with walls of flint and plaster. A tallow torch burns in an iron bracket, filling the air with an oily, animal smell. Nicholas feels a sense of impending dread. He's heard the rumours: that the great men of England who serve the queen – men like the Cecils – have their own private places for interrogating those they believe a threat to her realm. Simon Cowper once told him that Sir Francis Walsingham kept a fully functioning rack in the cellar of his house on Seething Lane, though how he'd known this, the unimpeachable Simon had never explained.

His fears are not eased when he and Bianca are pushed unceremoniously down a narrow, winding set of stone steps into a dank cellar space below ground level. It has the same, forlorn smell of despair and desolation he'd encountered at the Lazar House. It's the smell of a freshly opened grave. Behind them an iron grille slams noisily into its frame. The lock turns. At last, they are alone.

For a while neither speaks.

Nicholas can barely see Bianca in the little light that spills down the stairs and through the grille door, but he senses her standing with her back to him, looking back the way they have come as if searching for someone lost in a crowd. He sits down wearily on a pile of hemp sacks filled with something hard and unyielding. He leans forward, head in hand, resting his elbows on his knees. He's in too much discomfort, too cold, too weary to say very much. Whatever lies ahead, Nicholas knows his ability to resist it is already beginning to drain away.

'Why has Robert Cecil issued a warrant for our arrest?' he asks at last, trying hard not to sound petulant, though it's a question he's been asking himself for six long days. 'I presume it's not because you refused to mix a balm for his crooked back.'

'What does it matter now?' Bianca replies, only the merest falter in her voice telling him she is struggling to hold back the tears.

'*What does it matter?* I've spent six days in the Marshalsea! And, by the look of you, you haven't been sleeping on silk and eating stuffed capon, either.' He tries to read her face in the semi-darkness – and fails.

'I'm so sorry, Nicholas. I never meant for any of this to happen, I swear it.'

He'd try anger, but he knows he wouldn't be able to sustain it beyond a moment or two. 'Did they harm you? Where did they take you?'

'The Queen's Bench. Asked me a lot of silly questions. But no, they didn't harm me. Timothy brought me food and extra clothing.' She runs her hands over her forearms, indicating the brown linsey cloak she's wearing over the green brocade kirtle.

'Timothy? How did he find you?'

'Bless him, he followed us – when we were taken up. When they separated us, he had to decide who to stay close to. He chose me. I suppose that's because I pay his wages. Don't be angry with him.'

The clang of the iron grille as it opens reverberates around the cellar. A cold knot of fear forms in Nicholas's stomach as a harsh male voice calls out, 'The woman is to stay. The physician is to come with me. Now!' He recognizes it as the voice of the sergeant-at-arms from the barge that brought them here.

'*Jesu*, what's going to happen to us, Nicholas?' whispers Bianca, grabbing his arm.

'I don't know. I suppose it depends on what they think we're guilty of,' Nicholas tells her, his throat dry, his fists clenched. And before he can stop himself, he adds, '*Are* we guilty, Bianca? Is there something you haven't thought to tell me – something in that travelling chest of yours they took from the Jackdaw?'

✠

Outside, the night has grown even colder. Nicholas hurries along one side of a wide courtyard, flanked by the sergeant-at-arms. The man has one hand cupped over the guard of his sword, just to let his prisoner know how easy it would be to run him through, should the thought of escape ever enter his mind.

Through leaded windows he catches glimpses of gowned clerks hard at work by candlelight. A chapel bell strikes ten. He hasn't eaten since breakfast and now hunger has attached itself to the litany of his miseries. If Eleanor were alive, he thinks, at least there'd be the hope of a return to cling to, the promise of comfort and solace. That at least would give me the strength to face whatever lies ahead.

An imposing façade of brickwork and mullioned glass. Tall chimneys that disappear before they ever reach the sky. Everything robbed of form by the night and the dark, suffocating clouds... These are the impressions reeling in his head as the sergeant shoves Nicholas through a side-door. Though he's relieved to be out of the night, he has no time to get his bearings. A steward in livery stands at the foot of a narrow spiral stairway. 'Follow me,' he commands, as if he were an executioner and the steps the way to the scaffold.

✠

It is a fine oak-panelled room hung with expensive Flanders tapestries. At one end is a tall window glittering with the reflected light of the fire blazing in the hearth. In front of the window is a desk piled high with documents. It is a government desk. A Privy Councillor's desk. Beyond the window: nothing but the night.

A slight man of about Nicholas's age stands behind the desk. His shoulders stoop like a falcon mantling over its prey. He has a pale, intense face that narrows from a broad forehead to a sharp, dagger-point of a beard. He appraises Nicholas through coldly intelligent eyes.

'Welcome to Cecil House, Dr Shelby. I am Robert Cecil.'

Nicholas is almost speechless. From the moment in the street when the sergeant-at-arms had called out 'Robert Cecil's men!', he's known that the Lord Treasurer's son is the instigator of tonight's events. But he has not once imagined he would stand before the courtier in the flesh. Stunned, he remains motionless for a few seconds, until the weight of the sergeant's hand on his shoulder and a savage jab to the back of his right leg forces him to bend his knee in an ungainly stagger.

'What have you done to him, Harris?' Cecil asks of the sergeant, who steps back a pace as Nicholas regains his balance. 'He looks as though he's already spent a week at the mercies of the Lieutenant of the Tower. I told you not to harm him.'

'I swear upon the holy cross, sir, we have handled him with restraint, as you commanded. He was in this condition when we took him from the Marshalsea.'

It dawns on Nicholas that, after six days in a cell, he must look again like the derelict he once was.

Robert Cecil regards him with amused interest. He seems to be sizing him up, measuring what he sees against an image he already has in his head. Then he turns his unsettling gaze towards the fire, where a second man sits in silence, his face hidden by the shadows.

'I trust he's not in his cups,' Cecil says, addressing the dark figure in the chair. 'You assured me he hasn't been seen cut with ale since before Christmas. He'll be no use to me otherwise.'

'I have it on good authority from the warden of St Thomas's hospital that he has been sober throughout his employment,' comes the reply in a loud, familiar boom. The man in the chair leans forward, his bearded, heavyset face emerging into the firelight. '"Wine is a lecherous thing, and drunkenness is full of noise; whoever delighteth in these shall not be wise",' quotes Sir Fulke Vaesy portentously. 'Is that not what the Bible tells us, Dr Shelby?'

30

Robert Cecil toys with the embossed face of a huge gold ring that he wears on his left middle finger. He raises one cloaked arm, giving Nicholas the impression he's preparing to flap those crooked shoulders and take flight. He snaps his fingers at the steward and says, 'Bring Dr Shelby some ease. He looks as though he's about to fall over.'

The steward fetches a chair from the far side of the study and Nicholas sinks into it without being aware of having moved.

'I take it this truly is Dr Shelby, Sir Fulke?' Robert Cecil says amiably. 'Harris hasn't snatched some cut-purse off the streets of Southwark by mischance?'

Vaesy leaves his chair and comes close to Nicholas, wrinkling his nose as though Nicholas was a cadaver at one of his dissections. 'It's him,' he says at length. 'Reduced somewhat from the last time I saw him. Lost a little around the face. But, without question, the same man.'

'Good. Then tonight we may hope for some satisfactory answers.'

'Answers? I have nothing to answer for,' Nicholas protests. 'And while we're speaking of answers, perhaps you could provide me with some of my own: like why I have been brought here? Why has Bianca Merton been brought here?'

Burghley's crook-backed son does not answer. He makes a show of spreading out the books on his desk, opening each one in turn and briefly studying the frontispiece. He looks like a lawyer assembling evidence. Then, without warning, he picks up one of the books and throws it towards Nicholas. Caught off-guard, Nicholas almost fumbles the catch. The pages of the book flutter like the wings of a startled bird.

'How is your Latin, Dr Shelby?' Cecil asks.

'There's not much call for it in Southwark,' Nicholas answers warily.

'I should imagine not. But you surely can't have forgotten it in only a matter of months. Please translate the title of that book for me. I want to hear it from your own mouth.'

'What is this about?'

'Just read, please, Dr Shelby.'

The book is about six inches by three, a little over two inches thick. The paper is crisp, the dense black type slightly tilted on the page, through either the carelessness or the hurry of the printer. On the frontispiece is a small illustration of Hippocrates treating his patients on the steps of a Greek temple. Nicholas translates: 'A miraculous insight into diverse and wondrous systems of physic.'

'Printed where?'

'Padua,' Nicholas says, reading the line at the foot of the page, 'in the year of Our Lord 1586.'

'Indeed – Padua.'

'It's in Italy.'

'I know where Padua is, Dr Shelby. I'm more interested in the author.'

Nicholas looks for the name and finds it written across the base of the temple. 'Simon—' He falls silent as his eyes focus upon the second word.

'You were about to say?'

'Merton. The author is Simon Merton.'

Robert Cecil smiles and stretches his 'thank you' almost to breaking point. He throws Nicholas a second volume, a little larger than the first. This time Nicholas catches it easily. He opens the cover and reads: 'A treatise on the efficacy of several ancient decoctions of flora, as practised in ancient times upon the Veneto.'

'Not a title that reads trippingly, I'll grant you,' says Robert Cecil. 'But it will suffice. The author again, Dr Shelby, if you please...'

Nicholas inspects the title page.

'Simon Merton,' he says, struggling to keep his voice empty.

'Again?'

'It's written by Simon Merton.'

'And are you familiar with this Simon Merton?'

'Not personally. I assume you're going to tell me he's related to Bianca Merton.'

'You're ahead of me already, Dr Shelby,' says Cecil, clapping his small, be-ringed hands. 'Well done. So, Mistress Merton has told you about this father of hers.'

'Her father? Yes, a little.'

'What do know of him?'

'He was an English merchant, an apothecary. He lived in Padua. He died on their voyage to England. That's all I know.'

'In fact, Dr Shelby, he died in a cell, accused of heresy and witchcraft. His heretical theories – which were apparently even too much for the papists to stomach – are contained in these books. We found them in the possession of his daughter.'

Nicholas flicks through the pages of the two volumes Robert Cecil threw at him. It doesn't take him long. 'You've read them, have you – these books? You understand them?'

'Sir Fulke has made a preliminary investigation. He will confirm everything I have just said.'

'Master Robert is indeed correct,' says Vaesy, nodding eagerly. 'Simon Merton was a charlatan, and in no small measure a medical heretic. So much so that the Romish authorities saw fit to arrest and imprison him.'

Robert Cecil makes a play of bewilderment. 'Mercy, to what level of sinfulness must a man sink before even the papist legionaries of the Antichrist find him too hot to the touch?'

Though he has no idea what Simon Merton looked like, Nicholas can imagine him brimming with Bianca's spirit, as he damns everyone from the Chancellor of Padua University to the Pope in Rome for not allowing him the chance to practise his physic openly.

'Do these titles suggest anything to you, Dr Shelby?' Robert Cecil asks.

'Of course they do. They're medical textbooks.'

'I was thinking more of the environment in which they were written and printed.'

'Italy?'

'The land wherein dwells the Bishop of Rome, in his foul pit of ungodliness. These are papist tracts, are they not?'

Nicholas tries desperately not to laugh at the preposterous notion that healing can have a religious dimension, let alone a political one. 'Medicine is not religious faith,' he protests, 'it's just medicine.'

'Just medicine?'

'Have you read Galen, sir?'

'I have attended dissertations at Cambridge and the Sorbonne. Of course I've read Galen.'

'Then you'll know he was a Roman – a pagan. Hippocrates was a Greek. Also a pagan. But we still believe everything they wrote. If I cross the Narrow Sea to France, fall over and break my leg, does that make the fracture Catholic?'

Cecil regards him with icy suspicion. 'Thought, Dr Shelby. That's what's in these books. *Foreign* thought. And even if what

you say is true, might not a papist physician – or even an apothecary – carry the message of the Antichrist hidden amongst words
of learning?'

'That's preposterous.'

'Is it? You have no idea how cleverly these people disseminate
their vile philosophy. Only last month we hanged and quartered
a Jesuit priest who'd disguised himself as a peddler. He had the
abominable devices of his ministry hidden in his box of ribbons!'

'These are just medical books!'

Robert Cecil leans back in his chair. He watches Nicholas with
practised detachment. Then he reaches down and lifts an object
from amongst the papers. Flashes of reflected firelight dart into
the shadows from its gleaming silver limbs.

'Has Mistress Merton ever shown you this before?' he asks,
holding up a silver crucifix barely the length of his hand.

Nicholas stares at the little figure pinioned to the cross, its
arms outstretched, its head tilted towards one shoulder. The way
the letters PP have been stamped into the metal show clearly the
way the crucifix is meant to be displayed: inverted.

Everything holy turned on its head.

31

Y ou appear a little lost for words, Dr Shelby. Here – take it,'
Robert Cecil says, holding out the crucifix. 'If your soul
is pure, it should not trouble your eternal sleep – much.'

'What is this?' whispers Nicholas as he turns the cold silver in
his fingers.

'It's a Petrine cross, or so I am informed by those who understand the meaning of papist symbols. The letters PP are the Latin
cipher for Peter the Fisherman.' Robert Cecil thrusts a finger in
the direction of the crucifix. 'That's him, hanging upside-down
like a common street acrobat. He desired to be martyred in that
manner because he thought himself unworthy to die in the same
way as Our Lord. We found it amongst your Mistress Merton's
possessions. Did you know she was a papist, a disciple of the
Antichrist, Dr Shelby?'

Nicholas hesitates, not because he thinks the silver crucifix
will endanger his soul, but because it's Bianca's secret and he
feels like an intruder. 'Oh, Bianca, why didn't you tell me? It
wouldn't have mattered,' he whispers. Then, to Robert Cecil:
'I will swear on the Bible that I never witnessed Bianca Merton
engage in any rite or practice contrary to the new faith.'

'That will not help her in the slightest,' says Robert Cecil,
taking back the crucifix and laying it down like a winning card
in a game of *primero*.

'I'll pay the recusancy fine. Whatever it is.' Beneath the bluster,
Nicholas loathes his own inadequacy.

'With what? I understand you're barely more prosperous than

the patients who come to see you at St Thomas's. I'd guess you'll have to swim back to Bankside, for lack of the wherry fare.'

'There's a bridge. I'll walk.'

Robert Cecil shakes his head in faux-admiration. 'What exactly is this woman to you? Are you in love with her?'

Nicholas colours. 'It's not like that.'

'Then tell me, what is it like? I'm eager to know.'

'She gave me a second chance – when I'd lost everything.'

'And consequently you feel you owe her a debt? Is that it?'

'Yes, I do. A *debt* – that's exactly what I owe her.'

Burghley's crook-backed son draws his gown around his shoulders, settles in his chair and smiles. 'You were right, Sir Fulke. Over-sentimentality. It's a grievous fault in the young. If ever Spain comes against us again, our young gallants will be too busy writing tearful sonnets to stop them.'

Nicholas has the urgent need to lean across Robert Cecil's desk and ram his fist into that manipulative face, to strike the entire head off those crooked shoulders.

'We also found this in your own chamber at the Jackdaw, Dr Shelby. Do you recognize it?'

Nicholas takes the expensive sheet of parchment Robert Cecil has lifted from his desk. As he reads the lines of neat script, his eyes moisten with tears of anger and frustration:

To Master Nicholas Shelby, right worthy gentleman of physic, greetings... Send to me a more detailed account of your spheres of interest... and should you seek the aid of far greater minds than mine own poor one, you are most heartily welcome at Nonsuch to avail yourself of the wisdom to be found in my humble library there...

'Revelation upon revelation,' says Robert Cecil in disbelief. 'Imagine it: the noble Lord Lumley in correspondence with a lapsed physician who's spent the last few months drunk under a hedge in the Pike Garden! Has God rearranged the social order while I was asleep?'

'John Lumley is a patron of the College of Physicians,' says Nicholas, ramming his fingernails into his palms to keep himself under control. 'He likes discussing new ideas.'

'Oh, I know who he is, Dr Shelby.' Robert Cecil turns his face to the panelled ceiling as though this knowledge is just one more trial he must bear. 'Let me suggest an alternative to you. It is this: Mistress Merton's papist masters send their seditious instructions to her disguised in medical books. You then convey those instructions – in your letters – to the noble lord, their true destination. To an observer: merely two medical men having a learned discourse by post. To me: *treason*.'

'As a diagnosis, that's the most ludicrous thing I've ever heard.'

'Good enough for a jury and a hanging judge, Dr Shelby.'

'I only wrote to him a couple of weeks ago. He barely knows me.'

'Yet he has invited you to Nonsuch; opened the doors of his abominable trove of heresies to you. How very generous of him. Why would he do that?'

'I wanted to seek his advice on a certain medical matter. And it's just a library, that's all.'

Robert Cecil studies Nicholas in silence for a while. Then he says with a reasonableness that takes Nicholas utterly off-guard, 'And all I ask of you, Dr Shelby, is to enter it for me.'

'Then why all this?' Nicholas says angrily with a sweep of his arm. 'Why not just ask me? I was going anyway.'

'Because I want you to spy for me. I want an informer in John Lumley's nest of heresy.' He casts a glance towards Fulke Vaesy. 'Sadly, my last one is not now as welcome as he once was.'

'Why would I turn informer, just to please you?'

'Have you so easily forgotten Mistress Merton – this woman to whom you owe such a debt?'

'Bianca?'

Robert Cecil sweeps a hand across the books and the Petrine cross. 'This is damning evidence, Dr Shelby. I can easily ensure Bianca Merton hangs for heresy and treason – *if* she's lucky. Otherwise, she will burn.'

The sickening realization of just how easily Robert Cecil has played him leaves Nicholas speechless.

'You can save her, if you desire. It's really up to you.'

Nicholas stares at Robert Cecil, open-mouthed. 'And if I agree?'

'You have it on my word that Mistress Merton will be returned unharmed to Bankside, where she may continue to gull the impressionable, along with all the other charlatans and knaves practising there.'

'And what exactly am I supposed to find at Nonsuch?' Nicholas asks. 'Being an informer wasn't on the curriculum at Cambridge.'

Robert Cecil leans back in his chair with a smile of self-satisfied innocence. 'You're the physician, Dr Shelby. Surely you know what contagion looks like when you see it.'

✠

Master Sprint is showing Betony how to pluck pigeons.

'Take a few feathers at a time, but briskly – like this,' he says gently. He knows she's understood him, but like a man having a conversation with his dog, he does not actually expect a reply.

Since the day he discovered the inverted crosses scratched into the soot by the bread-ovens, Sprint has watched the girl they have named Betony closely. He's watched for the slightest sign of malignity or devilry. He has seen none. Joanna, his assistant – beside whom Betony sleeps at night – reports that the girl appears diligent in her prayers, always kneeling with her hands clasped and her head bowed, though what she actually says to God remains a secret only they share. As to who Betony is, and where she's come from, no one at Nonsuch is any the wiser.

Though Sprint does not know it, Elise has come close to breaking her own self-imposed silence several times in recent days. For a start, she wants everyone to know how wonderfully warm she is, warmer than she can ever remember being. The thick walls of the Nonsuch kitchens trap the heat, and the embers in the central hearth are high enough to take a martyr waist-deep. Her whole body seems aglow. If only little Ralphie were here, she would be content – almost.

As she works she watches the scullions scrubbing grease off the roasting spits. They look just like the lads she used to play with on the banks of Battle Abbey creek. She sneaks a brief upward glance at Sprint. He's standing close to her, closer than she would have ever tolerated barely days ago. Even in his blood-stained apron, he is surely no Devil's minion. He's far too kind.

The men and women of the household treat her civilly now. That's taken a deal of getting used to. And the womenfolk especially are beginning to grant her their minor secrets, secure in their belief she cannot reveal them.

And what of their master, Lord Lumley – the man she had once assumed was foremost amongst these servants of Satan? He is never less than kind to her. True, he seems to think of her as an object to be studied, her dimensions and character measured and catalogued. Yet he shows no displeasure at her refusal to speak. Never even raises his voice – unlike his friend, the great physician who had come from the queen to make her talk and is now apparently unwelcome at Nonsuch. She hasn't seen him for days.

Yet despite the warmth and the kindness, Elise still can't quite lay aside her fears. Like the hind supping from the stream, a part of her is still alert for the rustle in the trees that warns of the hunter's approach.

✠

A misty morning, the tide low and the stink of mud and carrion drifting up from the river. In mid-stream the barges drift towards the city under slack sails. Beyond them Nicholas can just discern the outline of Lambeth Palace. It appears to be settling into the marsh.

He makes his way towards the private river stairs where they landed the previous night. Bianca, flanked by two bored servants in Cecil livery, watches him approach. She's wearing the same serge overgown and the brocade kirtle in which she was taken from the Jackdaw. Her hair looks as wild as Medusa's. She puts her hands to the sides of her brow and runs the fingers back to untangle it. The familiar habit is like an accusation to him.

'Marry, someone has turned the night to his profit!' she observes with a raised eyebrow, taking in the smart doublet of London russet trimmed with black lace that Robert Cecil has given him to wear, because he doesn't want one of his people walking around Cecil House looking like a vagabond.

'You should have told me, Bianca. It would have meant nothing to me. I would have kept your secret.'

'Told you what?' she asks, looking him up and down. 'Where to find a good tailor?'

'That you practised the old faith.'

'That's my concern, not yours.'

'Robert Cecil threatened to use your father's books and his Petrine cross to hang you for sedition,' he tells her, his anger burned out almost before the words have left his mouth. 'I struck a deal. He's changed his mind.'

'A deal? What are we to Robert Cecil that he makes deals with us?'

'It's me, Bianca. I'm the one he wanted. You're being sent back to Southwark, a free woman. You're to say nothing other than that the charges were a false denunciation.'

She looks so small, standing between the two Cecil men. Yet she stands squarely on the jetty as though she means to stop an army passing. 'Really? And how much of himself did Mister Nicholas Shelby have to sell to arrange that?'

There is no other way Nicholas can think of couching it, so he tells her, 'There is a man he wants me to betray.'

She almost laughs. 'You're not the betraying kind, Nicholas. You're too honest. Who is this man anyway?'

'It's John Lumley. The man I wrote to. The one I thought could help us.'

'Am I permitted to know why?'

Nicholas hopes she cannot see the lie in his eyes. 'It's complicated.'

From the gilded Cecil barge moored to the jetty comes the command for Bianca to board. Four rowers lift their oars into the rowlocks. The two liveried servants make to assist her onto the deck.

'Shall I see you again, Nicholas Shelby?' she calls out as she steps aboard. 'I don't even know where you're going.'

'I am to stay at Cecil House until I leave for Nonsuch.'

'Mercy, Nicholas Shelby is going to live in a palace!' The bright amber eyes are teasing him again. 'You *have* come up in the world.'

'I'm just going to visit for a while. I don't know how long.'

'Will I see you again? Do I need to look for another handy fellow to help me out at the Jackdaw?'

'I don't know. But yes, you will see me again, Mistress Merton. You may count on it.'

'Will you write?'

'When I can.'

'You were safer on Bankside than you knew, Nicholas. Please take care.'

He doesn't see it coming: the sudden overwhelming need to jump onto the barge, follow her back to the Jackdaw and take her to his lonely bed in the attic.

But even as the urge hits him, the barge vanishes into the mist, the only evidence it was ever there the fading sound of oars breaking the water – and the guilt of betrayal in his heart.

32

Candlemas, 2nd February 1591

In the meadow beside Cheam church a band of militia is at drill practice. They wield the heavy pikes like the farm-boys and seed merchant's clerks they are. Their sergeant is a small fellow in a battered, hand-me-down breastplate. In a shrill voice he's warning them their ineptitude will cost England dear, should the Spanish ever come to Surrey. Nicholas Shelby watches them go through their postures as he rides past on one of Robert Cecil's palfreys, loaned for the journey. He knows the sergeant's threat is not an idle one. In the Low Countries he'd seen the well-drilled armies of Spain cutting through lads much like these with the ease of a buttery maid scooping curd. It makes him think again of the infant he'd seen pitchforked onto a midden, and that leads his thoughts inevitably to Ralph Cullen. He looks away to the fields, the hedgerows and the occasional thatched house. Where, on the journey from the Cardinal's Hat to Cuddington, did the killer find you? he wonders. Was it hereabouts? And what of you, Elise? Did you make it? Or are you merely waiting your turn to wash ashore?

It's a week since Nicholas bade farewell to Bianca Merton. For most of that time he's been a virtual prisoner at Cecil House, though his incarceration has not been arduous. On the day Bianca returned to Southwark, Robert Cecil had stood over him while he wrote another letter to Nonsuch, taking up John Lumley's offer. Then had followed the random summons to Robert Cecil's study, delivered whenever the courtier was able to tear himself away from the onerous burden of saving England from heresy. During these sessions Nicholas had received instruction on the nature of the beast he was to confront. Now his head is full of details: Lumley's youthful allegiance to Bloody Mary; how he and his first wife, Jane FitzAlan, daughter to old Arundel, had ridden in the entourage at Mary's marriage to the Catholic Philip of Spain; how Lumley and his father-in-law had plotted to wed Mary Stuart, the Scots queen, to the Duke of Norfolk to strengthen a papist claim to the throne. Now he can recite the dates of Lumley's sojourns in the Tower with accuracy. He can name the exact amount Lumley still owes to the Crown for getting into bed with Florentine bankers. He knows the rents due to the privy purse for which Lumley keeps seeking respite. Now he feels like one of those spies who used to flit in and out of the camps in Holland: furtive, secretive fellows, their lives little else but a paid-for procession of lies and betrayal.

How did I make the journey from healer to informer so seamlessly?

What would Eleanor think of me now?

As he rides leisurely up the gentle, grassy slope towards the gleaming white-walled outer court of Nonsuch Palace, another troubling image insinuates itself into Nicholas's mind. It's the image of some helpless soul – as yet unknown to him – chained, frightened, waiting alone in the dark interior of the Lazar House for the moment the door opens and a new nightmare begins. And he wonders how he can ask for Lumley's help in stopping it, while at the same moment scheming to betray him.

✠

'We need new sheets,' says Rose apologetically. She is un-accustomed to speaking obliquely, but what exactly does one say to a mistress who disappeared a heretic and a traitor and returned in a gilded barge, like Queen Dido of Carthage? What she really wants to ask Bianca – has wanted to asks for days – is *did they harm you?*

Now that the mistress of the Jackdaw is safely home, the tavern has returned almost to its former state. But there is still work to do. Much of the linen recovered from the floor and the street is badly torn, and lodgers must now sleep on their cloaks and not mind the gaping wounds in the straw pallets where Robert Cecil's men went rummaging for hidden papist tracts.

'At least we still have our customers,' Rose observes. 'When they raided the Knight's Shield on Bermondsey Road, it took a whole month for trade to recover. Looking for Jesuits, they were.'

'Did they find any?' Bianca asks.

'No. Only a fugitive from Bedlam.'

'How did they recognize him? All the Shield's customers look as though they've escaped from Bedlam.'

'There's only a few haven't come back here,' says Rose, laughing. 'That Walter Pemmel – the one who only pays every other tab – he hasn't shown his miserable face again. And old Leicester and Walsingham haven't been seen or heard of since.'

'I'm not surprised. They're probably the reason the Privy Council turned us over in the first place,' Bianca retorts harshly. 'And as for Walter Pemmel, he was a Puritan hypocrite anyway. Wore out his knees in the pews at St Saviour's each Sunday; back in the taproom on Monday, trying to drown all that guilt he got from lying with whores. We're better off without him.'

'He hasn't written yet, then? You'd have told me if he had, Mistress.'

'Why on earth would Walter Pemmel write to me?'

'I wasn't speaking of Walter Pemmel, was I?'

Bianca gives Rose's left knee a gentle slap. 'Nicholas probably doesn't have the time. He's an eminent physician now, didn't you know? Get on with your sewing, girl.'

Rose does as she's told – for all of two minutes. Then she announces defiantly, 'I don't care what the Bishop of London says! I don't think papists are the Devil's own spawn. My grandmother was of the old faith, and a goodlier person you never met.' It's her way of saying whatever Bianca has been accused of, it doesn't matter.

'I'm sure she was, Rose.'

'I'd light a candle for her soul, too, if it were allowed. She always liked candles.' Rose considers this small heresy for a moment, then asks, 'Do you think they'd come back and arrest me, if I did?'

'I shouldn't imagine so,' says Bianca. 'If they do, I suggest you take Timothy with you. After what's happened to Nicholas, Tim might come back as master of the Brewers' Company and you as a lady-in-waiting to the queen.'

'Was it dreadful – in the Tower?'

'We weren't in the Tower, Rose dear. We were at Cecil House, near the Strand. A very different place.'

'Did they put burning irons to your flesh?'

'No, they didn't.'

'Nor rack you?'

'Never saw a rack all the time I was there.'

'I shouldn't like to be racked. The extra inches might be nice, though.'

Bianca lets out a gasp of exasperation. 'I'll rack you myself, if you don't hurry up with your needlework. *Jesu*, girl – you're a monstrous trial to me!'

Rose sets to work viciously with her bodkin, making little hissing noises as she jams the end against the linen, as if it were an instrument of hot torture and the fabric human skin.

Yes, life at the Jackdaw is almost back to normal.

✠

Nicholas has barely crossed the spacious lawn – complete with neatly trimmed box hedges and its own bowling green – before he's entranced. He lets his eyes wander in disbelief over the gleaming white towers, the soaring minarets, the high walls topped by stone gods and heroes of antiquity. Christ's wounds, he thinks, whatever they say about King Henry, the old monster knew what he was doing when he built mystical, soul-lifting Nonsuch.

He rides beneath the arch of the gatehouse and enters a wide courtyard. The sides are two storeys high. They're set with herringbone brick under a blue slate roof, the windows framed with exquisite carvings of fantastical beasts. Glancing back, he sees a great bronze sundial emblazoned with the signs of the zodiac set above the arch. It's supported by three brightly painted stucco lions, quartered with fleurs-de-lys and flanked by a greyhound and a dragon – the coat of arms of Henry Tudor. A servant approaches and takes the bridle of his horse while he dismounts. A lanky man with a shaven head and pockmarked face bustles towards him, dressed in a formal gown. Nicholas recognizes him at once.

'I give you good day, Master Shelby,' says Gabriel Quigley, without extending a hand in greeting. 'Follow me, please. We expected you some time ago.' Silently Quigley leads Nicholas through a second gatehouse opposite the first.

They emerge into the heart of Nonsuch.

For a moment Nicholas thinks he's standing in some magnificent Italian palazzo. The inner face of the second gatehouse is a high clock tower set with six golden horoscopes, while ahead of him is a great fountain capped by a rearing marble horse. Beyond it gleam the painted plaster walls of the royal chambers. Two stucco Roman emperors gaze imperiously past him into eternity, one a mature man with a beard, the other much younger. Nicholas assumes they are meant to depict Henry and his short-lived son, Edward.

'Hurry, Master Physician,' Quigley says, turning at the top of the entrance steps to see Nicholas staring around like a country green-head newly arrived in the city. 'Lord Lumley is waiting.'

✤

John Lumley is sitting in a high-backed chair that is very nearly a throne. His private study is a fine panelled chamber off the empty royal apartments, draped with expensive Flemish tapestries. It seems to be the only room with a lit fire. Lumley's hose-clad feet are stretched out towards the hearth. He sports a long spade-cut beard and a pearl-studded cap on his head. The dark folds of a scholar's gown flow out below a neatly starched ruff.

'Mr Shelby! It is a pleasure to wish you God's good day. Welcome! Come in, please *do* come in,' he says without rising. His voice has a distinct Northumbrian burr to it.

Nicholas makes an extravagant bend of the knee. He might be invited, but his host is still a lord.

'Master Baronsdale is most fulsome in your praise,' Lumley says, lifting a parchment from a small table beside the chair. 'He sent this letter of recommendation.'

Nicholas is forced to admire Robert Cecil's preparation. He guesses the President of the College of Physicians has no idea he's written any such letter – men like the Cecils employ clever servants skilled in forgery. 'I'm sure it's quite unwarranted, my lord,' he says uncomfortably.

'Nevertheless, it is always good to have the opportunity to converse with the younger fellows in the profession,' says Lumley, one lugubrious eye coming close to a wink. 'If the only people

I listened to were the likes of Baronsdale and Vaesy, my understanding of science would like as not go backwards rather than forwards.' He rises from his chair and shakes Nicholas by the hand. 'Forgive me if your welcome is not as warm as might be thought proper, only Lady Elizabeth is in London. She keeps on at me to light a fire in almost every room. I don't think she has the slightest idea of how many rooms we actually have, or how many men we need to gather the firewood.' He laughs affectionately. 'She's a D'Arcy – from the county of Essex. You'd think she'd be used to a draught or two.'

'Your invitation alone is worth a thousand warm welcomes, my lord. It is far more than I expected.'

Lumley turns to Gabriel Quigley. 'Dr Shelby has had a long ride, Gabriel. We should fetch him some hippocras.'

'I don't take spirits, my lord,' says Nicholas, trying to keep the consternation out of his voice, and fearing he just sounds rude as a consequence.

'A young physician who doesn't sup? Whatever next? Don't tell me you're a Puritan, Dr Shelby.'

'No, of course not. It's just that—'

'Fear not, the inebriation is quite boiled out of it,' Lumley says. 'It won't bring you harm.'

He knows, thinks Nicholas. Vaesy, or someone else, has told him about what happened to me after Eleanor. The understanding does not bode well. What kind of informer will he be, if the man he's been sent to spy on can see through him so easily?

✠

Supper that evening is taken in Lumley's privy apartments. It proves something of a mixed pottage. Quigley remains taciturn, barely engaging in the scientific discourse, even when Lumley asks for his opinion. In the candlelight his pockmarked skin looks like the surface of one of Rose's puddings. Why is Quigley so sullen? Nicholas wonders. Has he already guessed why I'm really here? Or is Lumley's secretary guarding his master's library a little too jealously? *An abominable trove of heresies*, that's what Robert Cecil thinks it is. Could he be right?

Lumley's clerk, Francis Deniker, proves to be little better company. A gentle-looking man in his fifties with little wings of grey hair curling behind his ears, his gaze seems directed permanently downwards. He looks like a priest or a schoolmaster. And he seems evasive, unwilling to talk much about himself. Nicholas gets the distinct impression that Deniker's reserved conversation is a coverlet designed to obscure what lies beneath. He's like a physician who doesn't want to give you bad news.

Only John Lumley seems completely at ease. He speaks with great knowledge on subjects that, on occasion, enter the realm of the positively dangerous: like who should reign when the queen is no longer alive, and whether science – rather than religion – might one day prove if there really is a place called Purgatory or not. At this, Deniker suffers an explosive fit of coughing.

Is John Lumley testing him? Nicholas wonders. Is he watching to see how his guest reacts to controversy? Whatever his motives, by the time the dessert arrives – a miraculous apple-and-cinnamon tart – it seems Nicholas has passed the examination.

'Stay as long as you like, Dr Shelby,' Lumley says. 'It pleases me to imagine what wondrous discoveries in physic are yet to be made, and it is good to have a receptive ear. You don't cluck like old Lopez, or try to tell me there's no new knowledge to be found, like Fulke Vaesy does.'

'No new knowledge, my lord? How can that be?'

'Fulke says we're only rediscovering what man used to know already – knowledge that was lost after the first sin.'

'That explains a lot.'

'Tomorrow I'll show you the library. I think you'll find it instructive.'

'I'm sure I will, my lord.'

'And when you're done, perhaps you and I might turn our minds to an issue that's been much troubling me of late. I've not found anything in the library that might shed a medical light upon it.'

'I'd be honoured, if you think I can help. What is it that concerns you?'

'Speech, Dr Shelby – the ability to make ourselves understood, the property that separates us from the beasts,' Lumley answers, wiping away a sliver of apple from the corner of his mouth. 'Or rather the *lack* of it.'

He looks Nicholas so squarely in the eye that for a moment Nicholas thinks by 'lack' he means wilful withholding – duplicity, evasion, secrecy or any of the other sins Nicholas is currently accusing himself of.

'Lord Lumley is referring to a servant newly brought to the household,' Francis Deniker says. 'A goodly soul, it seems, but mute.'

'Sir Fulke Vaesy believes the Devil has stopped up her mouth,' says Lumley. 'I don't believe him, not for a moment. But I would like to discover why someone who has a perfectly functioning tongue should deliberately deny themselves the use of it, when they know full well it was put into their mouth by the very same God who made the rest of them.'

33

His chamber in the inner gatehouse is one of the rooms the courtiers use when the queen visits. If Lumley were selling Nonsuch, his agents would call it 'well appointed'. It has Flanders hangings on the wall, and a comfortable mattress. But Nicholas cannot sleep. He lies awake while Henry's great clock on the outside wall chimes every half-hour, its mechanism making the floorboards tremble like an ailing heart.

'Henry built the house for his one true love, Jane Seymour,' John Lumley had told him over supper, barely three hours ago. 'What a tragedy she did not live to witness the magnificence of the gift he intended for her.'

It occurs to Nicholas now that the king must have been grieving even as he watched the first stones being raised, barely six months after Jane Seymour's death in childbirth. A house conceived in love, built on grief. The image is not lost on him. He wonders what its creator would make of Nonsuch now.

Nicholas had expected to find the place alive with activity. But with only the Lumley household in residence, it's all but empty. And there's an air of disquiet, despite the magnificence. It's as if Nonsuch is bracing itself for impending catastrophe, frozen in the very moment joy turns to despair. He imagines the very bricks can sense why he's come.

And Nicholas knows full well the ghastly procession of tragedy that will follow, if he finds what Burghley's son hopes he will find. And not just for Lumley, but for his wife, and for Quigley and Deniker too – and who knows how many more of Lumley's friends and acquaintances? He can imagine all too easily the arrests in the dead of night, the river journeys taken in fear, iron-bound doors slammed shut to extinguish the light – and the hope with it. *Give us the dates upon which you visited the traitor Lumley... What treason did you hear uttered? Who else was present? Give us the names...* When the indictment is finally read before the Privy Council, it will contain a long list of sworn statements, even if the signatures are a little unclear, due to the writers' fingers mysteriously no longer functioning as they once did. Meanwhile Elizabeth Lumley will sit weeping in the solitude of Nonsuch, tormented by dreadful images of her husband's suffering, and wondering if she will be allowed to see him just one more time before the hooded executioner beckons him forward. And I, Nicholas Shelby, will have set the whole grizzly parade in motion.

Is Bianca Merton's life worth all that? Is there a tariff to be set for betrayal – one life worth more, another a little less? How did I, a man dedicated to serving the sick, come to bring about such pain?

There are so many troubling questions disordering his thoughts that he quite forgets John Lumley's comments at supper about the mute in the Nonsuch kitchens. His last conscious thoughts are of the letter he hasn't yet written to Bianca. He tries to compose the lines in his mind, but his impressions of the day are too disordered to marshal.

A quiet tapping on the door makes him turn his head. It's Harriet, his maid from Grass Street, bearing breakfast. She's struggling not to giggle at her master and mistress lying entwined in the chaos of the sheets like vines in the summer sun. He leans across the bed, the better to delight in the salty tang of Eleanor's skin, expecting the scent of rose oil in her hair.

His hand meets nothing but cold linen. Only the tapping on the door is real. And the guilt that, in the moment before waking, he was unsure exactly whose face would have turned towards him on the pillow.

✠

When Nicholas enters the library he finds Gabriel Quigley stooped over a desk, making entries in a ledger with a quill. The secretary does not acknowledge him, other than to wave him to a window seat. It seems daylight has not lightened the secretary's mood.

While he waits for John Lumley to arrive, Nicholas takes in the view from the windows. It's as though he's gone to sleep in Surrey and woken in Caesar's Rome. In the watery sunlight he can see arches of close-cropped holly, classical columns, statues of gods and emperors. There's even a small pavilion where – he assumes – the queen may sit when she views the chase.

Turning away from the view, he begins to inspect the library. It takes only a few paces for him to see that the rumours were based on fact. There's Bright's *Treatise of Melancholy*; Bullein's *Dialogue against Fever Pestilence*; Vicary's *Anatomy*; three works by Thomas Gale... The ancients are here, too: Galen in the original Latin, Aretaeus in the Greek. More pages of medical knowledge than Nicholas has seen since he left Cambridge. And beyond the books on physic he can see treaties on cosmology, philosophy, theology – a store of wisdom so vast it humbles him.

But there are also books here that only a man with powerful friends – or a carefree attitude to his own safety – might possess. Volumes on necromancy... on occult practices... on matters that the new religion would consider highly detrimental to one's immortal soul. He sees the words 'Thomas Cantuarien' embossed in gold leaf on a spine and realizes it's by Archbishop Cranmer, Henry's reforming Protestant prelate, sent to the flames by

Bloody Mary Tudor. It stands alongside Pope Innocent's polemic against witches. John Lumley, it seems, is walking a very dangerous tightrope.

A voice from behind him breaks into his thoughts. 'I'll wager the lost library of Alexandria can't have had many more works in it than this.'

Nicholas turns. Lord Lumley is watching him from the doorway, severe in his scholar's gown, a pearl pendant hanging on a gold chain around his neck. He looks more like one of Nicholas's tutors at Cambridge than Robert Cecil's version of a disciple of the Antichrist.

'But then Alexandria never had Gabriel to keep it in order, or I dare say it would never have become lost in the first place. I trust you slept well, Dr Shelby.'

Better than the innocent, Nicholas assures him, hoping Lumley won't notice the tiredness in his eyes.

'In your letter you wrote of an interest in the carriage of blood through the human body.'

'I believe I did, my lord.'

Lumley selects a shelf and extracts a large leather-bound book. He places it on a lectern. The stiff velum parts reluctantly, the pages rocking slowly as though the book can't quite make up its mind which of its secrets to reveal.

It decides upon an exquisite woodcut showing a man standing in a landscape of trees and ancient temples. He is leaning nonchalantly on a stick. But Nicholas can see this is no simple Arcadian scene. The man's skin has been flayed open to show the interior of the body in minute detail: muscles, veins and arteries perfectly drawn, the ink a dark and lustrous lifeblood. The head is in fact a skull, tilted upwards, the bulbous eyes fighting to pull themselves free of the surrounding muscle fibres as they seek a glimpse of heaven.

'By Carolus Stephanus. Published in Paris less than one man's lifetime ago,' says Lumley proudly.

'It's extraordinary,' Nicholas whispers, bending forward to inspect the illustration. 'Look at the detail, the way he depicts the veins—'

'Yet it's already out of date, I fear. And, worse, inaccurate.'

'Inaccurate? It looks perfect.'

'Aye, it's a fine piece of work, I'll grant you. But when Stephanus published it, he did not know that in just a few years he would discover these very veins have *valves* in them. Now he's bickering with Fabricius and the others over who discovered them first. Sir Fulke Vaesy tells me that when he went to Padua to learn from the masters, he found it worse than trying to separate two women squabbling over ribbons at a market stall.'

Nicholas shakes his head in wonder. 'When I was in Holland, one of our German doctors had studied under Stephanus,' he says, remembering a jovial Lutheran from Saxony named Gunther. 'He said these valves were like sluices in a river, managing the tide of the blood around the body. We all thought he was in error.'

'And why, if I may ask?'

'Well, if these valves are truly like sluices, when a man is wounded why do they not simply shut? Such a mechanism would prevent him bleeding to death?'

One of Lumley's wintery eyebrows lifts a little. 'A young physician barely out of Cambridge disputing with the great Stephanus?'

'No dispute, my lord. Merely a question.'

Lumley returns the book to its place on the shelf. 'There's nothing shameful about questions, Dr Shelby,' he says, 'particularly in an age that demands certainty. Certainty of faith, certainty of allegiance. Equivocation is to be stamped out wherever it is found. Is that not so?'

'So the bishops would tell us, my lord.'

'Yet in these volumes are contained a thousand different opinions, all vehemently disagreeing with one another. This library could not exist if it were not for questions. The times have made natural philosophers of us all, have they not?'

'I'm not a philosopher, my lord,' Nicholas says, looking at his feet and feeling again that John Lumley is somehow testing him. 'I'm just a humble physician.'

Lumley looks at him like a man inspecting a gem for a hidden flaw. 'So humble, in fact, that Dr Baronsdale has never spoken of you before, though now he sends me a fulsome recommendation. How is that?'

'I c-cannot say, my lord,' Nicholas replies, his voice faltering. Has Lumley seen through him so easily? Is he so singularly unsuited to the role of spy and informer that his inner thoughts are as easy to read as a playbill? He's even more certain now that Baronsdale's letter is one of Robert Cecil's clever forgeries.

'A coincidence then?'

'A very generous coincidence, my lord.'

Lumley studies him a while. Then he shrugs, his suspicions apparently forgotten. 'Well, a fortunate one, to be sure – for both of us, I hope. Had Baronsdale been even slightly unsure of your qualities, I cannot imagine he would have recommended you. So I will trust to his judgement. And you seem like an honest man. Are you honest, Dr Shelby?'

'In my heart I believe so, my lord,' says Nicholas, sickened by the prospect of being the agent of this man's destruction. He has the sudden, overwhelming urge to confess to Lumley why he's been sent, to beg his forgiveness, to leave Nonsuch as quickly as he can, before he brings yet more grief to this beautiful but ill-starred place.

✠

Next day, under a pale sky streaked with fine white mare's tails, Lady Elizabeth returns to Nonsuch. She has come from the Lumley town house in London, sending a rider galloping ahead with news of her progress. He's spotted miles off by a servant John Lumley has posted high in one of the two great minaret-like towers that flank the southern face of Nonsuch. The news sends a wave of anticipation surging through the palace. Even Francis Deniker's priestly face seems to lighten a little.

The household gathers in the inner court. The grooms and servants line up on one side of the gatehouse, the maids and scullions are assembled on the other. Nicholas joins Quigley and Deniker by the fountain while they wait for the little party to ride in. John Lumley has put on a fine bottle-green velvet doublet trimmed with gems for the occasion. He looks every inch the senior courtier. His wintry face glows with anticipation. All eyes are on the archway at the foot of the clock tower and its six golden horoscopes.

'His lordship always makes a goodly greeting when Lady Elizabeth has been away,' says Francis Deniker in Nicholas's ear as the party rides in. 'He scarcely welcomes the queen with greater show. Look at her, she is a returning angel, a veritable angel.'

If she is, thinks Nicholas, it is only her eyes that show it. They are grey, but warm and generous, fine lines spreading out from the corners where the wind has tightened her skin. The rest of her is swaddled in a warm riding cloak with a genet-trimmed hood. As she pulls it free of her face, Nicholas sees a comely woman in her middle thirties, her fair hair gathered up beneath a linen coif, her jaw resolute, yet by no means given to seriousness. With a ready smile and easy manner, she seems the perfect counter-balance to John Lumley's stern Northumbrian gloom. Nicholas takes to her immediately.

'I trust my husband has put you somewhere warm, sir,' she says with a mischievous gleam in her eye. 'He is notorious for being parsimonious with firewood.' She turns to John Lumley and kisses his cheek. 'A little more warmth around the place might soothe away some of those furrows on your brow, Husband.'

'These, madam, come from trying to govern an unruly household,' Lumley replies with a theatrical wag of one forefinger.

They are an oddly mismatched couple, Nicholas thinks. There must be a full twenty years between them. On the surface they seem complete opposites. Yet they clearly adore each other. Nicholas's heart sinks – Robert Cecil had not warned him that the man he is to destroy is a doting husband to an adoring wife.

As he watches Lady Lumley greeting the rest of the assembled household, Nicholas's attention is caught by one of the servants. Standing beside the man he now knows to be Sprint, the head cook, is a girl of perhaps thirteen or so. She keeps looking around uncertainly from within the wide wings of a bonnet. It's clearly not her own – it's an adult's bonnet and far too big for her. She looks like a fox cub that's woken from a deep sleep to find itself in an unfamiliar place.

And he can't help but notice that while everyone else is chattering, exchanging pleasantries, rejoicing at Lady Elizabeth's safe return, the child remains silent. She doesn't even join in when the chamber-maids begin to sing a pretty hosanna to welcome their mistress home. Is this the mute servant John Lumley had mentioned at that first supper? For a reason Nicholas can't explain, he'd assumed Lumley was talking about an adult. He studies the girl more closely.

Her silence has an almost physical strength to it. It's far more than shyness, it's as though something inside her has been fashioned not from flesh, but stone. She seems clearly part of the household, yet as distant from it as he is from Eleanor. He cannot take his eyes off her. For an instant he even harbours the wild notion she might be Elise Cullen. But there are several girls of her age amongst the Lumley staff, so he quickly rejects the idea as his own wishful thinking.

As Nicholas watches, Lady Lumley reaches into her cloak and pulls out a small ivory comb. She clearly means it as a gift, a trinket brought from London for a favoured member of the household. The girl takes it, studying it intently as though she had never seen such a thing before. 'Does it please you, Betony?' Nicholas hears Lady Elizabeth ask gently.

The child makes a discreet bob of acknowledgement.

But she utters not a single word in reply.

34

I n the Jackdaw's parlour Rose is repairing Bianca's best doro-thea. When Robert Cecil's men tore it from her clothes chest, along with her spare kirtle and nightgown, they'd com-pounded the outrage by trampling it underfoot. Several of the bone-stiffeners have been shattered beyond resurrection.

'Look at it!' cries Bianca as she holds the corset against her body. 'It's supposed to flatter. Now it looks more like something you'd constrain a dangerous lunatic in!'

'Your Haarlem linen is almost dry,' says Rose. 'And I've brushed the carnelian bodice. He likes you in those. I've seen it in his eyes.'

'Who, Rose? *Who* likes me in my carnelian bodice? Walter Pemmel, the Puritan rake? Will Slater, the wherryman who smells of waterweed? Tell me, Rose – I'm all ears.'

Rose decides it's best to change the subject. Her mistress has developed an uncommonly raw nerve recently. 'And all because *someone* does not write,' she whispers – just loud enough for Bianca to hear.

Timothy comes in with a pensive look on his face. 'Pardon, Mistress, but there's a fellow becoming fractious in the taproom. Shall I have Ned Monkton throw him out?'

The fractious fellow turns out to be a grubby-bellied man with lank grey hair, claret-coloured cheeks and eyebrows that curl down over his eyelids like wood-shavings.

'He's the overseer at the Magdalene almshouse,' Ned tells her softly. 'Came in a few times while you were – away. No trouble, till now.'

Bianca can see at once the man is a practised souse-head. You could warm your hands on the veins that illuminate those cheeks, she tells herself. 'Marry, what's all this? – troubling my poor overworked taproom boy,' she says pleasantly.

'I know you,' the fellow says, as Bianca sits down beside him. 'You're that maid what got herself invited to Whitehall for sack and sweetmeats.'

'That's me.'

'They say you came back in the queen's golden barge. I heard all about it.'

'Then you won't be surprised if I tell you the owner sends her affections and counsels you to be her mild and obedient subject,' Bianca says with a laugh, deciding that's a better reputation to have than flying down the street at night in the form of a bat. 'And that includes being obedient in taverns.'

The man squawks with derision. 'The queen? I'd rather she gave me a decent annuity for looking after them addle-pates I've been set in charge of at the Magdalene,' he says, breathing fumes of knock-down over her, ''cause the parish pay me fuck-all for it – if you'll pardon my grammar.'

Bianca decides Timothy and Ned are right – the Jackdaw can do without this particular patron. 'I think it's time you went home, don't you? Careful of the cut-purses on the way. I wouldn't want you to come to harm.' She lifts one hand, intending to signal to Ned. But then the Magdalene's overseer kicks the world out from under her feet.

'That husband of yours is a right enough fellow, though – ain't 'ee?'

Bianca stares at him. Last time she checked, matrimony was a state utterly unfamiliar to her.

'My *husband*?'

'Aye, the physician. Where is 'ee? Call 'im out – I ain't too proud to sup with the bone-setter from St Tom's.'

Ned Monkton's huge arm is already reaching out, in antici-pation of Bianca's command. She stops him.

'Do you mean Nicholas Shelby?'

'Aye. The one who came down from St Tom's – for the ceremony.'

Bianca gives him the eyes of death. 'Firstly, I'll have you know Nicholas Shelby works for me. Well, he *did*. And secondly, there's been no marriage ceremony, unless I was asleep with a pillow over my head when it happened.'

The overseer vents more fumes into the already fuggy atmosphere of the taproom. Bianca shifts sideways an inch or two. 'Listen, Mistress, I'm talking about the ceremony at the Magdalene a few weeks back. The one with the fish.'

'Fish?' Bianca is beginning to feel her command of this exchange slipping through her fingers.

'Aye, St Tom's sends a physician for the inmates. The Bishop of Winchester gives the hospital a sack of fish in return. Dates back to King Canute. Fuck knows what good it does any of them.'

'I have not the faintest idea what you're talking about.'

Unconcerned, the overseer ploughs on. 'Mostly, the physic don't work, and the fish stinks worse than the Magdalene does. But we have to do it, else the inmates don't get the medicine. More's the point, I don't get to keep the alms money. Your hus-band was the physician, last time. I hadn't seen his face there before.'

'Dr Shelby is *not* my husband,' Bianca says indignantly.

The overseer decides of his own accord that it's time to leave. He rises uncertainly to his feet, bestowing a parting belch of knock-down fumes on her. 'Well, if he ever should be, you want to keep him on a tight leash. That Lady Katherine Vaesy was all over him like an outbreak of the buboes.'

✠

At breakfast Lord Lumley announces that the household will attend Cheam church for a thoroughly conventional, approved Protestant Sunday sermon.

Nicholas's relief is palpable. Robert Cecil is deluded, just as I'd hoped, he tells himself. John Lumley's library is merely eclectic, not heretical. His conversation at supper is designed solely to provoke. His mind encourages discourse, not sedition. He is no threat to the realm.

Now I can now safely broach the subject of the Bankside killer, he decides. I can enlist John Lumley's help. Then I can go back to Southwark, having discharged Robert Cecil's instructions to the full. I'm off the hook.

He joins the household as they assemble in the outer courtyard with a lighter conscience than he's had since the day he arrived. It occurs to him – with a guilty start – that he still hasn't written to Bianca.

✠

The winter sun flecks the chalk-and-flint walls of Cheam's Saxon church with slivers of golden light. The hamlet is a cluster of houses and barns, some as old as England itself, others new with whiteboard fronts and straight chimneys, all lying in a small valley between Cheam Common and the Banstead Downs. At the church porch a serious-looking man in a rector's gown greets them. He bows deeply before John Lumley. 'My lord, you are – as always – doubly welcome. And the Lady Elizabeth.'

'Reverend Watson, I trust I find you in God's good peace, sir,' Lumley answers. 'This is Dr Nicholas Shelby, a young man of physic. He's come from London to study a while at Nonsuch.'

'A physician?' says Watson. 'Oxford or Cambridge?'

'Cambridge.'

'Brothers then, eh? I was at Christ's.'

Nicholas remembers his first year there – a sizar, little better than an unpaid servant for the students of better breeding, darning their hose and carrying their hawks when they went hunting. The divinity men had been the worst. He smiles thinly and shakes the priest's hand. It feels as dry and dead as the stones of his church, though he can't be much older than forty.

The local squires and the more prosperous yeomen line up to be acknowledged by the master of Nonsuch, according to their standing. Then their women. Then their children. The conversation is confined to the banal: the current price of wool; how it's such a shame the Earl of Leicester isn't around any more to see off Spanish impertinence; why it's not worth going to see a comedy in London, now that Dick Tarleton is dead. It's a scene, he thinks, that must be playing out in just about every parish church across England. Robert Cecil should be happy.

Inside, the air smells as old as the stones themselves. The walls have been hastily whitewashed to hide the painted images of the saints venerated by the old religion. The little window behind the altar screen has been stripped of its coloured glass and now admits nothing more majestic than the insipid light of a February afternoon. The Reverend Watson, it appears, is a stout defender of the new faith.

Lumley stops before a stone monument about the size of a large sideboard set against the chancel wall. On the top is a handsome plaque on which a woman kneels at prayer. Around the base stand three small children, hands clasped in eternal piety. Nicholas understands at once what he's looking at: it's the memorial to Lumley's first wife and their long-dead children.

He fears for a moment that Lumley is going to kneel and offer prayers for the immortal souls of his dead children. Prayers to speed the departed out of Purgatory are forbidden. Purgatory as a real place no longer exists – the bishops have decreed it so. And if he does, it means everyone in the little church is complicit in the heresy. Robert Cecil will want to know. And if he learns of it from another source, he'll know Nicholas has kept it from him.

Don't ruin it now, he pleads silently.

To his immense relief, John Lumley merely reaches out and lays one hand briefly on the cold stone, before quoting to Watson, '"And God shall wipe away each tear. Death shall no more be, neither mourning, neither crying, neither sorrow".'

'The Book of Revelations,' says Reverend Watson, nodding approvingly. 'Shall we begin?'

⚜

The sun has almost sunk below the treetops. Watery beams of light spill between the branches. Nicholas waits by the church porch while John Lumley and Elizabeth finish taking their leave of the Reverend Watson and the congregation.

He smiles now to think he'd once been afraid of cemeteries. At ten, his brother Jack had bet him he couldn't stay longer than an hour in the Barnthorpe churchyard at night. Jack had fled at the first owl's hoot. Nicholas had lasted about ten minutes longer. But since his icy vigil on Christmas Eve he's found they can be strangely comforting places. While he waits for Lumley he fills the time idly inspecting the nearer headstones.

Most of the inscriptions are illegible, the graves ancient. But one, close to the path, is newer. It's a very ordinary headstone, flecked with a patchy dusting of moss. The words carved into the stone catch his eye:

Mathew Quigley
Laid in earth 13th May 1572
No gentler man ever spilt his blood for Christ

The grave of Gabriel Quigley's father? Or perhaps an uncle. Maybe a distant relative. But Quigley does not strike him as a Surrey name, and indeed there are no other Quigleys buried nearby. And something about the last line of the eulogy troubles him: *No gentler man ever spilt his blood for Christ.*

It's the sort of memorial he'd expect to find on the tomb of a Christian warrior, or perhaps even a martyr.

But Lumley's secretary doesn't seem like a man born of warrior stock.

A martyr then? Was this particular Quigley one of the three hundred or so Protestants burned by Bloody Mary Tudor when she temporarily returned the realm to the Pope's authority? A moment's thought tells Nicholas that cannot be. The date places Mathew Quigley's death firmly in the present reign. He's still puzzling when a voice hails him impatiently.

'Physician, are you with us or no? His lordship is leaving!'

Nicholas looks up to see Gabriel Quigley beckoning – John and Elizabeth Lumley are almost out of the lych-gate. He puts the eulogy out of his mind and hurries after them, but not before he notices the look on Quigley's damaged face. He's caught Nicholas looking at the grave. And for some reason he seems to consider it an intolerable offence.

✠

The following day Nicholas continues his deception. He labours in the Nonsuch library, ostensibly studying the medical books. And though it's a pretence, it's a productive one. It's rare for a young physician to have such a trove of learning at his fingertips.

He studies voraciously, even though a part of him questions what he's reading. After all, what use was this wonderful knowledge when he was trying to save Eleanor?

How long must he stay at Nonsuch? he wonders. If he leaves now, Robert Cecil will say he hasn't done his job. It will make Bianca's safety even more precarious. And he still has to find the right moment to enlist John Lumley's help in bringing the killer of little Ralph Cullen and the others to justice.

By late afternoon a gentle breeze from the west has made the air mild enough to entice him to take a break from his reading. He decides upon a stroll through the ornate Italian gardens, hoping it will clear his mind. Perhaps then he can compose his long-overdue letter to Bianca. If he's honest with himself, he's been dreading even picking up nib and quill. He fears that if he begins to write, unbidden thoughts will come – like the moment he stood watching her board the Cecil barge that day, when raw desire stole into his grief like an act of betrayal.

Nevertheless, as he walks he marvels. To a Suffolk yeoman's son, the earth is made for ploughing and seeding, for pigs to grub and fatten upon. At Nonsuch the ground gives up a very different harvest: fine classical statues, leafy arbours, trellised walks and tight-clipped hedges. He passes Venus standing atop a pillar. He sees birds with their stone wings frozen at the moment of flight. There's even a prancing marble horse like the one in the inner courtyard. He knows his father would scratch his head and wonder what possible use this inedible bounty could be. But looking back towards the palace, Nicholas notices they have all been set carefully. They provide a pleasing vista from the windows of the royal apartments. Monarchs, he realizes, have the power to remake the very world itself – merely to get a better view.

In a mood that comes remarkably close to contentment, Nicholas wanders down a gravel path along the side of the palace.

Glancing through a mullioned window twice his own height, he sees Christ staring back at him from the Cross. He walks over, stands on his toes and peers in.

He's looking into the shadowy interior of a private chapel, past stone pillars that seem to support an upper gallery. But there's nothing much to see: a half-panelled wall, a few rows of simple wooden pews, a pulpit and an altar no more elaborate than the one at Cheam church. Everything properly modest, properly Protestant. Not a trace of Rome anywhere.

A soft, happy chattering causes him to jump back onto the path.

Elizabeth Lumley emerges from an arch of close-cut privet. She has two women of her household in train. She wears a gown of sober winter Kendal, her face bright and flushed with laughter. It's like Bianca's when she's teasing me, he thinks.

'I give you good day, Dr Shelby,' says Lizzy. 'What a pity it is not yet spring. The privy gardens look so much more beautiful then. The queen herself says so. Doesn't she, ladies?'

Nicholas replies with a smile, a formal bend of the knee and a ladleful of poetic flattery. 'Madam, here is beauty enough for any man.'

It's how he assumes the comely wives of eminent courtiers expect to be greeted.

'A physician *and* a gallant,' says Lizzy Lumley, turning to her ladies and clapping her gloved hands in delight. 'So much more pleasing in manner than gruff Sir Fulke. If I am taken poorly, do you think he might read me poetry while he prescribes the physic?'

A spasm of delighted twittering from the ladies.

Nicholas blushes. He's utterly out of his depth. 'I fear you would soon find me tiresome, Lady Lumley. I read poetry as romantically as I order firewood,' he says.

'I can't believe that, Dr Shelby.'

'Oh yes – without question. My wife tells me so.'

My wife tells me so.

The words slip out so easily. Yet each one is like a stitch torn unexpectedly from a still-raw wound.

'Mercy, whatever is the matter, Dr Shelby?' Lizzy asks, noticing the pain in his eyes.

'It is nothing, madam. Nothing of consequence.'

Nothing of consequence.

It is everything. It is everything and then everything again. He fights to regain his composure, knowing that if she were to press him, he'd have to tell her about Eleanor. And once that secret's given up, who knows what others will follow?

'Then in the absence of consequence, will you walk with us, Dr Shelby?'

His instinct is to make some excuse; courtly talk eludes him at the best of times. But he fears he'll simply appear rude. 'Gladly, madam, though I fear the profit of it will be mine alone,' he replies.

This seems a suitable answer, for Lady Lumley's women fall back with a swirl of their gowns to take up station a few paces behind.

'It is good to see my husband enjoying his conversations again,' Lizzy says conspiratorially as they set off along the path. 'He thrives on the views of the younger fellows. Sir Fulke drives him almost to madness.'

'There are physicians I used to sup with who would dare to say Lord Lumley is not alone in that regard.'

Lady Lumley grins engagingly. 'To share a confidence with you, Dr Shelby, it will be a relief not to see him at Nonsuch for a while. Especially after that dreadful business with Betony.'

The name means nothing to Nicholas. 'You have me at a loss, madam. Betony?'

'Our silent talisman. Our mute kitchen maid.'

'Oh, the girl you gave a gift to on your return from London.'

'Mercy, were you spying on us, Dr Shelby?' Lizzy asks with a smile.

'No!' says Nicholas, just a little too vehemently. 'I just happened to notice – that's all. Lord Lumley told me about her over supper one night.'

'Indeed – that was our Betony. The more impressionable servants believe her silence to be saintly, Dr Shelby. Though why she will not speak is a mystery that no one in Nonsuch has been able to explain – not even my very learned and sometimes infuriatingly inquisitive husband.'

'Has she suffered this malady long?'

'Who can tell, Dr Shelby? My husband only found her this last St Wulfstan's Day – hiding in Cheam churchyard. She came to us a vagabond. What her *real* name is, only Our Lord in heaven knows.'

✠

How long does Nicholas make small talk with Lizzy Lumley after that?

He himself will never be certain. At the time it felt like hours, though it couldn't have been more than a few minutes. Certainly no longer than it took to walk to the pretty grove of Diana with its mossy statue of the huntress, then back again to the privy garden.

His overriding memories are of the rattling clamour of his thoughts – and of Alice Welford's voice coming out of nowhere: *They was always inseparable... That's what she'd do – find a haven... Elise wouldn't let nothing this side of Satan's front door stop her.*

35

Nicholas enters Master Sprint's cavernous realm of heat and noise with Alice Welford's words still ringing in his ears. He's here because Elizabeth Lumley says if anyone has come close to ending Betony's silence, it is the Nonsuch head cook. At once he's assailed by shooting flames, acrid smoke and spitting fat. The air is rent by the hammering of cleavers and the quivering thwack of knife blade against bone and muscle.

Along one wall he can see four huge brick fireplaces. In one of them a carcass of venison roasts slowly on a spit-iron, turned by two kitchen-hands stripped to the waist and sweating in the fierce heat. At a long table women sieve flour through cloths stretched tight over wooden frames, while the younger scullions variously pluck, trim, pare and generally clean up the mess.

'You should see it when the queen comes to Nonsuch,' Sprint replies when Nicholas asks him how he can stand it hour after hour. 'It gets so hot then that Satan himself would cut off his own pizzle for a cold bath.'

'Lady Lumley suggested I speak to you – about Betony. She says you know more about the maid than anyone.'

'Aye, and that's little enough, Master Physician. Joanna and I have coaxed all we can.' As he shakes his head the folds of his neck appear to rotate the other way. 'Our reward? Not a single word. All we can do is guess.'

'And what's your guess, Master Sprint?'

'I can tell you one thing – that child wasn't born to live in empty echoes.'

'What do you mean?'

'I think she could speak, if she desired it. I think she's frightened to.'

'Where is she?'

'Out with Joanna, cleaning the hen coops. I can call her, if you like.'

'In a while. I thought I'd speak to you first; you seem to have taken her under your wing.'

Sprint smooths his apron self-consciously. 'My belly might not suggest it, Dr Shelby, but I had a hard start in life too – much like Betony, I suspect. I'm told the parish found me under my mother's corpse in a ditch. Lord Lumley made me a scullion's help in the kitchen. I'd be white bones, if not for him. He's a good Christian man. He who says nay is welcome to debate the issue with me.'

'I'm sure he is. Were you there when the child was found?'

'No, sir, I was not. But I must tell you plainly, when she came into the household I wondered what manner of creature she might be.'

'Why say you so, Master Sprint?'

'I'm a God-fearing man, Dr Shelby. I do not fear Him because the queen or the Privy Council tell me I must; I fear Him because He knows when we seek to hide our hearts from Him. So in truth, when Betony first came here, I wondered if He hadn't sent her to test my faith.'

'That's quite an accusation to make of a maid,' Nicholas says, trying not to smile at Sprint's superstitious confession.

'A few days after she arrived, I discovered some marks by the bread ovens,' Sprint tells him, casting a glance towards where two kitchen women are kneading manchet dough, slamming the white slabs against the table with their broad, floury fists. 'No one here would have dared do it. Betony must have made them when Joanna left her alone for a while.'

'Marks? What sort of marks?'

'Satanic images, Dr Shelby. Crosses – turned on their heads. Scratched with her fingernails, I reckon.'

Suddenly from the hearth comes the rattle of hot fat spilt on even hotter iron. A wave of heat sears the side of Nicholas's face. At once Alice Welford's voice jumps clear from the clamour in his head: *One of Mary's customers at the Cardinal's Hat managed to set fire to the mattress Elise was sleeping on, burned her on the face...*

'Tell me something, Master Sprint,' he says, trying to keep the rising surge of hope from his voice. 'Betony was wearing an adult's bonnet when Lady Lumley returned from London. I couldn't see her that well. Does she have a scar of any kind on her face?'

'Indeed she does, Dr Shelby,' says Sprint. 'A burn mark—' He touches his beard. 'Right here, on her jaw.'

✠

Once again Southwark has decanted all its flavours into the Jackdaw. But this evening there is a change in the air; there has been for some days now. The customers sup their ale in a somewhat less boisterous manner. The fire seems a little less warm. When anyone asks Rose and Timothy what's the matter with Mistress Merton, they receive only evasion in reply.

The truth is, the drunken overseer's casual remarks have turned the Jackdaw's mistress into a stalking gorgon.

As Bianca works the tables she recalls her father's stern warning. 'Never become any man's chattel,' he'd told her when the local Paduan boys began to really notice the daughter of the *commerciante Inglese*. 'I'm a merchant, young lady, I know how prices can fall when the goods are too plentiful.'

Soon there had been a steady procession of young gentlemen discovering an urgent need to visit the house of the English merchant, Simon Merton. But his daughter had never liked the way Italian men made such a great play of venerating the Virgin while counting real women barely more important than their hawks or their hounds. She'd known instinctively how her life would be, if she married one of them – sewing and gossiping, gossiping and sewing, day after day, while her husband took boat rides on the Bacchiglione river with his courtesan. She'd decided then she would become a physician. She would do good in the world.

Bianca can remember walking hand-in-hand with her father in the Palazzo Bo. She couldn't have been more than fourteen. The air had been full of the noise of carpenters sawing and hammering, putting up temporary wooden stands for a public dissection in honour of the great Vesalius. The senior professor of anatomy at the university was to give the lecture. The subject was the body of a hanged criminal. With the ghoulish innocence of the young, Bianca had asked to watch. Her father had refused.

'But Julio and Esperanza's parents took them to watch a heretic being burned in the Piazza del Santo,' she'd protested angrily. Instead of answering, he'd introduced her to a terrifyingly august Italian in a black gown who'd turned out to be the university chancellor. 'It appears my daughter wants to be a physician,' Simon Merton had said. 'Can you help her?'

The chancellor had given Bianca a patronizing smile. 'Signorina, it will be one hundred years at the very least before a woman is allowed to graduate with a doctorate from Padua.' He'd made it sound like some sort of achievement.

'But Dorotea Bucca was professor of physic at Bologna almost two hundred years ago,' she'd protested. 'I read it in a book.'

Her father had beamed with pride.

Not so the Paduan. 'The Bolognese would elect a toad as a professor if they thought it would bring a few more ducats through the door,' he'd told her scornfully.

When she'd come to England – after her father's death – she'd rapidly discovered that it would be more like five hundred years before anyone would allow a woman to study medicine, let alone practise. Not only that, but the Grocers' Guild wouldn't even let her set up as an apothecary.

What would her father make of it: his daughter, the would-be physician, now mistress of a Bankside tavern? Worse still, what would her mother say? Bianca thinks she knows. She can hear her mother's wildfire Italian voice saying, 'I don't care two figs that you're a tavern-mistress in the city of the ungodly – only that you're an *unmarried* tavern-mistress!'

Why have the overseer's drunken ramblings upset me so? she wonders. Nicholas Shelby is already wed. He is a partner – whether willing or otherwise – in an indissoluble marriage, one that cannot be fractured even by death. He is not mine to love, even if I were to allow myself the luxury of that emotion.

But then just *who* is this Lady Katherine Vaesy – the one that rogue from the Magdalene says is all over Nicholas like a plague rash?

✠

Nicholas's feet beat out a tattoo that echoes beneath the arch of Henry's great clock tower as he runs. The sun is setting, the towers and minarets of Nonsuch silhouetted against the sky like some fabled palace in far-off Araby.

Ahead of him he can see the entrance to the royal apartments, flanked by statues of ancient gods and heroes – myth made solid by the mason's hand.

Myth made solid.

Ever since the moment Alice Welford told him about the existence of Elise Cullen, Nicholas has sought to put flesh on her insubstantial bones. But she's always remained tantalizingly indistinct, a whisper calling to him from within a great silence. Now she is real.

He's only minutes away from John Lumley's privy study. He has a truth to tell. He has a key with which to turn a lock. A name to break open a cipher.

He bounds up the steps, throws open the heavy oak door and takes the great staircase three steps at a time.

He hurries along the upper gallery, the fresh rushes on the floor deadening his footfall. The startled faces of the few servants he passes make no impression on him. He has no interest in the magnificent straight-backed chairs set along the corridor where the awed of Surrey can wait while Lord Lumley considers their petitions and their suits, even though each chair cushioned with cloth-of-gold costs more than Nicholas has ever earned in a year. He does not turn his head to admire the paintings – three Holbeins, a brace of Dürers, an Antonio Moro and a Frans Floris. They leave him unmoved. The artists might as well have left the pigment unmixed in the mortar. The *Passion of Christ*, carved from black marble, and which Francis Deniker's inventory values at £117 6s. 10d., if it's worth a farthing, leaves him cold. He has thoughts only for what he intends to say to John Lumley.

He already knows it will be part revelation, part confession. For the revelation: everything he knows about Elise Cullen and her murdered brother. His confession will be that he's come to Nonsuch on a pretence, that his real intention was to enlist Lumley's help in finding the man who killed Ralph, Jacob Monkton and the others. He will say nothing about Robert Cecil. And therein lies the guilt. Confession always comes with a price attached. And Robert Cecil will expect him to pay it. Find a killer. Abandon Bianca.

✠

Gabriel Quigley opens the privy-chamber door to Nicholas's erratic knocking. The way Lumley's secretary stands in the frame, his arms folded across the breast of his gown of legal black, makes Nicholas remember all the aldermen's clerks, the churchwardens, the petty officials who have barred his way so far. He struggles to remain polite.

'Master Secretary, forgive the intrusion, but I really must speak to Lord Lumley.'

'Lord Lumley is not here,' says Quigley, a little too quickly. The slight tightening of his pockmarked cheek makes him look as though he's just winced. It's an evasion, revealed before the muscles of the face can smother it. Nicholas knows he's lying.

'It's important I see him, Master Quigley,' he says, trying to look past the secretary without appearing distrustful.

'I shall tell you again: he's not here.'

'Then where is he? I'll go and find him.'

'Lord Lumley is not to be sought out like some common ostler or journeyman, Master Physician. If you have something of import to convey, I will pass it on when I next see him.'

And he shuts the door in Nicholas's face.

Nicholas is momentarily at a loss. He stands staring at the door while his breathing settles. What to do? His secret – Betony's secret – cannot be contained a moment longer.

At the far end of the passage stands a reedy servant lad. He's lounging in the way servants do when they think they're not observed. As he spots Nicholas, he straightens up. He smooths his tunic with the three Lumley popinjays stitched onto the breast. But if he has work to do, he doesn't seem inclined to set about it. He just stands there, looking a little sheepish. Almost as if he's been set to guard something and has been caught napping.

'Do me a service, lad,' Nicholas says. 'Tell me where I might find his lordship at this hour.'

'Sir, I cannot.'

'You mean you can't or you won't?'

The lad is unable to prevent the nervous entwining of his slender fingers. 'Forgive me, sir,' he pleads. 'I cannot help you.'

Nicholas thinks, I don't need to be Robert Cecil's spy to know I've been lied to twice inside a minute. Why is John Lumley suddenly a secret in his own house?

Then the answer comes to him: there's no secret. Lumley is merely taking his customary evening swim through the nurturing waters of learning. He's in his privy reading room and he's told his household he doesn't want to be interrupted.

Well, my noble lord, thinks Nicholas, you're about to learn something you couldn't possibly have imagined.

✣

Nicholas is familiar enough with Nonsuch now to know that to reach Lumley's privy reading room he must first pass the chapel he'd noticed from the outside, barely an hour ago. When he turns into the corridor on the first floor he sees another liveried Nonsuch servant ahead of him, not exactly blocking the way but standing motionless as he gazes out of a window at the privy gardens, now in deep shadow.

Two servants in the space of fifty paces. Both apparently with nothing to do but idle away the time. Now he's sure they're keeping a watch. But over what?

He can hear a faint voice. There's a strange rhythm to it. It seems to be coming from a door opposite where the servant stands so casually. By its place in the corridor, Nicholas reckons it must be the entrance to the upper gallery of the private chapel. Perhaps it's the Lumleys at prayer. Again? It's possible; he knows the devout pray often.

But although the voice is faint, it's quite unlike Lumley's

northern burr. It's a different sound entirely. And why, he wonders, didn't Gabriel Quigley simply tell me Lord Lumley was at his devotions – come back later?

'I'm sorry, sir, this corridor is denied to all but the family,' the servant says, turning from the window as he senses Nicholas approach.

One last deceit, Robert Cecil, says Nicholas to himself. After this I'm done with you.

'Master Quigley set you to guard here, is that correct?' he asks, taking an inspired gamble.

'Yes, sir, he did,' says the man.

'Well, he's sent me with new orders. He wants you on the other side of the royal apartments. And hurry.'

The servant looks at him in confusion. 'But that's not possible, sir. I must be here.'

Don't give him time to become bold, says a voice in Nicholas's head. It sounds suspiciously like Bianca's. 'Do you defy Master Quigley?' he asks in a tone as icy as he can make it. 'He has sent me directly with the instruction.'

The servant's eyes are moist with indecision. His jaw works as if he's chewing on a nut.

'Well, do you?'

The man looks over his shoulder towards the door. Then back to Nicholas. 'No, sir, of course I do not,' he sighs wretchedly and sets off at a lope in the direction of the royal apartments, leaving Nicholas struggling to calm a heart that's beating a wild *volta* of relief and anticipation.

The door is emblazoned with the Lumley crest: the three popinjays, their wings about to open for flight. Above the lintel is Henry's royal coat of arms.

The door is too thick for Nicholas to judge how many people are in the chapel. But there's no lock.

No lock – and careless guards. A secret, then, barely worth protecting. Or has complacency caused its keeper to under-estimate the threat? Easing the door open as gently as he can, Nicholas slips inside.

He already knows the layout of the chapel – he's observed it through the ground-floor windows before he took that astonishing walk with Lizzy Lumley. But the gallery above is new to him. And it's in almost complete darkness. The only illumination comes from the trembling glow of candles rising from the floor. It takes his sight a moment or two to adjust. And while it does, he's captivated by a single voice. A strong male voice. High Latin, chanted sweetly. It sounds too beautiful to be so sinful.

Slowly, the detail of the gallery offers itself to him. He can tell that it runs the full width of the chapel, some seven or eight paces in length, a good ten feet above the floor. A finely carved screen rises before him to chest height. There's a narrow stone stairway to his far right. He thinks, this is where guests must sit if they're not important enough to be part of the congregation.

Edging to the wall opposite the stairwell, Nicholas moves silently to peer over the screen.

What he sees makes his mouth gape open in astonishment.

Go, now! Turn around and walk away. Pretend you've seen nothing. Leave Nonsuch immediately. When you get to Cecil House, tell them you were somewhere else when John Lumley and his wife were taking the papist Mass before a fully robed father-confessor of the Romish heresy.

36

Nicholas can't drag his eyes away.

For a start, Francis Deniker – the one doing the chanting – appears to have undergone some form of magical transformation. His formal clerk's tunic has somehow turned itself into vestments of silk and damask. They glint opulently in the candlelight. Tied around his waist is a braided girdle. In one hand he holds a silver chalice. On a low table before him is a small, grey flat square of stone: a miniature second altar. A papist altar. And beside the table stands an empty travelling chest, an innocent wooden box – home for it all. Robert Cecil's words flood into Nicholas's head like a breaking wave: *You have no idea how cleverly these people disseminate their vile philosophy. Only last month we hanged and quartered a Jesuit priest who'd disguised himself as a peddler. He had the abominable devices of his ministry hidden in his box of ribbons!*

And then Nicholas hears another voice, much closer this time, and not in Latin but in very angry English. He feels the sharp press of a knife-point against his back – not enough to stab, but enough to get his full attention.

'I knew you were a spy from the moment you came here,' says Gabriel Quigley in his ear like a spurned lover. 'You're not the physician, you're the disease.'

✠

'I suppose you'd better come down, Dr Shelby – if you think your immortal soul can withstand the peril,' Lumley says, his voice remarkably firm as he looks up at the gallery.

It can't be easy, thinks Nicholas, for a man of advanced years to rise from his knees to a standing position in the same instant all his secrets are exposed, and still maintain some semblance of dignity. But John Lumley achieves it with some grace.

Lizzy Lumley is still kneeling. She stares up at Nicholas, a look of terror on her face. Francis Deniker, for all his priestly apparel, looks like a man caught in the act of purse-diving a judge of the Queen's Bench.

'Don't blame yourself, Gabriel,' Lumley calls out, trying to spot his secretary in the semi-darkness of the gallery. 'Close the door. Stay outside until I call. And say nothing of this to anyone – understand?'

'But, my lord, this man is an informer, I'm sure of it. I've had my fears about him since he arrived,' Quigley calls back.

'And I should have heard them, Gabriel. But what is done is done. Let Dr Shelby and I speak awhile.'

Quigley hesitates. He wants to ram the dagger into Nicholas's back as deep as the hilt will allow.

'Gabriel—'

'Very well, my lord,' says Quigley reluctantly. He steps back. But not before he gives Nicholas a parting jab with the tip of the blade. Nicholas feels a hot, sharp pain low down on his right hip, and a warm trickle of blood running down over his right buttock. 'You're lucky, *spy*,' Quigley rasps in his ear. 'If this were not a holy place—'

The stinging pain stays with Nicholas as he descends the stairs at Lumley's command. Reaching the bottom, he steps out into the candlelight as bravely as he can.

'Merciful heaven, Husband. We are utterly undone,' Lizzy Lumley whispers when she sees him.

'That rather depends on Dr Shelby, Mouse.'

Francis Deniker is packing away his vestments in the pine reliquary like a travelling haberdasher at the close of a country fair. Perhaps he thinks he can make Nicholas un-see what he has seen. His hands are shaking and his skin has the pallor of a man about to face the axe – which is almost a certainty, if Nicholas survives to tell Robert Cecil what he has witnessed.

'I should have taken more heed of Gabriel, Mouse,' Lumley says with a slow shake of his head as he helps his wife to stand. 'We've been at this young man's mercy since the moment he arrived at Nonsuch. Isn't that so, Dr Shelby?'

Nicholas doesn't know how to answer.

'I always knew my enemies would send someone here to shatter all this,' Lumley says, the merest hint of a wry smile on his lips. 'The question is, Dr Shelby, which one of them was it?'

Lady Katherine Vaesy.

Bianca has heard Nicholas speak only of Sir Fulke, the great but apparently incompetent anatomist. Is Katherine his wife? Or his winsome daughter? A fair cousin, perhaps? Whatever her connection, Bianca imagines her suffocating in silk, crushed under a weight of pearls, troubled by nothing worse than which of her many maids to call upon first to comb her hair.

But you can't claw like a Veneto maid when she's faced with a rival, Bianca tells herself with a tight smile. You'd be as much use with a blade as Vaesy himself, if what Nicholas says about you is true. In a dark piazza in Padua, surrounded by a bunch of over-enamoured gallants, you'd have no idea which bit of them to kick first.

She scolds herself for this jealousy, which will not let her be. She thinks, you're probably just a decent woman who gives alms to the distressed poor at the Magdalene. So why do I care what ceremony you performed with Nicholas Shelby when I wasn't there to protect him from himself?

But why has he still not written?

✠

'I care not for myself, Dr Shelby,' says Lizzy Lumley in astonishment when Nicholas has recounted in full the true story of how he has come to be at Nonsuch, 'but to think you would betray my husband to save a tavern-mistress!' She seems uncertain whether to regard him with compassion or fury.

Nicholas stands there like a felon pleading his case before the bench. The jab from Quigley's dagger makes him want to massage his hip, but he thinks that would simply make him appear furtive. He wonders if he's dripping blood on the chapel floor.

'Bianca Merton saved my life, Lady Lumley,' he tells her, giving the only defence he can – the truth. 'When my wife and infant died, I was utterly lost. I would have committed the sin of self-destruction, had not Mistress Merton taken pity on me. How could I then abandon her? I bear neither you nor your husband malice of any sort. Your faith is of no concern to me. I've already lost mine.'

John Lumley walks to the chapel windows, draws the hangings and stares pensively out at the setting sun. 'From what he's told us, Mouse, he could have done no less and kept his conscience clean. And Robert Cecil is adept at coercion. We know that only too well.'

'I assure you, my lord, there was no deceit in my original letter,' Nicholas says. 'I really was seeking your help. But then Robert Cecil got his talons into me and all went awry.'

'Do the Psalms not tell us that a man who deceives shall not abide in God's house, Dr Shelby?' asks Lizzy Lumley, less forgiving than her husband.

'Madam, that is a place in which I have not dwelt for some considerable time,' Nicholas replies softly.

Lumley turns back from the windows and appraises him silently. Then he says, 'For Lizzy and myself, I am not overly troubled by what you have discovered here, Dr Shelby. The queen knows of my adherence to the old faith. She tolerates it as the eccentricity of a man living in the past. I suppose the Privy Council might persuade her to a fine—'

'You can't afford a fine, Husband,' Lizzy protests angrily. 'You owe enough to the Crown already! Francis, tell him he can't afford a fine.'

'Hush now, Mouse. If not a fine, then perhaps a few months in the Tower. That can be less tiresome than it sounds. I've been there before – as I suspect you already know, Dr Shelby. I'll survive. It is gentle Francis I fear for most.'

Nicholas understands that fear only too well. It's not just their altars and their vestments – the outward trappings of their hated religion – that damn these Jesuits to a traitor's death. It's not their taking of confession or their dispensing of indulgencies. It's not even their Masses. It's the fact that they carry with them the Pope's message to all the English: that God will excuse them when they rise up and overthrow their heretical, excommunicated queen.

'You underestimate the danger to yourself, my lord,' says Nicholas. 'I'm sure I don't have to remind you that hiding a Jesuit priest is a felony. And to hide one in a place the queen visits often, to allow him to give the Mass in a chapel she herself may even pray in, is tantamount to treason. If Robert Cecil has his way, it will mean the scaffold not just for Master Deniker, but very probably for you, too.'

'The question is: are you going to tell him?' asks Lizzy Lumley. 'Will you condemn these two good souls to the torment their enemies will demand – all to save this tavern-mistress of yours?'

Before Nicholas can answer, Francis Deniker says 'That is a fate I have been prepared to suffer since I first entered a seminary. I am prepared, and strengthened.' He glances at Lumley. 'But I would beseech you, sir, do not be the cause of this good man's destruction.'

Nicholas takes a deep breath, gathering up his conscience with it. He imagines the fate in store for Deniker and Lumley: dragged through the city streets so that good men and women of the new faith may spit upon them; half-hanged on the gibbet, then cut down to enjoy with the baying mob the spectacle of what follows: their disembowelling, their privy parts burned before their dying eyes, mercy coming only when the axe slams into their limbs for the final quartering. 'None of you need fear me,' he says. 'Robert Cecil will never learn from me what I saw here. You have my word on it.' Then he offers up a silent promise to Bianca that he will find some other way to protect her from Burghley's hunch-backed son.

'Thank you, Dr Shelby. My trust in you was justified,' says Lumley, exhaling in relief. He takes his wife's arm and draws her close. 'I think we may consider our own devotions at an end, Mouse – for today. But that does not absolve us of our duty. If Dr Shelby is right, there is someone else here at Nonsuch much in need of our prayers.'

37

S he sits in one of the broad bay windows of the Nonsuch library, a small figure set against the fading glow of fiery sunset. She makes Nicholas think of a handmaiden patiently awaiting her fate while behind her back Rome burns.

She wears a plain woollen kirtle, her hair tied neatly back from her face. Now Nicholas can see the livid burn mark along one cheek. In the light from the candles that John Lumley has had placed in the sconces, her skin gleams as though an artist has just this minute finished painting her upon his canvas.

Lizzy Lumley kneels on a cushion in front of her. Nicholas hangs back a little, in awe of this young maid whose courage and endurance he cannot even begin to measure. Gabriel Quigley waits nearby. He's been commanded by his master to make a written record of what transpires, Francis Deniker's hand being still a little less than firm. Lumley has taken Quigley aside and told him that Nicholas is no enemy. He seems unconvinced. He casts malevolent glances in Nicholas's direction, as though he's considering calling up a couple of the handier servants and having him dropped down the nearest well. Perhaps he's regretting he didn't make better use of his knife. Nicholas massages his hip. The bleeding has stopped and he's sure the wound is not substantial. But it still smarts.

No one present can be certain the girl they call Betony will be persuaded from her self-imposed silence. Everything is down to Nicholas now. He runs his tongue around his mouth so that the dryness in this throat will not rob him of a clear voice at the critical moment. His heart pounds in his chest. He begs Eleanor to give him the courage to act, to give him the wisdom not to shut off Elise Cullen's voice for ever by a thoughtless word or gesture.

'There is no need to be afraid, child,' says Lumley gently. 'We have summoned you here only out of love. You are in no trouble – none. You are amongst friends. You are safe. Do you understand that? Quite safe.'

The girl has made fists of her hands. She gently rubs the knuckles together. Still she says nothing in reply. Then, to Nicholas's immense relief, she gives the faintest of nods.

'Good,' says Lumley, smiling. 'Now then, child, I would beseech you to listen carefully to what Dr Shelby has to say to you.'

Quigley casts Nicholas a glance that says: what fresh deceit are you about now? But he takes paper, nib and inkpot from his scrivener's box and lays them out carefully on a table by one of the windows. 'I'm ready, my lord,' he says.

'Gentlemen, in mercy's name be careful,' urges Lizzy in a whisper.

'I've been sent by a woman named Alice Welford,' Nicholas begins, realizing that his first words to Elise Cullen are a lie – Alice Welford has not the slightest idea he's here.

Sometimes a lie is what we have to tell if that's what it takes to reach a greater truth, Eleanor tells him. You lied to John Lumley to get here. But now the truth is right here in front of your eyes. Don't start fretting about your conscience now, Husband.

'Alice Welford told me a story,' he continues, stepping out into clear view, 'about a young girl named Elise—'

The girl's head turns towards the sound of his voice, as though she were a wooden manikin connected to his hand by an invisible cord.

'Alice would look after this girl when her mother Mary could not. She'd make sure she had a bowl of paplar for breakfast, that her clothes were washed regularly. And it wasn't only Elise that Alice looked after. This girl had a little brother named Ralph. You remember Alice Welford, don't you... Elise?'

He means this to put her at ease; but the foolish grin that takes over his face comes from somewhere he did not expect. It has stolen up on him. It has ambushed him not with joy, but with a complicit agony. It is the smile he realizes he's been saving for the child Eleanor was to have given him. It's been sitting inside him all this time with nowhere to go.

'Alice told me that Elise Cullen had a fine voice,' he says, feeling the tears stinging his eyes. 'Elise used to trill like a pipit – that's what she told me. A pipit. Never silent. Not for a single moment.'

Now the girl's face is fixed so intently on his that her eyes seem to be boring into him.

'A pipit is such a little bird,' he says, narrowing the thumb and index finger of his left hand to illustrate, 'but by Jesu, how our good Lord loved to hear her sing.'

The effect of his words takes even Nicholas by surprise.

One moment the girl is sitting as inanimately as a carved saint in a shrine, the next she hurls herself from her seat. The cushions go flying. A candle sconce clatters against the floor, the wax splashing like blood. Nicholas ducks into a run before he even knows it, anticipating the chase – a pursuit he knows will silence the pipit's song for ever.

But Elise does not flee. Instead she throws herself into Lizzy Lumley's arms. The sorrow and the fear come bursting out of her in a torrent of heaving sobs. Her body writhes as though a host of invisible demons is beating her with rods of fire. She clings so tightly to Lizzy that Nicholas must struggle to confirm there's something else spilling from her mouth other than her cries of anguish: words!

Ralphie... oh, little Ralphie... I'm so sorry, Brother — so sorry... Forgive me... I should never have called to the angel...

38

Night has slipped in before Elise Cullen recovers enough to tell her story. At first her voice is so weak, so faltering, that Nicholas fears it cannot possibly bear the weight of the words it must carry. But Elise Cullen is no stranger to burdens. She has endured the weight of her little brother on her back along weary miles of country lanes, borne the trials of living in the open, through summer heat and winter chill. She's faced hostility and violence from almost everyone she's met on the way. So – quickly – the voice begins to strengthen. Soon Elise Cullen is all but singing like the songbird Alice Welford said she was. And she confirms everything Alice had told him: the journey through a succession of increasingly rundown stews and tenements of Bankside; the sudden decision, made one day last summer, to take herself and little Ralph away, to the place her mother had often told her about: Cuddington, where a rich and kindly relative lives in a great house. As he listens, Nicholas hears in her voice the desperate longing for a better life than the one she'd been dealt. He thinks of his own – the future he'd anticipated with Eleanor and their children. Why is it so easy, he wonders, to build our lives on such treacherous hopes?

Lizzy lays a hand on the girl's knee. 'But you have found your refuge now,' she says gently. 'It is here.'

Does Elise know what has happened to her brother? Nicholas wonders. And how did she herself escape Ralph's fate? He would ask her directly, but how do you speak of murder and mutilation to a maid who's suffered what Elise has suffered? Instead he asks, 'Who was the angel, Elise? You spoke of an angel – said you should never have called to her.'

At this, Lizzy says, 'She's tired, Dr Shelby. Let her rest.'

But Elise has too many words inside her still waiting to be let out. 'He was my brother, sir. I was carrying him on my back. It was hot, and I couldn't manage another step. Then the angel found us.'

'An angel?' says John Lumley, wondering if the child is about to claim divine visitation.

'We had left London by the Fleet Bridge, three days before, I think it was. I was so tired, so hungry. We were crossing a stream. Then a woman came to help us. I thought she must be an angel – I'd been praying so hard for one to come.'

'And did you go with this woman?' Nicholas asks.

'Yes. She gave us shelter and food, let us play in her garden...'

'Do you know where this was?'

'In the country. I remember the smell of the warm grass. There was birdsong and the humming of the bees.'

'And why did you leave?' Nicholas enquires, catching the hurried rasp of Quigley's nib as he writes.

'We didn't leave. She took us – to somewhere bad.'

'What happened there, Elise? Can you tell us?'

'Have we not taxed her enough?' asks Lizzy. 'She should sleep.'

But Elise is not ready for rest. 'I began to realize she wasn't an angel after all,' she says.

'Can you describe this new place she took you to?' Nicholas asks.

'High walls. Dark, and dusty. Very dusty. Even the Cardinal's Hat was cleaner.'

'The Cardinal's Hat?' enquires Lumley. 'Is that a tavern?'

'A bawdy-house on Bankside, my lord,' Nicholas explains. 'It's where her mother took the children when she fell into drunkenness and penury.'

Lumley closes his eyes for a brief moment. A bawdy-house named the 'Cardinal's Hat' – his Romish faith has taken more insults today than he can stomach.

'By then I was very sleepy most of the time,' Elise continues without prompting, 'and I had nightmares, even during the day. I think it was the angel working magic upon me. But I do remember there were other people there.'

'How many people, Elise?' asks Nicholas, trying to sound almost uninterested.

'There was a blind woman and her sister, and an old man with only one hand. They were kind to me. And then there was Jacob.'

He squats down beside her. 'This Jacob – was he a young man with a round face, a face like the moon? A young man who was very much like a little child?'

Elise smiles at the memory. 'Jacob is sweet. I've known him a long time, since I was small. He lived on Scrope Alley. His father was a poulterer. He used to bring us a chicken once a month, until he stopped coming because my mother frightened him.'

'Do you know where Jacob is now, Elise?'

'Yes, of course. Jacob is still with the Devil.'

A muttered *Kyrie eleison, Christie eleison* from Francis Deniker, followed by an *Amen* from John Lumley. Lizzy covers her mouth with her hands.

'And your brother, little Ralph?' asks Nicholas.

Elise's eyes become wet and extraordinarily bright as the anguish floods back into them. 'Yes, Ralphie also. Ralphie is still with the Devil.'

The sound of Gabriel Quigley's pen as it scratches has slowed. Nonsuch seems too perfect a place in which to write of Satan.

'How do you know it was the Devil, child?' asks Lumley cautiously. 'Did he manifest himself to you?'

A sudden tremor runs through Elise's body. 'No, sir, he did not. But only the Devil would be about such work as I saw there.'

And then she tells them of a night, shortly after she had arrived in the place she now begins to call the Devil's house – the night she went in search of her brother.

'There was an archway, just beyond the dormitory where we were being kept. There were steps, leading down. I was afraid to go, but I knew Ralphie would be even more afraid down there without me. You see, I thought I might find him at the bottom.'

'And did you?'

'No.'

Elise begins to rock back and forth as the memories hem her in. Lizzy moves closer to her, defensively.

'What did you find there, Elise? Will you tell us?'

'I found a dead man,' she says in a coldly matter-of-fact voice. 'A dead man in a chamber lit by a thousand candles.'

Lizzy stifles a gasp. The scratching of Quigley's pen has stopped entirely.

'He was on a cross, like our saviour, but turned all about,' Elise continues in a matter-of-fact voice. 'There was blood. I think it must have been old blood, because it came from high up on his leg and ran all the way down to his head, like wax on a candle, only black, as black as the river at night. There was a bucket close by his head. The bucket was full of his blood. I did not know that a man had so much blood in him. I knew then why the angel had brought us to this place.'

39

D o we have this aright?' asks John Lumley sometime
later. He is sitting at his study desk like a justice of the
peace at the quarter assizes, kneading the collar of his
gown as if he's been called upon to deliver a particularly complex
judgement. 'Will the words do?'

Elise is asleep in the servants' quarters, after much gentling
and soothing by Sprint, Joanna and the other members of the
household, along with more fortifying hippocras than a thirteen-
year-old should rightly drink.

'They may "do", John,' says Lizzy from her seat at the window.
'But not for a moment can they accurately convey what the poor
child has suffered.'

For his part, Nicholas is retelling Elise's story in his head, mar-
velling at her courage, appalled by what she has seen, what she
has endured. Her words are seared into his mind. He wonders if
the body she'd described hanging upside-down in the cellar was
that of the old man with the stump for a hand, or a victim yet
unknown. He remembers the wheals on Jacob Monkton's wrists
and ankles – evidence that he, too, had suffered on this monstrous cross. He wonders how Elise could have seen what she'd
seen and not gone mad. And he wonders if he's right – that it all
happened barely ten minutes' walk from the Jackdaw, in the grim
heart of the Lazar House.

'How can we be sure these words are nothing but fantasy, mere
dreams?' Quigley asks. 'The maid confessed she was often very

sleepy and suffered nightmares, even in the daytime. Yet on this particular night, she was apparently in full possession of her wits. Explain that.'

'I believe the woman she thought was an angel came and went at intervals,' Nicholas says. 'Whatever she was giving to Elise and the others to keep them compliant, the effect was dependent on constant replenishment. Elise believed it was magic – "the angel's magic" is what she called it. Bianca Merton and I suspect it was a concoction of henbane or some other powerful essence.'

'And who exactly is Bianca Merton?' asks Quigley, scanning his notes for her and failing.

'She's mistress of the Jackdaw tavern, on Bankside,' Nicholas tells him.

'Mistress Merton, apparently, is the reason Dr Shelby has come to Nonsuch,' Lumley tells his secretary. 'It's a long and somewhat troubling story, and we have Robert Cecil to thank for it.'

'A tavern-mistress?' says Quigley to Nicholas contemptuously.

'We're close friends. She knows all that I know.'

Lumley says, 'Gabriel, do me some service and recount the part where the girl escaped her confinement.'

Quigley does, as though reading a shopping list. 'Here it is, my lord. "When I heard the sound of the Devil's footsteps returning, I went back up the stairs. I did not want to leave Ralph, but I knew not where they had taken him. I knew I had to get away from the Devil's house. I tried to get Jacob to come with me, but he didn't understand." Then Dr Shelby asks her how she found a way out. The child states, "I discovered a window, high up. It was boarded, but the boards were loose. Just beyond the window were the branches of a tree." Then comes some trivia about how the maid used to climb trees when she was younger, how her brother would watch her, laugh and shout "squirrel" – or some such nonsense.'

'Thank you, Gabriel, you appear to have it down pat,' says Lumley. 'What is your view of her story?'

'If you want my professional opinion, my lord, it's nothing but invention. Pure childish fantasy.'

'And if it's not?'

'If you put the child before a magistrate she'll likely revert to her former silence. What use will this supposed testament of hers be then?'

'It's all we have,' says Nicholas, 'and it fits with everything I know.'

'Which is precious little of substance,' Quigley says contemptuously. He turns to Lumley. 'I make the observation only as a lawyer might, my lord. She didn't even see the face of the man she claims had done these things.' He scans the sheet of paper. 'Here it is: Lord Lumley asks the child if the Devil manifested himself to her. Her reply: "No, sir, he did not." There – she didn't actually *see* anyone. If the Devil is at work here, I suggest he has done nothing but toy with a young girl's powers of imagination.'

'She's telling the truth,' Nicholas counters. 'I've seen three of the bodies myself.'

Quigley looks at him sharply.

John Lumley turns to his secretary and says, apologetically, 'Dr Shelby told me of Elise's story, privily, while you were waiting outside the chapel. It would appear that everything the maid says is true – God forbid.'

Nicholas holds up three fingers of his left hand. 'I saw Ralph Cullen's body on the dissection table at the College of Physicians last August,' he says. 'He'd been pulled from the river by a waterman. I saw Jacob Monkton's body at Mutton Lane stairs last Accession Day. And I saw the corpse of a preacher who'd been found by Battle Abbey creek just after Twelfth Night. All three had the same wounds to the leg. One victim had been bled dry, one bled out and the liver excised, one victim wholly eviscerated.'

Lumley frowns. 'And the marks you and Master Sprint saw scratched into the soot by the bread ovens, what of them?'

'At first I thought they described the wounds on the bodies. Now I think she was drawing what she saw in that cellar – the man hanging on the frame like an inverted crucifixion.'

'So these wounds have nothing to do with devilry?' Lumley asks.

'They're just the way the killer makes sure the artery is properly found and severed.'

'Someone is going to have to tell Elise about her brother, Dr Shelby,' says Lizzy. She shudders. 'The poor, poor child – to have witnessed such a thing.'

'I suspect she already has a pretty good idea of what's happened to Ralph,' Nicholas says. 'But I think we should wait until her mind is strong enough to bear the burden.'

'A justice of the Queen's Bench must hear of this,' Lumley says, reaching out to take the testimony from his secretary. 'Or, better still, the Privy Council.'

Quigley shakes his head, giving up the papers almost grudgingly. 'Again, my lord, I must counsel you to caution. I need hardly remind you how tenuous this will appear if you present it before a jury. Just look at the witnesses: a vagrant female child, a mortuary clerk and a woman who owns a tavern.' He looks directly at Nicholas. 'Not to mention a physician who's also a paid informer. I understand from my contacts at the College that he has a recent history that can best be described as questionable.'

'It's the truth,' says Nicholas. 'And don't think I haven't had it refuted by any number of clerks and parish officers already.'

'It's late,' says Lumley. 'Gabriel, as usual you've been uncomplainingly dutiful. I shall decide what to do in the morning. As for you, Dr Shelby, I think you've provided us with more than enough shocks for one day. God grant us both an untroubled rest.'

✠

In his chamber, Nicholas dips the hem of his shirt into a water bowl and cleans the dried blood from hip and buttock, washes the neat puncture made by the tip of Quigley's dagger. It's a small wound; he's suffered worse bringing in the harvest at Barnthorpe. It seems a small price to pay for the gift Elise Cullen has given him. He climbs into bed, lies on his front for comfort and falls into an exhausted sleep.

Eleanor is waiting for him. She's standing on the far bank of a river, her gown harried by the wind, her hair loose and billowing. The sky at her back is a boiling cauldron of dark cloud. She is calling to him, one arm outstretched like the doomed heroine of a Greek tragedy. Nicholas knows she is in terrible danger. He must cross the river to reach her. To save her. But there are things lurking just below the surface, things even worse than his own dread of failing her. A magnificent barge is moored nearby. In the prow, Robert Cecil is hunched over Francis Deniker's writhing body. He's hauling out the Jesuit's bloody entrails while Fulke Vaesy stands at his shoulder, quoting the Bible and pointing to each organ with his ivory pointer.

Nicholas awakes with an anguished groan. His shirt is soaked in sweat, ice-cold against his back. The wound from Quigley's knife throbs like a wasp's sting in his hip. He sits up in bed and waits for his breathing to settle, for the hammering of his heart to soften. What has caused him to wake? Was it the dream, or a noise from the corridor outside his chamber? He has no idea of the time, though by the amount the candle on his table has burned down he can't have been asleep more than an hour. The last wakeful moment he can remember was spent staring at the wall, wondering how he was going to protect Bianca once he'd told Robert Cecil that life hadn't equipped him for the role of informer.

There it is again – a noise just loud enough to wake a habitually light sleeper. Less than a full tapping on the door, more than just a draught pushing it against its hinges. He calls out. 'Who's there?'

Silence. Or not quite silence. Then the distinct sound of feet hurrying away down the passage.

Nicholas throws back the covers and goes to the door, his way lit only by the candle and the muted glow from the embers in the hearth. He lifts the latch and looks out into the corridor. It's empty. Cursing his overactive imagination, he turns back towards the bed.

As he does so, he sees in the candlelight a small sheet of parchment on the floor. He bends to retrieve it, cursing at the sudden sharp pain in his hip. Carrying it back to the bed, he reads the words scrawled in spidery black ink:

> I know who killed the maid's brother and the others. Come
> to me in the storeroom at the end of the mews. I shall wait
> no longer than cockcrow. Despite your promise before
> Lord Lumley not to denounce me, I must go out of England
> before the day's end or perish.

40

Tonight is the first night the dreams do not come. Tonight Ralph's weight does not fatigue her shoulders. Jacob Monkton does not disturb her ears with his gibberish. The eyeless woman who rocks to and fro incessantly has departed. The old, one-handed man who cannot remember where to find his mattress or the piss-pot has vanished. Tonight the sturdy walls of Nonsuch do not transform themselves into briary thickets and hedges. Elise is warm in her bed. Her stomach is full. She is not chilled to the bone, cramming discarded scraps of bad meat into her mouth, drinking from muddy puddles. All these trials have begun to fade from her consciousness like pain from a wound as it heals. In their stead comes a strange noise, which at first sounds like someone calling to her in a foreign language, calling from a long way off. It is the sound of her own voice.

When she'd returned to the servants' dormitory, on the ground floor of the Nonsuch inner gatehouse, no one had thought to ask her why she'd been summoned to Lord Lumley's privy apartments. They'd known she wouldn't answer. Since when had the girl they called Betony ever answered a question?

Sprint had been wise enough to let her go in and find her own way of making landfall. She'd busied herself in preparation for sleep, washed under her linen kirtle with a rag wetted from the water tub in the corner, cleaned her teeth with leaves of eglantine. Then the familiar ritual: Joanna leading the women in their

329

evening prayers: *Our Lord which art in heaven, hallowed be thy name...*
let thy kingdom come...

It took a few lines for someone to realize they had been joined
by an extra voice.

The result couldn't have been more dramatic. Joanna stopped
dead in her tracks, as though she'd forgotten the words. Someone
gasped. Every bowed head lifted and turned towards the girl.
And then everyone was urging her on, as though they feared that
if she stopped, the old impenetrable silence would come back to
reclaim her.

And after that: much hugging and dancing and singing, which
Joanna avowed was a most ungodly way to behave after the Lord's
Prayer, but joined in with anyway. Followed – at least for Elise –
by the sleep of the saved.

But enough of the old wariness – the alert stringing of the
senses for the faintest hint of danger – remains with her. Some
two hours after she first closed her eyes she awakes to the
murmur of voices in the corridor. The first she recognizes at
once. It is Joanna's.

'Mercy, what time is this for you to be calling for the child
again? She's asleep. Let her rest.'

The answering voice is less familiar to her, and in her drowsiness she struggles to give it a face. 'This cannot wait until
morning. The child is to come now. Wake her, please.'

'And what am I to tell the poor chub when I do?'

The voice is low and full of a dark urgency. 'It is a privy matter,
Mistress Joanna.'

'Well, good or ill, it can wait until morning,' says Joanna
protectively.

'Do you defy Lord Lumley?'

'In no measure. But if he wishes to disturb the well-deserved
sleep of our little talisman, he can come and speak to her here.

She's not a dog to be woken from the hearth whenever a body feels like making a pet of her. Have you any idea of the hour?'

Elise does not hear the reply, if indeed there is one. The call of her dreamless sleep is irresistible.

✠

A full moon hangs in a sky rent with fragments of scudding cloud. In the lapping of its light, the Nonsuch mews lie along one side of the kitchen yard like the pale wreck of a ship cast upon a reef. In this simple wooden cloister Lord Lumley's falconer keeps his master's birds of prey. Nicholas wonders why Francis Deniker has chosen here, of all places, to meet.

The priest's note has set his mind racing. How can Deniker possibly know the identity of the killer? Surely he can't be here at Nonsuch – Elise Cullen would have bolted like a startled hind at the first sight of him. And if he is, why has he not taken care to remove the one soul who can identify him?

And then he remembers Quigley reading from Elise's testament in John Lumley's study: *Lord Lumley asks the child if the Devil manifested himself to her. Her reply:* 'No, sir, he did not.' Elise Cullen hasn't seen the face of the killer. But nor has the killer seen hers.

And then another thought occurs to him: what if the note is a lie? It could be nothing more than a morsel of bait laid to lure him here. The Jesuit might appear a gentle fellow on the surface, but the brave words he spoke in the Lumley chapel will bring him little ease in the face of martyrdom on the scaffold. With Nicholas dead, Francis Deniker would be safe.

But try as he might, Nicholas can't cast Francis Deniker in the role of assassin. And anyway, if it is a trap, he's forewarned. The priest is no match for a Suffolk yeoman's son.

Cautiously, he opens the door and enters the mews. There's a soft rustle of feathers as the birds wake from their sleep. They make a strangely gentle sound, these creatures of talon and razor-sharp beak. Like cats meowing. Has he disturbed their dreams of aerial slaughter – or do they just think he's come to feed them?

Shafts of moonlight penetrate the unshuttered windows. Scattered across his path are streaks of white mute – hawk-shit. The birds stand upon low wooden blocks like executioners waiting for a commission. They watch him with fierce yellow eyes that hold no discernible emotion other than the desire to kill. One of them hops down onto the ground, skips to the limit of the long leather cord that secures him by one leg, spreads his wings and disgorges a small pellet from his beak. Nicholas can smell a pungency of digested shrew and mouse, of coney flesh, of blood and gore. He thinks, thank God these birds don't work for the Cecils, or we'd all be dead.

The storeroom lies at the end of the mews, almost invisible in the darkness. Nicholas feels his way along one wall, past shelves containing the paraphernalia of the falconer's world: punches and shears for cutting the leather jesses that hang from the birds' talons, imping needles for repairing broken feathers, rolls of padding and wire for the construction of bow perches. Reaching the end, he stumbles over a knee-high pile of dusty sacking, before recovering his balance and trying the storeroom door.

It's unlatched and ajar.

'Deniker, are you there?' he calls softly. 'It's me, Nicholas – Nicholas Shelby.'

The only reply is a short, unearthly mewling from one of the falcons. He calls again.

Still no reply.

Nicholas pushes the door open a little further. It yields into utter blackness. A musty smell from within reminds him of the ancient threshing barn on his father's farm in Suffolk. It comforts him, helps keep his breathing calm. He steps cautiously inside, almost blind in the darkness.

And as he does so, he senses a sudden disturbance in the night air – the sleepy stretching of a hawk's wing somewhere behind him. He turns to look back over his shoulder, assuming Deniker has entered the mews.

And then a blinding white light floods into him. The moon has fallen from the sky, crushing him, forcing his senses into the unyielding Surrey clay, driving him down into black nothingness.

41

What if Shelby is lying to us? He's done so before,' says Lizzy, sensing John shifting fitfully in the darkness against the bolster of the great bed. 'We can't let him destroy us, Husband. Not after all you've been through.'

'I trust him to keep his word, Mouse. I think he's an honest man.'

'Who lied to you from the very beginning!'

'That's not true – he swore there was no deceit in his first letter, remember?'

'And you believe him? A man who works for Robert Cecil?'

'He does not *work* for Cecil. He was coerced by him. I thought you liked him.'

'I thought him charming when he came here. Now I'm not so sure.'

'Did you not witness him with Elise, Mouse? Those weren't the actions of a man whose soul is chained to the Cecils' ambition.'

'But there's something about him – I fear he may carry chaos in that smile of his.'

'Hush, Mouse. Sleep awhile.'

'How can I, when all I can think of is what might yet happen to you and Francis, if he's lying? And when I'm not thinking of that, I can't free myself from imagining how that poor young girl has suffered – her brother and the others, too.'

'Nicholas Shelby is an honest man, Mouse. From what he's told us, has he not grieved enough to win your trust?'

Lizzy sits bolt upright in bed. 'You're right. I need to lay these fears of mine to rest. I shall start with a clear conscience – I'll have Francis hear my confession.'

'Now? It's not even dawn, Mouse,' John says, turning over yet again. 'Give the poor man his rest. Let him hear what's in your soul when the sun is up. Our sins are easier borne in the light.'

✠

Bianca stands in the physic garden, pale as death in the pre-dawn moonlight. She's come to hear her thoughts. It's easier to do so here.

Beyond the garden wall looms the black bulk of the Lazar House. She wonders if Nicholas is right – is this really where the man who killed young Jacob Monkton goes about his monstrous business? If so, he couldn't have chosen a more fitting place.

But there have been no more bodies washed up on Bankside since Nicholas left – save for a customer from the Good Husband who'd decided upon a swim after an injudicious three quarts of stitch-back. Perhaps the killer has moved out of the parish. Perhaps he's discovered a conscience. Perhaps he's died.

And where is Nicholas now? she wonders. Is he asleep in some goose-down bed in fabled Nonsuch? Does he share it with Lady Katherine Vaesy?

She reaches down and rubs her fingertips over the winter herbs. And as she savours the rich aromas that cling to her skin, for the first time since she planted them they bring her not comfort, but a dreadful premonition.

✠

It is some indeterminate time since the moon fell in on Nonsuch. It could be one minute; it could be one hundred years. Nicholas cannot be certain.

He is lying on the storeroom floor. Waves of pain ripple through his body. The stench of old straw and hawk-mute assaults his confused senses. He can see nothing. The darkness seeps into him, filling him from his extremities inwards, so that he doesn't know where the darkness ends and his skin begins. Is this how death comes stealing up? he wonders.

Then he hears the rasp of a bolt sliding home. It's followed by the agitated striking of a flint against steel. A thin glimmer of light appears, low down near the floor where he thinks the corner of the door might be.

With his sense of time fractured, he thinks the dawn must be breaking.

The light brightens – and the back of his throat catches the first sharp stab of smoke.

42

Young Tom Parker, Lord Lumley's apprentice falconer, wakes to the impression that someone's boot has just brushed the edge of his mattress.

He sits up, bracing himself for a cuff to the head for neglecting his duties. He should be in the mews, keeping watch over Lady Lumley's merlin, Salome. The hawk has recently fallen victim to sour crop. It needs a small medicinal feed every three hours. Falconer Hilliard has arranged a rota, and as usual Tom has drawn the night watch. Being the apprentice, he always draws the worst jobs – like scrubbing the mutes off the floor or disposing of the half-digested mouse carcasses when the birds are off their food. But it's cold in the mews tonight and Tom doesn't have a coat of feathers to keep him warm. A hearthside mattress in Master Sprint's kitchen is a far more agreeable spot in which to rest between visits.

Tom is not lazy. He did not mean to fall asleep. Indeed, until a couple of hours ago he'd hardly had the opportunity. Whenever anyone had entered the kitchens, the cry had gone up: 'Have you heard the news? Betony has spoken! Master Sprint heard her with his own ears!'

The details of exactly what Betony has spoken are still hazy. Tom has heard the most implausible stories: that the girl has admitted to being the daughter of a Spanish noble drowned with the Armada, and that she's wandered here from Devon where her father's galley was wrecked; that she's the love-child of the

Bishop of London; even that she's Lord Lumley's bastard daughter returned to the fold. With all this excitement going on, Tom Parker is surprised he's managed to shut his eyes at all.

He's already muttering a sleepy apology before he realizes falconer Hilliard is not standing over him, demanding to know why he's not at his post. Whoever's foot it was that woke him, it must have belonged to someone else.

Looking around in the hearth-light, he sees the kitchens are still, the scullions snoring peacefully nearby. The only movement is a fleeting shadow in the far corner, someone slipping out into the corridor beside the door to the buttery. Gathering his wits, Tom hurries out into the icy yard to bring Salome her medicine – just in time to see the fiery glow spreading at the far corner of the mews.

Close. Almost too close.

Nicholas stands precariously on the cobbles of the kitchen yard on legs that appear to belong to an infant who hasn't yet learned to walk. He takes great gulps of clean, cold pre-dawn air. Above his head the stars appear to dance in long silver ribbons. Tears stream down his cheeks from the acrid sting of the ash in his eyes.

And then everything becomes increasingly fractured and untrustworthy. He has but a blurred impression of John Lumley in his nightshirt, telling the assembled crowd that if King Henry's architects hadn't put a well and a hand-pump in the kitchen yard, this could all have ended very badly indeed. He catches the blur of Lizzy Lumley's face, pale and suspicious, as she asks what he's doing skulking around the mews at this time of the night. He sees indistinctly Gabriel Quigley staring at him, with even more loathing burned into his pocked face than before.

He captures only fragments of the walk back into the palace and what follows: Sprint's great arms supporting him... the icy splash of water against his skin and the smell of wild clary as one of the Nonsuch women bathes his eyes with a soothing tincture... someone easing him back against the comforting bolster of a bed and pulling the covers over his chest...

After that, nothing. Not even dreams.

It will take till mid-morning to entice Lord Lumley's peregrine, Paris, down from one of the Nonsuch minarets with the offer of a particularly bloody slice of beef. Even then he will sit reluctantly on Hilliard's glove and glare at poor Tom Parker, as if to say, *It's all your fault.*

The bird has the most powerful wings of all the Nonsuch hawks. If he hadn't been one of the first out of the mews when Tom opened the door, the apprentice swears he might never have heard the hammering of a fist against the storeroom door.

✠

The pale light of late afternoon spills over the casement like the dying flow of a dammed-up stream. Nicholas wakes, convinced his lungs are trying to claw their way out of his chest. When the retching subsides, the physician in him goes to work.

First he'll need the juice of purslain seeds. That will ease the burns in the throat. Then priest's pintle and hoarhound, to bring up whatever debris the smoke has carried into him. It's what he would have prescribed for the men he'd tended in the army of the Prince of Orange when they'd inhaled too much of the smoke of battle. There's bound to be a medicine chest somewhere in Nonsuch.

For the rest of it, including the drum-roll of pain when he touches the back of his head and feels the hardness of hair matted with dried blood, he wishes Bianca were here with her theriac. At least the wash of wild clary that the Nonsuch maids used to clean the soot from his eyes has done the trick: he can see well enough.

Not that Nicholas needs the faculty of sight to know that Nonsuch has suddenly become a very dangerous place for him. Whoever has tried to kill him is still at large. They might try again. He leans back against the bolster. His brow is clammy with sweat.

How can I have been so stupid? he asks himself. Why did I blunder into the mews, certain that Francis Deniker was no threat? He flails himself with recrimination. But then he thinks: I can't prove Deniker wrote the note. It could have been someone else entirely. An awful thought assails him: there's another at Nonsuch with a motive to silence me. What if the master of Nonsuch himself was behind the attempt on my life?

John Lumley might seem like a cultured man of learning, but Nicholas knows – from all Robert Cecil has told him – that in the past the courtier has gambled for very high stakes indeed. Perhaps the hand that wrote the words *I know who killed the maid's brother and the others* wasn't Francis Deniker's at all, but John Lumley's.

✠

Lumley is alone in his privy chamber when Nicholas is shown in. He sits in a high-backed chair by the fire, his mournful brows knitted in concentration. There's a slim leather-bound book open on his knees and a pair of spectacles perched on the bridge of his long nose. In his black gown he looks like a Northumbrian abbot in a wintry Lindisfarne cell.

'Marcus Aurelius, the *Meditations*,' he explains. 'Printed in Heidelberg. Greek into Latin. Not particularly accurately, I fear. I'm gladdened to see you alive, young man.'

'I was lucky, my lord,' Nicholas says, suddenly aware of a hoarseness in his voice.

Lumley waves the book at him as though it were evidence in a lawsuit.

'Aurelius tells us we are foolish to be surprised when bad things happen, or to weep when we suffer loss. He says it is wiser to expect these things and find the bravery to bear them. But as far as I can tell, he says nothing about going in search of them. I assume your presence in the mews at the dead of night was not happenstance, Dr Shelby? Or have you discovered a sudden unaccountable interest in falconry?'

'No, my lord.'

'Then what were you about, sirrah? You were somewhat incoherent when we found you.'

'I was there because of a note, my lord, apparently from Master Deniker. It was pushed under my door during the night.'

'This?' Lumley asks, taking a fragment of paper from the folds of the book. 'We found it in your chamber when we carried you there.'

One glance confirms it. 'Yes, my lord, this is the note. But the words on it are a lie. That's not why I was lured to the mews.'

'And the true reason is?' asks Lumley, frowning.

'Because last night someone panicked when I mentioned I'd seen the bodies washed up on Bankside, when I said I knew Elise Cullen's testimony to be true. That person decided the safety of their secret required my immediate death – however risky that might be.'

'Do you comprehend what you imply, Dr Shelby?'

'Yes, my lord,' says Nicholas firmly. 'It means someone here is involved in the killings. It must be Francis Deniker, Gabriel Quigley, Lady Elizabeth or *you*.'

Nicholas can scarcely believe what he's said. Barely hours

ago it would never have occurred to him. Can it possibly be? Is John Lumley – the patron of physic, the man of medicine, the collector of dangerous books – behind the drained and eviscerated carcasses washing up on Bankside? Is this dour, studious man sitting before him responsible for a series of ghastly pseudo-medical experiments carried out on the living? Has John Lumley killed, merely to satisfy his unbounded hunger for new knowledge?

For a long while Lumley says nothing. Then he slips the note back into the Aurelius. 'I can see now why Robert Cecil chose you, Dr Shelby. You have an inquisitor's tenacity about you.'

'I take not the slightest pleasure from it, my lord.'

'Yet you wish to add murderer to the list of accusations my enemies would hurl in my face.'

'Not unless I have to, my lord.'

Lumley's long, grey face colours with anger. 'Shelby, if I'd wanted you dead, it would have cost me less money than Lady Elizabeth makes me spend on firewood for a single hearth! I could have had you waylaid on the ride back to London. Why in the Lord's name would I make a confection of notes and assignations at the dead of night?'

'That's what I've asked myself several times, my lord.'

John Lumley slams his fist down on the Meditations. 'God's blood, Shelby! You have brought me pain indeed by coming here.'

Nicholas stands firm. 'Through no desire of my own, my lord. But I have found myself caught up in a tempest. And no matter how much I might wish it, I cannot stop the wind from howling.'

Lumley closes his eyes and exhales, purging himself of rage. He says, 'God has not yet made a storm that does not eventually abate, Dr Shelby.'

'Indeed so, my lord. But how many more innocents will have to die before this one does?'

With a weary shake of his head, Lumley says, 'At least one. We found Francis in his chamber this morning. It seems he didn't trust your assurances. He's hanged himself.'

43

Halfway down Black Bull Alley the front wall of the Magdalene almshouse sags out into the narrow street. An open sewer borders it like an insanitary moat. Bianca can smell the place from a hundred yards away. The front door is open. An old woman in a grubby, patched woollen kirtle sits on the step peeling vegetables with a blunt knife, her face raked with ancient furrows.

'Is the overseer here?' Bianca asks. 'I wish to speak to him.'

The woman looks up. One of her eyes is glazed milk-white. There's an abscess under the other the size of a half-angel coin. 'If he is, he'll be dead-drunk in his cot, snoring like a leviathan,' she says, glancing to the far end of the almshouse where the overseer's official dwelling spills out from the wall like a ruinous cattle byre. Bianca thanks her and leaves the old woman to her paring. When she reaches the place, she has to lean across the open drain to peer in through the tiny window. The squalid chamber is empty. On her return she asks the old woman, 'Do you know when he'll be back?'

'Who can say, duck?'

'Then can you tell me where he might be?'

'How should I know? Try the jumping-shop at the sign of the Blue Bear.'

'But surely his duties are here, with you?'

'Duties? He don't know the meanin' of the word. Sometimes he attends to them, sometimes he don't. Mostly he don't.' She carefully gathers the vegetable peelings from the step and drops them into a fold in her kirtle for later use.

'Then who looks after you?'

The woman laughs through her gums. 'Us Magdalenes know how to fend for ourselves, duck. Every now and awhile the parish sends a churchwarden to look us over. Couple of times a year a physician comes down to give us ease—'

'That's dreadful,' says Bianca with a guilty blush. While she's sent salves and balms to the Magdalene when she's been asked, she's never actually been inside.

'We manage,' the woman says contemptuously, and directs a gobbet of phlegm into the drain. 'Last time the pestilence came, they shut us away completely – for a fortnight. No food, no water, other than what we managed to save before they nailed up the door and painted a fucking great cross on it.'

'This physician – when did he last come?' asks Bianca, telling herself the question has nothing whatsoever to do with Katherine Vaesy.

'Not long ago. A few weeks – a few days. Once you've been in the Magdalene a while, time don't really work the same way it does for others.'

'Can you remember what he looked like?'

'Handsome enough, saving he looked more like a day-labourer than a quack. I had this elbow, see. Got a bit raw.'

Bianca squats down, heedless of the fact that the hem of her serge overgown is now firmly in the mire of the street. Looking through the open door, she gets a murky, insubstantial view of human bodies lying about listlessly in the fetid semi-darkness. She's almost grateful for the open drain between her and the old woman.

'He came with someone, I believe.'

'That he did.'

'A rich lady. A titled lady.'

The old woman shrugs as she slices at the vegetables. 'Aye, she's here every now and then.'

'So you've seen Lady Vaesy before?'

'Vaesy – is that her name?'

'Does she bring you charity?'

'Sometimes she brings charity, sometimes she brings us new friends.'

Bianca has to put a hand down to the earth to steady herself. 'She brings you *what*?'

'Friends, duck. Folks like us – down on their luck, troubled in the wits or the body. Must think we're some sort of midden: a place to dump God's cast-offs.'

In a moment of inspiration Bianca asks, 'Did she happen to bring a young girl and a boy – a crippled boy – sometime last summer?'

'Aye, I remember them. A sweet young thing she was.' She frowns as she searches her memory. 'Name began with an L—'

Bianca begins to rise to her feet, disappointed. Then it strikes her – this old crone can't read. 'Was her name *Elise*?'

'That's it – L for Elise,' says the old woman with a fond smile. 'And the poor little mite was called Richard, or Rolland, or something like that.'

'Ralph. His name was Ralph,' says Bianca, her heart beating fast. 'And can you recall if ever there was a young lad with a moon face, about fifteen – slow in the wits? His name would be Jacob.'

'Oh, I remember Jacob well enough, the poor little addle-pate.'

'How long was he here?' Bianca asks, remembering the long, desperate search Ned and his father had made for Jacob. 'It must have been about a month—'

'No! Three or four days at the most.'

'Are you sure?'

'I'm not entirely witless, duck. None of them she brings here stay long.'

'Do you know where they go when they leave?'

'No. They just go. The Magdalene ain't a prison, duck. We's all free subjects of our sovereign majesty here,' the woman says proudly, waving her paring knife at Bianca to make her point. 'If we want to up and leave, there's nothing to stop us – less you count the open road and likely starvation.'

✳

John Lumley's private chapel is a very different place in daylight. And it's a world away from Ned Monkton's grim vault at St Tom's. Not a shared coffin or a dirty winding sheet to be seen. But today it's still a place of death.

Deniker's corpse is laid out on a makeshift table, draped in a linen shroud. Lumley stands beside it in contemplation for a while. Then, defiantly, he makes the sign of the Cross over the body. 'You may as well know, Dr Shelby, that I intend to pray for the soul of Francis Deniker, whether the law permits it or not,' he says harshly, his eyes taking on a dull, watery sheen. 'Robert Cecil may call me a heretic if he wishes. My conscience and my heart are not his playthings.' He lays one palm against the side of Deniker's covered face. 'Poor, gentle Francis – that he should come to such an end,' he says. Then, to Nicholas: 'God's wounds, Shelby! I never knew a man bring more tumult in his wake than you.'

Somewhere in Nicholas's mind a dam breaks, releasing a torrent of helpless rage. How dare Lumley – rich and well connected enough to choose what faith he embraces, to indulge his curiosity with books that a lesser man would find himself in a cell for reading – blame him for any of this? Wasn't it Lumley who used his influence to procure Ralph Cullen's body for Fulke Vaesy to toy with, in the name of physic? Wasn't it Lumley who brought

Francis Deniker down from Durham, knowing full well what would happen to him if his true identity was discovered? What would he have had me do – look the other way? Pretend I never saw those wounds on the child's leg?

Lumley pulls aside the shroud. He stares into Deniker's face. He begins to quietly sob, the tears melting into his beard like hailstones on hot sand.

But Nicholas barely hears him. He's too busy cataloguing the telltale signs of Francis Deniker's struggle: the bruises on the forearms, the scratches around one eye, the nostrils clogged with dried blood, the tiny fragment of cloth stuck between two teeth like the remains of a hastily consumed meal – probably a scrap of pillow cover.

'I don't recall him having a wrestler's nose when he was in your privy chamber,' Nicholas says brutally. 'He's been smothered, probably by a pillow held down over his face. Look: the force has crushed the nasal bone and the septal cartilage.'

Lumley puts a fist between his own nostrils and his upper lip to staunch the sniffling. When he's composed himself he says, 'Smothered? I thought these hurts were caused when he was cut down and laid on the floor. Francis hanged himself – there was a written testament lying on his bed.'

'A suicide note?'

'Yes.'

'A suicide note from a Jesuit priest who presumably believed self-destruction was the fastest way to an eternity of sulphur and brimstone?'

'Dr Shelby, I can see the words he wrote seared into my mind every time I close my eyes. He sought your death because he feared you would betray him to the Privy Council.'

'Yesterday I assured everyone present in your privy chamber that I would not reveal what I witnessed there. I meant it.'

'Clearly not all of us believed you, Dr Shelby.'

'So, after much fervent prayer, Francis Deniker decided he couldn't carry the weight of all that sin and live? He must have been a busy man last night – plotting my murder, all that writing of notes.'

'Have a care for where you are, sirrah! Do you doubt the account?'

'Even the players at the Rose couldn't make a fiction like that convincing. This cord about his neck – it's the one he wore around his vestments yesterday, is it not?'

'I ordered it left in place, for when the coroner comes.'

'And what will you tell him – that your secretary hanged himself with a Romish trinket, after he'd tried to kill one of Robert Cecil's agents? Who, by the way, discovered him giving his master the papist Mass?'

'I'll take a leaf out of your book, Dr Shelby. I'll lie.'

Some blows, Nicholas thinks, have to be taken without flinching. He softens his tone. 'May I ask who found him?'

'His servant, at dawn. The door to his chamber was jammed by an overturned chair. We had to break in. He'd hanged himself from a beam.'

'Were you present?'

'No, but they called me at once.'

'So you saw him hanging?'

'Not exactly. I helped get him off the floor.'

Nicholas looks puzzled. 'The floor?'

'That's where he was found. Look at the cord, Dr Shelby. It must have held just long enough, then broken under his weight.'

Nicholas takes up the frayed end of the cord and inspects it more closely. He sees immediately how some of the strands have been cut through. He imagines the killer rolling Deniker's smothered body off his bed, wrapping the cord around his neck, pulling it tight, then picking away with the point of a blade until the material rips into a plausible tear.

A sudden jolt of dread courses through his body. 'Where is Elise? Has anyone seen her?'

'She's with Master Sprint in the kitchens, I think.'

'Are you certain? Have *you* seen her?'

'No, but Lizzy has.'

Nicholas has to fight the urge to seize Lumley by the collar of his gown and shake him. 'When? *When* did she see her?'

'Within the hour.'

'And Quigley?' asks Nicholas, the relief breaking in him like a wave.

'Quigley? What of him?'

'Where is he?' Nicholas's voice is raised almost to a shout. He suspects it's the first time a lord has been spoken to in such a manner by a humble Bankside dispenser of physic. But protocol is the last thing on his mind.

'On his way to London – to my house on Tower Hill,' Lumley replies passively.

'Did you send him? Or was it his idea?'

John Lumley's face pales as he realizes what Nicholas is implying. 'He was due to leave on the morrow—'

'And I suppose he suggested to you that he should leave early, report Deniker's death to the coroner on the way?'

'Dr Shelby, what are you suggesting: that Gabriel is behind this?'

'Francis Deniker didn't attempt to kill me. He wasn't the type. And he didn't kill himself. We both know that, my lord. I'm guessing Lady Lumley is not a practised murderer. So if it wasn't you, that only leaves Quigley.'

✠

By the time they reach the library all the strength seems to have flowed out of John Lumley. He's teetering like a frail old man. His hands shake as he lifts the latch.

Once inside the study, Nicholas sees the fire has been freshly built and candles lit for Lumley to take his habitual evening journey amongst the shelves. 'Forgive me,' he says, 'but I'm not well versed in the way of courtiers, my lord. I assume a man of your high position keeps records.'

'Records, Dr Shelby? What sort of records did you have in mind? I keep many private papers.'

'A journal of household business: what your servants do on your behalf, who they meet, where they go upon your commission – that sort of thing. A man of your rank would have to, wouldn't he, if only to provide an alibi when someone like Robert Cecil has him examined by the Privy Council?'

Lumley crosses to his desk. Beside his quills, inkwell and pounce-pot is a handsome leather-bound book, his business journal. 'If you're right, Dr Shelby – which I cannot accept – why did Gabriel not simply kill the child when she came into Nonsuch – remove the only living witness?'

'He didn't know who she was. And on Bankside, Elise never actually saw him. She told us so. Until yesterday, all Quigley knew was that she was a vagrant mute found under a hedge – until I persuaded her to tell her story.' The self-recrimination in Nicholas's voice is clear to both men.

'What do you want to know?' Lumley asks, unlocking his journal and opening the leather cover.

'Fulke Vaesy's dissection of Ralph Cullen took place on Lammas Day last year. Where was Quigley then?'

Lumley flicks through the pages until he finds what he's looking for. 'He was in London for me. He was meeting Signor Carrapelli, the agent of my Florentine bankers. He returned to

Nonsuch on' – his finger traces the entries – 'the twenty-ninth of July.'

'Just before Ralph Cullen was taken from the river.'

'It could be mere coincidence.'

'Try last Accession Day.'

Again John Lumley riffles through the journal. 'There you are, Dr Shelby – he was here, at Nonsuch, visiting my tenant farmers.'

'Try a few days before. Jacob Monkton had been in deep water awhile.'

Lumley flicks back a page or two. Just for a moment he closes his eyes. 'He was in London. Returned via Kingston on the sixteenth.'

'Jacob's body was taken from the river the next day.'

'But Gabriel goes often to the city, to my town house on Tower Hill – always on my commission,' Lumley protests. 'It means nothing.'

'What about the end of January this year? That's when the preacher was found.'

Reluctantly Lumley reads: 'January twenty-fourth. Rode in from London at four of the clock G.Q. with documents from Sir Joseph Laslet regarding the sale of my holdings in Sussex.'

'From London.'

'It's entirely circumstantial!'

'The Privy Council has hanged men for less circumstance than this.'

Lumley shakes his head. 'I cannot countenance what you are implying.' He's struggling to keep the growing despair out of his voice, and failing. 'Gabriel has been with me since he was a lad. I trust him implicitly – with my life, if necessary.'

'Face it, my lord: he's been in London around the time each body washed up on Bankside. If we take Elise's testimony as accurate, there have been at least six victims, including her brother. Then there's Father Deniker, the seventh – I think it's fair to count him amongst them. I would have been the eighth.'

'This *cannot* be, Dr Shelby—'

'When Quigley found out I'd seen some of the bodies, he panicked. In his extremity he came up with an insane idea to kill me and make it look as though Francis Deniker was to blame. You would have believed him, too – for all your enquiring mind.'

'Oh, merciful Jesu—'

'All this time I've been searching for a monster without a soul, an implacable creature I thought I couldn't even begin to touch,' Nicholas says, shaking his head in wonder. 'And he turns out to be just an angry little man with a pockmarked face who panicked the moment he thought he might be exposed. If he'd had a fraction of Francis Deniker's fortitude and courage, I'd still be looking for him.'

Lumley slowly closes his journal, like a man shutting away a life that's been lost to him. He goes to the window and stares out at the gathering darkness. Nicholas hears him mutter: 'Oh, Gabriel... *Gabriel...* what have you done?'

✣

The first thing that strikes Nicholas about Gabriel Quigley's chamber is the monkish austerity of it. Nothing on the walls, no personal items on the simple wooden chest beside the bed. It could be a cell. He can smell the man now: the flat odour of severity and denial, of plain wool and unyielding leather.

'How long has he lived in the household?' Nicholas asks. 'It looks as if he's barely been here.'

'Since he was a lad, apart from when he went to study medicine,' Lumley says bleakly.

'He's a *physician*?'

'When he was seventeen I paid for him to attend Oxford. But

he struggled, poor lad. In the end they rejected him. So no, Dr Shelby – Gabriel is not a physician.'

'But he has access to enough knowledge to think himself one, doesn't he? Enough to think he can use a scalpel.'

'I suppose so.'

'And after Oxford?'

'A couple of years studying law at Lincoln's Inn. Then he returned to Nonsuch and became my secretary. His failure weighed much on his mind – I know that. All he had ever wanted to do was match the promise of his brother, Mathew.'

Suddenly Nicholas is standing in the graveyard at Cheam church, that Sunday after the sermon. He's looking down at a eulogy carved into a headstone: *Mathew Quigley... Laid in earth 13th May 1572... No gentler man ever spilt his blood for Christ.*

Now the dates make sense to him.

'So Mathew Quigley was Gabriel's brother?'

'Yes – the older by a couple of years.'

'I saw the eulogy on his headstone in Cheam churchyard – but I couldn't work it out. "Spilt blood" – what does that mean? How did Mathew die?'

Lumley's eyes moisten. Nicholas thinks he's going to weep again. But he controls himself. 'Is it not a form of martyrdom to die so young? To be cut off with so much left to do, to leave behind only memories that bring everlasting pain to those who loved you? You would know about that – from what Sir Fulke Vaesy told me.'

'What does it mean? I need to know.'

'Mathew suffered from the Hebrew malady, Dr Shelby. I'm sure you're familiar with it. When he cut himself, he would bleed so profusely that the flow was almost unstoppable. It left him very weak and sorely troubled. In the end it killed him.'

A wave of ice-cold nausea sluices through Nicholas Shelby's

belly. 'Dear Jesu!' he whispers. 'Gabriel's killing them because he thinks he's going to find a cure!'

☩

Lumley shouts for a servant to bring an iron crow. Inside five minutes Nicholas is prizing the lock from the only secure hiding place in Quigley's chamber – a wooden chest beside the bed. Lumley doesn't attempt to stop him. The man once bold enough to politic with earls, to risk his very neck to strengthen a Catholic claim to the throne of England, now seems completely in thrall to a Suffolk yeoman's son with a crowbar.

Nicholas scatters Quigley's possessions across the floor, as though he means to cast away all trace of their owner. It's a pitifully meagre haul: a spare formal gown, some of Quigley's books from his days at Oxford – amongst them, Nicholas notes, Breferton's *Treatise into the ungovernable diseases of the blood.*

At the bottom of the chest Nicholas finds an almanac – is it for astrology, or to predict the tides at Bankside? – and a few sheets of parchment filled with incomprehensible notes laid into a diagonally drawn grid, all scribbled in a small, tight hand.

And then he lifts out a fragment of paper. It's about the size of a *primero* card. It looks as though it's been torn from a larger sheet. He holds it up to get a closer look. It's covered with what at first glance are random symbols and words:

… ♈ *3 qtr. moon… imperfect flow…* Ω *»Σ… dominant black bile… three onz. / one turn glass…* ♉ *new moon / mortem / three turns glass…*

John Lumley leans over his shoulder. 'What does it mean? It looks like an incantation. Is it a spell? Is it witchcraft?'

Nicholas reads again. And suddenly the meaning of the message takes on an awful clarity.

'The symbols are astrological,' he says.

'A horoscope?'

'Oh, it's much more than that. Look: there's Aries, and Libra... then the phase of the moon. That fixes the date on which the observations were recorded. The last line is the clearest. If I'm right, on the night of the new moon during the ascendancy of Taurus – sometime in late April, early May last year – it took three turns of the sandglass for one of Quigley's victims to bleed to death. Little Ralph Cullen – God save his soul – wasn't even the first.'

✠

In Lumley's privy chamber Lizzy sits as still as a statue, gripping her husband's hand for support. She is wondering if King Henry built Nonsuch strong enough to withstand the shocks it has endured of late. Nicholas watches them both, detached, like a passer-by at a funeral.

'It grieves me beyond sufferance, Mouse, but I cannot fault Dr Shelby's reasoning. I have been harbouring a monster at Nonsuch.'

'I always thought him a cold and secretive man, John. But this—'

'He never got over Mathew's death; I've always known that. But what terrible corruption in his soul made him take this course, only Satan himself knows.'

'Something Joanna told me this morning – it makes sense now.'

'Joanna?'

'She said Gabriel came to her in the small hours. He told her that you'd called for Elise. He said he was to bring her to you.'

'I never did such a thing, Mouse. We were together, you know it.'

'She sent him packing – told him if you needed her so urgently at such an hour, you should come yourself.'

'Why didn't you tell me?'

'Husband, have you quite forgotten the night's commotions? Besides, at the time it meant nothing to me.'

'But why would Quigley need to do her harm?' Lumley asks. 'He knows Elise can't identify him. She didn't see him. She said so in words he himself wrote down.'

'Because she *can* identify his accomplice – the woman who imprisoned her and her poor brother. She can identify Quigley's "angel".'

'So if Tom Parker hadn't managed to raise a cry, she might have suffered the same fate as the one intended for Dr Shelby,' Lumley says, appalled. 'Thank Jesu I have such contrary servants.'

'What will happen to Gabriel now, Husband?'

'I don't know, Mouse. I can't imagine the Queen's Bench will ever have tried such a case before.'

'I know exactly what will happen,' says Nicholas, remembering his footsore days trying to get the authorities to take an interest. 'Absolutely nothing. He'll use a lawyer's defence: Prove it.'

'But that fragment of parchment you found—?'

'He could claim they're observations of just about anything – the amount of water the shrubs in the privy garden need,' Nicholas says cynically.

'But I can bring the case to the ear of Sir John Popham, the Attorney General, if needs be.'

'Do you remember, my lord, when Quigley advised you against placing Elise before a court? Well, he was right. With my history, I'm an unreliable witness. Bianca Merton has been accused of heresy and witchcraft. Elise Cullen is the bastard child of a Bankside bawd. Do I need to continue?'

'You must ride to Tower Hill and confront him, John,' Lizzy orders.

'He hasn't gone to Tower Hill, madam,' says Nicholas. 'He knows I'm alive. He'll be wondering how long it will take for your husband to accept the truth of what I've told him. He's probably already on his way to the coast. He'll cross over the Narrow Sea and start again. They'll find the next corpse in Bruges or Rotterdam.'

Silence, while the pale walls of Nonsuch wait patiently for the next assault.

'Kat will be quite undone if she learns of this,' Lizzy says. 'It will destroy her. You know how much she loves him.'

'Kat?' echoes Nicholas. 'Are you telling me Quigley had a wife?'

'*Jesu*, no,' says Lumley with a grim laugh. 'Even I'm not so blind as to think Gabriel's heart had space for such affections.'

'Then who's Kat?'

'Katherine Warren,' says Lumley, his grey eyes misting over with old memories. 'Blessed with an angel's beauty – that's what we all used to say of Kat. She was a young maid sent to my late wife by her father, to learn a woman's duties in a great household. She fell in love with Mathew – would have married him. Nothing would have pleased us more.'

'*Would* have married? What happened?'

'Her father forbade the match, because of Mathew's sickness.' Lumley pauses, a foolish look on his face as if he's realized he's telling a story Nicholas has heard before. 'But of course you probably already know her, Dr Shelby. Kat Warren is now Lady Katherine Vaesy.'

44

At Vauxhall pale shafts of evening light cut through the mist rolling off the river. Kat Vaesy pulls her gown tighter against her body as she walks. Lost in thought, she barely notices the figure in a mud-stained riding cloak hurrying towards her from the house. When he calls to her harshly, she fears for a moment it's Fulke. But this man is much leaner, there's no bombast to his gait. And then she sees his face – and knows this is something far, far worse than any unannounced visit from her husband.

'I *had* to see you, Kat,' Gabriel Quigley says, seizing her arm.

'Gabriel, let go, you're hurting me!' Kat demands, unnerved by the intensity in Quigley's eyes. 'Why have you come here? We agreed never to—'

'The vagrant child you took up from the Effra ford last summer,' he says, interrupting her, 'the crippled boy—'

'What of him?'

'Did he have a sister?'

'Yes, of course he did. I left her for you at the Lazar House, with the others.'

'Well, I never saw her there. And now she's at Nonsuch. We are discovered!'

'At Nonsuch? How can she be? I ensured she was tranquil before I left. All you had to do was take her—'

'She's told Lord Lumley everything. It's only a matter of time...'

Kat Vaesy takes Quigley by the shoulders of his riding cloak and – though she loves him for being Mathew's brother – shakes him, like the little boy she has always suspected him to be. 'Gabriel, the child cannot be at Nonsuch. The child is dead. Afterwards, you put her in the river with the others. *Didn't you?*'

✠

'It was the summer before my first confinement in the Tower, Dr Shelby,' Lumley tells Nicholas solemnly. 'I'd returned from London to find Nonsuch in a state of great joy and celebration. Jane met me at the gatehouse. She told me Kat Warren and Mathew were to be wed. I couldn't have been happier for them.'

'And then Katherine's father got in the way?' Nicholas says.

'Aye. He could not be moved by their love, or by my attempts to intercede on their behalf. I tried to reason with him. But a father's governance is sacrosanct, is it not? That's what God has ordained. And to be blunt, Mathew's future was indeed bleak.'

'So she married Vaesy instead.'

'There was twenty years between them. I suggested a delay, until Kat was a little older. I hoped a postponement might cause Fulke to look elsewhere. But John Warren said he didn't want his daughter sitting in a bower all day plucking forget-me-nots and moping over lost love, not when she could be bearing sons.'

Lizzy gently rests her fingertips on her husband's arm. 'John, there was something Kat said to me at Cold Oak, when we last dined together – something about never letting Fulke Vaesy near me, if I should' – she pauses to glance at Nicholas, colouring at the thought of revealing intimacies to a near-stranger – 'if I should find myself bearing your child. What did she mean by that?'

Lumley stares at his feet and slowly shakes his head. 'After the marriage, Kat soon fell with child. At the birth Vaesy intervened. Something went wrong – he never told me what.'

'I know she lost the infant. I know she almost died,' Lizzy says. 'But I didn't know it was Fulke's fault.'

Lumley seizes a fistful of his beard as though he intends to rip it from his flesh in a gesture of atonement. 'Vaesy was my physician then,' he says. 'He was also my friend. I hold myself partly to blame. I should have tried harder to persuade John Warren to listen to his daughter.'

Lizzy waits for him to look up. Then she says, 'Fulke Vaesy's actions were his own, Husband, not yours. You were not culpable.'

'But I could have stopped all this, a long time ago – if I'd understood,' he says bleakly, looking around the privy chamber as though it's suddenly become a prison cell. He puts his head in his hands and whispers, 'Not dearest Kat as well – not the two of them together. Does this nightmare have no end?'

✣

In the darkening orchard the mist is spreading like the creeping fingers of a ghostly hand. 'Merciful Jesu, how did you let this happen?' whispers Kat Vaesy into the shadows.

Quigley is unsure if Kat is addressing him or the spirit of his brother. 'I'll find another way to silence Shelby and the child, I promise you,' he assures her.

'How?'

'When he returns to Bankside. I'll pay someone to stage a quarrel, or a robbery. That's easy enough to arrange in Southwark.'

'And the maid?'

'I'll try to think of an enterprise to get her away from Nonsuch. But she's not the immediate danger. After all, she's a whore's daughter – who will believe a word that comes out of her mouth? We'll say the Devil has put a vile mischief into her heart.'

'That still leaves John Lumley,' says Kat. 'I'm loath to do it, but there's no alternative. I'll have to denounce him to the Privy Council – anonymously, of course. I'll claim he's plotting an act of treason. He'll be too busy defending himself from a cell in the Tower to interfere. It's a shame, of course – I've always admired him.'

Quigley has to lean against a tree to steady himself. He can't believe what he's just heard. 'But Lord Lumley has been your friend and champion for some twenty years! And what of Lady Elizabeth – your friend?'

'Oh, Gabriel, do you still not understand? If some hard things must be done to honour Mathew's memory, then they must be done without flinching. Did you not fortify yourself with that thought, every time you pressed home the scalpel blade? Or were you only ever doing this for the sport of it?'

The accusation stings. Quigley shakes his head violently, as though he's trying to throw off the memory of Ralph Cullen, Jacob Monkton and the others. 'Perhaps we should lie low for a while. Or we could go out of England, into France or Holland, continue our work there. Europe is more open to new science.'

'We don't have time, Gabriel. We've come so far. We're so very close. We cannot let these people stop us.' Kat's face is as close to his as a lover's. 'Imagine it: you and me – revealing to the great scholars of Europe's universities the true wellspring of the blood. How it is *really* propelled through the veins and the arteries. How it nourishes the organs. Where it goes when it has worked its miracle.' Her voice becomes soft, urgent, enticing him with its promise. 'You and I will overturn a thousand years of medicine! Think how foolish my husband and the rest of them will look – these masters of physic who have only ever studied a dead criminal, or cut open some poor stray dog.' She searches Quigley's eyes for the resolve she used to see in Mathew's. 'Don't you remember what he used to say to us when we doubted?'

'I hear it every time I close my eyes to sleep. *Sapere aude* – dare to know.'

'Then you know we owe it to Mathew to go on. It's all been for Mathew!'

Quigley is spellbound. He stares into Kat's face with open adoration – not secretly, the way he's done for twenty years, always hoping she'd return his gaze the way she'd returned his brother's.

'Gabriel,' she says, her voice an urgent caress, 'is there anyone else who knows? Anyone?'

And then he remembers.

'Shelby spoke of a woman – she owns a tavern on Bankside. I believe they are close... very close.'

✠

I have found myself caught up in a tempest... no matter how much I might wish it, I cannot stop the wind from howling...

It's howling now, inside Nicholas's head. He lies in his chamber at Nonsuch trying to seize hold of the swirling memories of the past forty-eight hours. But like all things storm-blown, they're almost impossible to chase down and catch.

He pictures Elise Cullen as she describes the horror she's witnessed. He sees John Lumley weeping over Francis Deniker's body in the chapel. He sees him again in his study, journal in hand as he tries to deny the truth that's in plain sight. He sees Elizabeth Lumley's despair as she finally accepts the truth about Katherine Vaesy. And, worse, he imagines Gabriel Quigley still at large, somewhere beyond his reach, preparing once more some helpless victim for his knife. Unable to sleep, Nicholas wishes he could catch these swirling thoughts and lock them away somewhere they cannot harm him – as Francis Deniker hid his heretical trinkets in a travelling chest with a good, solid lock on it.

And then John Lumley's voice says softly in his ear: *God has not yet made a storm that does not eventually abate, Dr Shelby.*

And Nicholas – to his astonishment – discovers he's right. The tempest stops howling. The competing thoughts in his head stop spinning. The chamber becomes utterly still, not even the trembling of Henry's great clock troubling the night air.

One of these swirling images has given Nicholas the answer he's been searching for. Throwing back the covers, he dresses hurriedly and sets off to rouse the master of Nonsuch, quite uncaring of the hour.

45

An hour before sunrise. Rush torches flare in the inner courtyard. Sleepy-eyed grooms check saddles and girth-straps, preparing the four horses for the fast ride to Richmond. From there it will be onwards by river to the city. Two servants, armed against cut-purses, have been sent ahead to wake the watermen.

Nicholas settles himself into the saddle. He's wrapped against the pre-dawn chill in one of Lumley's fur-lined riding cloaks. He leans forward and runs a hand along the palfrey's neck, wondering quite who he's trying to comfort: the horse or himself.

Lizzy reaches up to take her husband's hand. Lumley leans down from the saddle and kisses her fingers. When the intimacy is over, Lizzy turns to Nicholas. 'I still say this is madness, Dr Shelby. You could be delivering my husband into the hands of his enemies. Carry this knowledge with you – I will take pains to destroy you, if you do.'

'In which case, madam, I will deserve it,' says Nicholas.

Lizzy shakes her head. 'To be honest, sirrah, I know not whether to count you amongst the saints or the sinners. If the plague comes again in the summer, I wouldn't be surprised if it has the name of Nicholas Shelby scratched into its scales.'

The little party rides out of Nonsuch as the pale arc of dawn turns the trees on the eastern edge of the park into a spidery weave of black branches. Nicholas has tested his plan against all manner of catastrophes. He tells himself there's no more he can do, that it's futile to keep weighing the morality of the idea that came to him just at the moment when his thoughts were at their darkest. He's resolved now.

He can think of no other way to stop Gabriel Quigley and Kat Vaesy, no other means of bringing them to justice. Fulke Vaesy wouldn't listen. The Queen's Coroner wouldn't listen. The parish authorities and the Church wouldn't listen. It's too late for pleading. Now there's no more time left.

This is the only way to be sure, he tells himself. And he must thank Francis Deniker for revealing it to him – even if it is from beyond the grave. Even if it proves what Quigley said in the gallery of the Nonsuch chapel was the truth: that Nicholas Shelby is not the physician, he's the disease.

Slowly, magnificent Nonsuch fades behind them, a place of myth, unable to endure long against the violence of the real world. Soon it's vanished from sight. 'I pray you're right, Nicholas,' says Lumley to a chorus of screeching rooks. 'Not so much for myself, but to stop them from further devilry.' Then, remembering the love he'd once borne for Gabriel and Kat, he adds, 'No, not devils – but good souls led astray. I know they have sinned mightily, but the price they shall pay will be a heavy one indeed.'

But Nicholas doesn't feel like soothing Lumley's conscience for him.

'They didn't stray, my lord. They're not leash-hounds who've caught a scent and gone deaf to the call; they chose this path of their own free will. They knew what they were about. They made a mockery of the eulogy on Mathew Quigley's grave.'

As they splash cross the Pyl ford, Lumley calls back to one of the two servants riding close behind, 'Careful, Adam – according to Dr Shelby, you're bearing the means of my deliverance. I don't want it dropped in the mud.'

✠

In the taproom, Rose believes her mistress is labouring over the tavern's accounts. Ned Monkton worries she might be crafting a spell. Some of the customers fear she's drawing up their reckonings. In truth, Bianca is planning her letter to Nicholas. She thinks, *if he won't write, then I will* – and, mercy, how my news will stop him in his tracks.

She taps one index finger on the paper to marshal her thoughts. *Tap*: Katherine Vaesy is harvesting victims for the killer. *Tap*: Maybe Katherine Vaesy *is* the killer. *Tap*: Fulke Vaesy – be he cousin, brother, husband or any other form of male irritant, is an eminent man of medicine. *Tap*: John Lumley is an eminent man of medicine. *Tap*: Nicholas is closer to the killer than he knows. *Tap... tap... tap...*

Where does this harvest of souls go when it leaves the Magdalene? she wonders. Because the Magdalene is not a prison. The old woman with the eye and the elbow has told her so. Even if the alternative *is* starvation, the Magdalenes are always at liberty to leave.

To the Lazar House, then? In which case, Nicholas is right. She can hear his familiar soft Suffolk burr: *How could we have been so blind? He's been doing it right under our noses!*

The rhythm of her tapping falters. Rose looks over from where she's been making moonbeam faces at Ned Monkton. 'Anything the matter, Mistress?'

'Nothing, Rose. It's nothing.'

Ned and Rose are getting on like a house on fire, she thinks. They're suited: Ned, who spends his day amongst the dead; Rose with her worrying interest in torture. Ghoulish, admittedly – but then what was it her mother used to say? There's always someone for someone.

She remembers when the English merchants visiting her father's house in Padua had started taking more than a passing interest in her. Her mother had warned her somewhat brutally, 'Cardinal or carpenter, bare-chin or greybeard, all they really want is to tup you till you've given them an heir, then have you cook them fishcakes for the rest of your days. They're all the same.'

'But what about Papa?' Bianca had protested.

'Ah, your father – he's different.'

'How so?'

'He doesn't like fish.'

Bianca smiles at the memory. Even now she doesn't know if her mother was joking. She turns her thoughts back to the letter. When it's written, she'll do what Nicholas did: have Timothy take it to Lord Lumley's town house near Tower Hill. Hopefully it will find its way to Nonsuch. She wonders what he'll make of Lady Katherine Vaesy then.

'Mistress, Mistress!'

Bianca looks up to see Timothy standing over her, his face flushed.

'Whatever's the matter? You sound as though the Spanish have landed.'

'There's a fellow outside, from the Magdalene almshouse,' Timothy tells her, carried away by the drama of the call. 'Says he's heard your physic is the best on Bankside.'

'And so it is, Timothy. If I say so myself. What does he want?'

'There's a woman – sick almost to death. He says, will you come?'

'It's not the warder, is it: the one we threw out?'

'No, Mistress. This one's got a face full of pox scars.'

She wants to say, tell him to try the jumping-shop at the sign of the Blue Bear – that's where the old woman who peels vegetables for her friends that the rest of the world has forgotten says he's usually to be found. But then she recalls the sense of shame she'd felt when she'd realized she'd never once stopped by in person to help.

'I'll go with you,' says Ned Monkton, laying down his ale. 'Master Nicholas would wish it.'

She thinks about it. She really does think about it. But I'm a healthy, strong young woman, she tells herself. I don't fit the pattern. What happened to Ralph Cullen and Jacob Monkton happened *after* they left the Magdalene. And I'm Veneto-born and bred; not some simpering, pasty, over-jewelled English buttercup. Besides, if Lady Katherine Vaesy is there, at least I'll have a face to point out to the constable when the time comes. But what really makes up her mind is this: why should she accept a guard dog just because Nicholas Shelby, who can't be bothered to write, wishes it?

She goes to the parlour for the bag of balms and ointments she keeps for emergencies. She slips in a small knife, just to be on the safe side.

'Stay here, Ned,' she says. 'I'll go on my own. You keep an eye on Mistress Moonbeam here.'

46

The wherry drops them at the Cecils' private water-stairs. At the Covent Garden house they're told Lord Burghley is at Whitehall. A brisk walk past Henry's old tilting ground takes them beneath the Holbein gatehouse and into the vast jumble of grand houses, government offices, gardens and chapels that's grown up around the spot where Edward the Confessor first raised his royal palace on the banks of the Tyburn. Somewhere inside this maze is the human incarnation of England's majesty. Everywhere there are guards, to ensure she doesn't end up like poor Prince William of Orange, shot by an assassin with a wheel-lock pistol in his own home. To carry a firing piece anywhere inside the palace boundary is now an act of treason. Nicholas and John Lumley find their way barred by two bearded halberdiers in full plate.

'Please be so good as to have your servant open that box, my lord,' says one of them.

Lumley signals for the servant Adam to open the pine chest he's carrying. Nicholas's heart starts rat-tat-tatting like a tambour in a parade.

'Samples of chamber hangings, sirrah,' says Lumley with an understanding smile that's meant to show he appreciates the difficulties a guard must face, when so many men of note pass through his gate every day. 'My lord Burghley much admired the ones in his room at Nonsuch when he came there last with our sovereign lady. I promised to bring him some samples from the weaver. Show the sergeant, Adam.'

The guard, who's heard only the words 'Burghley' and 'our sovereign lady', takes a cursory look inside the chest and signals his mate to stand aside.

✠

They track down Burghley and his entourage to a row of chambers next to the Court of Requests. Even then their quarry proves elusive. 'His Grace is presently in discourse with members of the Privy Council, my lord,' says an unforgiving face whose tone reminds Nicholas of an examination of competence before the College of Physicians: *What ancient scholars have you studied?... Quote from them, in defence of your treatment for choler... What does Brasbridge have to say on the subject of serpiginous ulcers?* He certainly has the same butterflies in his stomach.

'I really do think my lord Burghley will wish to see me, no matter how pressing the discourse,' says Lumley, with a courage Nicholas can only admire.

'And why would that be, my lord?' asks the unforgiving face.

'Why don't *you* tell him, Nicholas?' says Lumley generously.

So, taking his cue from the surroundings, Nicholas does. He whispers his poison into the man's ear, in the best tradition of a practised courtier.

✠

Burghley is old and tired. The marrow in his bones aches at the slightest whiff of treason and sedition. How did it happen, he wonders – how did my lifelong service to my sovereign turn the birdsong outside my window into a never-ending warning?

These days he can't sleep much beyond a couple of hours at a stretch. His mind brims with fear for the future. His greatest dread is that one simple act of inattention – perhaps the churchwarden in some remote village failing to notice that one of his flock has suddenly started avoiding sermon on a Sunday – may lead to an English traitor taking the road to London. It's happened before. All it takes is a head full of the Pope's edict that killing your queen is no crime, because she's a declared heretic – and a pistol in the saddlebag.

So when four men – one of whom he recognizes as his son's nemesis, John Lumley – are ushered into his presence, following the uttering of the dread word 'treason', Lord Treasurer Burghley fears the worst.

'A Jesuit – in hiding at Nonsuch!' he exclaims when Lumley has delivered the news. He could be speaking of some particularly lethal species of serpent.

'An agent of the Pope, Your Grace. A deceiver,' Lumley says without the slightest trace of theatricality. 'Though I've known him for many years, he was able to hide his infamy even from me. Had I even the slightest suspicion, I would have denounced him instantly.' He turns to Nicholas. 'Perhaps you know Dr Nicholas Shelby – I understand your son Robert employs him on matters of extreme sensitivity. Nicholas, show His Grace what we discovered.'

Like a street entertainer performing a trick, Nicholas slowly withdraws Francis Deniker's vestments from the pine chest now lying open on Burghley's desk. He lays them out carefully for the Lord Treasurer to inspect. The crosses of gold thread and the jewels sewn into the heavy damask gleam like beacons lit to warn of an approaching enemy. Next, he takes the altar stone from its cloth wrapping and sets it down. He pulls back the covering from the chalice and places the gleaming silver bowl on the altar stone. All that's missing is the sound of a celestial choir singing the Benedictus. He glances at Lumley's long face. There's not a flicker of emotion on it, though what it's costing him to see the symbols of his faith used in such a manner, he can't begin to imagine.

Burghley stands up with surprising speed for such a stately old man. For one extraordinary moment, Nicholas fears the octogenarian Lord Treasurer is about to jump onto his chair like a parlour maid surprised by a mouse.

'Merciful Jesu!' he cries. 'The whole heretical set!'

'And hidden in the bosom of my household!' agrees Lumley, allowing his Northumbrian burr free rein to show what a simple, straight-dealing fellow he really is. 'I can only reproach myself for not having uncovered this heresy earlier.'

'And you knew nought of this deception?' Burghley asks, a last bubble of suspicion lingering on the surface of his revulsion.

'Nothing at all, Your Grace,' says Lumley sadly. 'I freely admit I have always been a church Catholic – but, as the law demands, I observe all that is asked of me by the new faith. I pay my recusancy fines. The queen herself knows it. But a hider of Jesuits, *never*. I would defend her faith to the death.'

Nicholas has the urge to applaud. Lumley has performed his part almost exactly as he's been coached.

'Do you have the rogue under guard, my lord?' asks Burghley.

'Sadly, no.'

'He's at large?'

'I fear so, Your Grace.' Lumley constrains himself to merely the barest wince. 'When Dr Shelby tried to take him, his violence knew no bounds. He killed my clerk, poor Master Deniker. Dr Shelby here was lucky to escape with his life. Show him, Nicholas—'

Nicholas turns his head to reveal the still-healing wound that he sustained in the Nonsuch mews.

'He must be hunted down without delay, without mercy!' says Burghley, calling for pen and paper so that he might draft the order. 'Does this agent of the Antichrist have a name?'

For the first time since they arrived at Whitehall, Nicholas detects a tremor of doubt in Lumley's voice, as if he's only now begun to comprehend how this will end for the man he once held so close in his affections. 'Indeed he does, Your Grace,' Lumley says slowly, regretfully. 'His name is Gabriel Quigley.'

✠

Black Bull Alley is empty when Bianca reaches the Magdalene. But she feels no alarm. If Katherine Vaesy is here, she can know nothing of what Bianca has discovered. Nevertheless, she's caught off-guard when the door is opened by a well-dressed but brittle-faced woman in her late thirties, wearing a smart winter gown of russell worsted. Can this be her: the woman who was all over Nicholas like a rash of the buboes?

'Mistress Merton – from the Jackdaw?' enquires the woman, peering past Bianca into the lane to see if she's brought company.

'Yes. And who are you?'

'Mistress Warren. I was passing by when I found the poor woman lying close to death on the doorstep. I had no idea what manner of place this was, but they told me you were skilled in apothecary. Come in – quickly.'

Her mind set at ease, Bianca ducks below the sagging lintel.

She finds herself in a press of hot, unwashed bodies. Fingers prod her skin. Stroke her gown. Tug at her hair, as if she's one of those exotic creatures that princes keep in their menageries. She recoils from the stench of sweat, rancid food and those human emanations that come with the flux. In the half-light from a small, high window all she can see is a moving huddle of rags and grey human limbs that look as though they belong to the already dead. And watching, while they mob her, is a man with a face like pitted slate.

'Come to join us, Mistress Purity?' calls one of the inmates in a voice harsh and throaty. 'We's all friends here!'

'I know *her* – she was here asking questions a while ago,' says the vegetable woman, the only remotely familiar face in the entire place.

'Come to rob us, more like!' shouts another voice.

'Quick, Gondall, hit her with your piss-pot!'

'I can't – it's been made away with,' cries the woman Gondall.

'The thief's stolen Gondall's piss-pot!' shrieks someone else.

'Mercy, it's not a thief,' says the first woman. 'It's the Virgin Mary come to wash away all our sins.'

'It shocked me too, at first,' says the woman who calls herself Mistress Warren, as she eases Bianca onto a small bench beneath a high casement that lets in minimal light. 'We shouldn't blame them. They're as deserving of God's love as the mightiest in the land.'

'Here, have some of this. It'll calm the nerves,' says the man with the pumice face, offering Bianca a clay jug. His mouth is a little too close to her ear for comfort. 'Not as fine as the Jackdaw's, I'm sure. But it will serve.'

Bianca takes a mouthful. It tastes unusual, but not at all unpleasant. It's sweet – refreshing. She takes another gulp. Then a few more, until her heart stops pounding.

'That's it – don't stop. It'll fortify you,' the woman says, smiling.

'No, really, I'm fine,' says Bianca, not wanting to appear like a wilting flower in the presence of such suffering.

'You'll feel better for it, I promise you,' says the woman kindly. 'I was the same the first time I came here.'

It's as though someone has slapped her. Bianca thrusts the jug at the woman. 'The first time? But you said just now you'd no idea what manner of place—'

'Drink,' snaps the woman in an altogether harsher tone than Bianca feels is called for.

And then – somehow without her noticing – the man has pinioned her arms. Her bag of balms and ointments falls to the floor. It's quickly snatched away by the woman called Gondall.

Mistress Warren pulls Bianca's head back by the hair. She starts pouring the liquid directly into Bianca's open, protesting mouth. Bianca slams her jaw shut. But the ale flows into her nostrils. She can't breathe. She can't stop her mouth from gaping open.

Her last clear sight, before her vision begins to blur, is of the inmate Gondall waving the balm bag to and fro – as if to say: who has your knife now, fool?

✠

Burghley is the most influential man in the realm, yet it takes even his great engine of power a while to lurch into motion.

The other members of the Privy Council present at the interrupted conference must be summoned: Hunsdon, the queen's chamberlain; Lord Howard of Effingham, her Lord High Admiral; Francis Knollys, the Puritan scourge of heretics everywhere, who appears sniffing like a deer-hound tracking a scent. Five minutes later the young Earl of Essex sweeps in on a tide of gloriously clad acolytes. They wear his tangerine ribbons on the tops of their boots and their beards are oiled and primped. They deliver the noble earl to Burghley's table and sweep out again, like a wave casting up a pearl on a beach.

The last to arrive is Robert Cecil. He comes in wearing a black silk gown and his boots crackle against the flagstones, reminding Nicholas of a cockroach scuttling over a kitchen floor. He glares impotently at John Lumley, like a schoolboy who's had his nose tweaked by his teacher. He does not acknowledge Nicholas.

But Nicholas has his own thoughts to keep himself occupied, thoughts that have been troubling him throughout the journey here; thoughts such as: does a new lock on an old door mean anything at all? And did I – or did I not – mention Bianca Merton's name when I told Gabriel Quigley I'd seen the bodies?

✠

She's in the open air. But where? And when?

The visions come to Bianca in waves: brilliant hallucinations at the crest, moments of near-lucidity in the troughs.

On one of the crests she's in the garden of her parents' house in Padua, bathed in eye-straining sunlight that makes everything around her twice as sharp as usual. She can hear the sounds of chickens pecking in the dirt. She can hear her mother telling her how to mix a draught to make your enemy do your bidding: *This much of hellebore root... lide-lilly for a pleasant smell... This many seeds of black henbane... and if still they persecute you, hemlock... until it rids you of their troublesome presence entirely...*

But she cannot be in Padua. Though there's sunlight, the air here is too cold. And it cannot be her mother speaking. Her mother is buried in the plot beside the old church on the hill, the plot that Father Rossi tends so lovingly – though he must be ninety now, if he's a day, and can barely lift the rake.

Once, aged nine, she'd dipped a finger in a concoction her mother had been mixing and lifted it to her lips. Her current fantasy had been that of a spurned lover determined upon death; she'd wanted to know what poison tastes like. Her mother had beaten her mercilessly – out of love, of course.

Now, in a brief interlude of clarity, she realizes what the man with the ruined face and the woman who seems to direct him have done to her. She knows what was in the liquid they forced her to drink. She knows also that she's standing in the wilderness surrounding the Lazar House, staring up at its forbidding walls.

How did I get here? she asks. There must be some passage-way or door, between the Magdalene and the Lazar House grounds, though she can't remember passing through one. 'Look, Nicholas,' she says out loud, her voice slurred, 'that's how they bring them here. In through the almshouse, out through the culvert and into the river. See? It's obvious now.' She's elated at having shown him a truth he'd been unable to find for himself. 'Didn't think of that, did you? – Master Nicholas Shelby, the oh-so-clever physician who lives in a palace and doesn't write. Hurry back, because soon it will be your turn to fish *me* out of the river. Only this time, you'll need more than theriac to cure me.'

And just before the next approaching wave of hallucinations breaks over her, the spinning of the world slows. The blurred earth comes again into sharp focus, its patterns once more familiar.

There – just a few yards ahead, slightly to the left! Is that what I think it is? Yes! Mother, let me lick my fingers, just this once – so I'll know for sure.

Bianca takes her chance. She breaks free from the man with the damaged face who is guiding her, but is not Nicholas. She runs as fast as she can – though she knows full well there's nowhere to escape to. He's not expecting her break for freedom and she manages to put a little distance between them. But there's no strength in her legs. She falls, sprawling headlong in the undergrowth.

But it's enough. She's made it. All she has to do now is hope they haven't understood. For a moment she just lies there, with slow, quiet sobs of relief racking her body, while her hands claw frantically at the decaying scrub around her as if she's trying to fashion herself a nest. When the man reaches her, she lashes out with her feet – not so much as to hurt him as to buy herself more time.

'Take care,' says Kat Vaesy gently into her left ear, arriving to help Quigley pin her to the ground. 'You don't want to harm yourself. Come, Mistress Merton – we have work to do.'

47

Having set a match to the powder trail, Nicholas discovers the resulting explosion doesn't go quite where he'd anticipated.

When he attempts to raise the matter of the Lazar House, not one head turns in his direction. It's as if men of this rarefied elevation have too much of their own sun in their eyes to see his sort. Hunsdon wants to send word to the ports and harbours to shut up the exits. Knollys wants to arrest every recusant in the land, just to be on the safe side. Essex wants to go to the queen and get put in charge of everything.

So Nicholas gets Lumley to intercede.

'My lords, Dr Shelby here has a view on where Quigley may seek refuge.'

The grand heads finally turn.

'I believe he sometimes uses the empty Lazar House on Bankside,' Nicholas says, his mouth suddenly tinder-dry. He adds for effect, 'It would be the ideal place for him to hold secret Masses.'

'In addition,' adds Lumley, setting his jaw against what he must say next, 'I would recommend someone rides to Cold Oak manor at Vauxhall. Lady Katherine Vaesy may well be harbouring him. She's an associate.'

'They can arrest that charlatan of her husband while they're about it,' grunts Knollys. 'Never did trust the fellow. Wouldn't let him physic a lame horse.'

Burghley nods his assent.

After that, Nicholas knows the powder blast will go where he intends. If Quigley is taken, he can protest that he's not a Jesuit until he's blue in the face. Denounced by Lumley, and with the contents of Francis Deniker's pine box for evidence, these men will not hesitate to deliver him to the mercies of one Master Richard Topcliffe.

The very thought of the man makes the hairs on the back of Nicholas's neck lift. When he was young, his mother would invoke the threat of Topcliffe whenever she wanted to frighten him into good behaviour. The boys in his class at petty school called their most feared teacher Topcliffe.

Richard Topcliffe – the man who will happily apply more than enough bone-breaking pressure to Gabriel Quigley's limbs for him to confess to whatever it is Knollys and the rest of them desire. Richard Topcliffe – the Privy Council's tame tormenter of the ungodly and the treasonous; the queen's gentleman tortur-er-in-chief. Once delivered into his clutches, Quigley can howl that he's only a harmless murderer until his screams beat against the walls of his cell like the clapper of the bell of doom. But the pain won't stop until Topcliffe hears the words 'I willingly con-fess to treason'.

After that, there will be no more eviscerated bodies troubling the wherry passengers of Bankside.

✠

They have brought her to a room high up in the eaves – a dark, dusty place with a small grimy window she can't see out of. They have chained her by one ankle. She can't move more than a short distance in any direction. Through some warped sense of com-passion, they've let her lie on one of half a dozen filthy mattresses scattered around the chamber.

'When will it be? We can't have much time left,' she hears the woman ask.

'Soon,' comes a harshly masculine reply. 'This is too important to hurry; I have to cast an astrological matrix for guidance. I'm not just going to cut her up like a village butcher. Mathew would not want it so.' Then they close the door on her and slide home the bolt.

Lying curled up on the mattress, Bianca fights against the waves of nausea and confusion that sweep over her as the poison she's drunk works on her body. She wonders if Ralph Cullen or Jacob Monkton slept on this very pallet, suffered these same wild visions, had their will and control of their limbs stolen away from them in the same manner. Then she decides it doesn't matter if they did – she does not intend to die like them.

But she knows that soon the hallucinations will return. She wonders how long she has: minutes? Hours? She slithers as close to the door as the chain will allow. Listening for footsteps beyond, she has to battle the noisy thudding of her heart. When she's satisfied there's no one nearby, she moves back to the mattress.

Reaching into her gown, Bianca pulls out a few of the leaves she'd gathered so frantically when she'd thrown herself headlong into the wilderness outside the Lazar House. She prays to all the saints that what she'd seen there was not a part of the hallucination; that the knowledge her mother has bequeathed her has not played her false. She holds the leaves to her nose, rubs them between her fingertips. At once the sharp scent of ginger rises like smoke from a chafing dish. She whispers just one word of blessed relief, like an incantation: *Asarabacca!*

In England, Bianca knows, they call the plant hazelwort. She hopes the English variety is as good a purgative as the one her mother used to give her when she'd eaten something she shouldn't have – like the time she tried to lick her poisoned fingers.

There's no possibility of making an infusion; she'll just have to eat the leaves raw. Look on the bright side, she tells herself: they'll work faster that way. The only question is: did I manage to gather enough?

She puts the leaves into her mouth and begins to chew. The taste of them makes her face pucker. Her whole body cries out to her: *Spit the vile stuff out – now!*

But there's no going back. This is her only hope. Bianca swallows the pulp and waits for the pain to start.

✠

Burghley has given Nicholas a private wherry for the journey to Bankside. He's detailed four of his men as crew – tough, weatherbeaten little fellows. Nicholas suspects they're former sailors from Effingham's fleet.

The captain of this small band is a leathery-skinned man named Brabant. He sports a pigtail and a brass earring. At his belt is slung a sword and buckler. There's a violent energy about him that seems barely constrained. He's one of those fearsome English privateers who keep the protests flowing from the Spanish ambassador, whenever a Don ship gets taken up and its cargo appropriated by the Treasury. The only thing that seems to give him pause is the thought of contracting leprosy.

'This lazar hospital – I've seen how quickly contagion can spread through a mess-deck,' he says as he settles himself deftly into the boat, leaving Nicholas to follow, in his own ungainly landlubber's way.

'It's been empty for years. There's hasn't been a leper living there since the queen was a young maid.'

'Are you sure?'

'Certain. You can't fall sick merely by entering it.'

'And the tide is against us,' says Brabant with the pessimism of a mariner who's spent too long at sea. 'We've a handy enough crew, mind. Davey over there was in *Ark Royal* when the Dons' Armada came sailing up the Channel in eighty-eight.'

Davey tips his cap to Nicholas.

'And Nikko Shugborough – that's him there, second oar on the leeward side – Nikko was in Henry Seymour's squadron, weren't you, Nikko?'

'Gunner's mate in the galleon *Rainbow*,' says a man in a dirty leather jerkin. Nicholas stares at his arms – each bicep is the girth of a boar's ham. 'Held the gun-deck record on the six-pounder *demi-culverin*, sir.'

'It's just one man,' says Nicholas, grateful that he's in serious company for the task in hand. 'Cannon might be somewhat of an excess.'

'Where do we land?' asks Brabant.

'There's a culvert between the place where Black Bull Alley reaches the river and the Mutton Lane stairs. You should be able to take us in under the lintel.'

The sky is beginning to darken. A wind that's had a clear run from the west batters Nicholas's face as the wherry lurches out into the river. The weight of having set this extraordinary play upon its stage is beginning to bear down upon his shoulders, sapping his confidence. As they head upriver towards the Lambeth marshes, he ponders his chances. He's almost sure that he never spoke of the Lazar House in Quigley's presence. He hopes he's right, otherwise Quigley will stay well clear of Bankside. Not even Burghley will be able to muster enough men to watch every escape route out of England.

✳

She'd hated getting sick when she was young. She'd loathed the indignity, the humbling of the will and the body, the feeling that some pitiless, angry beast had taken control of her and was forcing her insides to dance to its tune. Now she longs for it. When the first stab of cramp comes, Bianca almost weeps for joy. The asarabacca is working. Her own pain is a blow struck against the two people responsible for her terror. She crawls into a corner and vomits up the contents of her stomach, desperately trying to limit the noise of her retching.

When the spasms stop, she drags over one of the straw pallets to cover the mess. She doesn't care about the telltale smell. This place stinks already. But she daren't let them see what she's achieved: the first small victory in her struggle to live.

Nicholas is suffering his own imprisonment. The river seems to have him bound in hoops of invisible iron. The swell pushes the little wherry backwards one yard for every two that Brabant's men manage to claw forward.

His worry that Quigley knows of his suspicions about the Lazar House has given way to another fear – did he speak Bianca Merton's name only in John Lumley's hearing, or did he mention it when Quigley was taking down Elise's testament? Try as he might, he can't be sure. His only comfort, as Brabant and his crew battle against the river and the wind, is that Ned Monkton is standing his simple, honest – and hopefully sober – guard.

48

The woman enters, bearing an earthenware bowl. She kneels beside Bianca, smiles and says kindly, 'You've been taken poorly, Mistress Merton. We've sent for a physician, but you need to get your strength back. You really must drink. Here—'

Bianca rolls her eyes and groans, in her best imitation of someone deranged. Then she takes the bowl. Better to feign compliance than have them force her.

Again: the scent of hellebore and henbane.

She allows some of the liquid to flow over her chin. But she must drink enough to satisfy the woman or they'll realize what she's doing.

When the woman leaves, Bianca waits for the sound of her footsteps to fade. Then she reaches into her kirtle and brings out the rest of the asarabacca. She makes a little pile of leaves on the mattress. It's a worryingly small pile. She halves it and stuffs one portion into her mouth.

This, she realizes, is going to come down to a battle of wills.

'I can't take us in, sir, not even with the likes of Davey and Nikko on the oars,' says Brabant from the wildly pitching prow of the wherry.

'Shit!' hisses Nicholas in a wholly uncharacteristic display of frustration.

It's taken him a lifetime to strike a flint and get a lantern ablaze; the wind has defeated every attempt till now. By its meagre, agitated light he can see the tide is almost up to the level of the lintel in the Lazar House river-wall. A lethal foam of dark-brown water surges around the entrance to the culvert. The whole bank is beginning to lose its outline in the gathering dusk, river and land becoming one. The hull planks of the wherry heave beneath his feet, threatening to hurl him into the racing water. He braces himself and points to a low, dark smudge on the river – the jetty where Jacob Monkton's eviscerated body washed ashore.

'The Mutton Lane stairs then!' he shouts against the wind. 'And for mercy's sake, hurry!'

On land, it's less than a hundred paces away. But the river has taken against them. The tide is running. It might as well be on the far side of the Narrow Sea.

✠

She remembers the day news reached the Veneto of the execution of Mary Stuart, the Scots queen. Father Rossi had given the Mass in the little church on the hill. He'd told the congregation the Pope would soon intercede with God to make the new martyr a saint. Then he assured them the Holy Father prayed daily for divine retribution upon the heretical English queen who had killed her.

Sitting beside her father, Bianca could have wept with pity for poor Mary. She imagined her alone in her cell, awaiting the dawn and the executioner; no one but her enemies to give her the Viaticum. But the tortured way in which Father Rossi had pronounced the English name of the castle where this dreadful crime against God had taken place – Fotheringhay – had caused her almost to giggle in the most solemn parts of the service. It had come out of his mouth sounding more like *hot-herring-guay*.

Now she knows that God had noticed that little sin of hers, just as He notices all sin. And now He's punishing her by turning the tables: it is Bianca herself awaiting the executioner.

She hears the bolt rasp again. The door opens and she lifts herself a little from the stinking mattress.

Is it time?

Have you come to lead me to the block at hot-herring-guay?

No laughing matter now.

The woman kneels beside her – takes her hand. 'Come, Mistress Merton—'

Bianca senses pumice-face close by. She feels him place one arm around her shoulders, feels the strength in him as he lifts her to her feet as though she were made of little more than air. There is no play-acting in the way she drags her heels and stumbles as they lead her through the door and out into darkness. True, the frightening visions have ceased for a while. She feels as though at least a small measure of her will has returned. But the pain in her belly, the raw burning in her throat, the ache of her ribs from the spasms, her exhaustion – all these are real.

When did I last take the asarabacca?

When was my last purge?

When will the hallucinations come again?

Bianca knows the wrong answer to any of these questions could kill her.

A tiny gleam of light dances in the shadows. They are leading her towards it, though to her mind it is she who is stationary and it is the light that's approaching her.

A candle burning behind a wooden grille. Another door opening. A room smaller than the one she has come from. A chapel, of sorts, set deep inside the Lazar House.

As her eyes grow accustomed to the glow of the candle's flame, Bianca sees faded images of the saints staring at her from the walls and wonders: Have they killed me already? Have the angels come to take pity on another martyr?

A low archway, barely more than a deeper patch of blackness. A yawing mouth with only the bottom teeth left in it – like Father Rossi's. But the teeth are a curving flight of ancient stone steps leading down into Purgatory.

She must break free *now*, before it is too late.

But where will she go? She has no knowledge of her surroundings. She'd just blunder about helplessly until they caught her again. Then they'd tie her hands and feet.

No, I must choose the moment carefully. I will get just one chance.

The Mutton Lane shambles is silent now, but Nicholas can smell the place from the wherry. The iron perfume of butchery still lingers in the air. It even rises from the river, where the unwanted offal of the day's slaughtering has been dumped. Nicholas takes it as a dreadful warning.

'You want to stop at a *tavern*?' says Brabant incredulously when they're standing on the jetty. 'How shall I tell His Grace we lost a Jesuit, all because you fancy a jug of knock-down?'

'I don't fancy a jug of anything,' says Nicholas hotly. 'Mistress Merton is a witness, and I fear Quigley may intend her harm. Besides, to reach the Lazar House from here you have to pass the Jackdaw. I just want to make sure.'

When he enters the taproom it feels like a homecoming. The tang of wood-smoke and hops, the dry scent of the rushes on the floor, the herbs Bianca sets in the nooks and crannies are more pleasing to him than the aroma of a prince's bejewelled pomander. Even Ned Monkton is there. Nicholas spots him at once, deep in conversation with Rose. Nicholas decides to bring him along. If anyone deserves to be in at the kill, it's Ned.

But when Nicholas hails him, Ned turns towards him with eyes harrowed by worry. 'God's wounds! Thank Christ you've come,' he growls. 'She's been gone since yesterday – and the woe is all my doing!'

✠

She has been led almost to the bottom of a deep, dark well.

She is buried so far in the earth that in the spring her limbs will turn into pale shoots, forcing their way upwards until she spills out into the sunlight in a profusion of sweet-smelling flowers. A girl with an interest in herbs will pass by, pluck her leaves, set them in a bowl and make a heady infusion to place beside her pillow to help her dream.

But first must come the small matter of her death.

49

'W' hen she didn't return, I went looking for her,' Ned says as they leave the Jackdaw behind, heading at a brisk pace for the physic garden. He's brought a blazing torch to augment Brabant's lantern. By its light Nicholas can see how much he blames himself. 'At the Magdalene they said she'd already left, with a man and a woman. I couldn't get any sense out of them. They're all much like my Jacob in there.'

'It's not your fault, Ned; you weren't to know it was a trap,' Nicholas says for at least the third time. 'When her mind's made up, that's it.'

'I found the overseer – but he was that drunk he wouldn't have noticed if the Pope had dropped by, asking for a bed for the night.'

They press on through the darkened lanes. Nicholas carries the key to the physic garden door, given to him by Rose. Both she and Timothy had wanted to come, but Brabant had refused: 'A maid and a callow boy with my crew? That's unlucky.' So Nicholas has left Rose to comfort Timothy in his own self-recriminating misery.

What he hadn't expected was the look that Rose bestowed on Ned as they parted company: a mix of admiration and anxiety. Clearly, life at the Jackdaw has been getting along just fine without him.

On Black Bull Alley he can count the lighted windows on the fingers of one hand. To the south, towards Winchester House, barely a dozen more points of light resist the darkness. The Lazar

House seems to have leached its black heart into the night.

In the physic garden Burghley's men begin inspecting the wall, looking for a suitable place to climb. Nicholas is acutely aware that the moving circle of light must be clearly visible to anyone chancing to look out of those eye-slit windows below the eaves of the ancient hospice.

Brabant chooses his spot. His men go over with ease – a stationary wall, even if it is ten feet high, holds no challenge for men used to swarming aloft from a heaving deck in a high sea. But for Nicholas, the prospect does not sit so lightly.

Ned comes to his rescue. He's the largest of any of them, and his huge cupped paws give enough impetus to minimize the scraped hands and knees as Nicholas sails over into the dark wilderness beyond.

And then, almost before he knows it, he's standing in the waist-high weeds, while before him the great black bulk of the Lazar House looms up into the night like some dreadful pagan temple.

✠

Brabant uses an iron crow he's brought along to take the lock off the door. He makes almost no sound. Nicholas guesses it's a privateer's skill – honed by years of climbing mooring ropes, prizing open cabin windows and storming aboard to commit violence with pistol and sword, all in the name of England's queen. Or perhaps the lock was just older than he thought. If that's the case – and Quigley's not inside the Lazar House – then Bianca is either dead, or soon will be. And there's not a thing he can do about it.

The same awful feeling of helplessness he'd known when he'd realized Eleanor's fate was completely out of his hands floods over him now. A trickle of sweat runs down his forehead.

Through pursed lips, he empties his lungs of air to relieve the tension. And the fear.

It wasn't a prison, it was a hospital. That's what he'd told Bianca. *Leprosy is a sickness, not a sin.* So why is he so grateful when Brabant goes ahead of him into a narrow pitch-black passageway?

They emerge into cloisters around a central courtyard. There's no sound, other than their own breathing. Brabant and the others now seem reluctant to move any further – like sailors everywhere, they're innately superstitious. Each one of them is already conjuring ghosts out of the darkness.

And Nicholas has no trouble understanding why. By the light from Brabant's lantern and Ned's flickering torch, he sees, scattered around the cloisters, poignant reminders that the Lazar House was once a community of outcasts shut away from the world. There's a handcart collapsed against a wall like a Bankside drunk; a reed basket all but unravelled, its contents of washing mallets forming a forlorn and jumbled altar in the centre; even a child's wooden study-book lying in its frame, the painted letters of the alphabet so badly faded they are little more than shadows on its face. It's as if the occupants of a house have fled impending catastrophe, not daring to stop to take their possessions with them.

In the central courtyard grows a miniature forest of fern, hart's tongue and buckler. Nicholas remembers the night at Barnthorpe when he and Jack first climbed out of the window to go coney-hunting in the barley by lantern-light. He'd been barely tall enough to see over the gently swaying crop, imagining that he was alone and adrift on a vast black sluggish ocean. Then an owl had swept low over his head in the darkness and frightened him clean out of his boots. He'd had nightmares for a month.

He wonders if he's having one now – because at the extreme edge of the flickering lantern light he can just make out a black hole cut in the cloister wall. It's the entrance to a stone stairway. It looks to Nicholas more like a tomb with the door ajar.

Under his breath, Nikko the gunner's mate starts muttering something about graves and ghosts. Brabant curses him and tells him to shut his mouth. But even he seems reluctant to take the next step.

'The dead won't bite you,' rumbles Ned Monkton, coming to the rescue once again. He heads purposefully towards the archway. 'Not unless you let them.'

✠

At the top of a stone stairway festooned with cobwebs is a gallery that extends into the darkness. The walls are streaked with bat droppings, the floor no longer solid stone but baulks of timber covered by a thick layer of dust. It drifts up in little clouds as they pass. Nicholas hears Elise Cullen's voice in his head: *High walls... dark, and dusty... even the Cardinal's Hat was cleaner.*

Brabant has commanded silence, and though Nicholas wants only to call out Bianca's name at the top of his voice, he knows that if she's here – and still alive – it could be a death sentence. Stepping carefully – far too slowly for Nicholas's liking – they cover three sides of the building without observing the slightest sign of recent habitation.

What am I looking for? Nicholas asks himself. What do I expect to find?

A dead man in a chamber lit by a thousand candles – that's what Elise had said.

Or a dead woman.

'There's nothing here, sir,' says Brabant. 'We're wasting our time. His Grace will have more profitable work for us than this.'

'Thank Christ's holy wounds for that,' says Nikko. 'I'll take a Don's broadside over this place, any day of the week.'

'Amen,' says Davey from the *Ark Royal*.

'We're done, then,' says Brabant.

For a moment no one speaks. The lantern light makes sharp-edged masks of their faces. Then Ned Monkton's voice rolls like a heavy millstone out of the darkness:

'There's still the fourth side.'

Again, silence.

Then Brabant, spitting into the dust. 'Fourth side of my arse! This place is giving my men the black dreads. It's not doing much for me, neither. If there's a Jesuit in here, he's welcome to it. He and his friend the Pope can kiss my pimpled arse – we're on our way out.'

Ned whispers hurriedly into Nicholas's ear, 'Do you really think this is where my Jacob died?'

Nicholas doesn't know whether to nod or apologize. But something in his eyes makes Ned Monkton turn to Brabant and say, 'Leave if you want, but you'll have to walk over me to find the way out.'

Brabant lets out a weary sigh. He glances rapidly at Davey and Nikko and says, 'You might be a big bastard, Monkton, but you're shit at arithmetic.' And draws a good length of steel from his scabbard – just to make his point.

'Let them go, Ned,' says Nicholas dispiritedly.

As Burghley's men disappear into the darkness beneath the fading glow of Brabant's lantern, Ned mutters, 'Poxy sods', and calls after them in a voice loud enough to be heard but not to carry: 'We came in somewhere over there. Or maybe it was that way. Oh, and remember when I told you the dead don't bite—?'

✠

With only Ned's guttering rush torch to light the way now, the two men make their way along the fourth wall of the Lazar House.

Nicholas guesses they must be facing the edge of the Mutton Lane shambles. Most of the tiny windows are either boarded up or stopped with grime-encrusted glass. Those that are open let in the east wind. It lifts the dust into a low, swirling cloud about their feet, which reminds Nicholas uncomfortably of the night he walked off the jetty and into the river. He remembers how he'd imagined Eleanor beckoning him, how in his delirium he'd convinced himself he was to blame for her death, for the death of their child – for the death of little Ralph Cullen, too. For no reason he can think of, other than his own heightened state and the effect the Lazar House is having on him, one of Fulke Vaesy's dire sermon-lectures jumps into his head:

'In the Book of Ezra,' Vaesy is saying, 'the prophet states that the issue of a man and woman who lay together during her menstrual purge may be born leprous... may be born monstrous...'

An innocent crippled child – born monstrous, or so Vaesy would have it – murdered solely for the story that his own blood has to tell. Ralph Cullen, Jacob Monkton, the preacher and the others Elise had described in her testimony, all of them destroyed, reduced to a few lines of faux-academic scribbles on a sheet of paper. Medicine become its own monstrosity, in the hands of a man and a woman driven by some twisted notion of love.

And one last death to come – if it hasn't come already.

Unless I'm right.

Unless this is the place.

Unless I'm in time.

Out of the darkness of the Lazar House, Nicholas sees something large and solid looming ahead of him. At first he can't make it out. But as he approaches he sees it's the entrance to a chapel, built out from the wall. The door is an elaborate wooden tracery, like an altar screen.

Ned lifts his torch to get the last light out of the dying flames.

Through the screen Nicholas sees a woman crucified upside-down, white as chalk.

But it's only the torchlight scattering the shadows across the painted figures of the saints on the far wall. He turns and starts to walk away.

✠

It is the little crypt where Father Rossi prays over the graves of her parents. It's her father's cell in Padua. It's a prison specially made for her by the Worshipful Company of Grocers because they're frightened of what will happen if they grant her a licence to practise apothecary. And it doesn't matter whether its walls are in Padua or in London, she was a fool to think she could ever climb over them. Yet for all that, this low crypt deep in the earth appears almost welcoming. The candles set around the little chamber paint the stone walls with a blush of warm gold.

At the centre stands a plinth of coarse-cut ragstone. This, she assumes in a moment of lucidity, is the place where the inmates of the Lazar House would be brought at the end of their lonely lives – lives lived beyond the sight of the rest of the world outside. Down here, no one but the priests who prayed over them would have to look upon the visible signs of God's displeasure.

On the plinth, the man with the pumice face has laid out all the holy relics of his obscene, perverted physic. The candlelight gleams on saw-edge and hook, on knife-blade and needle. She sees an hourglass – polished till it seems to hold not sand, but a myriad tiny stars. She sees pewter bowls, a set of scales and weights, astrological symbols and calculations drawn out in chalk on the walls.

But the items that terrify her most are not on the plinth, but set to one side: a wooden frame supporting what looks like an inverted cross, leather straps fixed to the extremities. And set around its base: a collection of glass jars containing things Bianca can barely permit to exist – things that might once have pulsed and throbbed inside a human body. She almost pleads for the return of the hallucinations. They must come soon – she'd swallowed the last of the asarabacca pulp several lifetimes ago. At least when they do, she thinks, they will take her clear away from this monstrous place.

'A tavern-mistress?' says Quigley, shaking his head in apparent disbelief. 'How can she possibly comprehend an endeavour such as ours?'

He comes very close to her. She can smell the musty scent of old books on him. And something else: a desiccated smell – as if he's anointed himself with the distillation of a lifetime's resentment.

'Very few have been permitted to enter our chapel of mysteries,' he tells her, as though she should be grateful to him. 'We do such great and blessed work here. And you will be part of it. You may well be the one who gives us what we've been searching for. But first we shall pray together.'

Bianca sways, feeling the bones and muscles in her legs beginning to liquefy. This time she's not play-acting. The hallucinations are starting to bubble up from beneath the surface of her terror. Small at first – a bending of shape and form, a thinning-out of substance – soon they will grow. She cannot prevent it.

A sudden brightening of everything around her forewarns of an oncoming wave. She knows that when it breaks, the man with the pumice face will set to work with his abominable collection of instruments.

In a moment of extraordinarily banal reflection, she wonders how Rose and Timothy will fare under a new landlord; where the regulars of the Jackdaw will get their balms, salves and tinctures now; and if Nicholas will ever learn what happened to her, or even care.

She stares at the woman she now knows is Katherine Vaesy. The woman's mouth is moving, but it's her own voice that Bianca can hear coming out of it:

But you can't claw like a Veneto maid when she's faced with a rival... you'd have no idea which bit of them to kick first...

'Come, Mistress, we must be about our task. Pray with me,' says Quigley, moving closer to take her by the arm.

But the voice hasn't done with her yet:

Bianca Merton, you didn't come all the way from Padua to wash up like a gutted fish on the Mutton Lane stairs – did you?

She lets Quigley lead her towards the plinth. In his tight grip she feels as though she's made of paper. One careless squeeze will crush her entirely. She tenses her body, as if trying to force a precious liquid out of a rag. And as the wave begins to swell, she acts.

Grabbing the nearest thing on the plinth, Bianca flails out at Quigley's face.

She has no idea what she's picked up. Her arm seems as light as a feather – no real force behind it. I'm too weak now to do any hurt upon him, she thinks. He'll brush me aside as though I'm nothing more troubling than a moth.

In fact, she's picked up a small saw. The teeth are cruel and sharp, like the teeth of a cornered rat. And the desperation in her is more powerful than she knows. The blade catches Quigley along the edge of his jaw, tearing away gobbets of flesh. He shrieks in pain, a piecing yowl that echoes around the crypt, up the stairway and out into the Lazar House. He staggers, falling back across the plinth and scattering the instruments onto the flagstones.

Katherine Vaesy's mouth gapes wide in astonishment. Bianca slices at her, too. But now she can barely keep her legs from giving way. The strike does not land. Nevertheless, Kat reels back. She leaves the way to the stairs open. As the crypt begins to transform itself into a vast hall draped with brilliant tapestries in which the beasts themselves roar and prance, Bianca makes a desperate dash for the steps.

She takes the first few on pure spirit alone. Then she is flying upwards, a creature of the air, free to sail high above the world and all its maladies. She would fly for ever if she could. But like every good dream, its life is all too brief. She feels herself falling back to earth.

Her hands scratch at the stone to get purchase. The saw drops away, clattering noisily down behind her. She feels hands seizing her ankles, pulling her back, sucking her down in a maelstrom of noise and light, to where the Devil's cross waits ready for her crucifixion.

And then she hears it: the sound of someone entering the chapel at the top of the steps.

A voice calling her name. A man's voice.

A familiar voice.

As the hallucinations sweep over her, Bianca imagines it's Nicholas, come to explain why he didn't write.

50

Shrovetide, February 1591

On Tower Hill the apprentice boys are playing football in the crisp winter sunshine. It's the Fishmongers' Company against the Weavers' Guild, and it's rapidly turning into a no-quarter-given grudge-match. Since Nicholas Shelby left the Lumley town house on Woodroffe Lane, he's patched up three split scalps and a fractured elbow. He's also come perilously close to being thrown into a water-trough for tending a Fishmonger in a crowd of Weavers.

Along the city wall the food vendors are doing a roaring trade. Pies and pancakes are flying off the stalls. There's much feasting and carousing to be done before Lent stalks in with his grim face of guilty self-denial.

'Your Widow Welford was right, Nicholas,' Lumley says as they break free of the crowd. 'Nonsuch has never heard trilling like it – we can barely keep Elise silent for one minute at a time.'

'That's good to hear. But she's suffered so much; it will be a long time before our pipit sits happy on her branch. Will she stay with your household?'

'Lizzy and I would not have it otherwise. Sprint and Joanna are to wed – they have asked to adopt her. Elise seems to approve of the plan. My gift to them will be her education: I shall find her a tutor, someone gentle. *Very* gentle.'

'Then at least some good has come out of this.'

'And your Mistress Merton – how does she mend?'

'Well, my lord. She mends well. Still a little weak, but each day sees improvement. One moment she wants to shower me with gratitude for saving her, the next she wants to finish what Quigley started' – Nicholas touches the wound on the back of his scalp – 'for putting her in danger in the first place!'

'She had a lucky escape, I understand. Had it not been for your determination... well, it doesn't bear dwelling upon, does it?'

Nicholas smiles. 'She was the instrument of her own salvation, my lord. A lesser heart might have given up.'

'I hear Captain Brabant's men had to prevent Monkton from killing Gabriel with his bare hands – is that right?'

'That might have been a better outcome. It would have been a kinder death than the one he faces now.'

'You must put that out of your mind, Nicholas. As you rightly told me that morning we rode out of Nonsuch, Gabriel knew the path he was taking.'

'Still, it's a little too much of an eye for an eye for my liking, my lord.'

'I still think of Kat,' Lumley says sadly. 'One cannot easily put so long a friendship out of mind. Tell me again, how did it happen?'

Nicholas shrugs. 'It's hard to say, my lord. It was dark. She was in the stern of the wherry. We were rowing back to Cecil House. One moment she was there, the next – gone. Somewhere off the Lambeth marshes, I'd guess.'

'Was she bound?'

'Brabant didn't think it necessary: Quigley was in too much pain from the wounds Ned and Bianca had given him to cause any trouble. And Katherine Vaesy had been sitting quietly all the way from the Mutton Lane stairs.'

'Did she drown? Or did she make it to the bank?' asks Lumley, addressing his question to the sky. 'Whatever the truth, wherever she is, I hope she's at peace. At least she's free of her husband.' A thought occurs to him. 'Speaking of Sir Fulke, did you know he's been dismissed from the chair of anatomy, stripped of his fellowship of the College? It was the Privy Council's doing. Nothing to do with malpractice – it was the scandal, and his connection to a Jesuit, that they couldn't stomach.'

Nicholas says nothing.

'The most extraordinary thing is,' Lumley continues as they walk, 'her disappearance has quite brought Lizzy out of her shell. It's as though some malign skein connecting her to the past has been cut. I know she was in awe of my first wife, Jane FitzAlan – never thought herself Jane's equal – but now Kat has gone, well, Lizzy's found a worth in herself she never knew she possessed. Why, the very day I last left Nonsuch, she barely noticed my departure because she was so engrossed in a book she'd taken from the library!' He shakes his head in sad reflection. 'Even so, I know Kat's crimes have troubled her deeply. We both thought Kat was an angel; but Jesu, what a malign mark she has left on so many lives.'

They walk on together in silence, towards Petty Wales and the great Bulwark Gate to the Tower. Halting in its shadow Lumley says, 'You must bring Mistress Merton to Nonsuch when she's fit to travel. Lizzy and I are of a mind to build a physic garden there. We would welcome her counsel.'

'I shall, my lord – with gratitude.'

'God protect us poor, weak men from redoubtable women, eh, Nicholas?'

'Indeed.'

'I keep asking myself: how did the two of them come to this? Could I have prevented it? Was I remiss in my care for Gabriel? For Kat?'

Nicholas can find little compassion for Quigley. But for

Katherine Vaesy? How had the Devil entered *her* soul? 'Twenty years is a long time to carry so much hate,' he says. 'Perhaps the child Vaesy destroyed with his incompetence was not his, but Mathew Quigley's. Have you thought of that possibility?'

Lumley's cold, grey northern eyes glisten. 'It's cruel, I know, but a part of me wishes John Warren was still alive, so he could see the consequences of breaking his daughter's heart.'

At the north end of Petty Wales the sky disappears behind a cliff-face of ragstone and flint. They've reached the forbidding entrance to the Bulwark Gate, on the western side of the Tower. Here even passers-by with nothing on their conscience lower their voices and avert their eyes. The shadows seem colder than elsewhere.

Lumley presents his seal and letter of admittance signed by William Cecil. As they pass through, Nicholas steels himself for what must come.

'Are you ready?' asks John Lumley. 'A man of healing may well find this too much to stomach.'

Nicholas reflects on Lumley's words for a moment. Then he says, 'Yes, I'm ready. What kind of man is a hunter who can't look his quarry in the eye?'

✠

By the light of the yeoman-warder's lantern they climb the spiral stairs, their footsteps on the worn stones sounding like a slow tally of lives ended and forgotten. Nicholas has the nightmare sensation that the stairwell is coiling itself up behind him, cutting off his escape, as though he were being worked through the gut of some monstrous worm.

'They say he made the wildest claims when Master Topcliffe first put him to the hard questioning,' says the warder as he climbs ahead of them.

'Claims? What sort of claims?' Lumley asks, breathing hard now with the effort of the climb.

'That he was no Jesuit, but a physician – engaged upon secret work that would raise England high in the eyes of posterity. That there was a plot against him. That he'd been betrayed by those he trusted.'

'Is that so?'

'Being a gentleman of the court, you must know how these papist traitors are, my lord. They'll lie to the last breath.'

If 'papist traitor' causes Lumley to grit his teeth, Nicholas is unable to detect it. All Lumley says in reply is, 'So I'm led to believe.'

The warder blunders on. 'Master Topcliffe himself told me he feared he'd never get this rogue to confess. But I said to him, "Master Richard," I said, "the Devil's not yet fashioned the Jesuit who can keep his vile intent from *you*, when you've a mind to winkle it out of him." I told him straight. No messing.'

'I'm sure you did,' says Lumley despondently.

Reaching a narrow landing, the warden puts his key to the lock with a great rattling of iron. The door, barely large enough to admit a child, swings open on ancient hinges. John Lumley stoops to enter. He's been here before, Nicholas remembers. He knows what it's like to be incarcerated in a chamber like this. Perhaps it's not just the climb that's causing him to breathe so hard.

The cell tapers like a carpenter's wedge, a narrow arrow-slit of a window at the far end. The walls are half-panelled. They're covered with countless carved messages, some little more than a weak scratching of despair, others scoured out in rage. One, Nicholas sees, is written in Latin: *Parce mihi, Domine, nihil enim sunt dies mei...* Spare me, O Lord, for my days are as nothing...

Gabriel Quigley's broken body kneels in the tiny space by the window, his back towards Nicholas. A length of chain snakes from a ring-bolt in the floor to an iron fetter around his right ankle. He seems to be at prayer, the soles of his feet turned outwards. Nicholas notices they are almost black with livid bruises. But it's not spiritual ease Quigley's seeking – he's licking moisture off the windowsill.

'Stand up for the gentlemen, you Romish dog,' growls the warder.

Richard Topcliffe has done his work with chilling efficiency. As if waking from a long hibernation, Gabriel Quigley tries to rise. But he can manage no more than a half-crouch. Using the casement sill for support, he turns to face them. He's dressed in a heavily stained linen shirt and soiled hose. His eyes are devil-red where the minor blood vessels have ruptured. Diagonally across one side of his face runs the black, festering furrow made by the teeth of the saw Bianca wielded. He stinks of his own piss, his own vomit and – irony upon irony – his own blood.

Something appears to be eating him away from within. Nicholas thinks he knows what it is: it's the rotting of the self that occurs when a man's been shown the previously unimagined possibilities of his own humiliation by a torturer.

I'm not the physician – I'm the disease.

'For the love of mercy, get him some water to clean himself with,' Lumley snaps to the warder. 'And a blanket. It must be colder than Hecate's tit up here at night.'

The warder is unmoved. 'Orders from the Privy Council, my lord. The Jesuit is to have no more ease than this. There are worse places here we could have put him in – trust me.'

'May we speak with the prisoner a while – alone?' Lumley asks.

'A *short* while, Masters,' says the warder.

The single chair is out of Quigley's reach. Lumley moves it to within the arc of his chain and helps him to sit. The setting of his limbs into the angle of the chair makes Quigley cry out in pain. He stares at the open door as the warder leaves, as though he fears something terrible is about to come through it.

It's a few minutes before he even acknowledges that Lumley is beside him. Then, in recognition, he lifts one hand to clutch Lumley's sleeve. Nicholas notices the fingers no longer line up. Nor do they have nails.

'I am forsaken, my lord,' Quigley cries in a hollowed-out voice. 'They made me say I was a Jesuit! They made me say I desired to deliver the queen in chains to the mercy of the Pope! That I plotted her death. I am condemned out of my own mouth. For the love I know you bear me, my lord, tell them they've made a mistake. Tell them it's not *true*.'

Nicholas stares at the creature hunched in the chair. If nothing but sudden blindness could shut out the sight of what Gabriel Quigley has become – of what he, Nicholas Shelby, has brought about – he thinks he might almost welcome it. Only the image of Ralph Cullen's body, of Jacob Monkton's eviscerated carcass, prevents him from calling for the warden to let him out of the cell.

I'm not the physician – I'm the disease.

With what little strength Topcliffe has left him, Quigley tugs at Lumley's gown. 'You are a man of great learning, my lord. Your library nurtured my skills. Part of the glory will be yours. Tell them to let me go. I *have* to go on.'

Lumley drags himself away from Quigley's grasp as Nicholas says, in a bitter voice, '*Glory?* What glory? There's no glory in what you've done, Quigley.'

Quigley's bloodshot eyes turn on Nicholas. A dull light of comprehension flickers in them – and loathing.

'Tell me, Quigley, when were your crimes going to end?' Nicholas asks. 'When you'd butchered the last crippled child in

London? When you'd bled the life out of the last helpless beggar? What were you going to do then? Find another malady to cure by murder?'

Quigley shakes his head violently. The pain of his injuries makes his mouth gape in protest. 'Murder? No! You *must* understand: I have learned wondrous things in this work. I have come so close to understanding how God's purpose works in the body: in mine, in yours—' Then, pleadingly, to John Lumley, 'in *Mathew's.*'

Lumley just looks on in horror.

'I lost someone I loved, too,' Nicholas says without pity. 'The grief almost killed me – I couldn't save her. But not once did I ever think of butchering someone else's wife to find out why!'

Quigley studies him for a moment, as though trying to read his thoughts. Then, utterly unrepentant, he says hoarsely, 'And you're the poorer physician for it, Shelby. No vision – that's the trouble with your sort. You should stick to prescribing balms for scrofula.'

It would be so easy, Nicholas thinks, to smash his fist into Quigley's already-ruined face. That his inevitable end will be unimaginably more painful is small recompense for not doing so. 'Did you know their names, Quigley?' he asks, crossing his arms lest the temptation prove irresistible.

'Names? *Whose* names?'

'The people you butchered. Ralph Cullen, for a start.'

Quigley shakes his head slowly, painfully. It dawns on Nicholas that his victims' humanity is something Quigley dare not allow himself even to glimpse.

'Ralph was the little boy with the withered legs,' he explains. 'Ralph's mother was a drunken bawd from Bankside. You'd think God might have given him a little more of His much-vaunted love. His sister Elise carried him on her back, all the way from

Southwark to Surrey, looking for a little hope in life. Instead she found Katherine Vaesy, and *you*.'

Quigley lowers his head and lets it sway gently in denial.

'Then there's Jacob Monkton, the lad you eviscerated. Did you learn much from him – other than how to torture an innocent lad who wouldn't harm a fly? Did you know his father and his brother have almost nothing in the world? And most of what they did have went on paying a charlatan like you to find a cure for his malady.'

The swaying of the head increases. Nicholas wonders if a small shard of guilt has found its way beneath Quigley's carapace.

'And what about the preacher? What about the blind woman with the bell around her neck – and her sister? Or the old man with one hand? I've no idea what they were called, Quigley. Have you? Perhaps you should have asked them, before you drained the blood out of them. At least you'd have been able to thank them properly for their contribution to your studies! Do you actually *have* any blood in your own veins, Quigley? Or is there just the piss of your own self-importance flowing there?'

Quigley looks up and meets his angry gaze. He reaches to his own breast with his feeble, twisted hands. 'We were almost *there*,' he says, in a voice that sounds as though it's being scratched out on glass with a rusty nail. 'Your woman was going to provide the final proof.'

'Proof? Proof of what?'

Quigley draws a long, slow breath. 'I believe the answer lies somewhere inside the heart. Galen and the others were wrong – the blood has no *tide*. It isn't heated in the heart. It doesn't flow from the liver to the organs. Somehow it's *propelled* around the body. If a vessel is cut and enough blood is lost, the heart will stop. Even Galen knew that, but he didn't know why. The heart and the blood are more connected than we ever thought. And if you had not intervened, I could have discovered how!'

Suddenly, for Nicholas, the cell is full of people. He can see his mother-in-law, Ann, wringing her hands out of fear for Eleanor... Harriet breathless from the run from the Cheapside fountain... the midwife with her holy stones... *Barely a single drop of blood discharged from the privy region – just some small quantity of her water.*

Nicholas sinks to his knees. He's so close to Quigley he can feel the man's sour breath on his face. 'Quigley, tell me, from what you've discovered, what would happen if the blood vessels ruptured internally – if there was no outside agency, no knife, no wound?'

When Quigley answers, it's not because he wants to hand the gift of knowledge to Nicholas, but because he's learned from Richard Topcliffe that not answering can swiftly bring a man more pain than he can possibly imagine. 'The heart would drive the blood out into the body cavity, until there was not enough left in the vessels to support its work.'

'And then?'

'Then it would stop.'

Nicholas closes he his eyes.

Eleanor: the thread in the weave of my soul. The sunlight on the water. The sigh in the warm wind.

And I didn't kill her. I didn't kill her child.

They died not because of what I'd forgotten, but because of what I never knew.

Lumley's voice makes Nicholas open his eyes again.

'The heart is the seat of reason, of courage and of love, Gabriel,' Lumley says, his words heavy with disgust. 'Mathew would have told you that, if you'd listened to him. It's the chalice into which God pours His mercy – not some merely mechanical *engine*.' He steps back outside the compass of Quigley's reach, as if he fears contamination. His last words to his secretary are filled with self-recrimination. 'If I'd known what use you wished to make of my precious library, Gabriel, I'd have fed every single page into the fire with my own hands.'

✠

Robert Cecil's carriage is waiting by the Bulwark Gate. The door is open. Burghley's crab-shouldered son watches Nicholas and John Lumley approach. He looks smaller than Nicholas remembers.

'My noble lord of Nonsuch,' Cecil says, with a courtier's smile that suggests there is no setback that cannot be turned to an advantage, 'I hear our sovereign lady is much in your debt.'

'Is that so?' There's a hint of bravado in Lumley's reply.

'You have denounced a dangerous Jesuit. The Privy Council – and my lord father – seem to think you're the most loyal man in England. Tell me, my lord, how did that happen?'

'I merely did my duty to our sovereign, Master Robert, as must we all.'

'What troubles me,' says Robert Cecil, giving Lumley a mistrustful squint, 'is quite how a Jesuit can hide himself away in your household for so long without you having the slightest idea he's there. Explain that, if you can.'

'The Devil is adept at disguise, Master Robert. As you yourself have said on many occasions.'

Cecil studies him the way the victim of a street-gulling studies the trickster with the dice – he knows he's been had; he can't quite see how. 'During his questioning Quigley claimed it was actually your clerk, Francis Deniker, who was the Jesuit. I'm informed that Quigley swore his innocence almost until the end – until Master Topcliffe persuaded him of the truth.'

'Well, wouldn't you,' says Nicholas, playing the trickster's apprentice, 'if you knew what you were facing?'

Robert Cecil offers Nicholas a smile so tight it would take a crowbar to prise it open. 'Why do I have the feeling you've played me a very fast match, Dr Shelby?'

Nicholas doesn't answer.

'I could make use of your talents, Physician. You should consider it.'

'I have employment, thank you, Master Cecil. At least, I think I still have.'

'Bringing comfort to the destitute at St Thomas's? What a wanton waste!'

'To you, perhaps.'

'Come now, clever men can prosper in this land – with the right patron. You may forget any hope of advancement under Fulke Vaesy. He'll never make queen's physician now – not after what that wife of his appears to have been up to. Is it true: human organs, blood, kept in jars for the purpose of witchcraft?'

But Cecil doesn't wait for an answer. He raises a bejewelled hand. The liveried coachman takes up the reins. As the coach door closes, Cecil's parting shot is full of malice. 'Take my advice, Lord Lumley – don't feel *too* comfortable at Nonsuch. I'll winkle you out of your shell yet.'

And with that, the Lord Treasurer's son is borne away in magisterial splendour towards Thames Street.

✣

John Lumley says not a word until he and Nicholas are free of the shadow of the Tower. Around their feet the last of winter's dead leaves dance in the strengthening breeze. An ox-waggon passes, laden with sacks of seed, heading for the wharves.

'He's right, of course,' says Lumley over the noise of the turning wheels.

'My lord?'

'Robert Cecil – about my "shell". He will prise me out of it eventually. The size of my debt to the Crown makes it inevitable.'

'I wish there was something I could suggest—'

'Lizzy tells me I should offer to make the queen a gift of Nonsuch.'

'You mean, give it up?'

'Make a contract: cancellation of my debts in exchange for the deeds of her father's palace. Lizzy and I to stay on, as life-tenants. That way, the library will be secure.'

'Then perhaps that's what you should do, my lord. Even Robert Cecil can't take away from you what's not yours to lose. Occasionally we must accept that *some* gifts are not ours to keep.'

John Lumley's wide smile catches Nicholas completely off-guard. 'You know, Nicholas, that's not a bad idea. And it would stick in the Cecil craw like a chicken bone, wouldn't it?'

Looking down towards Galley Quay, Nicholas can see the wherries and the tilt-boats battling against the swell as they make their way upriver to Whitehall and Richmond, downstream to the city and the ships moored in the Pool. The tide is up. The water looks angry.

'Perhaps, Nicholas, when you come to see you cannot blame yourself for things you have not the power to prevent, you might consider becoming my private physician. After all, you've barely scratched the surface of the library.'

'That's generous of you, my lord. But I think St Tom's might have more need of me.'

Lumley smiles. It's something he's begun to do more of recently. 'I understand. Should you ever change your mind—'

'There is one favour I would ask of you, my lord.'

'Then ask it.'

'That you intercede with the Guild of Grocers.'

'The Grocers? Whatever do you wish of them?'

'A licence, my lord.'

Lumley looks at Nicholas in bemusement. 'A licence?'

'To practise as an apothecary.'

'An honest trade, Nicholas, but a waste of your talents, if I may say so.'

Nicholas smiles. 'It's not for me, my lord,' he says, 'it's for Mistress Merton.'

✳

Heading west, alone now, Nicholas crosses New Fish Street towards St Paul's. He does not hurry. For the first time in months there is no urgency driving him. Disjointed fragments of the great city's life come to him as he walks: the smell of boiling pig skin from the scalding house on Pudding Lane, the shouts of the day-labourers touting for work on East Cheap. He is just one man among the crowd, unremarkable, drawing no one's eye, catching no one's attention.

On Grass Street he pauses to look up at the window of his old lodgings. A woman he does not recognize is leaning out, airing bed sheets that flap noisily in the breeze. After a while she gives up and pulls them back inside.

He stops for a while at Trinity church, but he does not enter the churchyard. He doesn't want Eleanor to hear the question that's been noisily troubling him since he saw Gabriel Quigley trying to quench his thirst at the windowsill of his cell: Would I kill a man – if by doing so I could cure the malady that took you away from me? He fears she will think him a monster if she catches his answer: *Without hesitation!*

Nicholas sits beneath the little thatched roof of the lych-gate until the bell chimes four. Then he gets to his feet and, with exaggerated care, brushes down his white canvas doublet. He begins to whistle a song he's heard often on the Southwark streets: 'On high the merry pipit trills'.

Turning his back on the city, he sets off down Fish Street Hill towards the bridge. Towards Southwark.

Historical note

In 1616, just seven years after John Lumley's death, the English anatomist William Harvey delivered his revolutionary thesis in which he showed that the heart was indeed the driving force behind the circulation of the blood. It ended fifteen hundred years of Galenic teaching, almost all of it wholly false.

By that time, the glorious palace of Nonsuch had been back in royal hands for a while. The year after this story ends, John Lumley, overwhelmed by debt and his questionable religious affiliations, did indeed sign Nonsuch over to Queen Elizabeth. In return, his loans and mortgages – worth, in today's currency, well over twenty million pounds – were cancelled. The queen allowed Lumley and his wife to remain there as custodians for the rest of their lives. Both outlived her. John died in 1609, Elizabeth Lumley eight years later. Their tombs are to be found in the Lumley chapel at Cheam, beside those of John's first wife, Jane FitzAlan, and their three children. Many of the surviving volumes of Lumley's priceless collection of books now reside in the British Library. The Lumleian Lectures are still presented each year by the Royal College of Physicians.

The forceps mishandled by Fulke Vaesy at his wife's childbirth were introduced into England by the Chamberlens, a family of refugee Huguenot physicians who fled Paris in 1569. In the long-running battle between the physicians, the barber-surgeons and the midwives, forceps were invariably kept hidden, lest they became commonplace and thus lost their financial value. The true nature of Mathew Quigley's haemophilia was not properly understood until the early nineteenth century.

In 1876 the Board of Examiners of the Royal College of Surgeons – the successor to the Company of Barber-Surgeons – resigned en masse rather than allow women to sit for a diploma in midwifery. It wasn't until 1909 that a woman became a fellow of the Royal College of Physicians. The surgeons caught up two years later. Neither event – though great achievements for the women involved – can be considered exactly ground-breaking: five centuries had passed since Dorotea Bucca was appointed professor of medicine and philosophy at the University of Bologna, a post she inherited from her father in 1390.

A little over a century after John Lumley returned Nonsuch to royal ownership, Charles II gave the estate to his mistress, Barbara Villiers. Just like Lumley, she too was burdened by immense debt. Her solution was somewhat more extreme than his: she had Nonsuch – renowned as one of the most glorious Renaissance palaces in Europe – demolished.

It is now a municipal park.

Author's note

This story is, of course, a fiction, though some of the characters in it did exist. We can never really know what it was like for them to live in Elizabeth's England. Like all their kind, they thought differently, spoke differently, understood their world differently. But I'm sure their emotions were no less vibrant, no less unruly, than ours.

Fortunately for us scavengers of history, so many superb historians and writers have thoughtfully left their best dishes lying alluringly within reach, to provide us with at least a taste of the world in which those characters lived. I am indebted to Ian Mortimer and Liza Picard, whose *The Time Traveller's Guide to Elizabethan England* and *Elizabeth's London* respectively are such wonderful gateways to the world in which my story is set. John Stow's *A Survey of London*, written in 1598, was equally indispensable; as was Jeffrey Forgeng's *Daily Life in Elizabethan England*. I should also make mention of Lauren Kassell's *Medicine & Magic in Elizabethan London*; Thomas Wright's *Circulation*, a fascinating account of how William Harvey discovered the true function of the heart; Roy Porter's *Blood & Guts*; and John Dent's *The Quest for Nonsuch*.

I must also offer deep gratitude – though, sadly, neither is alive to receive it – to my English teacher, Mr Mortimer, and to Mr Pugh, my history teacher; both from Enfield Chase Secondary School. It's indicative of schooling in the 1960s that I have absolutely no idea of their first names.

Nor must I fail to acknowledge the immense help I've received from my agent, Jane Judd, and from Sara O'Keeffe, Susannah Hamilton and the team at Corvus. I must also thank Mandy Greenfield for her eagle's eye.

But the greatest debt – given that the writing life can be uncomfortably solitary, and not just for the author – I owe to my wife Jane. Without her belief and encouragement, I doubt a word of this tale would have survived to reach the printed page.

Read on for an extract from ...

Tilbury, England. Winter 1591

I n the dusk of a desolate November evening an urchin in a mud-stained and threadbare jerkin, long-since stolen from its rightful owner, hurries along the Thames foreshore beneath the grim ramparts of Tilbury Fort. The chill east wind claws at his puckered pale flesh. The hunger that has driven him down to the narrowing band of shingle gnaws within him, as if it would tear itself out of his belly and go crawling off by itself in search of sustenance elsewhere. He is risking the tide because he knows a place where the oysters are plump and good. On balance, the strand is a safer route than striking inland in the gathering darkness.

His destination is a small channel that runs deep into the Essex shore, a wilderness of marsh and reed, of dead-end tracks that lead to creeks where you can drown in stinking mud before you can get to the *Amen* at the end of the Lord's Prayer. He knows this because the wasteland is where he lives, on its southern fringe, in a ramshackle camp of vagabonds and peddlers, swelled by the destitute and the maimed from the wars in Holland and by discharged sailors from the queen's fleet.

The river is the colour of the lead coffin he once saw when he broke into a private chapel to get out of a storm. It is studded with ships: hoys and flyboats from Antwerp and Flushing, barques from the Hansa ports of Lübeck and Hamburg, fur traders from the white wastes of Muscovy. As night approaches, they are beginning to dissolve before his eyes, like old coins tossed into oil of vitriol. All they leave behind is the tarry smell of caulked timber and the tormenting scent of food cooking on galley hearths.

Before the boy can reach the channel he must first climb over the great iron chain that runs out into the water, the boom that blocks the river lest the Spanish come again, as they did in '88.

He is unwilling to jump the chain because the hunger has given him cramps in the stomach. He'd crawl under it, but that would mean slithering through pools of rank green slime. So instead he puts one tattered boot into a slippery iron link and starts to ease himself over.

And as he does so, something amongst the rotting kelp that clings to the chain detaches itself and drops to the pebbles.

A crab! A dead crab.

Dare he eat it? He's ravenous enough. But how long has it been there, trapped amongst the weeds and the barnacles? The urchin knows you can die from eating bad food. It makes you double up like a sprat being fried in a pan. It makes you scream. He's seen it happen.

But famine has made him canny. He knows exactly what to do. He'll wash the crab clean of mud in the nearest pool, take a long sniff beneath the carapace and judge then if it's worth breaking open.

It is only when he lifts the crab from the pebbles that the boy realizes it is not a crab at all.

It is a human hand.

PART 1

✠

The Physician from Basle

1

Nine months earlier. 23rd February 1591

It is a day made for second chances, a day ripe for confession, for penitence, for admitting your sins and seizing that unexpected God-given chance to start afresh. A dying storm has left thin wracks of ripped black cloud hanging in the saturated air, above a pale empty world awaiting the first brushstroke. It is simply a matter of applying the paint to the canvas. Let today slip by unused, and Nicholas Shelby – lapsed physician and reluctant sometime spy – knows he must return to London, no nearer to accepting the new life he's been so cruelly dealt than when he left.

His father has sensed it, too.

'Your Eleanor died in August last,' Yeoman Shelby observes with devastating calmness, as the two men shelter from the last of the downpour in the farm's apple press. 'It's now almost March. *Seven* months. Where were you, boy? Where did you go?'

How much of an answer does a father need? Nicholas wonders, close to shivering inside his white canvas doublet. Would it help to know that for a while I was busy drinking myself stupid in any tavern I could find that hadn't already banned me? Or that I was losing every patient I had, because word had soon spread that Dr Shelby was raging in his grief like a deranged shabberoon? Or that I was busy rejecting everything I learned at Cambridge – attended at a cost you could scarcely bear – because when the time came and Eleanor and the child she was carrying had need of it, my medical knowledge turned out to be little more than superstition? Or that, on top of everything else, there had been a murderer I had to stop from killing again?

There are some questions, Nicholas thinks, that should remain for ever unanswered, if only for the sake of those who ask them.

'How could you do that to us, boy – vanishing off the face of God's good earth like that?' his father is saying, his words delivered to the dying rain's slow drumbeat. 'Your brother wore himself thin, searching that godless place called London for a sign of you. Your mother wept like we'd never heard her weep before. Do you not know *we* loved Eleanor, too?'

Nicholas has been dreading this moment ever since he returned to Suffolk and the Shelby farm. Now he sits on the cold stone rim of the press, straight-backed, head up, a damp curl of wiry black hair slick against his brow, unable to give in to the desire to slump, because a Suffolk yeoman's son is not grown to wilt, even if the weight of all that's happened since Lammas Day last is almost too much for his broad countryman's shoulders to bear. Sickened by the excuses he hasn't even tried to make yet, at first all he can bring himself to say is 'I know. I'm sorry.'

Yeoman Shelby has rarely struck either of his sons, and not at all since they've grown to manhood. But as he comes closer, Nicholas wonders if he's about to land a blow in payment for the extra pain his youngest has caused the family by his vanishing. He catches the heavy, musty smell of his father's woollen coat, the one he's worn in winter for as long as Nicholas can remember. Dyed a now-faded grey, it smells as though it's been buried in a seed basket for all of Nicholas's twenty-nine years. But the scent is oddly comforting. Nicholas has the overwhelming urge to reach out and cling to the hem, as if he were an infant again.

'The only way I can explain it is this,' he says, staring at his hands and thinking how his fingers, nicked and coarsened by boyhood summers helping with the harvest, seem so unsuited to healing work. 'Imagine if you woke up one morning and discovered that all the wisdom accumulated over fifteen hundred years of husbanding the land didn't work any longer – that you couldn't grow anything any more; that you couldn't feed your family.'

'It's called an evil harvest, boy. It's happened before.'

'Exactly! And there was absolutely nothing you could do about it, was there?'

Nicholas looks up at his father with moistening eyes. He snorts back the tears, frightened that he's about to weep in the presence of a man who has always seemed immune to sentiment. 'That's how it was when I tried to save Eleanor and our child,' he says thinly.

His father lays a hand on his son's shoulder. 'I know you well enough, Nick. You would have moved heaven and earth, if you but could. But sometimes, boy, it's just the way God wants things to happen.'

Nicholas gives a cruel laugh. 'Oh, I've heard that said before. Did you know the great Martin Luther – fount of this new religion we're all supposed to embrace so unquestioningly – tells me in his writings that God *designed* women to die in childbirth! He says it's what they're for! Well, for the record, I'll have none of such *knowledge*.'

'Parson Olicott would say that what you learned at Cambridge is God's wisdom revealed through man,' his father replies, caution in his runnelled face. 'He'd say our Lord would offer us no false remedies. He'd call you a blasphemer for suggesting otherwise.'

'The remedies Parson Olicott gets called upon to administer, Father,' says Nicholas, running his fingers through a tangle of hair that the rain has flattened to his scalp like black ribbons discarded in a ditch, 'are for ills of the soul, not the body.'

'But if the soul is in good health, does not the body follow?'

Though a humble farmer, a man who only learned to write when he was forty, his father has just summed up the current thinking of the College of Physicians in a nutshell.

'That's what we've thought for centuries,' Nicholas says. 'That's what the books tell us: bring the body into a balance pleasing to God. They instruct us to bleed the patient from a particular part of his body if the sanguine and choleric humours are out of kilter; purge him if the melancholic humour suppresses the phlegmatic; read the colour of his water – and always make sure the stars and the planets are in favourable alignment, before you do any of it. Then present the bill. And if it all goes wrong, say it was God's will – or the stars were inauspicious.'

His father kneels and stares into his son's eyes with the stoic acceptance of the cycle of life and death, of hope and disappointment, that a man who relies on the fickleness of the earth for his survival must learn. His face looks carved out of holm oak. You're barely fifty, thinks Nicholas, yet you look like an old man. Is it the toil? Or have my own actions aged you? He settles for what his mother and his sister-in-law, Faith, have always claimed: grubbing away at the earth makes Shelby men look older than their years.

'Listen to me, boy,' his father says with a surprisingly gentle smile that looks out of place on such a hard-used face. 'Thrice in my lifetime I've heard Parson Olicott tell me I'm to forget my religion and believe in a different one. Every Sunday – until I was about fourteen – he'd tell me the Pope was a fine Christian man, an' that for my spiritual education I was to study the pictures of the saints in St Mary's...'

Nicholas wonders what that weathered stone Saxon barnacle, where the Shelby family now have their own pew almost within touching distance of the altar, has to do with his present agony; but he's learned long ago that when his father embarks on one of his homilies it's best not to interrupt.

His father continues. 'Then one Sunday shortly after King Henry died, I hear Parson Olicott announce, "King Edward says the Pope is the Antichrist!" Well, you could have knocked me down with a feather. After the sermon, Parson Olicott hands us lads a bucket of whitewash.' He makes a painting gesture with one hand, the fist clenched. '"Cover up those paintings of the saints," orders old Olicott, "'cause now they be heretical!"'

Nicholas has stared at the plain walls of St Mary's every Sunday for as long as he can recall, usually with intense boredom. It has never occurred to him that his father was one of those who'd done the whitewashing.

'Took us lads ages, I can tell you,' Yeoman Shelby says. 'But the next thing I know – around the time I was paying court to your mother – there's Parson Olicott proclaiming that Edward is dead, Mary is queen, and the Pope is once more our father in Christ. Imagine it!'

Nicholas indulges his father and imagines.

'"Change the prayer book!" says Olicott. "Bring out the choir screens again" – we'd hidden them in Jed Arrowsmith's barn. "Scrub off the whitewash! The bishops what made us paint over those saints are all now heretics and must burn for it!"' Yeoman Shelby sighs, as though all this variable theology is beyond the understanding of a simple man. 'To tell the truth, Nick, when we got the whitewash off, I was surprised those paintings had survived. But survive they had. Stubborn buggers, those Catholic saints. Didn't last, of course. Barely five years on, Bloody Mary is dead, we're all singing hosannas for Queen Elizabeth, and the Pope is the Devil's arse-licker again. And what's old Olicott preaching?'

'Fetch the whitewash?'

His father nods. 'Exactly. What I'm saying to you is this: there ain't ever such a thing as *certainty*, boy. Maybe in the next world, but not in this. So don't you worry your young head about whether or not your old father can handle it when his clever physician son has a crisis of belief. Because what really grieves us, Nick – what *really* makes us weep – is that when *your* world was turned on its head, when you had need of us most, you didn't come home.'

For a moment there is only the slow dripping of water on the pressing stone. Then Nicholas is in his father's arms, his chest heaving like a man drowning, sobbing with a child's bewilderment at unjustified injury.

Outside, the rain is starting to ease. The old thatched houses of Barnthorpe are beginning to take on their newborn, sharper forms. When the two men walk back to the Shelby farmhouse, Nicholas feels somehow lighter. Certainly more resolute. Confession has done him good – even if it's only a partial confession.

Because there's something else Nicholas hasn't admitted to his father. He hasn't told Yeoman Shelby that a part of his son – a small part to be sure, but even the smallest canker can still presage a greater infection – now belongs to one Robert Cecil.

✠

'Careful now, Ned. Master Nicholas is not here to set your bones if you fall!'

Bianca Merton grasps the ladder with both hands, letting her weight bear down on her left foot, which is set firmly on the bottom rung. Above her, Ned Monkton sways precariously as he leans out over the lane. He looks like a bear that's climbed to the top of a maypole and got stuck there. Cursing, he tries to attach the newly made board beside the sign of the Jackdaw. It takes him a few minutes and an excess of profanities, but before long the new banner is in place: the unicorn and the jackdaw swaying side-by-side in the breeze. Southwark now has a tavern *and* an apothecary, all in one. You can forget your tribulations with a quart of knock-down, and get colewort and hartshorn for the resulting hangover, in the same place.

'Don't that look a fine sight?' says Rose, Bianca's maid, as she admires the scene – though whether it's the apothecary's sign or the sight of Ned's hugely muscular legs wrapped around the ladder is somewhat unclear to Bianca.

'I wish I could have seen the faces of the Grocers' Guild when they signed my licence,' Bianca says, sweeping her proud, dark hair from her brow. 'They've been trying to shut me down since the day I arrived. And now I'm legal! Who would have imagined it? Bianca Merton of the Jackdaw, a licensed apothecary!'

Whatever her curative talents, Bianca makes an unlikely tavern-keeper. She's slender, with a narrow, boyish face topped by a trace of widow's peak, and extraordinarily amber eyes that gleam with a mischievous directness. Having been born of an Italian mother and an English father, her skin still boasts a healthy lustre infused by the Veneto sun, despite all that three years in Southwark have contrived against it.

'Shame a *someone* isn't here to see it,' says Rose, a plump, jolly young woman with a mane like tangled knitting. 'How did he manage it? I thought he were out of all regard with them physicians in their pretty college on Knightrider Street.'

'He called in a favour, Rose,' Bianca says wryly. And beyond that she will not go. The memories of the horror she and Nicholas endured together are still too raw. Before he left for Suffolk to make his peace with his family, they'd scarcely spoken of it between themselves, let alone with outsiders. The nightmares still come to her, though less frequently now. When they do, they have a terrifying fidelity about them. Once again she is back in that vile place deep in the earth, feeling her flesh tense as it awaits the draw of the scalpel. She consoles herself with the knowledge that no more bodies will wash up on Bankside. The man who put them in the river has met his just reward, thanks to Dr Nicholas Shelby, who came to her as a talisman from out of that very same river.

She wonders what Nicholas is doing now. Is he reconciled with his family? Do the ghosts of his wife and child haunt him still? Will he return to Bankside, as he promised? And how will she feel about him, if he does?

He's so very different from the men she'd known in Padua. A yeoman's son from the wilds of Suffolk who'd found the intellectual courage to battle the stultifying hand of tradition during his medical studies is as unlike a fashionably clad *libertino* as she can possibly imagine. She scolds herself for the sudden, unexpected surge of jealousy that comes with knowing how capable of love Nicholas is, despite his stolid roots. It would be so much better, she thinks, if he could devote that love to the living, and not the dead.

Her reverie is broken by the sole of Ned's boot on her hand as he descends the ladder.

'God's mercy!' she cries, snatching her hand away and shaking it vigorously. 'Have a care where you're putting your feet, you clumsy buffle-head!' Catching herself using the vocal currency of the London streets, she smiles. She thinks, soon I shall have lost that accent Nicholas says he can hear in my voice whenever I get fractious. Soon I shall be as English as Rose.

Ned Monkton, just turned twenty-one, built like King Henry's great *Mary Rose* – and just as liable to capsize, if too much liquid flows in through an open port – steps back to earth. He scratches his fiery auburn hair and slaps his belly with his great fists. 'There now, Mistress,' he says, looking up at the two signs, 'they can't beat *that* at the Turk's Head or the Good Husband, eh?'

'You've hung it upside-down,' says Rose.

And for just a moment Ned is taken in.

They're an odd pair. Rose is as ungovernable as a sack of wild martens. Her idea of a day's leisure is a trip to Tyburn to watch a good hanging. Ned used to be the mortuary warden from St Thomas's hospital down by Thieves' Lane. Smiling, Bianca remembers her mother's firm conviction: there's always *someone for someone.*

It's good to see Ned above ground now, she thinks, instead of deep in the hospital crypt, surrounded by the dead. He's even getting some colour back in his face. Since Nicholas set off for Suffolk, Ned has taken his place as the Jackdaw's handyman and thrower-outer-in-chief. There's been not a jug spilt in anger since. And with Rose beside him, he's beginning to recover a little from what befell young Jacob, his younger brother, whose death gave Nicholas his first lead in tracking down the man they all now describe – in lowered voices that still have an echo of dread in them – as the 'Bankside butcher'.

Bianca looks up at the two signs again, satisfaction welling in her breast. A measure of cautious contentment stirs within her. She waves happily at a *fee* of young lawyers – the invented collective noun slips into her head, unbidden. They've come across the bridge for the stews and the cock-fights. They'll be lucky to get back to Lincoln's Inn with the hose they put on this morning. She receives their clumsy, ribald replies as down-payment and ushers them towards the Jackdaw's entrance.

And then her taproom boy, Timothy, comes running down the lane. In the excitement of raising the apothecary's sign, she'd almost forgotten she'd sent him down to Cutler's Yard to pay the sign-maker.

'Mercy, young Timothy, what's the alarm?'

'The watermen say a new barque will drop anchor in the Pool tomorrow,' he tells her breathlessly. 'She's coming up from the

Hope Reach on the morning tide. Four masts!' He raises the appropriate fingers to indicate the wonder of it. 'Imagine it: *four!*'

For the denizens of Southwark, a newly arrived ship is like a freshly killed carcass to a wolf. There are victuals to be replenished at twice the going rate; goose-feather mattresses for men who've spent months sleeping on salty boards; a predictable uncertainty of the legs, which makes lifting a purse that much easier; an outlet for desires that until now have been only solitarily satisfied. It's been this way since the Romans were here, and Bianca Merton isn't about to pass on the opportunity.

'From which state is she? Do they say?' she asks, factoring translation into the equation – French and Spanish mariners take less time to serve than those from Muscovy, and Moors don't take drink at all.

'Venice,' says Timothy eagerly, with not the slightest comprehension of just how much powder he's about to ignite. 'She's the *Sirena di Venezia.*'

Praise for The Angel's Mark

'A gorgeous book – rich, intelligent and dark in equal measure. It immerses you in the late 16th century and leaves you wrung out with terror. This is historical fiction at its most sumptuous.'

Rory Clements

'Wonderful! Beautiful writing, and Perry's Elizabethan London is so skilfully evoked, so real that one can almost smell it.'

Giles Kristian

'A strong and convincing debut.' Antonia Senior, *The Times*

'I knew before I got to the bottom of the first page that *The Angel's Mark* was the real thing. In an increasingly crowded field, this one is going to stand out.' S. G. MacLean

'An impressively dramatic and gripping debut novel. Elegantly written, thoroughly researched, *The Angel's Mark* draws us into the murky world of Elizabethan London where life is a game of chance, and savage death a close neighbour, quick to pounce on the unsuspecting. I predict that we will be seeing much more of Nicholas Shelby, physician and reluctant spy.' Anne O'Brien

'An engaging Elizabethan thriller.' *Sunday Times*

'*The Angel's Mark* has the pace of a thriller... S.W. Perry is a welcome addition to the ranks of historical crime novelists.' Simon Brett

'A tense whodunit and a fine debut.' Weekend Sport

'A remarkably assured and classy debut. Perry grabs your attention from the first paragraph and holds it throughout a fascinating journey into high and low life of Tudor London. This could, hopefully, be the start of an addictive series.' L C Tyler

'[A] sad, compassionate story, beautifully told.' *Daily Express*